REMOTE CONTROL

Also by Andy McNab

BRAVO TWO ZERO
IMMEDIATE ACTION

REMOTE CONTROL

ANDY McNAB

BANTAM PRESS

LONDON • NEW YORK • TORONTO • SYDNEY • AUCKLAND

TRANSWORLD PUBLISHERS LTD
61–63 Uxbridge Road, London W5 5SA

TRANSWORLD PUBLISHERS (AUSTRALIA) PTY LTD
15–23 Helles Avenue, Moorebank, NSW 2170

TRANSWORLD PUBLISHERS (NZ) LTD
3 William Pickering Drive, Albany, Auckland

Published 1997 by Bantam Press
a division of Transworld Publishers Ltd
Copyright © by Andy McNab 1997

A catalogue record for this book is available from the British Library
ISBN 0593 042360 (cased)
ISBN 0593 04360X (tpb)

Typeset in 11/14pt Palatino by Falcon Oast Graphic Art
Printed in Great Britain
by Mackays of Chatham Plc, Chatham, Kent.

Glossary

ASU	active service unit
ATO	ammunitions technical officer
basha	improvised shelter
bergen	pack carried by British forces on active service
BG	bodyguard
blue-and-white	US police car
CTR	close target reconnaissance
CT	counter-terrorism
DA	defence attaché
DEA	Drug Enforcement Administration
Det	abbreviation for detachment. Sub-unit of 14 Intelligence Group, which is a covert intelligence-gathering organization operating in Northern Ireland
the Firm	Secret Intelligence Service
gypy's warning	final warning
head shed	nickname for anyone in authority. From Malaya days, this is what any form of leadership in the Regiment has been called, after the term for the start of the river course
K	operator on deniable ops
LCN	La Cosa Nostra
LOSO	liaison officer, special operations
MoD	Ministry of Defence
OPSEC	operational security
PIRA	Provisional Irish Republican Army

RHQ	regimental headquarters
RV	rendezvous
sat comm	satellite communications
scaleys	signallers
security blanket	an operator's 'insurance', often documentary evidence of a government's complicity in deniable ops
SF	Special Forces
SIS	Secret Intelligence Service
sit rep	situation report
slime	Intelligence Corps
SOP	standard operating procedure
SWAT	special weapons and tactics
VDM	visual distinguishing mark

REMOTE CONTROL

Gibraltar: Sunday, 6 March 1988

I pinged him straight away.

I got on the net. 'Alpha, Delta. That's confirmed – Bravo One, foxtrot on the right approaching Blue Two. Brown pinstripe on faded blue.'

He always wore that brown pinstriped suit jacket; he'd had it for so long that it sagged in the pockets, and there were constant creases in the back from where he'd been wearing it in a car. And the same old faded and threadbare jeans, the crotch halfway down between his bollocks and his knees. He was walking away from me, stocky, slight stoop, short hair, long sideboards, but I recognized the gait. I knew it was Sean Savage.

I got back on the net. 'Delta still has – that's Blue Two towards Blue Seven.' Before Simmonds gave the briefing, the whole Rock had been marked out with the spot system. Junctions and major landmarks were identified by a colour and a number.

Savage was now at the library junction. Blue Seven was a small square at the bottom end of Main Street, near the Governor's residence. It was also the car park where the band of the resident infantry battalion would fall out after the changing of the guard. This was where the bomb must be.

Alpha, the base station controlling the operation for now, repeated the message so that everyone knew which direction

Savage was walking in. I knew that Kev and Slack Pat would soon start moving on behind me.

There were six or seven cars parked up against the wall of an old colonial building, taking advantage of the shade. As he headed towards them, I saw Bravo One push his hand into his jacket pocket. For one split second I thought he was going for the initiation device and my mind flashed back to the briefing.

Simmonds hadn't been able to tell us the exact make or model of car they'd be using; all he knew was that the bomb was a big one, and it would be an RCIED – a remote-controlled, improvised explosive device. His closing words had echoed around the smoke-filled room. 'Remember, gentlemen, any one of the PIRA team, or all of them, could be in possession of the initiation device. That bomb must not detonate. There could be hundreds of lives at risk.'

Without checking his stride, Savage focused on one vehicle in particular and headed towards it.

'Alpha, Delta,' I said. 'That's Bravo One now at Blue Seven . . . Plate check, Mike Lima 174412.'

I pictured Alpha with the bank of computers in front of him in the control room. He confirmed, 'Roger that, Mike Lima 174412. That's a white Renault Five.'

'It's the third car on the right from the entrance,' I said. 'That's nose-in.'

By now the keys were in his hands.

'Stop, stop, stop. Bravo One at the car; he's at the car.'

I was committed to passing him quite close now – I couldn't just change direction. His side profile showed me that his chin and top lip were full of zits, and I knew what that meant. Under pressure, his acne always blew up.

Savage was still at the Renault. He turned, now with his back to me, pretending to sort his keys out, but I knew he'd be checking the tell-tales. They could be just a sliver of Sellotape across a door or things arranged in a certain way inside the vehicle. Whatever, if they were not as he had left them, Savage would lift off.

Golf and Oscar – Kev and Slack Pat – would be somewhere near the entrance to the square, ready to 'back'. If I got over-exposed to the target, one of them would take over, or if I got in the shit and had a contact, they would have to finish it.

The buildings were casting shadows across the square. I couldn't feel any breeze, just the change in temperature as I moved out of the sunlight. Savage still had his back to me.

I was too close to him now to transmit. As I walked past the car I could hear the keys going in and the click of the lock.

I headed for a wooden bench on the far side of the square and sat down. There were newspapers in a bin next to me; I picked one out and sat watching him.

I got back on the net. 'Alpha, Delta – that's now Bravo One complete Charlie One. No, he's not . . . wait . . . wait . . . that's his feet outside, he's fiddling underneath the dashboard, he's fiddling under the dashboard. Wait . . .' I had my finger on the pressel, so I was still commanding the net.

As I was doing my ventriloquist act, I saw an old boy wandering towards me, pushing his bike. The fucker was on his way over for a chat. I took my finger off the pressel and waited. I was deeply involved in the local newspaper, but I didn't have a clue what it said. He obviously thought I did. I didn't want to stick around and discuss the weather; but I wasn't just going to fuck him off either, because he might start jumping up and down and draw Savage's attention.

The old boy stopped, one hand on his bike, the other one flailing around. He asked me a question. I didn't understand a word he was saying. I pulled a face that said I didn't know what the world was coming to, shrugged and looked down again at the paper. I'd obviously done the wrong thing. He said some angry shit and then wheeled his bike away, arm still flailing.

I got back on the net. I couldn't see exactly what Savage was doing, but both of his feet were still outside the Renault. He had his arse on the driver's seat and was leaning over underneath the dash. It looked as if he was trying to get something out of the glove compartment – as if he'd forgotten something and gone back to get it. I couldn't confirm what he was doing, but his hands kept going into his pockets. Was he making the last connection to the device?

I was caught up in my own little world, everything closing in. The air was crisp and clean under a blindingly blue Mediterranean sky, the morning sun just starting to make it comfortable enough for shirtsleeves. The trees that lined the square were packed with birds so small I couldn't see them amongst the thick foliage, but they made enough noise to drown out the sound of traffic going up and down the main drags, just out of sight.

I felt like a boxer – I could hear the crowd, I was listening to my seconds and the referee, I was listening for the bell, but mostly I was focused on the boy that I was fighting. Nothing else mattered. Nothing. I was totally detached from what was going on around me. The only important people in the whole world were me and Bravo One.

Euan was still working like a man possessed, trying to get on top of the other two targets. I knew this guy like a brother – in fact probably better; I hadn't seen any of my family for over twenty years. He was dedicated to the job. I knew exactly the way he thought. I knew that what he said on the net would be very calm, very precise and very clear.

Kev and Slack Pat were still backing me; the other two, Zulu and Lima, were with Euan. All four would still be satelliting, listening on the net so as to be out of sight of the targets, always close enough to back us if we got in the shit.

We could all hear Euan on the net, closing in on Bravo Two and Echo One. The two players were coming in our direction.

Bravo Two was Daniel Martin McCann. Unlike Savage, who was well educated and an expert bomb-maker, 'Mad Danny' was a butcher by trade and a butcher by nature. He'd been expelled from the movement by Gerry Adams in 1985 for threatening to initiate a campaign of murder that would have hampered the new political strategy. It was a bit like being kicked out of the Gestapo for cruelty, but McCann had supporters and soon got himself reinstated. Married, with two children, he had twenty-six killings linked to his name. Ulster Loyalists had tried to kill him once, but failed. They should have tried harder.

Echo One was Mairead Farrell. Middle-class and an ex-convent schoolgirl, she was, at thirty-one, one of the highest-ranking women in the IRA. See her picture and you'd think, Aah, an angel. But she'd served ten years in prison for planting a bomb in Belfast, and as soon as she was released she'd reported back for duty. Things hadn't gone her way: a few months earlier, her lover, another terrorist, had accidentally blown himself up. As Simmonds had said at the briefing, that made her one very pissed-off Echo One.

Euan was giving commentary on the route they were taking. Everybody knew where they were; everybody would keep out of the way so they had a clear run in. 'That's Bravo Two and Echo One at Blue Two – left to right – straight towards Blue Seven.' They were crossing the road, on their way to the Renault.

I recognized the other two as soon as they turned the corner. Farrell, with her petite, almost innocent, features, and McCann, blond curly hair and mean mouth. I knew them both well; I'd been working against them for years. I got on the net and confirmed the ID.

Everybody was in place. The only problem was that the situation still hadn't been handed over to the military. Alpha, our controller at the moment, would be with the senior policeman, people from the Foreign Office, people from the Home Office; you name it, every man and his dog would be there, everybody wanting to put their tuppenceworth in, everybody with their own concerns. We could only hope that Simmonds would be looking after ours. I'd only met the SIS desk officer for Northern Ireland a couple of days earlier, but he certainly seemed to be running our side of the show. His voice had confidence that was shaped on the playing fields of Eton, and he measured his words slowly, like a QC with the meter running.

All *our* concerns were on the ground: we'd got three players together, and, if we weren't careful, they were going to kill every fucker in this square – including us. We wanted the decision made now. But I knew there would be big debates going on in the ops room; you'd probably have to cut your way through the cigarette smoke with a knife. Our liaison officer would be listening to us on his radio and explaining everything that we were doing to the police, confirming that the team was in position. At crunch time, it was the police, not us, who would decide that we went in. Once it was handed over to the military, Kev would control the team.

The frustration was outrageous. I just wanted to get this over.

By now Farrell was leaning against the driver's door, the two men standing and facing her. If I hadn't known differently I'd have said they were trying to chat her up. I couldn't hear what they were saying, but their faces showed no sign of stress and, now and then, I could hear laughing above the traffic noise. Savage even got out a packet of mints and was passing them round.

I was still giving a running commentary.

'Alpha, Delta, that's no change, no change.'

'Alpha, roger that.'

Alpha came back on the net. 'Hello, all call signs, all call signs, I have control, I have control. Golf, acknowledge.'

Kev acknowledged. The police had handed over; it was Kev's show now.

To my left, I heard, 'Oh, let's have a sit-down here, let's have a rest.'

An old British couple came bimbling over and sat down next to me. They were both carrying newspapers and little bottles of Evian water and, as they settled onto the bench, they unscrewed the tops of the bottles and took a sip. Then all I could hear was some shit about it being a lot warmer now and something to do with losing a coat.

At the same time, what I had coming from Golf was, 'Delta, send a sit rep, send a sit rep.'

I couldn't do anything. I couldn't talk on the net and I didn't want to move; there was nowhere to go anyway. Golf was now flapping. 'Delta, check. Delta, check.'

I pressed twice. He now knew I couldn't talk.

'Is that Bravo One, Two and Echo One still at Charlie One?'

Click, click.

'Are they aware?'

Nothing.

'Are they looking unaware?'

Click, click.

'Are the doors on the vehicle still closed?'

Click, click.

'Are they locked?'

Click, click.

'Are they talking?'

Click, click.

'Does Echo One still have her bag?' He was concerned that the firing device could be in her bag.

Click, click.

'Did they get anything out of the vehicle?'

Nothing.

In the same ear I'm getting these old people talking to each other. They're sitting there reading the newspaper, something about a pop star and sex-crazed orgies with sixteen-year-old girls, loads of pictures of old slappers in stockings and suspenders on the front page. 'Have you read this? Oh, look at this. There's no smoke without fire, that's what I say.' She was tucking into a half-pound bar of Fruit & Nut.

The targets started to move away from the vehicle and I clicked the pressel four times.

Golf came back, 'Standby, standby!'

'Is that them foxtrot?'

Click, click.

'Are they going towards Yellow Six?'

Nothing.

15

Of course not. They're going back the way they came, towards the bottom of Main Street. Ask again.

'Are they going back towards Blue Two?' That's better.

Click, click.

'Roger that. Do you have?'

Click, click.

'Roger that. Hello, all stations, Delta has – Bravo One, Two and Echo One foxtrot back towards Blue Two.'

That was it, we were off.

I let them walk towards the main square and then I got up. I knew we wouldn't lift them here. There were far too many people. For all we knew the players might want to go out in a blaze of glory and start dropping the civilians or taking them hostage, or, even worse, go into kamikaze mode and remotely detonate the device.

I was now out of earshot of the old couple. 'Standby, standby! That's Bravo One, Two and Echo One foxtrot. Halfway, Blue Seven to Blue Two.'

They were under control; the others didn't have to close in yet. I'd take them out of the square, back on to the main street.

But all of a sudden Alpha came back on the net. 'Hello, all call signs, all call signs – cancel, cancel, cancel! I do not have control! Cancel! Golf, acknowledge.'

I could almost hear him thinking. Then we heard Kev's not-so-correct reply.

'What the fuck's going on? Tell me – what's going on?'

The desk came back on the net. 'Wait . . . wait . . .' He sounded under pressure. There were voices in the background. 'All stations, all stations, this is Alpha. The police need another ID; they need to be sure. Golf, acknowledge.'

What did they want, introductions? 'Hi, I'm Sean, IRA bomber and murderer, I enjoy travelling and working with children.'

We were in danger of losing them across the border into Spain if we didn't act soon.

Alpha came back on the net. 'All stations, ATO is moving to

check the vehicle. Delta, we need that confirmation.'

I gave two clicks. There was obviously some flapping going on in the ops room. The boss was getting a hard time from the police and it sounded like a chimps' tea party in there.

They would be crossing the border within minutes. I was now on the other side of the road. I wanted at least to get parallel to them so that I could see their faces again. I had to reconfirm the players, then stick with them. I got back on the net. 'Roger that. That's confirmed, Bravo One, Bravo Two, Echo One, foxtrot on the right, at Red One, towards Blue Six.'

To allow a natural gap to develop between me and the players, I bent down and pretended to do up the lace on one of my trainers. As I did so I got a jab in the ribs from the hammer of the 9mm Browning. The holster was covert, inside my jeans; that way only the pistol grip would be in view if I pulled back my black nylon bomber jacket. I preferred to have my pistol at the front. A lot of the blokes wore theirs on the side, but I never could get used to it. Once you find a position you like, you don't change; you might be in the shit one day, go to draw your weapon, and it isn't there – it's several more inches to the right and you're dead.

In the Browning I had an extended twenty-round magazine protruding from the pistol grip. I also had three standard thirteen-round mags on my belt, and reckoned that if fifty-nine rounds weren't enough I shouldn't be doing this for a living.

Alpha left the net open. I could hear all the tension in Alpha's voice now, telephone lines ringing, people milling about.

Golf cut on to the net. 'Fuck the ops room, let's keep on top of them until someone somewhere makes a fucking decision. Lima and Zulu, can you get forward of Blue Six?'

Zulu came on the net for himself and Lima, very much out of breath. 'Zulu and Lima, we . . . we can do that.'

'Roger that, move up, tell me when you're there.'

Kev wanted them to go beyond the health centre at Blue Six. That way the players came to them. They were running hard to get beyond the targets; they didn't care who saw them, as long as the players didn't. We still hadn't got control. What the fuck were we going to do if they got over the border?

Kev came back on the net. 'Alpha, Golf. You need to get your finger out now; we're going to lose them. What do you want us to do?'

Alpha was straight back on the net: 'Golf, wait, wait . . .'

I could still hear noise in the background: lots of talking, more telephones ringing, people shouting instructions to each other.

Everything went quiet, just waiting for Alpha to come back.

'Wait . . . wait . . .'

All I could hear now were the background noises of Alpha on my radio, plus my pulse pounding in my head, very, very slowly. There seemed to be an unnatural pause, then, at last, in the background, I heard a decision being made. It was Simmonds's voice, very clear, a voice you wouldn't argue with, very calm and slow in the confusion. 'Tell the ground commander he can continue.'

'All call signs, all call signs, this is Alpha. I have control. I have control. Golf, acknowledge.'

Kev got on the net and, instead of acknowledging, said, 'Thank fuck for that. All call signs, if they get as far as the airport, we'll lift them there. If not – on my word, on my word. Zulu and Lima, how's it going?'

They came back on the net. 'That's us static at the junction, Blue Nine. We can take at Blue Nine.' That was the end of Main Street and the start of Smith Dorrien Avenue, the main approach road to the crossing into Spain. The players were just a few hundred yards from the border.

Golf came back. 'Roger that, Delta acknowledge.'

'Delta, roger that, I still have Bravo One, Bravo Two, Echo One on the right, Blue Six to Blue Nine – that's about halfway.'

'Golf, roger that, lift off, lift off at Blue Nine.'

'Delta, roger that, still on the right, still towards Blue Nine.'

Zulu came back. 'Roger that, I can take at Blue Nine.'

'Delta, roger that, still straight.'

That was me nearly finished, I could lift off soon. I'd done the job I'd been brought here to do. I was preparing myself for the handover as the players turned right onto Smith Dorrien Avenue, still towards the border.

But then they stopped.

Fuck! 'Stop, stop, stop!' I said. 'That's Bravo One, Two and Echo One static twenty metres past Blue Nine, still on the right.'

Everybody was closing in. *Come on, let's lift them here and now!*

All of a sudden, Savage split from the other two and headed back the way they'd come, towards the town centre.

It was all going to rat shit. We had two groups to control now and we didn't know who had the initiation device.

I could see Kev arrive to back me as I moved in to take Savage. All he and I were worrying about was Bravo One.

It was now up to the rest of the team to take Bravo Two and Echo One, with Euan as the trigger. On the net, I could hear the other two players being followed along Winston Churchill Avenue by the rest of the team. From my days as a young garrison soldier, I remembered that it was a dual carriageway, running north–south, that led to the border. On one side was an apartment complex called the Laguna Estate. Between the estate and the road was a Shell petrol station. Kev and I stayed with Savage back towards the town centre.

He turned left down an alleyway. I was just about to get on the net when I heard a police siren, followed by gunfire behind me.

At the same time I heard Euan on the net. 'Contact! Contact!'

Then more shots.

What the fuck was going on?

Kev and I looked at each other. We ran round the corner and saw Savage. He'd heard the shots, too, and turned back the way he had come. Even from this distance I could see his eyes, as big as plates, and jerking as if he was having a seizure.

There was a woman between us. Savage turned again and started to run.

Kev shouted, 'Stop! Security forces! Stop!'

With his left hand, he had to push the woman over to the side and bang her against the wall to keep her out of the way. She was going down, blood pouring from her head. At least she wouldn't get up and become a target.

She began screaming. We had Kev hollering and screaming at Savage and all the people in the area were starting to scream. It was turning into a gang fuck.

Kev flicked back the right side of his sports jacket to reach the pancake holster over his kidneys. We always put a bit of weight in a pocket – a full mag is good – to help the jacket flick back out of the way.

But I wasn't really looking at Kev, I was looking at Savage. I could see his hand moving to the right side of his jacket. It was decision time. He must not use that detonation device.

Savage was aware. He wasn't some knuckle-dragging moron from the back streets. The moment he saw us, he knew his time had come.

Kev drew his pistol, brought it up and went to fire.

Nothing.

'Stoppage! Fuck, Nick, fuck, fuck!'

Trying to clear his weapon, he dropped on one knee to make himself a smaller target.

Now is when everything seems to go into slow motion and you really can't hear what's happening. It sounds as if you have ear-muffs on.

Savage and I had eye-to-eye. He knew what I was going to do; he could have stopped, he could have put his hands up.

My bomber jacket only looked as if it was zipped up, in fact it was held together with Velcro, so at times like these I could just pull it apart and draw my pistol.

The only way a weapon can be drawn and used quickly is by breaking the whole movement into stages. Stage one, I kept looking at the target. With my left hand I grabbed a fistful of bomber jacket and pulled it as hard as I could towards my chest. The Velcro ripped apart.

At the same time I was sucking in my stomach and sticking out my chest to make the pistol grip easy to access. You only get one chance.

We still had eye contact. He started to shout, but I didn't hear. There was too much shouting going on, from everyone on the street and the earpiece in my head.

Stage two, I pushed the web of my right hand down onto the pistol grip. If I got this wrong I wouldn't be able to aim correctly: I would miss and die. As I felt my web push against the pistol grip, my lower three fingers gripped hard around it. My index finger was outside the trigger guard, parallel with the barrel. I didn't want to pull the trigger early and kill myself. Savage was still looking, still shouting.

Savage's hand was nearly there, nearly where his weapon or the firing device was concealed. It didn't matter which; he had to be stopped.

Stage three, I drew my weapon, in the same movement taking the safety catch off with my thumb.

Our eyes were still locked. I saw that Savage knew he had lost. There was just a curling of the lips. He knew he was going to die.

As my pistol came out, I flicked it parallel with the ground. No time to extend my arms and get into a stable firing position.

Stage four, my left hand was still pulling my jacket out of the way and the pistol was now just by my belt buckle. There was no need to look at it, I knew where it was and what it was pointing at. I kept my eyes on the target and his never left mine. I pulled the trigger.

The weapon report seemed to bring everything back into real time. The first round hit him. I didn't know where, I didn't need to. His eyes told me all I wanted to know.

I kept on firing. There is no such thing as overkill. If he could move, he could detonate the bomb. If it took a whole magazine to be sure I'd stopped the threat, then that was what I'd fire. As Savage hit the ground I could no longer see his hands. He was curled up in a ball, holding his stomach, a natural reaction to the rounds he had taken there. I moved forward and fired two aimed shots at the head. He was no longer a threat.

Kev ran over and was searching inside Savage's pockets and coat.

'It's not here,' he said. 'No weapon, no firing device.'

I looked down at Kev as he wiped the blood off his hands onto Savage's jeans.

'One of the others must have had it,' he said. 'I didn't hear the car go up, did you?'

In all the confusion and noise I couldn't remember. It wasn't important at the time. 'No, I don't think so.'

I stood over them both. Kev Brown's mother came from southern Spain and he looked like a local: jet-black hair, about 5 feet 10 inches and the world's bluest eyes. His wife reckoned he was a dead ringer for Mel Gibson, which, being thirty-eight going on seventeen, he scoffed at but secretly liked. Right now his face was a picture; he knew he owed me one. I wanted to say, 'It's OK, these things happen,' but it just didn't seem like the time. Instead I said, 'Fucking hell, Brown, what do you expect if you have a name the same colour as shit?'

As I spoke, we put our safety catches on, and Kev and I swapped weapons.

'I'm glad I won't be at any inquest,' I said. 'You'd better start getting your shit together.'

Kev smiled as he got on the net and started to send a sit rep. It was all right for him, but Euan and I had to get away before the police arrived.

I tucked his weapon inside my jeans and started walking. Euan and I had been seconded from the Regiment to work on undercover operations with 14 Intelligence Group, known as the Det. Its remit only extended to Northern Ireland. It was illegal for its members to operate anywhere else.

1997

1

If you work for the British intelligence service and get formally summoned to a meeting at their headquarters building on the south bank of the Thames at Vauxhall, there are three levels of interview. First is the one with coffee and biscuits, which means they're going to give you a pat on the head. Next down the food chain is the more businesslike coffee but no biscuits, which means they're not asking but telling you to follow orders. And finally there's no biscuits, and no coffee either, which basically means that you're in the shit. Since leaving the Regiment in 1993 and working as a K on deniable operations I'd had a number of interviews at every level, and I wasn't expecting a nice frothy cappuccino to be on the cards this particular Monday. In fact, I was flapping quite severely, because things hadn't been going too well.

As I emerged from the tube station at Vauxhall the omens weren't exactly with me either. The March sky was dull and overcast, preparing itself for the Easter holiday; my path was blocked by roadworks, and a burst from a jackhammer sounded like the crack of a firing squad. Vauxhall Cross, home of what the press call MI6 but which is actually the Secret Intelligence Service, is about a mile upstream of the Houses of Parliament. Bizarrely shaped, like a beige and black pyramid that's had its top cut off, with staged levels, large towers either side and a terrace bar overlooking the river, it only needs a few swirls of neon and you'd swear it was a casino. It wouldn't look out of place in Las Vegas. I missed Century House, the old HQ building near Waterloo station. It might have been 1960s ugly, square, with loads of glass, net curtains and antennae, and not so handy for the tube, but it was much more homely.

Opposite Vauxhall Cross, and about 200 metres across the wide arterial road, is an elevated section of railway line, and beneath that are arches that have been turned into shops, two of which have been knocked through to make a massive motorbike shop. I was early, so I popped in and fantasized about which Ducati I was going to buy when I got a pay rise – which wasn't going to be today. What the hell, the way my luck was going I'd probably go and kill myself on it.

I'd fucked up severely. I'd been sent to Saudi to encourage, then train, some Northern Iraqi Kurds to kill three leading members of the Ba'ath party. The hope was that the assassinations would spark everything up and help dismantle the regime in Baghdad.

The first part of my task was to take delivery in Saudi of some former Eastern-bloc weapons that had been smuggled in: Russian Dragunov sniper weapons, a couple of Makharov pistols, and two AK assault rifles – the parachute version with a folding stock. All serial numbers had been erased to make them deniable.

For maximum chaos, the plan was to get the Kurds to make three hits, at exactly the same time, in and around Baghdad. One was going to be a close-quarters shoot, using the Makharovs. The idea was for the two boys to walk up to the family house, knock on the door, take on whatever threat presented itself, make entry into the house, zap the target and run.

The second was going to be a sniper option. The target saw himself as a big-time fitness freak; he'd come out and have a little jog round a running track, all of about 400 metres. He emerged from his house every day in a lime-green, fluffy velour shell suit, did one lap, and that was his training for the day. The boys were going to hit him just as he started to sweat and slow down – which, by the look of him, would be after about 100 metres. I would be on this one to co-ordinate the hit so that both fired at once.

The third target was going to be taken out on his way to the ministry. Two bikes would pull up at traffic lights and give him the good news with their AK47s.

I landed up in northern Iraq without any problems, and started the build-up training. At this stage not even the Kurds knew what their task was going to be. The Dragunov sniper rifles were a heap of shit. However, the weapon is never as important as the ammunition, which in this case was even worse, Indian 7.62mm. Given a free hand, I would have wanted to use Lapua, manufactured in Finland and the best in the world for sniping because of its consistency, but Western rounds would have given the game away.

The Indian ammunition was hit and miss, mostly miss. On top of that the Dragunovs were semi-automatic rifles. Ideally, you need a bolt-action weapon, which is not only better for taking the hit, it also doesn't leave an empty case behind because it stays in the weapon until you reload. However, it had to be Russian kit that they were zapped with and it had to be deniable.

Once all three jobs went down, the weapons were dumped in a hide and should have been destroyed. They weren't. On the AK there is a forward leaf sight, and underneath that is scratched a serial number. I had been told that all serial numbers had been removed at source and had taken the information at face value. I didn't check – I fucked up.

The only way to retrieve the situation as far as London was concerned was to kill the Kurd teams I'd been training. It was damage limitation on a drastic scale, but it had to be done. Detail counts. If the Iraqis could trace the weapons back, they might make the UK connection. If they then captured the Kurds, who just happened to mention the fact that they had been trained by a Westerner called Nick Stone, it wouldn't take a mastermind to work out which country he came from. It actually pissed me off to have to kill them because I'd got to know these boys really well. To this day, I was still wearing the G Shock watch one of the snipers had given me. We'd had a bet when we were on the range, and he lost. I knew that I could beat him, but still cheated because I had to win. I'd really got to like him.

Back in the UK there had been an inquiry and everybody was covering their arse. And, because I was a K, they could land it all on me. The armourers and technicians from the intelligence service said it was my fault for not checking. What could I say? I didn't even exist. I was bracing myself to take the hit.

I entered Vauxhall Cross via a single metal door that funnelled me towards reception. Inside, the building could be mistaken for any high-tech office block in any city: very clean, sleek and corporate. People who worked there were swiping their identity cards through electronic readers to get in, but I had to go over to the main reception desk. Two women sat behind thick bulletproof glass.

Through the intercom system I said to one of them, 'I'm here to see Mr Lynn.'

'Can you fill this in, please?' She passed a ledger through a slot under the glass.

As I signed my name in two boxes she picked up a telephone. 'Who shall I say is coming to see Mr Lynn?'

'My name is Stamford.'

The ledger held tear-off labels. One half was going to be ripped off and put in a plastic badge-container, which I would have to pin on. My badge was blue and said, 'ESCORTED EVERY-WHERE.'

The woman came off the phone and said, 'There'll be some-body coming down to pick you up.'

A young clerk appeared minutes later. 'Mr Stamford?'

I said, 'All right, mate, how yer going?'

He half smiled. 'If you'd like to come with me.' He pressed the lift button and said, 'We're going to the fifth floor.'

The whole building is a maze. I just followed him; I didn't have a clue where we were going. There was little noise coming from any of the offices apart from the hum of the air-conditioning ducts, just people bent over papers or working at PCs. At the far end of one corridor we turned left into a room. Old metal filing cabinets, a couple of 6-foot tables put together, and, as in any office anywhere, the kettle and cups, jars of coffee, packets of sugar and a milk rota. None of that for me, though – in free-fall talk, I'd just stand by and accept the landing.

Lieutenant-Colonel Lynn's office was off to one side of the larger area. When the clerk knocked on the door there was a crisp and immediate call of 'Come!' The boy turned the handle and ushered me past.

Lynn was standing behind his desk. In his early forties, he was of average build, height and looks, but had that aura about him that marked him out as an absolute flier. The only thing he didn't have, I was always pleased to note, was plenty of hair. I'd known him on and off for about ten years; for the last two years his job had been liaison between the MoD and SIS.

It was only as I walked further into the room that I realized he wasn't alone. Sitting to one side of the desk, obscured until now by the half-opened door, was Simmonds. I hadn't seen him since Gibraltar. What a switched-on boy he'd turned out to be, sorting out the inquest and basically making sure that Euan and I didn't exist. I felt a mixture of surprise and relief to see him here. He'd had nothing to do with the Kurd job. We might be getting the kettle out after all.

Simmonds stood up. Six feet tall, late forties, rather distinguished looking, a very polite man, I thought, as he extended his hand. He was dressed in corduroy trousers the colour of Colman's mustard, and a shirt that looked as if he'd slept in it.

'Delighted to see you again, Nick.'

We shook hands and Lynn said, 'Stone, Would you like a brew?'

Things were looking up.

'Thanks. Coffee, white, no sugar.'

We all sat down. I took a wooden chair that was on the other side of the desk and had a quick look round the office, while Lynn pressed the intercom on his desk and passed the order on to the clerk. His office was at the rear of the building and overlooked the Thames. It was a very plain, very functional, very impersonal room, apart from a framed photograph on the desk of a group which I presumed were his wife and two children. There were two Easter eggs and wrapping paper on the window sill. Mounted on a wall bracket in one corner was a television; the screen was scrolling through Ceefax world news headlines. Under the TV was the obligatory officer's squash racquet and his jacket on a coat-stand.

Without further formalities, Lynn leaned over and said, 'We've got a fastball for you.'

I looked at Simmonds.

Lynn continued, 'Stone, you're in the shit over the last job, and that's just tough, but you can rectify that by going on this one. I'm not saying it'll help, but at least you're still working. Take it or leave it.'

I said, 'I'll do it.'

He'd known what I was going to say. He was already reaching for a small stack of files containing photographs and bits of paper. As a margin note on one of the sheets I could see a scribble in green ink. It could only have been written by the head of the Firm. Simmonds still hadn't said a word.

Lynn handed me a photograph.

'Who are they?'

'Michael Kerr and Morgan McGear. They're on their way to Shannon as we speak, then flying to Heathrow for a flight to Washington. They've booked a return flight with Virgin and they're running on forged southern Irish passports. I want you to take them from Shannon to Heathrow and then on to Washington. See what they're up to and who they're meeting.'

I'd followed players out of the Republic before and could anticipate a problem. I said, 'What happens if they don't follow the plan? If they're on forged passports, they might go through the motions just to get airside, then use their other passports to board another flight and fuck off to Amsterdam. It wouldn't be the first time.'

Simmonds smiled. 'I understand your concern and it is noted. But they will go.'

Lynn passed me a sheet of paper. 'These are the flight details. They booked yesterday in Belfast.'

There was a knock on the door. Three coffees arrived, one in a mug showing a Tasmanian devil, one with a vintage car on and a plain white one. I got the impression Lynn and Simmonds were on their second round.

Simmonds picked up the plain one, Lynn picked up the car, and I was left with the Tasmanian devil running up a hill.

'Who's taking them from Belfast to Shannon?'

Simmonds said, 'Actually, it's Euan. He has them at the moment. He'll hand over to you at Shannon.'

I smiled to myself at the mention of Euan's name. I was now out of the system and basically just used as a K on deniable operations. The only reason I did it was to finance other things I wanted to do. What they were, I didn't know yet; I was a thirty-seven-year-old man with a lot on his mind but not too much in it. Euan, however, still felt very much part of the system. He still had that sense of a moral responsibility to fight the good fight – whatever that meant – and he'd be there until the day he was kicked out.

Simmonds handed me a folder. 'Check that off,' he said. 'There are thirteen pages. I want you to sign for it now and hand it over to the aircrew when you've finished. Good luck,' he added, not meaning it at all.

'Am I going now?' I said. 'I don't have my passport with me – fastball isn't the word.'

31

Lynn said, 'Your passport's in there. Have you got your other docs?'

I looked at him as if I'd been insulted.

Passport, driver's licence, credit cards are the basic requirements for giving depth to a cover story. From there the K builds up his own cover by using the credit cards to buy things, or maybe paying direct debits for magazine subscriptions or club memberships. I had my cards with me, as always, but not my passport. The one Simmonds handed me had probably been specially produced that morning, correct even down to visas and the right degree of ageing.

I didn't have time to finish my coffee. The clerk reappeared and took me downstairs. I signed for the documents in the outer office before I left; thirteen bits of paper with the information on, and I had to sign each sheet. Then I had to sign for the folder it was in. Fucking bureaucracy.

A car was waiting for me outside. I jumped in the front. When I was a kid I'd look at people being chauffeured and think, Who the fuck do they think they are? I talked shit with the driver, probably bored him rigid; he didn't really want to talk, but it made me feel better.

A civilian Squirrel was waiting on the pad at Battersea heliport, rotors slowly turning. I had one last job to do before boarding: from a wall phone I called up the family who covered for me, people who'd vouch for me if I was ever up against it. They'd never take any action on my behalf, but if I got lifted I could say to the police, 'That's where I live – phone them, ask them.'

A male voice answered the phone.

'James, it's Nick. I've just been given a chance to go to the States and visit friends. I might be a week or two. If it's more, I'll call.'

James understood. 'The Wilmots had a break-in next door two days ago, and we're going to see Bob in Dorset over the Easter weekend.'

I needed to know these things because I would if I lived there all the time. They even sent the local paper to my accommodation address each week.

'Cheers, mate. When you see that son of yours at the weekend, tell him he still owes me a night out.'

'I will . . . Have a nice holiday.'

As we skimmed over the Irish Sea, I opened the briefing pack and thumbed through the material. I needn't have bothered. All they knew for certain was that two boys had booked tickets to Washington and they wanted to find out why. They wanted to know who they were meeting and what was happening once they met. I knew from experience that the chances of failure were big-time. Even if they kept to the script and went to Washington, how was I going to follow them around? There were two of them and one of me; as a basic anti-surveillance drill they were sure to split up at some point. But, hey, at the end of the day, the Firm had me by the bollocks.

Judging from one of the documents, it seemed that we'd reached the time of the year when all good PIRA fund-raisers headed for the dinner circuit in Boston, New York, Washington – even down as far as Tucson, Arizona, to catch Irish-American sympathizers who'd retired to the sun. It seemed that the seizure of 10 tons of explosives and weapons during the search of a warehouse in north London in September 1996 had produced a financial crisis. PIRA weren't exactly asking their bank for an overdraft yet, but the increase in legitimate fund-raising in Northern Ireland was an indication that they were flapping. There were also other, less public, ways of raising cash. I was sure my new friends were part of that.

Apart from that, I was still none the wiser about the job. I had no information on the players' cover stories, or where they might be going, within or outside Washington. All I knew was who they were and what they looked like. I read that Michael Kerr had been a member of the South Armagh ASU. He'd taken part in four mortar attacks on SF bases and tens of shoots against the security forces and Prods. He'd even got wounded once, but escaped to the South. A hard boy.

The same could be said for Morgan McGear. After a career as a shooter in the border area of South Armagh, the thirty-one-year-old jobbing builder had been promoted to PIRA's security team. His job there was to find and question informers. His favoured method of interrogation was a Black & Decker power drill.

2

The helicopter was operated by a civilian front company, so the arrivals procedure at Shannon was no different than if I'd been a horse breeder coming to check the assets at his stud farm in Tipperary, or a businessman flying in from London to fill his briefcase with EU subsidies. I walked across the tarmac into the arrivals terminal, went through Customs and followed the exit signs, heading for the taxi rank. At the last minute I doubled back into departures.

At the Aer Lingus ticket desk I picked up my ticket for Heathrow, which had been booked in the name of Nick Stamford. When choosing a cover name it's always best to keep your own Christian name – that way you react naturally to it. It also helps if the surname begins with your real initial because the signature flows better. I'd picked Stamford after the battle of Stamford Bridge. I loved medieval history.

I headed straight to the shop to buy myself a bag. Everybody has hand luggage; I'd stick out like the balls on a bulldog if I boarded the aircraft with nothing but a can of Coke. I never travelled with luggage that had to be checked in, because then you're in the hands of whoever it is that decides to take bags marked Tokyo and send them to Buenos Aires instead. Even if your baggage does arrive safely, if it then reaches the carousel five minutes after the target's you're fucked.

I bought some toothpaste and other odds and ends, all the time keeping an eye out for Euan. I knew that he'd be glued to Kerr and McGear, unless they'd already gone airside.

The departure lounge seemed full of Irish families who were going to find the Easter sun, and newly retired Americans who'd come to find their roots, wandering around with their brand-new Guinness sweatshirts, umbrellas and baseball caps, and leprechauns in tins and little pots of grow-your-own shamrock.

It was busy and the bars were doing good business. I spotted Euan at the far end of the terminal, sitting at a table in a café, having a large frothy coffee and reading a paper. I'd always found 'Euan' a strange name for him. It made me think of a bloke with a skirt on, running up and down a glen somewhere, swinging a claymore. In fact he was born in Bedford and his parents came from Eastbourne. They must have watched some Jock film and liked the name. Euan was short and had an acne-scarred face and the world's biggest motorbike; the problem was that he could only just keep upright on it because his toes barely brushed the ground.

To the left was a bar. Judging by where Euan was sitting I guessed that was where the players were. I didn't bother looking; I knew Euan would point them out. There was no rush.

As I came out of the chemist's I looked towards the coffee shop and got eye-to-eye. I started walking towards him, big grin all over my face, as if I'd just spotted a long-lost pal, but didn't say anything yet. If somebody was watching him, knowing he was on his own, it wouldn't look natural for me just to come up and sit next to him and start talking. It had to look like a chance meeting, yet not such a noisy one that people noticed it. They wouldn't think, Oh, look, there's two spies meeting, but it registers. It might not mean anything at the time, but it could cost you later.

Euan half got to his feet and reciprocated my smile. 'Hello, dickhead, what are you doing here?' He gestured for me to join him.

We sat down, and since Euan was sponsoring the RV he came up with the cover story. 'I've just come to see you from Belfast before you fly back to London. Old friends from school days.' It helps to know you both have the same story.

'Where are they?' I said, as if asking after the family.

'My half left and you've got the bar. Go right of the TV. They're sitting – one's got a jean jacket on, one a black three-quarter-length suede coat. Kerr is on the right-hand side. He's now called Michael Lindsay. McGear is Morgan Ashdown.'

'Have they checked in?'

'Yes. Hand luggage only.'

'For two weeks in Washington?'

'Suit-carriers.'

'And they haven't gone to any other check-in?'

'No, it looks like they're going to Heathrow.'

I walked over to the counter and bought two coffees.

I could tell they were the only Irishmen at the bar, because everybody else was wearing Guinness polo shirts and drinking pints of the black stuff. These two were on Budweiser by the neck and watching the football. Both had cigarettes on the go and were smoking like ten men; if I'd been watching them in a bar in Derry I'd have taken it as nervousness, but Aer Lingus have a no-smoking policy on their flights and it looked as if these boys were getting their big hit before boarding.

Both were looking very much the tourist, clean-shaven, clean hair, not overdressed as businessmen, not underdressed as slobs. Basically, they were so nondescript you wouldn't give them a second glance, which indicated that they were quite switched on – and that was a problem for me. If they'd been looking a bag of bollocks or at all nervous, I'd have known I was up against second- or third-division players – easy job. But these boys were Premier League, a long way from hanging around the Bogside on kneecapping duty.

There were kids everywhere, chasing and shouting, mothers screaming after two-year-olds who'd found their feet and were skimming across the terminal. For us, the more noise and activity the better. I sat down with the drinks. I wanted to get as much information as I could from Euan before they went airside.

On cue, he said, 'I picked McGear up from Derry. He went to the Sinn Féin office in Cable Street and presumably got the brief, then to Belfast. The spooks tried to use the listening device but didn't have any luck. Nothing else to report, really. They spent the night on the piss, then came down here. Been here about two hours. They booked the flight by credit card in their cover names. Their cover's good. They've even got their Virgin cabin-luggage tags on, they don't want anything to go wrong.'

'Where are they staying?'

'I don't know. It's all very last-minute and Easter's a busy time. There are about ten Virgin-affiliated hotels in Washington and it's probably one of them – we haven't had time to check.'

'Is that all?' I said.

'That's your lot. I don't know how they're going to transfer from the airport, but it looks like they're off to DC, big boy.' Subject closed, as far as Euan was concerned. It was now time to talk shit. 'You still see a lot of Kev?'

I took a mouthful of coffee and nodded. 'Yeah, he's in Washington now; he's doing all right. The kids and Marsha are fine. I saw them about four months ago. He's been promoted and they've just bought a plastic mansion on this naff estate. It's what you'd call executive housing.'

Euan grinned, looking like Father Christmas with white froth on his top lip. His own place was a stone-walled sheep-farmer's house in the middle of nowhere on the Black Mountains in Wales. His nearest neighbour was 2 miles away on the other side of the valley.

I said, 'Marsha loves it in Washington – no-one trying to shoot holes in the car.'

Marsha, an American, was Kev's second wife. After leaving the Regiment he'd moved to the States with her and had joined the DEA. He had three grown-up kids from his first marriage and two from this one, Kelly and Aida.

'Is Slack Pat still over there?'

'I think so, but you know what he's like: one minute he's going to learn how to housebuild and the next minute he's going to take up tree-hugging and crocheting. Fuck knows what he's doing now.'

Pat had had a job for two years looking after the family of an Arab diplomat in DC. It worked out really well – he even got an apartment thrown in – but eventually the children he was minding grew too old to be looked after. They were off back to Saudi, so he binned his job and started bumming around. The fact was, he'd made so much money during those two years he wasn't in a hurry.

We carried on chatting and joking, but all the time Euan's eyes flickered towards the targets.

The players ordered another drink, so it looked as if we were going to be sat there for a while. We carried on spinning the social shit.

'How's year ten of the housebuilding programme?' I grinned.

'I'm still having problems with the boiler.'

He'd decided that he was going to put in the central heating himself, but it was a total balls-up. He'd ended up spending twice as much money as if he'd got someone in.

'Apart from that, it's all squared away. You should come down some time. I can't wait to finish this fucking tour, then I've got about two more years and that's me out.'

'What are you going to do?'

'As long as it's not what you're doing, I don't care. I thought I'd become a dustman. I don't give a fuck really.'

I laughed. 'You do! You'll be scratching to stay in, you're a party man. You'll stay in for ever. You moan about it all the time, but actually you love it.'

Euan checked the players, then looked back at me. I knew exactly what he was thinking.

I said, 'You're right. Don't do this job, it's shit.'

'What have you been up to since your little Middle Eastern adventure?'

'I've been on holiday, got some free-fall in, did a bit of work for a couple of the companies, but actually not much, and to tell you the truth it's great. Now I'm just waiting for the outcome of the inquiry. I think I'm in the shit – unless this job gets me out.'

Euan's eyes moved again. 'It looks like you're off.'

The two boys must have started to sort themselves out at the bar.

I said, 'I'll give you a ring after this is finished. When are you back in the UK?'

'I don't know. Maybe a few days.'

'I'll give you a call, we can arrange something. You got yourself a woman yet, or what?'

'You've got to be pissed! I was going out with someone from the London office for a while, but she wanted to make me all nice and fluffy. She was starting to do my washing and all sorts of shit. I really didn't get into it.'

'You mean she didn't iron a crease in the front of your jeans?'

Euan shrugged. 'She didn't do things my way.'

Nobody did. Euan was the tidiest man in the world. If you sat on a cushion he would puff it up again the moment you stood up. He folded his socks instead of putting them inside each other, and stacked his coins in their denominations. Since his divorce he'd turned into Mr I'm-going-to-have-the-best-of-everything. People even started to call him Mr Habitat – you name it, spotlights, three-piece suite, the lot. The inside of his sheep-shagger's house was like a showroom.

I could tell Euan was watching the two players pick up their kit and walk from the bar.

I took my time, no need to get right up their arse. Euan would tell me when to move.

'Do a one eighty,' he said. 'Look half right, just approaching the newsagent's.'

I casually got to my feet. It had been great to see him. Maybe this job would turn out to be a waste of time, but at least I'd seen my bestest mate. We shook hands and I walked away. Then I turned, looked half right, and pinged them, suit-carriers over their arms.

The departures lounge looked like an Irish craft fair. I was starting to feel out of place; I should have got myself a Guinness hat.

What was I going to do once I got to Washington? I didn't know if somebody was going to pick them up, whether they were taking a cab or the bus, or, if they'd managed to get a hotel, whether it included a transfer. If they started moving around the city, that would be fun, too. I knew Washington a bit, but not in any great detail.

They were still smoking like beagles in a lab. I sat in the lounge and picked up a paper from the seat. McGear started scrabbling about in his pocket for change as they talked to each other standing at the bar. He was suddenly looking purposeful; he was going to either the fruit machines or the telephone.

He got out a note and leaned over to the barman, and I could see him asking for change. I was sitting more or less directly behind them and about 20 feet back, so even if they turned their heads 45 degrees either side I still wouldn't be in their peripheral vision.

McGear walked towards the fruit machines, but carried on past. It must be the telephone.

I got up and wandered over to the newsagent's, pretending to check the spinning rack of paperbacks outside.

He picked up the phone, put a couple of pound coins in and dialled. He got the number from a piece of paper, so it wasn't one that was well known to him. I looked at my G Shock; it was 16:16. The display was still on dual time; if there were any Iraqis in the lounge needing to know the time in Baghdad, I was their man.

I checked my pockets for coins: I had about two and a half quid; I would need more for what I was going to do, so I went in and bought a newspaper with a £20 note. The woman behind the counter looked well impressed.

McGear finished his call and went back to the bar. These boys weren't going anywhere; they ordered another beer, opened their papers and lit another fag.

I gave it a couple of minutes, then strolled over to the phone McGear had been using. I picked up the receiver, threw in a couple of pound coins and looked for a number on the set. I couldn't find one; not to worry, it would just take a bit longer.

I dialled a London number and a woman's voice said, 'Good afternoon. Your PIN number, please?'

'2422.' The digits were etched into my memory; they were the first half of the army number that I'd had since I was sixteen.

She said, 'Do you have a number?'

'No. This line, please.'

'Wait.'

I heard a click, then nothing. I kept my eyes on the players and fed the phone. Within a minute she was back.

'What times are you interested in?'

'I'd like to book it from 1613 up till now.'

'That's fine. Do you want me to call you or will you call back?'

'I'll call back. Ten minutes?'

'Fine. Goodbye.'

And that was it. No matter where you are in the world, you can dial in and the Firm will run a trace.

I phoned back ten minutes later. We went through the same PIN-number routine, then she said, 'Nothing until 1610 hours. A Washington, DC number, 703 661 8230. Washington Flyer Taxis, USA.'

I jotted down the number, hung up and immediately dialled it.

'Good morning, Washington Flyer Taxis, Gerry speaking. How may I be of assistance today?'

'Yes, I wonder if a Mr Ashdown or Lindsay has booked a taxi? I just want to check they're going to get to a meeting on time.'

'Oh, yes, sir, we've just had the booking. Collect from Dulles, arriving on flight number—'

I cut in. 'Are you going to drop them off at the hotel, or are they coming straight to me at Tyson's Corner?'

'Let me see, sir . . . they're booked for the Westin on M Street.'

'All right, that's fine. Thank you.'

Now all I had to do was try to get to the Westin before them. Everything seemed to be going to plan. Either that, or the fuckers had pinged me and were putting in a deception.

The flight to London Heathrow was getting ready to board. I watched them get up, find their passes and walk. I followed.

On something like this you always travel Club Class, so you're at the front of the aircraft. Then you can choose either to sit down and watch people boarding, or let them through ahead of you and come in later on. At the destination, you can wait for the target to come off the aircraft and naturally file in behind, or get out of the way beforehand so that you're ready to do the pick-up once you're out of arrivals.

I thought about a drink, but decided against; I might have to start performing as soon as we got to the other side. These boys seemed switched on and professional, so chances were they weren't going to be doing any work after all the Bud they'd been putting away. But, still, no drink for me.

As I settled into my seat I started to think about Kev and his family. I'd been there when he'd first met Marsha, I was best man at their wedding and was even godfather to Aida, their second child. I took the job seriously, even though I didn't really know what I was supposed to do on the God front.

I knew I'd never have any of my own kids; I'd be too busy running around doing shit jobs like this. Kev and Marsha knew that and really tried to make me feel part of their set-up. I'd grown up with this fantasy of the perfect family and as far as I was concerned Kev had it. The first marriage went a bit dodgy, but this one seemed absolutely right. His job with the DEA was now mostly desk-bound in Washington. He loved it. 'More time with the kids, mate,' he'd say. 'Yeah, so you can be one!' I'd reply. Luckily Marsha was the mature and sensible one; when it came to the family, they complemented each other really well. Their house at Tyson's Corner was a healthy, loving environment, but after three or four days it would get too much for me and I'd have to move on. They'd make a joke of it; they knew I loved them, but somehow couldn't handle people showing so much affection. I guessed that was why I'd always felt more comfortable with Euan. We were both from the same job lot.

And Pat? 'Slack' was younger than Kev, early forties, and really annoying – blond-haired, blue-eyed, good-looking, clever, articulate, funny – everything I hated. He was 6 feet 2 inches, very well toned, hardly ever needing to do any training, one of those people who naturally shit muscle. Even his hair was immaculate; it never seemed to move. I'd seen him climb into his sleeping bag looking groomed and perfect and wake up in the same condition. As far as I was concerned Pat's only saving grace was that there was nothing where his arse should have been. We used to call him Slack because he had lots of it.

When he started the BG job in Washington, a real-estate agent took him out to look at an apartment in Georgetown, by the university. The way he told the story, he saw a building with people coming in and out.

'What's that, then?' he asked.

'One of the best restaurants in Washington,' she said. 'Half of Congress seems to go there.'

'Right, I'll take it,' he said. The moon was in a new quarter or some shit like that, and I thought for a while that he reckoned he'd turned into Terence Conran. He told me he used to eat there every day and knew every waitress by name. He'd even started going out with one of them. Maybe it was her that got him into drugs. I hadn't seen it myself but I'd heard he had a problem. It made me feel sad. We'd all seen the results of addiction during our time in Colombia. Pat had called them losers, now it seemed he was one himself. Hopefully it was just one of his phases.

3

The transfer at Heathrow had been easy. The boys didn't get stopped at the security checks – probably because Special Branch had been informed – and the flight to Washington had taken off on time.

Now, as we started the approach, I put on my belt, made the seat upright and looked out of the window at America. The view always made me feel good. There's such a sense of opportunity and space, of all things being possible, and it's contagious.

I hoped McGear and Kerr were going straight to the hotel. I hoped they'd be playing the good tourist boys and wouldn't blow it by not booking in. If I ever lost a target, I'd look in all the places where he might be – his place of work, the pub, where the kids go to school, even the betting shop. I needed to know as much as I could about them, because once you're inside your target's mind you can second-guess every movement, even understand why they do what they do. Unfortunately, all I knew so far about McGear and Kerr was that they liked drinking Budweiser and must be gagging for a fag. So I had to start with the hotel.

I needed to get forward of them. That shouldn't be a problem, since Club had its own shuttle bus to get us to the terminal ahead of the herd. However, since they'd pre-booked a transfer, I'd need to grab a cab pretty sharpish if I was going to beat them to M Street. I could have booked one of my own when I spoke to Washington Flyer, but I'd tried to do that in Warsaw once in similar circumstances, only to come out and find the two drivers fighting over who to take first, me or the target. It was the taxi rank for me from then on.

I came out of arrivals through two large automatic doors and into a horseshoe of waiting relatives and limo drivers holding up name boards, all held back by steel barriers. I carried on through the bustle, turned left and walked down a long ramp into heat and brilliant sunshine.

There was a queue at the rank. I did a quick calculation and the number of passengers didn't go into the limited number of cabs. I wandered towards the rear of the rank and waved a $20 bill at one of the drivers. He smiled conspiratorially and hustled me inside. A further $20 soon had me screaming along the Dulles access road towards Route 66 and Washington, DC. The airport and its surroundings reminded me of a high-tech business park, with everything green and manicured; there'd even been a lake as we exited the terminal. Suburbia started about 15 miles from the airport, mainly ribbon development on either side of the Beltway – vast estates of very neat wooden and brick houses, many still under construction. We passed a sign for the Tyson's Corner turn-off and I strained my neck to see if I could see Kev's place. I couldn't. But, as Euan would have said, executive housing all looks the same.

We crossed the Potomac and entered the city of monuments.

The Westin on M Street was a typically upmarket American hotel, purpose-built, slick and clean, and totally devoid of character. Walking into the lobby, I got my bearings and headed left and up a few stairs to a coffee lounge on a half-landing that overlooked the reception area and the only way in and out. I ordered a double espresso.

A couple of refills later, Kerr and McGear came through the revolving door, looking very relaxed. They went straight to

46

the desk. I put down my coffee, left a $5 bill under the saucer and wandered down.

It was just a matter of getting the timing right; there was a bit of a queue at the desk, but the hotel was as efficient as it was soulless and now had more people behind the reception desk than were waiting to be served.

I couldn't hear what McGear and Kerr were saying, but it was obvious they were checking in. The woman looking after them was tapping a keyboard below desk level. Kerr handed over a credit card for swiping and now was the time to make my approach. It makes life far easier if you can get the required information this way rather than trying to follow them, and there was no way I was going to risk a compromise by getting in the lift with them. I only hoped they were sharing a room.

To the right of them on the reception desk was a rack of information cards, advertising everything from restaurants to trolley-bus rides. I stood about 2 metres away, with my back to them. There was no big flap about this; it was a big, busy hotel, and they weren't looking at me, they were doing their own stuff. I made it obvious I was flicking through the cards and didn't need help.

The woman said, 'There you are, gentlemen, you're in room 403. If you turn left just past the pillars you'll see the elevator. Have a nice day!'

All I had to do now was listen to their conversations while they were in their room, and to make that happen I went to the bank of payphones in the lobby and dialled the Firm.

A woman's voice asked me for my PIN number.

'2422.'

'Go ahead.'

'I'd like a room, please. The Westin on M Street, Washington, DC – 401 or 405, or 303 or 503.'

'Have you a contact number?'

'No, I'll call back in half an hour's time.'

They would now telephone the hotel using the name of a front company and request one of the rooms I'd specified. It didn't really matter whether the room was above, beside or below the targets', as long as we could get in and plant surveillance devices.

I went back to the raised lounge area and read a few of the leaflets and cards I'd picked up, all the time watching the exit on to M Street.

I ran through a mental checklist of surveillance equipment to ask for. I'd fit the first wave of kit myself – wall-mounted listening devices, phone-line devices, both voice and modem, and cables that fed into the TV in my room to relay pictures. They'd only take me about three hours to rig up once the Firm had dropped them off.

The second wave, once McGear and Kerr had vacated their room for the day, would be fitted by technicians from the embassy. In their expert hands, a hotel-room TV could become a camera, and the telephone a microphone.

Half an hour later I rang the contact number and again gave my PIN number. There was a bit of clicking, then the strains of a string quartet. About five seconds later the woman came back again.

'You are to lift off and return today. Please acknowledge.'

I thought I'd misheard her. There was a conference at the hotel given by the Norwegian board of trade and all the delegates were exiting for coffee.

'Can you repeat, please?'

'You are to lift off and return today. Please acknowledge.'

'Yes, I understand, I am to lift off and return today.'

The phone went dead.

I put the phone down. Strange. There had even been a memo in green ink from the head of the service about this – the fastball job that had now come to a sudden halt. It wasn't unusual to get lifted off, but not so quickly. Maybe Simmonds had decided these people weren't that important after all.

Then I thought, So what. Who gives a fuck? At the end of the day, they wanted me to do the job and I've done it. I called the booking agency and tried to get a flight out of Washington. The only one I could get on was the British Airways at 2135, which was hours away. Kev and Marsha were only an hour down the road towards the airport, so why not?

I dialled another number and Kev answered. His voice was wary, then he recognized mine. 'Nick! How's it going?' He sounded really happy to hear me.

'Not too bad. I'm in Washington.'

'What are you doing? Nah, I don't want to know! You coming to see us?'

'If you're not busy. I'm leaving tonight, back to the UK. It'll be a quick stop and hello, OK?'

'Any chance of you getting your arse up here right away? I've just got the ball rolling on something, but I'd be interested to know what you think. You'll really like this one!'

'No problem, mate. I'll hire a car at the hotel and head straight over.'

'Marsha will want to go into cordon bleu overdrive. I'll tell her when she gets back with the kids. Have a meal with us, then I'll take you to the airport. You won't believe the stuff I've got here. Your friends over the water are busy.'

'I can't wait.'

'Nick, there's one other thing.'

'What's that, mate?'

'You owe Aida a birthday present. You forgot again, dickhead.'

Driving west along the freeway, I kept wondering what Kev could want to talk to me about. Friends over the water? Kev had no connection with PIRA that I knew of. He was in the DEA, not the CIA or any anti-terrorist department. Besides, I knew that his job was far more administrative than field work now. I guessed he probably just needed some background information.

I thought again about Slack Pat and made a mental note to ask Kev if he had a contact address for the arseless one.

I got on the interstate. Tyson's Corner was the junction I had to get off at; well, not really, I wanted the one before but I could never remember it. The moment I left the freeway I could have been in leafy suburban Surrey. Large detached houses lined the road, and just about every one seemed to have a seven-seater people-carrier in the drive and a basketball hoop fixed to the wall.

I followed my nose to Kev's estate and turned into their road, Hunting Bear Path. I carried on for about a quarter of a mile, until I reached a small parade of shops arranged in an open square with parking spaces, mainly little delis and boutiques specializing in scented candles and soap. I bought sweets for Aida and Kelly that I knew Marsha wouldn't let them have, and a couple of other presents.

Facing the shops was a stretch of waste ground, which looked as if it had been earmarked as the next phase of the development. On and around the churned-up ground were Portakabins, big stockpiles of girders and other building materials, and a couple of bulldozers.

Far up on the right-hand side amongst the large detached houses, I could just about make out the rear of Kev's and Marsha's 'de luxe colonial'. As I drove closer I could see their Daihatsu people-carrier – the thing she threw the kids into to go, screaming, to school. It had a big furry Garfield stuck to the rear window. I couldn't see Kev's company car, a Caprice Classic that bristled with aerials – such an ugly model only government agents used them. Kev normally kept his in the garage, safely out of sight of predators.

I was looking forward to seeing the Browns again, even though I knew that, by the end of the day, I'd be more exhausted than the kids. I got to the driveway and turned in.

There was nobody waiting. The houses were quite a distance apart, so I didn't see any neighbours either, but I wasn't surprised – the commuter belt of Washington is quite dead during work and school days.

I braced myself; on past form, I'd get ambushed as soon as the car pulled up. The kids would jump out at me, with Marsha and Kev close behind. I always made it look as if I didn't like it, but actually I did. The kids would know I'd have presents. I'd bought a little Tweetie-Pie watch for Aida, and Kelly's was a handful of *Goosebumps* horror books. I wouldn't say anything to Aida about forgetting her birthday; hopefully she'd have forgotten.

I got out of the car and walked towards the front door. Still no ambush. So far, so good.

The front door was ajar about 2 inches. I thought, Here we go, what they want me to do is walk into the hallway like Inspector Clouseau, and there's going to be a Kato-type ambush. I pushed the door wide open and called out, 'Hello? Hello? Anyone home?'

Any minute now the kids would be attacking a leg each.

But nothing happened.

Maybe they had a new plan and were all squared away somewhere in the house, waiting, trying to stifle their giggles.

Once through the front door there was a little corridor which opened up into a large rectangular hallway, with doors leading off to the different downstairs rooms. In the kitchen, to my right, I heard a female voice on the radio singing a station logo.

Still no kids. I started tiptoeing towards the noise in the kitchen. In a loud stage whisper I said, 'Well, well, well – I'll have to leave . . . seeing as nobody's here . . . what a shame, because I've got two presents for two little girls . . .'

To my left was the door to the lounge, open about a foot or so. I didn't look in as I walked past, but I saw something in my peripheral vision that at first didn't register. Or maybe it did; maybe my brain processed the information and rejected it as too horrible to be true.

It took a second for it to sink in, and when it did my whole body stiffened.

I turned my head slowly, trying to make sense of what was in front of me.

It was Kev. He was lying on his side on the floor, and his head had been battered to fuck by a baseball bat. I knew that because I could see it on the floor beside him. It was one he'd shown off to me on my last visit, a nice, light aluminium one. He'd shaken his head and laughed when he'd said the local rednecks called them 'Alabama lie detectors'.

I was still rooted to the spot.

I thought, Fucking hell, he's dead – or should be, looking at the state of him.

What about Marsha and the kids?

Was the killer still in the house?

I had to get a weapon.

There was nothing I could do for Kev at the moment. I didn't even think about him, just that I needed one of his pistols. I knew where all five of them were concealed in the house, always above child level and always loaded and made ready, a magazine on the weapon and a round in the chamber. All Marsha or Kev had to do was pick up one of the weapons and blat anyone who was pissed off with Kev – and there were more than a few of those in the drug community. I thought, Fuck, they've got him at last.

Very slowly, I put the presents on the floor. I wanted to listen for any creaking of floors, any movement at all around the house.

The living room was large and rectangular. Against the left-hand gable wall was a fireplace. Either side of it were alcoves with bookshelves, and I knew that on the second shelf up, on the right, was the world's biggest, fattest thesaurus, and on top of that, tucked well back out of view, just above head level, but close enough to reach up for, was a big fat gun. It was lying so that, as you picked it up, it would be in the correct position to fire.

I ran. I didn't even look to see if there was anyone else in the room. Without a weapon, it wouldn't have made much difference.

I reached the bookcase, put my hand up and took hold of the pistol, spun round and went straight down onto my knees in the aim position. It was a Heckler & Koch USP 9mm, a fantastic weapon. This one even had a laser sight under the barrel – where the beam hits, so does the round.

I took a series of deep breaths. Once I'd calmed myself, I looked down and checked chamber. I got the topslide and pulled it back a bit. I could see the brass casing in position.

Now what was I going to do? I had my car outside; if that got reported and traced there'd be all kinds of drama. I was still under my alias cover; if I got discovered, that meant the job got discovered, and then I'd be in a world of shit.

I had a quick look at Kev, just in case I could see breathing. No chance. His brains were hanging out, his face was pulped. He was dead, and whoever had done it was so blasé they'd just thrown the baseball bat down and left it there.

There was blood all over the glass coffee table and the thick shagpile carpet. Some was even splattered on the patio windows. But strangely, apart from that, there wasn't much sign of a struggle.

4

I had to make sure Marsha and the kids weren't still here, tied up in another room or held down by some fucker with a gun to their heads. I was going to have to clear the house.

If only room-clearing was as easy as Don Johnson made it look in *Miami Vice* – run up to the door, get right up against the door frame, jump out into the middle of it, pistol poised, and win the day. A doorway naturally draws fire, and if you stand in one you're presenting yourself as a target. If there's a boy waiting the other side for you with a shotgun, you're dead.

The first room I had to clear was the kitchen; it was the nearest, plus it had sound.

I was on the opposite side of the living room to the kitchen door. I started to move along the outside wall of the room. I stepped over Kev, not bothering to look at him. The pistol was out in front of me; it had to be ready to fire as soon as I saw a target. Where your eyes go, the pistol goes.

I mentally divided the room into bounds. The first was from the settee halfway across the lounge, a distance of about 20 feet; I got there and went static by a big TV/stereo set-up, which gave me a bit of cover while I cleared the door that led back to the hall-way. It was still open.

There was nothing in the hallway. As I moved through, I closed the door behind me. I approached the one to the kitchen. The handle was on the right-hand side and I couldn't see the hinges, so it had to open inwards. I moved across to the hinged side and listened. Just above the sound of my breath and that of my heart thumping I could hear some bonehead on the radio, 'Injured at work? Fight for compensation through our expert attorneys – and remember, no win, no fee.'

My pistol arm wasn't completely stretched out, but the weapon was still facing forward. I leaned over to the handle, turned it, gave the door a push and moved back. Then I opened it a bit more from the hinge side to see if there was any reaction from inside the kitchen.

I could hear more of the radio and also a washing machine – turning, stopping, turning. But nothing happened.

With the door now open just a few more inches, I could see into a small part of the kitchen. I moved forward and pushed the door fully open. Still no reaction. Using the door frame and wall as cover, I edged round slowly.

As the angle between me and the frame increased, I gradually saw more of the room. I took my time so I could take in the information in stages. If I had to react, the fact of being 2 yards away from the door frame would not affect my shooting, and, if it did, I shouldn't be in this business anyway. Using my right thumb, I pushed the laser-sight button. A small dot of brilliant-red light splashed on the kitchen wall.

I leaned my body over to present as small a target as possible. If anyone was in the kitchen, all they'd see was a very nervous bit of head, and that would be what they'd have to react to, not the full Don Johnson.

The room was like the *Mary Celeste*. Food was still on the side in the middle of preparation. Kev had said Marsha was going to cook something special. There were vegetables and opened packs of meat. I closed the door behind me. By now the radio was playing some soft rock and the washing machine was on spin. The table was half laid, and that really upset me. Kev and Marsha were very strict on the kids' chores; the sight of the half-laid table made me feel sick inside because it heightened the chances of the kids being either dead, or upstairs with some fucker with a 9mm stuck in their mouth.

I moved slowly to the other end of the room and locked the door to the garage. I didn't want to clear the bottom of the house only for the boys to come in behind me.

I was starting to flap big-time. Were Marsha and the kids still in the house or had they made a run for it? I couldn't just leave. The fuckers who'd done that to Kev would be capable of anything. I was starting to feel my stomach churn. What the fuck was I going to find upstairs?

I went out into the hallway again. As I moved, I had my pistol pointing up the stairs, which were now opposite me. The last room uncleared downstairs was Kev's study. I put my ear to the door and listened. I couldn't hear anything. I did the same drill and made entry.

It was a small room, just enough space for some filing cabinets, a desk and a chair. Shelves on the wall facing the desk were full of books and photographs of Kev shooting, Kev running, that sort of stuff. Everything was now on the floor; the filing cabinets were opened and paper strewn everywhere. The only thing not ripped apart was Kev's PC. That was lying on its side on the desk, the screen still showing the British Army screen saver I'd sent him for a laugh. The printer and scanner were on the floor beside the desk, but that was where they had always been.

I went back out and looked at the stairs. They were going to be a problem. They went up one flight, then turned back on themselves for the second before hitting the landing. That meant that I'd have to be a bit of a Houdini to cover my arse getting up there. I wouldn't use the laser now; I didn't want to announce my movements.

I put my foot on the bottom stair and started to move up. Fortunately Kev's stair carpet was a thick shagpile, which helped keep the noise down, but still it was like treading on ice, gently testing each step for creaks, always placing my feet to the inside edge, slowly and precisely.

Once I got level with the landing, I pointed my pistol up above my head and, using the wall as support, moved up the stairs backwards, step by step.

A couple of steps; wait, listen. A couple more steps; wait, listen.

There was only one of me and I had only thirteen rounds to play with, maybe fourteen if the round in the chamber was on top of a full magazine. These boys might have semi-automatic weapons for all I knew, or even fully automatic. If they did, and were waiting for me, it would not be a good day out.

The washing machine was on its final thundering spin. Still soft rock on the radio. Nothing else.

Adrenalin takes over. Despite the air-conditioning I was drenched with sweat. It was starting to get in my eyes; I had to wipe them with my left hand, one eye at a time.

The girls' room was facing me. From memory there were bunk beds and the world's biggest shrine to *Pocahontas* – T-shirts and posters, bed linen and even a doll whose back you pressed and she sang something about colours.

I stopped and prepared myself for the worst.

I reached for the handle and started to clear the room. Nothing. No-one.

For once the room was even clean and tidy. There were piles of teddies and toys on the beds. The theme was still *Pocahontas*, but *Toy Story* was obviously a close second.

I gradually came out onto the landing, treating it as if it was a new room because I didn't know what might have gone on in the half-minute since I'd left it.

I moved slowly down to the next bedroom, with my back nearly touching the wall, pistol forward, eyes watching front and rear, thinking, What if? What do I do if they appear from that doorway? What if? . . . What if?

As I got nearer to Kev's and Marsha's room I could see that the door was slightly ajar. I couldn't actually see anything inside yet, but, as I moved nearer, I started to smell something. A faint metallic tang, and I could smell shit as well. I felt sick. I knew that I'd have to go in.

As I inched round the door frame, I got my first glimpse of Marsha. She was kneeling by the bed, her top half spreadeagled on the mattress. The bedspread was covered in blood.

I sank to my knees in the hallway. I felt myself going into shock. I couldn't believe this was true. This was not happening to this family. Why kill Marsha? It should have been Kev they were after. All I wanted to do was throw my hand in and sit down and cry, but I knew the kids had been in the house; they might still be here.

I got a grip on myself and started to move. I went in, forcing myself to ignore Marsha. The room was clear.

The next job was the *en suite* bathroom. I made entry, and what I saw made me lose it, totally fucking lose it. *Bang,* I went back against the wall and slumped onto the floor.

Aida was lying on the floor between the bath and the toilet. Her five-year-old head had been nearly severed from her shoulders. There was just 3 inches of flesh left intact and I could see the vertebrae still holding on.

Blood was everywhere. I got it all over my shirt and hands; I was sitting in a pool of it, soaking the seat of my trousers.

Turning my head away and looking out of the *en suite*, I could now see more of Marsha. I had to hold back my scream. Her dress was hanging normally, but her tights had been torn, her knickers were pulled down and she had shat herself, probably at the point of death. All I saw at this distance of about 15 feet away was someone I really cared for, maybe even loved, on her knees, her blood splattered all over the bed. And she'd had the same done to her as Aida.

I was taking deep breaths and wiping my eyes. I knew I still had another two rooms to clear – another bathroom and the large annexe above the garage. I couldn't give up now because I might land up getting dropped myself.

I cleared the other rooms, and half collapsed, half sat on the landing. I could see my bloody footprints all over the carpet.

Stop, calm down, and think.

What next? Kelly. Where the fuck was Kelly?

Then I remembered the hiding place. Because of the threats to Kev, both kids knew where they had to go and hide in the event of a drama.

The thought brought me to my senses. If that was where Kelly was hiding, she was safe for the time being. Better to leave her there while I did the other stuff I had to do.

I got up and started to move down the stairs, making sure that, as I moved, I had my pistol pointed. As I descended I could see the blood I had left on the wall and carpet where I'd sat. I was almost willing the attackers to appear. I wanted to see the fuckers.

I got a cloth and a bin liner from the kitchen and started to run round the house, wiping door handles and any surfaces where I might have left fingerprints. Then I went over to the patio sliding doors and closed the curtains. I didn't want anybody to discover an alien set of fingerprints before I was well out of it, hopefully on a plane back to London.

I took a quick look at Kev and knew I was back in control. He was now just a dead body.

I went back upstairs, washed the blood off my hands and face, and got a clean shirt and pair of jeans and trainers from Kev's cupboards. His clothes didn't fit me but they would do for now. I bundled my own bloodstained stuff into the bin liner that I'd be taking with me.

5

Kev had shown me the 'hidey-hole', as he called it, built under an
open staircase that led up to a little makeshift loft stacked with
ladders. If ever Kev or Marsha shouted the word 'Disneyland!'
the kids knew they had to go and hide there – and they were not
to come out until Daddy or Mummy came and got them.

I started making entry into the garage. Pushing the door
slightly, I could see the rear of the large metal up-and-over doors
to the right. The garage could easily have taken three extra
vehicles besides Kev's company car. 'Fucking thing,' I remembered Kev saying, 'all the luxury and mod cons of the late
Nineties in a car that looks like a Sixties fridge.'

The kids' bikes were hanging from frames on the wall, together
with all the other clutter that families accumulate in garages. I
could see the red laser splash on the far wall.

I moved in and cleared through. There was no-one here.

I went back to the area of the staircase. Chances were she
wasn't going to come out unless her Mum and Dad came for her,
but as I moved I started to call out very gently, 'Kelly! It's Nick!
Hello, Kelly, where are you?'

All the time the pistol was pointing forward, ready to take on
any threat.

Moving slowly towards the boxes, I said, 'Oh well, since you're not here I'll go. But I think I'll have one more look and I bet you're hiding in the Disneyland place. I'll just have a look . . . I bet you're in there . . .'

There was a pile of large boxes. One had contained a fridge freezer, another a washing machine. Kev had made a sort of cave with them under the staircase and kept a few toys there.

I eased the pistol down my waistband. I didn't want her to see a gun. She'd probably seen and heard enough already.

I put my mouth against a little gap between the boxes. 'Kelly, it's me, Nick. Don't be scared. I'm going to crawl towards you. You'll see my head in a minute and I want to see a big smile . . .'

I got down on my hands and knees and carried on talking gently as I moved boxes and squeezed through the gap, inching towards the back wall. I wanted to do it nice and slowly. I didn't know how she was going to react.

'I'm going to put my head round the corner now, Kelly.'

I took a deep breath and moved my head round the back of the box, smiling away but ready for the worst.

She was there, facing me, eyes wide with terror, sitting curled up in a foetal position, rocking her body backwards and forwards, holding her hands over her ears.

'Hello, Kelly,' I said very softly.

She must have recognized me, but didn't reply. She just carried on rocking, staring at me with wide, scared dark eyes.

'Mummy and Daddy can't come and get you out at the moment, but you can come with me. Daddy told me it would be OK. Are you going to come with me, Kelly?'

Still no reply. I crawled right into the cave until I was curled up beside her. She'd been crying and strands of light-brown hair were stuck to her face. I tried to move them away from her mouth. Her eyes were red and swollen.

'You're in a bit of a mess there,' I said. 'Do you want me to clean you up? Come on, let's go and get you sorted out, shall we?' I got hold of her hand and gently guided her out into the garage.

She was dressed in jeans, jean shirt, trainers and a blue nylon puffer jacket. Her hair was straight and just above her shoulders, a bit shorter than I remembered it, and she was quite lanky for a seven-year-old, with long, skinny legs. I picked her up in my arms and held her tight as I carried her into the kitchen. I knew the other doors were closed, so she wouldn't see her dad.

I sat her down on a chair at the table. 'Mummy and Daddy said they had to go away for a while, but asked me to look after you until they come back, OK?'

She was trembling so much I couldn't tell if her head was nodding or shaking.

I went to the fridge and opened it, hoping to find some comfort food. Two large, half-eaten Easter eggs were on the shelf. 'Mmm, yum – do you want some chocolate?'

I'd had a good relationship with Kelly. I thought she was a great kid, and that wasn't just because she was my mate's daughter. I smiled warmly, but she stared at the table.

I broke off a few pieces and put them on one of the side plates that she'd probably been setting earlier with Aida. I found the off switch on the radio; I'd had enough relaxing soft rock for one day.

As I looked at her again I suddenly realized I'd fucked up. What was I going to do with her? I couldn't just leave her here; her family were lying dead all over the house. But, more importantly, she knew me. When the police arrived she'd be able to say, 'Nick Stone was here.' They'd soon find out that Nick Stone was one of Daddy's mates and the house was full of photographs with me in them. And, if they did arrest the grinning drunk in the barbecue shots, they'd find that, for some strange reason, he wasn't Nick Stone at all, he was Mrs Stamford's little boy. As they used to say in the Harp commercial, time to make a sharp exit.

Kev's jacket was hanging over one of the chairs. I said, 'Let's wrap you up in your dad's coat; that'll keep you nice and warm.' At least she'd have something of her dad's; with luck it would cheer her up.

There was just a little bit of whimpering in reply. She was

almost in rigor mortis with shock, though at least she had turned her head to look at me now. This was where normally I would have let Marsha take over, because a child's mind was far too complicated for me to work out. But I couldn't do that today.

I wrapped the coat around her and said, 'Here you are, get this around you. Look, it's your dad's! Don't tell him, eh, ha ha ha!' I felt something solid in one of the pockets and checked. 'Oh good, look, we can phone him up later.'

I looked out of the window – no movement. I picked up the bin liner, grabbed Kelly's hand, then realized that, to reach the front door, I'd have to come out of the kitchen and into the hallway.

'Just sit there a second,' I said, 'I've got to do something.'

I had a quick check to make sure the doors were closed. I thought again about fingerprints but, if I'd missed a set, there was nothing I could do about it now. My only thought was to get out of the area and keep Kelly away from the police until I'd sorted things out.

I went back and got her and checked the front of the house again for movement. She seemed to be finding it hard to walk. I had to grip Kev's coat by the collar and half drag her towards the car.

I put her in the front passenger seat and smiled, 'There you go, that's nice and warm. Better look after your dad's coat for him. Keep it nice for when you see him.'

Then I threw the bin liner in the back, settled into the driver's seat, put my seat belt on and turned the ignition. We drove off at a really sensible pace, nothing outrageous, nothing likely to be noticed.

We'd only gone a few hundred yards when I thought of something; I looked across at her and said, 'Kelly, put your seat belt on. Do you know how to do that?'

She didn't move, didn't even look at me. I had to do it for her.

I tried to make small talk. 'It's a nice day today, isn't it? Yep, you'll stay with me a while; we'll get everything sorted out.'

Silence.

My mind switched back to the matter in hand. What was I going to do? Whatever I decided, I knew it was no good where we were at the moment; we needed to lose ourselves in a crowd. I headed for Tyson's Corner.

I turned to Kelly and smiled, trying to be happy-go-lucky Uncle Nick, but it just wasn't happening. She was staring anxiously out of the window, as if she thought she was being wrenched away from all her familiar landmarks and seeing them for the last time.

'It's OK, Kelly.' I tried to stroke her hair.

She jerked her head away.

Fuck it, just let her get on with it; with luck I'd be able to offload her before too long.

I turned my thoughts to Kev. He'd said he had some information about my 'friends over the water'. Could it have been PIRA who'd killed him? What the hell for? It was highly unlikely that they'd start messing about like that, not in America. They were too switched on to bite the hand that was feeding them.

Other things weren't adding up. Why wasn't there a struggle? Both Marsha and Kev knew where the weapons were. Why weren't they used? Why was the front door ajar? There was no way that would have happened. People didn't just wander in off the street into Kev's house, they had to be invited in.

I felt a rush of anger. If the family had been killed in a car crash, fair one. If the killers had come in and maybe shot them, I'd be upset, but, at the end of the day, if you live by the sword, you must be prepared to die by the sword. But not this way. They'd been hacked about for no reason that I could see.

I forced myself to think rationally. There was no way I could phone the police and explain my version. Although I'd been lifted off, I was still operating in another country without its consent. It goes on in the UK, too, but getting caught would be a big no-no. The operation here would be seen as a sign of betrayal and would create distrust between the two security communities.

There was no way SIS would back me up; that would defeat the whole purpose of deniable ops. I was on my own.

Looking at my passenger I knew I had a problem. As we drove towards Tyson's Corner I realized what I had to do. I saw a Best Western hotel on the left and an open-plan mall on the right. I had to dump the car because, if I'd been seen, that was one of the connections between me and the house. I needed somewhere to leave it that wasn't isolated, somewhere without video cameras. As well as the shopping mall and its massive car parks, satelliting it was a drive-thru Burger King with its own parking.

It's all very well abandoning a vehicle in the middle of hundreds of others in a car park during shopping hours, but at night it might be the only car left there; it's going to stick out, and will be checked over by police patrols. What I was after was an area that was really busy, day and night. Multi-storey car parks were out, because nine times out of ten they have video cameras to stop muggings and car theft. Many multi-storey car parks have a camera that takes a picture of the number plate and driver as you drive in. At any major junction and along most major thoroughfares, there are traffic video cameras. If my car had been pinged outside Kev's house, the first thing they'd do was study the traffic videos and car-park photography.

'Shall we get a burger and some shakes?' I suggested. 'Do you like milk shakes? I tell you what, I'll park up and maybe we'll even go shopping.'

Again it would be no good driving into the Burger King car park, stepping out and then walking a few hundred metres to the shopping mall – that isn't normal behaviour. It might register in people's minds and be triggered off at a later date, so I wanted to make the two of us look as natural as possible.

'Strawberry or vanilla – which one do you want?'

No reply.

'Chocolate? Go on, I'm going to have a chocolate.'

Nothing.

I parked up. The place was pretty full. I cupped my hand under her chin and gently turned her face so that she was looking at my big smile. 'Milk shake?'

There was a faint movement of her head, or maybe it was a nod of appreciation. Not much, but at least it was a reaction.

I carried on with the bullshit. 'You just sit here, then. I'll get out, I'll lock the car and go and get the milkshakes. And then, I tell you what, we'll go into the shopping mall. How about that?'

She looked away.

I carried on as if she'd given me a positive response. I got out of the car and locked her in. I still had the pistol tucked into my waistband, concealed by Kev's jacket.

I went into the Burger King, got two different-flavoured milk-shakes, and came straight back to the car.

'Here we go, then, chocolate or vanilla?'

She kept her hands by her sides. 'I'll tell you what, I'll have the vanilla; I know you like chocolate.'

I put the shake in her lap. It was too cold for her legs and, as soon as she lifted it up, I said, 'Come on, then, let's go to the shops. You can bring that with you.'

I got her out, closed the door and locked up. I did nothing about our fingerprints; no matter how hard I tried I'd never get rid of them all, so what was the point? I opened the boot, pulled out the bag with the bits and pieces I'd bought at Shannon, and threw in the bin liner full of bloodstained clothing.

It looked like rain. We walked towards the shopping mall and I kept on talking to her because the situation felt so awkward. What else do you do, walking along with a kid who doesn't belong to you and doesn't want to be with you?

I tried to hold her hand, but she refused. I couldn't make an issue of it with people around, so I gripped the shoulder of the jacket again.

There was everything in the shopping centre, from a computer discount warehouse to an army surplus store, all housed in long, one-storey, purpose-built units that were like islands in a sea of car park.

We went into a clothes store and I bought myself some jeans and another shirt. I'd change as soon as I'd had a shower and got Aida's blood off my back and legs.

At an ATM I drew out $300, the maximum allowed on my credit card.

We came back out to the car park, but didn't return to the car. I kept a firm grip on her as we walked towards the hotel across the road.

6

As we got nearer I could see that the Best Western was in fact separated from the main drag by a row of single-storey office buildings. Our view was of the rear of the hotel.

Looking each way, it was obvious that the junctions that would lead us round to the front of the hotel were miles away. I decided to take a short cut. The traffic was busy and the road system hadn't been designed for people on foot. With the number of lanes and volume of traffic, it was like crossing a motorway in the UK, but at least there were traffic lights slowing the vehicles and creating gaps. I gripped Kelly's hand as we dodged to the central reservation and waited for another gap. I looked up at the sky; it was very overcast; rain couldn't be far away.

Drivers, who had probably never seen pedestrians before, hooted furiously, but we made it to the other side and scrambled over small railings onto the sidewalk. More or less directly in front of us was a gap between two office buildings. We went through and crossed a short stretch of waste ground that brought us into the hotel car park. As we walked past the lines of vehicles I memorized the number of letters and numbers for a Virginia plate.

The Best Western was a large, four-storey rectangle, the architecture very 1980s. Every elevation was concrete and painted a sickly off-yellow. As we walked up to the reception area I tried to look inside. I didn't want them to see us coming from the direction of the car park, because it would be odd to walk all that way without first checking that they could take us, and then unloading our bags. I hoped Kelly would stay silent when we were inside; I just wanted to do the business and walk out again as if we were going to see Mummy back in the car.

Inside the lobby I got hold of her and whispered, 'You just sit there. I'm going to get us a room.' I gave her a tourist freebie that was lying on one of the chairs, but she ignored it.

In one corner, by the coffee percolator and cream, was a large TV. A football game was on. I went over to the receptionist, a woman in her mid-forties who thought she was still twenty-four, who was watching the screen and probably fancying her chances with one of the quarterbacks.

All smiles, I said, 'I need a family room just for one night, please.'

'Certainly, sir,' she said, a graduate with honours from Best Western's charm school. 'If you'd like to fill out this card.'

As I started to scribble I said, 'How much is a room anyway?'

'That's sixty-four dollars, plus tax.'

I raised an eyebrow to make it look as if that was a lot of money to a family man like myself.

'I know,' she smiled. 'I'm sorry about that.'

She took my credit card to swipe and I filled in the form with crap. I'd been doing this for donkey's years, lying on hotel forms, looking relaxed as I wrote, but in fact scanning about four questions ahead. I filled in a car reg, too, and, for number of occupants, put two adults and a child.

She handed back my card. 'There you are, Mr Stamford, it's room 224. Where's your car?'

'Just around the corner.' I pointed vaguely to the rear of the hotel.

'OK, if you park by the stairs where you see the Coke and ice machines, turn left at the top of the stairs and you'll see room 224 on the left-hand side. You have a nice day now!'

I could have described the room even before I ran the key card through the lock and opened the door – a TV, two double beds, a couple of chairs and the typical American hotel designer's obsession with dark wood veneers.

I wanted to get Kelly settled quickly so I could use the phone. I pressed the remote and flicked through the channels, hoping to find Nickelodeon. Eventually I found some cartoons. 'I remember this one, it's good – shall we watch it?'

She sat on the bed, staring at me. The expression on her face said she didn't like this outing too much and I could understand that.

'Kelly,' I said, 'I'm going to leave you for just a couple of minutes because I've got to make a phone call. I'll get a drink while I'm out. What would you like? Coke? Mountain Dew? Or do you want some candy?'

There was no reaction, so I just carried on. 'I'm going to lock the door and you're not to answer it to anybody. Nobody at all, OK? I'll use the key to get back in again. You sit there and enjoy yourself and I'll just be about five minutes, OK?'

Still there was no reaction. I hung the Do Not Disturb sign on the door, made sure I had the door swipe card and left.

I was heading for a call box I'd seen in the street because I didn't want her to hear the telephone conversation I was about to have. I didn't know much about kids, but I knew that when I was seven nothing had gone unnoticed in my house. On the off-chance that it wasn't PIN-protected, I took Kev's mobile from his jacket pocket. I pressed the power button and it demanded a PIN number. I tried two basic ones – the usual factory default, four zeros, and then 1 2 3 4. Nothing. I couldn't try any more; with some phones you can only try the wrong PIN three times and then it automatically cuts out and you need to go back to the dealer to get it rectified. I turned off the power and put it back in my pocket. I'd ask Kelly about it later.

I turned left via the car park and headed for the call boxes out on the road. I spent a few moments sorting out in my mind what I wanted to say, and then I dialled London.

In veiled speech I said, 'I've just finished work and I'm in Washington to visit an old friend. I used to work with him ten years ago. He's now working here for the US government.' I outlined the problem and said that Kelly and I both needed help.

Veiled speech is not some magical code; all you're trying to do is intimate what is going on, yet at the same time put off a casual listener. You're not going to fool any professional eavesdroppers – that's what codes and one-time pads and all the rest of it are for. But all London needed to know was that I was in the shit, I had Kev's child and needed sorting out. Quick-time.

'Fine, I'll pass that message on. Have you a contact number?'

'No. I'll ring you back in an hour.'

'OK, goodbye.'

These women never ceased to amaze me. They never, ever got worked up about anything. It must be hard work being their husbands on a Saturday night.

I put down the phone and felt a bit better as I strolled over to a filling station. I knew the Firm would work everything out. They might have to call in some big-time favours in the US to detach me from this shit, but what are friends for? They'd pull out all the stops, not so much to get me off the hook, more to make sure their operation was covered up.

I was trying to look on the bright side, which was more than the weather was doing. It had been starting to drizzle when I left the hotel and that had now turned to light rain. With luck, the Firm would pick us both up tonight. Kelly would be taken care of, and I would be whisked back to the UK for another interview without coffee and biscuits.

I bought some food and drink at the filling station so we could stay in the room and out of the public eye, together with a few other goodies to pass the time, then crossed the road and went back to the hotel. At the drinks machine, I went up the stairs, turned left and knocked on our door.

As I opened it I said, 'I've got loads of stuff – I've got candy, sandwiches, chips – and I've even got you a *Goosebumps* book to read.'

I reckoned it was better to buy loads of stuff to keep her mind off things, rather than trying to cuddle or console her; I'd have felt really uncomfortable with that sort of stuff anyway.

She was lying on the bed exactly where I'd left her, staring in the direction of the television set, but not really watching, her eyes glazed over.

As I put the stuff down on the other bed I said, 'Right, I reckon what you need now is a nice hot bath. I've even bought some Buzz Lightyear bubbly stuff.'

It would give her something to do and maybe relax her out of the catatonic state she was in. Apart from that, when I handed her over to the Firm, I wanted them to see that I'd made an effort and that she was all nice and clean. After all, she was my mate's kid.

I turned the taps on and called back into the room, 'Come on, then, get undressed.'

She didn't reply. I went back into the bedroom, sat at the end of the bed and started undressing her. I thought she might resist, but instead she sat placidly as I pulled off her shirt and vest. 'You do your jeans,' I said. She was only seven, but I felt awkward about taking those off. 'Come on, undo your buttons.' In the end, I had to; she was miles away.

I carried her into the bathroom. Good old Buzz had done his job and the bubbles were halfway to the ceiling. I tested the water, lifted her into the bath, and she sat down without a word.

'There's loads of soap and shampoo,' I said. 'Do you want me to help you wash your hair?'

She sat, stock-still, in the water. I gave her the soap, which she just stared at.

It was nearly time to call London again. At least I wouldn't have to go to a call box for this one; she'd be out of earshot in the bath. Just in case, I kept the TV on.

There was some weird and wonderful cartoon on – four

characters in jeans, half-man, half-shark, who said things like, 'Fin-tastic!' and 'Shark time!' and apparently didn't kick ass, they kicked dorsal. *The Street Sharks*. The opening credits finished and I dialled London.

Straight away I heard, 'PIN number, please?'

I gave it. She went, 'One moment.'

A few seconds later the phone went dead.

That was strange. I dialled again, gave my PIN number and again got cut off.

What the fuck was going on? I tried to reason with myself, tried to tell myself that this was just a fuck-up. But really, inside, I knew the truth. It had to be deliberate. Either that, or maybe, just maybe, the phone line was down. No good thinking about it. Take action.

I went into the bathroom. 'The phone's not working,' I said. 'I'll just go down to the one in the street. Is there anything we need from down the shops? I'll tell you what, we'll go down there later on, the two of us together.'

Her gaze didn't leave the tiles at the end of the bath.

I lifted her out and put a towel around her. 'You're a big girl now. You can dry yourself.' I took the hairbrush from the wash kit and dragged her into the bedroom. 'Once you've done that, brush your hair, and make sure you're all dry and dressed when I come back. We might have to go somewhere. Don't open the door for anyone, OK?'

There was no answer. I pulled out the phone line and left.

7

I was feeling apprehensive as I walked across the car park. I'd done nothing wrong, so why were they cutting me off? Were the Firm going to stitch me up? I started to go through all the scenarios in my head. Did they think that I was the killer? Were they cutting away now as a prelude to denying everything?

I got to the phone, dialled, and the same thing happened. I slowly put down the receiver. I went and sat down on a low wall that made up part of the entrance to the hotel; I needed to think hard. It didn't take long to decide that there was only one option and that was to phone the embassy. I'd be breaking every rule in the book. I wouldn't even bother going through all the protocol; I dialled 411 for directory enquiries and got the number. I got straight through.

'Hello, British Embassy. How may I help you?'

'I want to talk to LOSO.'

'Excuse me?'

'LOSO. Liaison officer, special operations.'

'I'm sorry, we don't have an extension number for that name.'

'Get hold of the defence attaché and tell him there's somebody on the phone who wants to speak to LOSO. It's really important. I need to speak to him now.'

'Hold on a moment.' She clicked off and a string quartet took her place. I listened and waited while the phone card was used up.

Another woman came on the line. 'Hello, how may I help you?'

'I want to talk to LOSO.'

'I'm sorry, we have no-one of that appointment.'

'Then put me through to the DA.'

'Sorry, the defence attaché is not here. Can I help you? Would you like to give me a name and contact number?'

I said, 'Listen in, this is the news. I want LOSO or the DA to pass this on. I've tried to phone up on my PIN number. My PIN number's 2422, and I'm getting blanked off. I'm in a really bad situation at the moment and I need some help. Tell LOSO or the DA that if I don't make contact with London I'm going to expose what I've got in my security blanket. I will call back in three hours' time.'

The woman said, 'Excuse me, could you repeat that?'

'No, you're recording – the message will be understood. All you've got to do is pass that on to the DA or LOSO, I don't give a fuck which one. Tell them I'll call London on the PIN line in three hours' time.'

I put the phone down. The message would get to them. Chances were the DA or LOSO was listening anyway.

Some of the operations I'd been on had been so dirty that no-one would want them exposed, but that could cut two ways: it also meant that someone like me would be expendable if things weren't working too well. I'd always operated on the basis that if you were involved in deniable operations for the intelligence services and hadn't prepared an out for the day they decided to shaft you, then you deserved everything you got. The head shed knew that Ks had security blankets, but everybody denied it – the operators denied it, SIS denied it. I'd always been sure that SIS put as much effort into trying to find where the blackmail kit was hidden as they did on the operations themselves.

I'd committed myself now. It was a card I could only play once. No way would I be living an easy existence after this. I was finished with the Firm and would probably have to spend the rest of my life in a remote mountain village in Sri Lanka, looking over my shoulder.

What if the Firm decided to admit to the Americans that there'd been an op they'd forgotten to mention? Would they take the rap on the knuckles, then say, 'This man killed one of your officers?' No, it didn't work that way. The Firm wouldn't know if my blanket was bluff or not, or, if used, how much damage it could do in the hands of the press. They'd have to take it as real, they'd have to help. They had no choice. We'd get lifted by the Firm, I'd be flown back to the UK, and then I'd take up tree-hugging until they forgot about me.

Kelly was lying on the bed with a towel wrapped around her when I got back to the room. The cartoon had finished and there was some sort of hard-hitting news-type voice on, but I didn't pay much attention to it. I was more interested in getting a response from this little girl. It seemed that I was fast running out of friends, and she might be just seven years old but I wanted to feel she was on my side.

I said, 'We've got to hang around for another hour or two, and then somebody's coming to . . .'

And then it hit me. The no-nonsense female voice was saying, '. . . brutal murders and a possible kidnap . . .' I switched my attention to the screen.

She was black and mid-thirties. Her face was in camera, with Kev's house in the background and the Daihatsu still in the drive. Police were milling around two ambulances with flashing lights.

I grabbed the remote and hit the off button. 'Kelly, naughty girl,' I grinned, 'you haven't cleaned your neck. Just you go and get back in the bath right this minute!'

I nearly threw her into the bathroom. 'And don't come out until I tell you to!'

I hit the on button and kept the volume low.

The woman said, '. . . neighbours report seeing a Caucasian man in his late thirties, around five ten to six feet tall, medium build, with short brown hair. He arrived at the house in a white Dodge with Virginia registration at approximately two forty-five today. We now have Lieutenant Davies from Fairfax County police department . . .'

A balding detective was standing beside her. 'We can confirm that there was a man fitting that description, and we're appealing for more witnesses. We need to know the location of the Browns' seven-year-old daughter, Kelly.'

A picture came up on the screen of her standing in the garden with Aida, with a spoken description. The broadcast cut back to a studio shot of two presenters saying that the family were victims of what appeared to be drug-related murders. A family portrait appeared on the screen. 'Kevin Brown was a member of the Drug Enforcement Administration . . .' The anchormen broadened the piece to a discussion about the drug problem in the Washington area.

There was no sound of splashing water from the bathroom. Kelly would be out again any time. I started flicking channels. Nothing more on the murders. I switched back to children's TV and went into the bathroom.

I hadn't heard any splashing because she wasn't in the bath. She was on the floor under the sink, in the same foetal position I'd found her in at Kev's, hands over her ears to block out the news she'd just heard on the TV.

I wanted to pick her up and comfort her. The only thing was, I didn't know how. I decided to appear unaffected by her condition. 'Hello, Kelly,' I smiled, 'what are you doing down there?'

Her eyes were shut so tight I could see the creases in her face. I picked her up in my arms and started to walk back into the bedroom. 'Hey, you look sleepy. Do you want to watch TV or just go to bed?' It sounded crap to me, but I just didn't know what to say or do. Best to pretend it hadn't happened.

I took off the towel to get her dressed. Her own body heat had dried her by now. 'Come on, let's get some clothes on and your hair combed.' I was really fighting for words.

She just sat there. Then, as I started to pull on her vest, she said quietly, 'Mommy and Daddy are dead, aren't they?'

Getting her arms into the vest suddenly became very interesting. 'What makes you say that? I told you, I'm just looking after you for a while.'

'So am I going to see Mommy and Daddy again?'

I didn't have the words to use or the guts to tell her. 'Yes, of course you will. It's just that they had to go away really quickly. I told you, it was too late to pick you up, but they asked me to look after you. As soon as they come back I'll take you to Mommy and Daddy and Aida. I didn't know it was going to take this long; I thought it was only going to be a couple of hours, but they will be back soon.'

There was a slight pause as she worked through it all. I got her knickers, placed her feet in them and pulled them up.

'Why didn't they want to take me, Nick?' She sounded sad at the thought.

I moved over to the chair and picked up her jeans and shirt. I didn't want her to see my eyes. 'It isn't that they didn't want to take you, but there was a mistake made, and that's why they asked me to look after you.'

'Just like *Home Alone!*'

I turned round and saw that she was smiling. I had to think about that one. 'Yeah, that's right, just like *Home Alone*. They left you by mistake!' I remembered watching it on a flight. Shit film but good booby traps. I busied myself with her jeans again.

'So when will we see them?'

I couldn't spend all day picking up two bits of clothing. I did a half turn and walked back towards the bed.

'That won't be for a while yet, but, when I spoke to them just now, they wanted me to tell you that they love you, and they're missing you, and to do everything I say and be a good girl.'

There was a beaming smile on her face. She was taking this all in and I wished I had the courage to tell her the truth.

I said, 'Kelly, you must do what I say, do you understand that?'

'Sure, I understand.'

She nodded and I saw a little child needing affection.

I gave her my best attempt at a smile. 'Remember, they wanted me to look after you for a while.' I looked into her eyes. 'Come on, cheer up. Let's watch TV.'

We both went back to watch *Power Rangers* with a can of Mountain Dew. I couldn't take my mind off the news broadcast. Kelly's photograph had been on the TV. The receptionist, the clothes-store keeper, anyone, might remember her. Surely the embassy had called London by now, surely every fucker knew what was going on because it was splashed all over the news? No need to wait three hours before making the call.

I'd have to go to the outside phone again because I didn't want Kelly to hear. I put Kev's jacket on, slipped the TV remote control into a pocket, told her where I was going and left.

As I came to the stairs by the Coke machine I looked down. Two cars had pulled up outside the reception lobby. Both were empty, but their doors were still open, as if the occupants had piled out in a hurry.

I looked again. Besides a normal radio aerial, both vehicles had two-foot antennae on the back. One of the cars was a white Ford Taunus, the other a blue Caprice.

There was no time to think, just enough to turn round and run like a man possessed towards the rear fire escape.

8

Now wasn't the time to worry about how they'd found us. As I ran, the options started to race through my mind. The obvious one was to leave Kelly where she was and let them pick her up. She was a millstone around my neck. On my own, I could get away.

So why did I stop running? I wasn't too sure; instinct told me that she had to come with me.

I doubled back and burst into the room. 'Kelly, we've got to go! Come on, get up!'

She'd been drifting off to sleep. There was a look of horror on her face because of my change of tone.

'We've got to go!'

Grabbing her coat, I picked her up in my arms and started towards the door. I snatched up her shoes and stuffed them into my pockets. She made a sound, half frightened, half protesting.

'Just hold on!' I said. Her legs were wrapped around my waist.

I came out onto the landing. I closed the door behind us and it locked automatically. They'd have to break it down. I had a quick check along the corridor, not bothering to look below to see what was happening. I'd soon know if they were behind us.

I turned left and ran to the end of the corridor, turned left again and there was the fire exit. I pushed the bar and it opened. We were on an open concrete staircase at the rear of the hotel, facing the shopping mall area about a quarter of a mile away.

She started to cry. There was no time to be nice. I got hold of her head so that her face came right up to mine. 'People have come to take you away, do you understand that?' I knew it would frighten her and that it would probably fuck up her mind even more, but I didn't care about that. 'I'm trying to save you. Shut up and do what I say!'

I squeezed her cheek hard and shook her face. 'Do you understand me, Kelly? Shut up and hold me very tight.'

I buried her face in my shoulder and lunged down the concrete stairs looking for my escape route.

Ahead of us lay about 40 metres of rough grassland and, beyond that, a 6-foot chain link fence that looked old and rusty. On the other side of that was the rear of the long row of office buildings that faced the main road. Some were brick, some were plaster, all different styles built over the last thirty years. Their rear admin area was strewn with clutter and large cylindrical skips.

There was a pathway running across the waste ground, and it went through at a point where a whole section of the chain link fence had crumpled or been pulled down. Maybe the hotel and office workers used it as a short cut.

Carrying Kelly was like having a bergen on the wrong way round. That was going to be no good if I had to run fast, so I threw her round onto my back, linking my hands under her arse so I was carrying her piggyback. I got to the bottom of the stairs and stopped and listened. No sound of them shouting or breaking down the door yet. The urge was just to run for it across the waste ground towards the gap in the fence, but it was important to do this correctly.

Still with Kelly on my back, not bothering to tell her what was happening, I got onto my hands and knees. I lowered myself to within about a foot of the floor and slowly stuck my head round the corner. There was a chance that, once I'd seen what was happening, I'd choose a different route.

The two cars had now been driven to the bottom of the staircase by the Coke machine. The fuckers were obviously upstairs. I didn't know how many of them there were.

I realized that they couldn't see most of the waste ground from where they were. I started running. The rain had been light but constant and the ground was muddy. It was reasonably well looked after, littered only here and there with bits of paper, old soft-drink cans and burger boxes. I kept heading for the gap in the chain link fence.

Kelly was weighing me down; I was taking short, quick strides and not bending my knees too much, just enough to take her weight, bending forward from the hips as if I was lugging a bergen. She made involuntary grunts, in time with the running movements, as the wind was knocked out of her.

We reached the broken section of chain link, which was buried in the mud. I heard the screech of car tyres, then the sound of protesting suspension and bodywork. I didn't bother looking round, just dug deep and lengthened my stride.

Once through the gap we were faced with the rear of the office buildings. I couldn't see the alleyway we'd come through earlier. I turned left, looking for any other route through to the main drag. There must be one somewhere.

Now on tarmac I could make good speed, but Kelly started slipping. I shouted, 'Hold on!' and felt her tense up more. 'Harder, Kelly, harder!'

It wasn't working. With my left hand, I got hold of both her wrists and pulled them down in front of me towards my waist. She was nice and tight on me now and I could use my right hand to pump myself forward. My priority was to make good speed and distance. They would be out and running soon. I needed that alleyway.

It's a strange thing when untrained people are being chased. Subconsciously, they try to get as much distance as they can between themselves and their pursuers, and, whether it's in an urban environment or a rural one, they think that means going in a straight line. In fact what you need to do is put in as many angles as possible, especially in a city or a town. If you come to a junction with four options, it makes the chasers' job more difficult: they have a larger area to cover and have to split forces. A hare being chased in a field doesn't run in a straight line; it has a big bound, changes direction and off it goes again – the pursuers are getting momentum in a straight line and all of a sudden they have to change direction, too, which means slowing down, re-evaluating. I was going to be that hare. As soon as I got to the end of the alleyway I was going to chuck a left or a right, I didn't even know which yet, and run as fast as I could until I hit other options.

I found the alleyway. No time to think if it was the right decision, just make one. I could hear shouting behind me, maybe 100 to 150 metres away. But it wasn't directed at me. They were too professional for that. They knew it wouldn't have any effect. I heard the cars turning round. They'd be trying to cut me off. I ran.

By now I was out of breath with this seven-year-old on my back. My mouth was dry and I was breaking into a sweat. Her head was banging on the back of mine, and I was holding her so tight that her chin was digging into my neck; it was starting to hurt her and she was crying.

'Stop, stop, Nick!'

I wasn't listening. I reached the end of the alleyway and ran into a totally different world.

In front of me was a minor road that ran the length of the office buildings and, on the other side of it, a grass bank that went downhill to the main drag. Beyond that lay car parks and the malls. Traffic noise drowned out Kelly's cries. The flow of vehicles was fast in both directions, despite the wet road. Most had their headlights dipped and their wipers on intermittent. I stopped.

We must have looked a sight, a man with a shoeless child on his back, puffing and panting down the grass slope, the child moaning as her head banged on the back of his. I climbed the railings at the side of the main drag and now we were playing chicken with the Washington traffic. Cars sounded their horns or braked sharply to avoid us. It seemed my new name was fuck, nut or jerk. I didn't acknowledge anybody, even the ones who saved our lives by braking, I just kept on running.

Kelly was screaming. The traffic scared her as much as the running. All her young life she'd probably been warned about playing near the road, and here she was on a grown-up's back, cars and trucks swerving all around her.

Crossing the railings at the far side, I, too, was starting to flap. Kelly was slowing me down, without a doubt, and I still had quite a distance to run to get to safety. I ducked and weaved through the car park, using the height of pick-ups and people-carriers to block us from their view.

At the far right of the mall was CompUSA, a computer super-store, and that was where I headed. There's always a good chance that a large store on a corner site will have more than one entrance. I'd expect there to be one on the other side, maybe at the rear, so even if they saw me going in they'd have problems.

I knew the store would be hard for them to deal with because I'd had to do this sort of thing myself in Northern Ireland. If a player went into the shopping centre, we would send only one bloke in with him, then rush to seal up all the exits. It was hard enough when we knew a target, let alone having to find and iden-tify him. If he was doing anti-surveillance drills, he could go up in a lift, leave by one exit, go back in through another and up two floors, down in a lift one floor, then wander out into a car park and he's gone. If these boys were switched on, they'd start seal-ing the exits as soon as they saw where I'd gone. I had to be quick.

We went in through wide automatic doors. It was like a mega DIY store, with aisles and aisles of office equipment, computers and software packages. I went past the checkout counters with-out taking a trolley, still with Kelly on my back. The place was packed. I was standing there drenched with sweat, chest heaving up and down as I fought for breath, and Kelly was crying. People started looking at us.

Kelly moaned, 'I want to get down now!'

'No, let's just get out of here.'

I took a look behind and I could see two boys coming across the car park. In their suits, they looked very much like plain-clothes police and they were running purposefully towards the store; they'd be heading to block off the exits. I had to put in some angles, had to get that confusion going.

I ran down a couple of aisles crammed with CD-ROM games, turned right and ran along the exterior wall, looking for an exit. Fuck it, there wasn't one. The warehouse seemed to be one big sealed unit. I couldn't go back out the way I'd come in, but if I didn't find another exit I was going to spend the rest of the day running around the shop in circles.

One of the young assistants looked at me, turned away and went trotting down the aisle, obviously looking for the manager or security guard. Seconds later, two men in shirtsleeves with name badges started to approach us. 'Yes, excuse me? Can we help you?' All very polite, but in fact meaning, 'What the fuck are you doing in our store?'

There was no time to answer. I ran towards the rear, looking for loading bays, emergency doors, open windows, anything. At last I saw the sign I was hoping to see: 'Fire Exit'. I ran at it, pushed it open, and the alarm went off.

We were outside. We were on a platform, obviously used for deliveries, where trucks could back in and unload.

I ran down the four or five metal stairs and hit the ground. As I started to run to the left I shouted at Kelly to hold tight.

The rear of the shopping mall was deserted, just a long stretch of admin areas, with skips, Portakabins, even a container detached from its truck and being used as a static storeroom. There were piles of cardboard boxes and bulging bin liners everywhere, a day's worth of garbage. Beyond the tarmac'd stretch was a chain link fence surrounding the whole area, and probably about 15 feet high. Then waste ground, with trees and bushes. On the other side of that, I guessed, would be more car parking and stores.

I felt like a trapped rat. I only had two exits now, the slip roads at either end of the long line of shops.

9

I couldn't get over the fence with Kelly on my back and if I tried to throw her over she'd break her legs. I started to run to the left, along the rear of the shops, heading towards the slip road. It was no good; they'd had too much time to react; the road would be sealed.

I had to make a decision quickly. I moved towards one of the collection areas of skips, bagged-up garbage and cardboard boxes.

I lifted her from my back and positioned her in amongst it all, throwing boxes over the top of her and moving others to fill in the gaps each side.

She looked at me and started to cry.

I said, 'Disneyland, Kelly! Disneyland!'

She stared at me, tears rolling down her cheeks, and I threw a couple of boxes over the top.

'I'll be back, I promise.'

As I ran, I looked at the container that was right up against the fence. It was a huge thing the height of a truck. Without 50 pounds of young girl on my back, running towards it was like floating on air. At last I was in control. I felt as if I'd lost a ball and chain.

Sprinting like a maniac, using the cover of the bins and skips, I suddenly spotted the boot of a car jutting out from one of the loading bays. It was a mid-1980s model, not one of the cars that had been chasing me. I'd check it for ignition keys and, if I was out of luck, I'd cross the open ground to the container.

A truck was parked up near another loading bay. I started to run past it. A guy was running full pelt the other way and we smashed our heads together. We both went down.

'Shit!' I looked at him through blurred eyes. He had a suit on. There was no way I was going to take a chance. I staggered to my feet and charged at him, banging him up against the car. He tried to wrap himself around me.

As I was pushing into him I could feel with the side of my face that his body was solid. This fucker had covert body armour on.

I pinned him up against the car, moved back a pace and pulled my weapon, flicking on the laser sight with my thumb.

Then, dazed, I sank back to my knees. I was seeing stars and my head was spinning, and he was probably in exactly the same state. He looked down at me, confused, but trying to make a decision. I aimed the sight onto his face.

'Don't do it,' I said. 'Don't waste your life on this, it's not worth it. Get your hands up – now!'

As his hands moved I could see he was wearing a wedding ring. 'Think about your family. It's not worth dying over this. Number one, you're wrong, it wasn't me. Number two, I'll kill you. Put your hands on your head.'

My brain was clearing. What the fuck was I going to do now? Their cars would be here soon.

'Stay on your knees,' I said. 'Turn right. Move to the back of the vehicle.'

I got up off the ground and stumbled behind him. My eyes were still smarting as if I'd been hit with CS gas.

We were between the loading bay and the car. He knew the score and hopefully was thinking of his wife and kids. I switched my pistol into my left hand, moved into him and quickly jabbed the pistol muzzle into his armpit, twisting it into the material of his jacket. I felt his body tense and heard a little grunt.

'I'll explain the facts of life for you,' I said. 'This weapon is screwed into your clothes. I've got my finger on the trigger and the safety catch is off. If you fuck about, you'll kill yourself. Understand?'

He didn't react.

I said, 'Come on, this isn't difficult. Do you understand me?'

'Yes.'

'Place your hands on your head.'

With my right hand I took his weapon. Mine had only one magazine. He was carrying a Sig .45 in a pancake holster over his right kidney, and three magazines on his belt. The Sig is an approved weapon of the FBI.

He was in his mid-thirties and straight off the set of *Baywatch*: blond, tanned, fit, good-looking, square jaw. I could smell baby lotion. This boy wanted to keep his skin soft. Or maybe he had a baby. Who cared? If he moved, he'd be dead.

There was a white wire behind his ear, linked to an earpiece.

'Who are you?' I said. Not that it made any difference whether he was FBI or plain-clothes police.

No reply.

'Listen, whatever you think, I did not kill that family. I did not kill them. Do you understand?'

Nothing. I knew I wouldn't get *Baywatch* man to talk. In any event, there wasn't any time to waste trying.

I took the radio, and cash from his wallet. Then, with the pistol still in his armpit, I whispered loudly over my shoulder, 'Stay where you are, Kelly! Don't worry, I'm coming!' I gripped him harder. 'Kelly, I said we're going to go in a minute!' If they thought Kelly was still with me when I legged it, maybe they'd move on and search a fresh area.

I turned back to him and said, 'I'm going to untwist this now. Don't fuck me about; it's not worth it.' I gradually released my pistol, making sure I could fire at any stage. I was

89

behind him, with the weapon now pointing at his head. He knew that.

I said, 'You know what I've got to do next, don't you?'

There was a slight nod of acceptance.

I picked up a lump of angle-iron from a pile of discarded shelving and gave him the good news where his neck met his shoulder. That took him down good-style. For good measure I gave him a few kicks to the head and bollocks. At the end of the day, he wasn't going to be more pissed off with me because of this kicking; he probably already wanted to kill me. But I had to stop him raising the alarm. A professional like this boy would be expecting it anyway; if the roles were reversed it would be him doing the honours. It would certainly fuck him up for about ten minutes, and that was all I needed.

I came out from behind the car and had a quick look around. Nobody in sight. I ran towards the container; there was a large bin beside it that I could use as a springboard. I jumped, threw myself upwards and got my arms onto the roof. I scrambled up. From there it was just a 15-foot drop to freedom.

A sign pointed the way to Maylords Boardwalk. I turned left and ran along the grass bank, past the bins and into another car parking area. I went straight towards the boardwalk because it promised cover. I was looking for a toilet; and, with luck, there would also be an exit to the other side of the mall.

The boardwalk seemed to be a mini mall with mainly shoe and greetings-card shops. I found the block of conveniences by the coffee shop about a third of the way down the arcade. Looking further down, I could see there was another exit to the boardwalk. I went into the toilets.

Two guys had had a piss and were now washing their hands. I went straight into one of the cubicles and sat there while I waited to calm down.

I put the earpiece in my ear and switched on the radio. I didn't get much at all, the sound was all broken up, but that meant nothing. I was probably in a dead spot.

I used toilet paper to wipe the blood and mud off my shoes and trousers, and cleaned myself up as much as possible. When I was sure the other two had gone, I went out to the basins and washed my hands and face. I still wasn't getting anything but mush on the earpiece.

I headed for the coffee shop, bought a cappuccino and sat down about three tables back. From there I could watch both exits to the boardwalk. I didn't look out of place with the wire in my ear because so many store detectives and security guards wore them.

They sparked up on the net. They were talking freely, as if the radio was secure, not using codes. I checked and there was a jack on the radio for the key gun – the device that sends the chosen encryption codes to the radio. Once this has been done to two or more sets they can talk together securely. Everybody else would just hear mush.

I listened to some of them checking round the back, where the boy had been dropped, and others in places that I couldn't identify. What I couldn't hear was a base station, a central control. I started to wonder about that. Then I thought, Why was it these guys and not uniformed police that had turned up at the hotel? I was supposed to be a kidnapping murderer; in situations like these I'd expect to see heavily armed SWAT teams leaping from Chevrolet vans. I realized it was this that had made me run back for Kelly without even knowing it. I should have checked the boy I'd dropped for any ID. Never mind, it was too late now.

How did they find me so quickly at the Best Western? Had my call to London been traced to our room? Impossible: too quick. Was it my credit card when I checked in? Unlikelier still. Only the Firm would have known the details of my cover documents and they wouldn't have turned me in because they'd be too worried about the Americans finding out about their deniable ops. So it must have been the receptionist. She must have watched the news and recognized Kelly's photograph. But, even then, it didn't add up somehow. I started to feel very uneasy.

91

These boys weren't a Mickey Mouse group. When I bumped into *Baywatch* man, he'd been wearing a double-breasted jacket and it was open. But it was only now, thinking about it, that I realized that, in fact, it hadn't been open at first. There had been a Velcro fastening.

I heard more radio traffic. They'd found him. *Baywatch* man's name was Luther; but, whoever the boss was on the ground, he didn't really care too much about Luther's condition. He just wanted to know if he was able to talk.

'Yeah, he's OK.'

'Is he alone?'

'Yeah, he's alone.'

'Did he see the target?'

'No, he says he didn't see the target but they're still together.'

'Does he know what direction they went?'

There was a pause.

'No.'

I imagined Luther sitting on the ground with his head against the car, getting patched up and feeling pretty pissed off with me. In the background I could hear him mumbling information. He sounded almost drunk.

The sender said, 'No idea of the direction. And one more thing – he's armed. He had a side arm with him and he's also taken Luther's . . . Wait . . .'

I heard a click, then whoever was with Luther came back on the net and his voice was very agitated. 'We've got a problem – he's got the radio! He's got the radio!'

The boss came back on. 'Fuck! Everybody, all stations, cut comms! Close down now! Out.'

The earpiece went dead. They were going to turn off the radios and refill with a new code. Luther's radio was obsolete. What I wouldn't have given now for a key gun.

10

Luther said he hadn't seen the target, so it was Kelly they were after, not me. My face burned with anger. These were the people who'd killed Kev, they must be. This chase was nothing to do with law enforcement; this was about people who wanted to finish the job. Maybe they thought Kelly had seen them.

By now I had finished my coffee and the waitress had whisked the cup away. I was starting to be a pain in the arse here; other people were waiting for my table. I went back into the toilets. The TV remote control was still in my pocket. That went into the waste bin, along with the useless radio.

What about Kelly? What did I have to gain by going back? What if they'd found her, disposed of her and were waiting for me to pick her up? That was what I would have done. I could think of lots of reasons why I shouldn't go back.

Bollocks.

I walked back towards the mall exit. Looking half left in the dead ground, I could just about see the roof of CompUSA. The car park was still full and it was raining harder now. I turned up the collar of Kev's jacket and looked towards the main drag. I could see a Wendy's like a desert island in the middle of the car park. It was coffee time again. I checked the route ahead for any sign of my new friends and again used tall vehicles as cover.

I took my burger and coffee over to a window seat. I couldn't see the rear of the buildings but I could see the nearer of the two slip roads, the one I'd been running towards when I met Luther. Better than nothing. The Wendy's had a play station, which was great cover; kids screamed around in a tub of multicoloured tennis balls while their parents sat it out, just like me.

I sat and stared out of the window at the rain. I remembered the times I'd been bad as a child and got a slapping from my step-father and been put in the shed for the night; I'd been terrified of the rain beating down on the clear plastic wriggly roof; I'd sat there curled up, thinking that if the rain could get me, then so could the bogeyman. As a soldier and a K I had been shot at, beaten up, imprisoned; I'd always been scared, but nothing like those times as a child. I thought of Kelly, abandoned in her makeshift hidey-hole, rain beating down on the cardboard. Then I cut it from my mind. She'd get over it. I shouldn't let it concern me; I'd done worse things.

Still looking out of the window, I saw the white Taurus come out from behind the mall onto the slip road, stop at the junction and turn with the flow of traffic. It was four up by the looks of things, all suits, though in the rain it was hard to be certain. Four up was a good indication that they were lifting off: if they were taking Luther to hospital, there'd be three at most inside, one driving, one looking after the casualty. The others would have stayed behind. I was beginning to feel a decision coming on.

I'd have to change my appearance and I'd have to do it on the cheap – I had about $500 in total and would be needing every cent.

I finished my coffee and went back into the boardwalk. I found a clothes shop and bought a thin cotton raincoat that folded up to about the size of a handkerchief. I also bought a Kangol cap, the sort it was fashionable to wear the wrong way round, so the peak was hanging down the back of your neck and the logo was in front.

Then I went to an Hour Eyes and bought a pair of display

glasses with thick rims. Glasses really change the shape of your face. Whenever I'd needed an appearance-change on a job, a haircut and glasses had always done the trick. Wearing a different colour and giving yourself a different shape was the minimum required.

I went back to the toilets to sort myself out. I ripped out the inside of the raincoat pocket with my teeth. My newly acquired Sig .45 was down the front of my jeans, with the mags in my pockets. If the shit hit the fan, I could draw the weapon and fire through the coat.

I wanted to use the last three-quarters of an hour of daylight doing a recce of the bin area; the lift-off might have been a ploy and I wanted to reassure myself that nobody was lying in wait. The idea would be to do a complete 360 degrees around the target area, but, before that, I wanted to go back and give the hotel a walk-past; I wanted to see if there were any police cars outside, to confirm whether or not it had been an official lift. If Luther and his friends were after a murder suspect, the police should be up there by now, dusting for prints and taking statements.

I put on my disguise and looked in the mirror at Washington's hippest dude – well, nearly. If people looked closely they would think I was the oldest swinger in town. I turned the cap round, with the peak forward, and off I went. I walked straight across the car park, crossed the main drag at the junction and worked my way back up to the Best Western, along the roads. I saw nothing. Everything looked perfectly normal; not a police car in sight.

As I walked back I thought about the state that Kev, Marsha and Aida had been left in. Why hack them to bits? Luther and his friends weren't dopeheads, they were pros; they'd do nothing without a reason. They must have wanted it to appear drug-related to cover their arses. Given the number of attempts on Kev's life in the past, it would have been perfectly reasonable for the police to assume that one of them had finally succeeded, and that the perpetrators had then gone overboard and slain the whole family as a warning to others. But I knew that wasn't the reason. They had killed Marsha because they'd have had to assume that Kev had passed on whatever he knew, and then they'd had to kill Aida simply because they didn't want witnesses. Kelly owed her life to the fact that they hadn't seen her. It was probably only after the news reports that they realized they hadn't finished the job, and that there might be a witness after all.

The way they'd butchered Aida brought back to me a story about the American hearts and minds programme in Vietnam. In one region they injected the children of a village against small-pox. The Viet Cong came along a week later and cut off each child's arm. It worked: no more hearts and minds programme for them. Sometimes the end justifies the means. I had a sort of respect for Luther and co, but I knew I mustn't fuck about with these people – they were too much like me.

Rush hour was now in full swing and it would soon be dark. The shops were still open and the area was packed with people. It was great for me, it made me just another punter.

As I walked I had my head down against the rain. I reached the Wendy's car park. This time I was nearer the fence; wiping my glasses, I looked across the low ground as the rear of the mall came into view.

There was a loud hiss of air brakes as a truck backed up to a loading bay. Three other trucks were already parked up along-side the car where I'd met Luther. But again, just as at the hotel, there were no police investigating the crime scene. Maybe they didn't like the weather.

Only the bays that were in use were lit. The huddle of skips where I'd hidden Kelly was pretty much in shadow. One was being filled up with the old metal shelving I'd used on Luther. Even from where I was I could hear the loud crash and clatter. Kelly must be petrified down there.

No need for a 360; I'd seen enough. As I looked forward, deciding where to go now, I watched a bus pull up by a shelter, take on passengers and drive off again. Maybe that was our way out of here.

But, if they'd found Kelly and set an ambush, where was I going to run? I had to work out an escape route. Hijacking cars doesn't work so well in a built-up area – it attracts too much attention. Better to use the crowds and confusion. I picked three possible routes.

Hanging around increased the chance of getting pinged, so I decided to lift off from the area for a while. I carried on to the shops. I thought I'd get some stuff for Kelly, because she'd be needing an appearance-change, too. She'd been on the news; she was famous now.

I bought her a nice big floppy hat. I wanted to tuck her hair up out of the way, and hide her face as best I could. I also bought her a thinly padded, pink three-quarter-length coat to cover those skinny legs, and a completely new set of clothes to fit a nine-year-old. She was tall for her age, so I thought I'd better get the larger size. Almost as an afterthought, I bought myself some new jeans and a T-shirt.

With a handful of carrier bags I retraced the route along the fence. As I walked away from the shops their lights reflected on the wet tarmac of the car park. The traffic was slow on the main drag, windscreen wipers on full speed.

As I got to the fence I looked left. There was no change.

I carried on walking. As I got level with the shops the slip road started to rise up to meet me. The fence stopped. I turned left down a slippery grass bank and onto the slip road that led to the back of the shops. I followed the fence again as I dropped down into the dead ground.

The rain had turned the dust into mush. I now had the fence to my left and the loading bays to my right. I kept on walking, fighting the temptation just to run to Kelly, grab her and fuck off out of it. That's what gets people caught or killed.

My eyes must have looked as if I was plugged into the mains. They were darting everywhere, getting as much information into my head as possible. I wanted to see this ambush before it was sprung. I was committed now. If push came to shove, I'd fucking shove.

What if Kelly wasn't there? I'd call 911 and say I'd seen that girl from the news wandering around the area. If she hadn't already been lifted, hopefully the police would get her before Luther's pals did. That was if they hadn't already. I'd then have to take my chances when the Nick Stone manhunt began. Whoever had her would also have my name.

I got to within about 20 metres of the bins, still walking at the same steady pace. I didn't even look around now because that took time and effort.

I came up to the bins and started to lift away the boxes. 'Kelly, it's me! Kelly! See, I told you I'd come back.'

The cardboard was soaking and came apart in my hands. As I pulled the last of it away I could see she was more or less exactly in the position I'd left her, curled up, sitting on some dry board. My mind flashed back to how she'd looked when I'd found her in the garage. At least she wasn't rocking, with her hands clamped over her ears. She was dry; maybe the bogeyman had got in, but at least the rain hadn't.

I stood her up and put her new coat around her shoulders. 'I hope you like pink,' I said. 'I got this for you, too.' I put the hat on her head to preserve whatever was left of her body heat.

She put her arms around me. I hadn't been expecting it and I didn't know how to react. I just kept talking to her. She cuddled me harder.

I readjusted the hat. 'There, that'll keep you nice and dry. Now let's go and get you a bath and something to eat, shall we?'

I had the bags in my left arm and she gripped my left sleeve as we walked. It was awkward, but I needed to keep my right hand free to draw my pistol.

11

The bus was about half full with shoppers and bulging carrier bags. Kelly was cuddled up beside me in the window seat. Her hat was doing its job; her hair was tucked up and the dropped brim covered her face. I was feeling good. I'd saved her from Luther and his mates. I'd done the right thing.

We were on our way to Alexandria, an area I knew to be south of central DC, but within the Beltway, and we were going there because that was what had been on the destination board of the first bus to arrive.

Everyone was fed up and wet, and the bus was well fugged up. I leaned across and used my sleeve to wipe the condensation from the window, but it didn't help much. I looked towards the front, where the windscreen wipers were working overtime.

The priority was a hotel, and we'd have to check into one within the next hour or so because the later in the day I left it, the more unusual it would look.

'Nick?'

I didn't want to look at her because I could guess what she was going to ask.

'Yes?'

'Why were those men chasing you? Have you done something wrong?'

I could feel her looking at me under her hat.

'I don't know who they are, Kelly. I just don't know.' Eyes still fixed on the clear patch of windscreen, I said, 'You hungry?'

I could see her hat moving up and down in the corner of my eye.

'Not long now. What do you want? McDonald's? Wendy's?'

She nodded for both, then mumbled something. I was still looking out of the window. 'What's that?'

'Micky D's.'

'Micky D's?'

'McDonald's! Get with the programme!'

'Ah, OK – that's what we'll get.'

I went back to my thoughts. I would only use cash from now on; I had to assume the worst, which was that we'd been traced through my credit card. Despite that, I'd still call London again. Deep down, I guessed that they'd probably already consigned my records to the shredder, but what did I have to lose?

We drove past a place called the Roadies Inn. It fitted the bill. I didn't have a clue where we were, but that didn't matter, I'd sort that out later. I signalled the driver that we wanted the next stop.

When the Roadies Inn had been built in the 1960s it had probably looked a million dollars. Now even the grass outside looked faded, and on the red neon vacancies sign the V and the N were flickering. Perfect.

I peered through the fly screen of the door to reception. A woman in her twenties was behind the desk, smoking and watching a TV on the far wall. I only hoped we hadn't had star billing on the news. Looking past her, into the back office, I saw a bald, overweight man, probably late fifties, working at a desk.

'I want you to wait just here, Kelly.' I pointed to the wall of the hotel under the upstairs landing that acted as a verandah.

She didn't like it.

'I won't be long,' I said, starting to walk backwards towards the doors. 'Just wait there, I'll be right back.' By now I was at the door. I pointed at her as if I was training a puppy. 'Stay, OK?'

The receptionist was wearing jeans and a T-shirt. Her hair was the blondest I'd ever seen, apart from the roots. She glanced away from the TV and said on autopilot, 'Hello, can I help you?'

'I'm looking for a room for maybe three or four nights.'

'Sure, for how many?'

'Two adults and a child.'

'Sure, one moment,' and she ran her finger down the booking register.

The news was on. I turned and watched, but there was nothing about the murders. Maybe we were already old news. I hoped so.

'Can I take an imprint of your card?'

I pulled a face. 'Ah, that's where we have a problem. We're on a fly-drive holiday and we've had our bags stolen. We've been to see the police and I'm waiting for replacement cards, but I'm just running on cash at the moment. I understand you have to take imprints, but maybe if I pay in advance and you disconnect the phone in the room?'

She was starting to nod her head, but her expression was still the wrong side of sympathetic.

'We're really stuck.' I played the wet and sorrowful Brit abroad. 'We've got to go to the British consulate tomorrow and sort out our passports.' I brought out some dollar bills.

It seemed to take a while for it all to sink in. 'I'm so sorry to hear about that.' She paused, waiting for more chemicals to inter-act in her brain. 'I'll get the manager.'

She went into the office and I watched her talking to the bald guy at his desk. From their body language I got the impression he was her father. I felt a drop of sweat roll down my spine. If they refused us a room, we were stranded maybe miles from the next motel and would need to start ordering taxis and raising our profile.

Hurry up! I turned and looked outside, but couldn't see Kelly. Fuck, I hoped Mr Honest Citizen wasn't about to storm in demanding to know who'd left a little girl all alone in the rain. I quickly walked to the door and stuck my head outside. She was still there, standing where I'd asked her to.

I came back to the reception desk just as Dad appeared from the back office. The girl was on the telephone, taking a booking.

'Just making sure our car isn't blocking the way.' I grinned.

'I hear you have a problem?' Dad had a vacant smile on his face. I knew we were OK.

'Yes,' I sighed, 'we've been to the police and contacted the card companies. We're just waiting for it to get sorted. Until then, all I've got is cash. I'll pay for the next three days in advance.'

'That's no problem.'

I was sure it wasn't. There was no way our little cash transaction would be finding its way onto the books. What some people call white trash, Kev used to call 'children of the corn'; they might take a while to understand things, but an earner's an earner in any language.

He smiled. 'We'll keep the telephone on for you.'

I played the grateful Brit and booked in, then Kelly and I traipsed up two flights of concrete and breeze-block stairs.

Kelly hesitated outside the room, then looked at me and said, 'Nick, I want to see Mommy. When can I go home?'

Shit, not that again. I wished more than anything that she could go and see Mummy. It would be one less problem. 'Not long now, Kelly,' I said. 'I'll get some food in a minute, OK?'

'OK.'

I lay down on the bed and thought out the priorities.

'Nick?'

'Yes?' I was looking at the ceiling.

'Can I watch TV?'

Thank God for that.

I reached over to the remote and quickly flicked the channels, checking I wasn't going to catch us both on the news. I found Nickelodeon and stuck with it.

I'd made a decision. 'I'm going out now to buy us something to eat,' I said, my mind on the one option that hadn't yet been closed. 'You stay here, the same as before. I'll put the Do Not

Disturb sign on the door and you make sure that you don't open it for anybody. Do you understand?'

She nodded.

The call box was next to a Korean food store. It was still drizzling; I could hear the noise of car tyres on wet tarmac as I crossed the road.

I pushed in a couple of quarters and dialled.

I got: 'Good evening. British Embassy. How may I help you?'

'I'd like to speak to the defence attaché, please.'

'May I say who's calling?'

'My name is Stamford.' Fuck it, I had nothing to lose.

'Thank you. One moment, please.'

Almost immediately, a no-nonsense voice came on the line. 'Stamford?'

'Yes.'

'Wait.'

There was a long continuous tone, and I was starting to think I'd been cut off again. Then, thirty seconds later, I heard Simmonds. My call must have been patched through to London. Unflappable as ever, he said, 'It seems you're in a spot of trouble.'

'Trouble's not the word.'

In veiled speech I told him everything that had happened since my last call.

Simmonds listened without interruption, then said, 'There's not really a lot I can do. Obviously you understand the situation I'm in?' I could tell he was pissed off with me big-style. 'You were told to return immediately. You disobeyed an order. You should not have gone to see him, you know that.' He was still cool about it all, but under the veneer I knew he was boiling.

I could just picture him behind his desk in his crumpled shirt and baggy cords, with the family photo and maybe Easter eggs for his family on his desk, next to a pile of red-hot faxes from Washington that had to be attended to.

'It's got nothing on the situation I can put you in,' I said. 'I've got stuff that would make your lot look not very British at all. I'll

103

blow it to whoever wants to listen. It's not a bluff. I need help to get out of this shit and I want it now.'

There was a pause; the patient parent waiting for a child to stop its tantrum.

He said, 'Your position is pretty delicate, I'm afraid. There is nothing I can do unless you have some form of proof that you're not implicated. I suggest you make every effort to discover what has happened and why, then we can talk and I might be able to help. How does that sound to you? You can carry out your threat, but I wouldn't recommend it.'

I could feel his hand tighten around my balls. Whether they complied or called my bluff, I'd be spending the rest of my life on the run. The Firm does not like being strong-armed.

'I've got no choice really, have I?'

'I'm glad you see it like that. Bring what you find.'

The phone went dead.

My mind racing, I wandered into the shop. I bought a bottle of hair tint – one wash in, twelve washes out – and a hair-trimmer gadget. I also bought a full washing and shaving kit because we couldn't look like a couple of scruffies at large in Washington. Then I filled the basket with bottles of Coca-Cola from the chiller and some apples and candy.

I couldn't find a Micky D's and ended up in a Burger King. I bought two mega-deals, then went back to the hotel.

I knocked on the door as I opened it. 'Guess what I've got? Burgers, fries, apple pies, hot chocolate . . .'

By the wall next to the window was a little circular table. The carrier bags went on the bed, and I dumped the burgers on the table with a flourish, like a returning hunter. Ripping the bags open to make a tablecloth, I tipped the chips out, opened the sauce, and we both dived in. She must have been starving.

I waited until she had a mouthful of burger. 'Listen, Kelly, you know how grown-up girls are always dyeing their hair and cutting it and all sorts of stuff? I thought you might like to try.'

She didn't look fussed.

'What do you fancy – a really dark brown?'

She shrugged.

I wanted to get it done before she understood too much of what was happening. The moment she'd finished her hot apple pie, I led her to the bathroom and got her to take off her shirt and vest. I tested the shower temperature and leaned her over the bath, quickly wet her hair, then towelled and brushed it. I got the trimmer going, but I wasn't entirely sure what I was doing. I realized it was for beards really, and by the time I'd got the hang of it her hair looked shit. The more I tried to sort it, the shorter it was getting. Soon it was up around her collar.

As I studied the bottle of dye, trying to read the instructions, she said, 'Nick?'

I was still reading the bottle and hoping I wasn't about to turn her hair into a ginger fuzzball.

'What?'

'Do you know the men who were chasing you?'

I was the one who should have been asking questions.

'No, I don't, Kelly, but I will find out.' I thought about it and put down the hair dye. I was standing behind her and both of us were looking at each other in the mirror. Her eyes were now not so red around the edges. That only made mine even more dark and tired-looking. I looked at her a while longer. Finally, I said, 'Kelly, why did you go to the hidey-hole?'

She said nothing. I could see that her eyes were starting to question my hairdressing skills.

'Did Daddy shout "Disneyland"?'

'No.'

'Then why did you go?' Already this was getting too intense for me. I needed to do something. I picked up the dye.

'Because of the noise.'

I started to comb the dye in.

'Oh, what noise was that?'

She looked at me in the mirror. 'I was in the kitchen but I heard a bad noise in the living room and I went and looked.'

'What did you see?'

'Daddy was shouting at the men and they were hitting him.'

'Did they see you?'

'I don't know, I didn't go into the room. I just wanted to shout to Mommy to come and help Daddy.'

'And what did you do?'

Her eyes went down. 'I couldn't help him, I'm too little.' When she looked up again, I saw her face was burning with shame. Her bottom lip started to quiver. 'I ran to the hidey-hole. I wanted to go to Mommy, but she was upstairs with Aida, and Daddy was shouting at the men.'

'You ran to the hidey-hole?'

'Yes.'

'Did you stay there?'

'Yes.'

'Did Mummy come and call for you?'

'No. You did.'

'So you didn't see Mummy and Aida?'

'No.'

The picture of the two of them dead flashed into my mind.

I put my arms around her as she sobbed. 'Kelly, you couldn't have helped Daddy. Those men were too big and strong. Probably I couldn't have helped him, and I'm a grown-up. It's not your fault Daddy got hurt. But he is OK and wants me to look after you until he is better. Mummy and Aida had to go with Daddy. There just wasn't the time to collect you.'

I let her cry a bit, then said, 'Did you see any of the men who were chasing us today?'

She shook her head.

'Did the men who were with Daddy have suits on?'

'I suppose so, but they had like painting things on top.'

I guessed what she meant. 'The sort Daddy would wear to paint the house?' I did the actions of putting on a pair of DIY coveralls.

She nodded.

'So do you mean they had suits on, but had the painting things over the top?'

She nodded again.

I knew it; these boys were good, they were players. They hadn't wanted to get nasty red stuff all over their nice suits.

I asked her how many men there were and what they looked like. She was confused and scared. Her lip started to quiver again. 'Can I go home soon?' She was fighting back the tears.

'Yes, very soon, very soon. When Daddy is better. Until then, I'm looking after you. Come on, Kelly, let's make you look like a big girl.'

After a rinse I combed her wet hair and got her dressed straight away in her new clothes. If we had to move, I needed her dressed, so I told her that the only things she could keep off were her hat, coat and shoes.

She inspected herself in the mirror. The new clothes were much too big and her hair was – well, she didn't seem too sure.

We watched Nickelodeon and eventually she fell asleep. I lay staring at the ceiling, going through the options or, rather, trying to kid myself that I had some.

What about Slack Pat? He would certainly help if he could, as long as he hadn't turned into some drugged-up New Age hippy. But the only way I could think of contacting him was through the restaurant he used to rave about. The way he described it, he practically lived there. The problem was I couldn't remember the name of it, just that it was on a hill on the edge of Georgetown.

What about Euan? He was no good yet because he'd still be operating in Ulster and there was no way I could make contact with him until he was back on the mainland.

I looked over at Kelly. That was how she would have to live for the next little while, always dressed, ready to run at a moment's notice. I put the eiderdown over her.

I piled all the rubbish together and put it in the bin, then checked the sign was still on the door and her shoes were in her pockets. I checked chamber in both weapons – the 9mm in Kev's jacket and the Sig in my waistband. No doubt Kelly was going to be in all of tomorrow's papers, but at least, if the shit hit the fan, we were ready to go. I knew my escape route and would not hesitate to shoot my way out.

I got my new clothes out of the bag and took them into the bathroom. I had a shave, then undressed. I stank; Kev's things were stained on the inside with blood. The sweat had thinned it, spreading it right up the back and shoulders of his shirt and the legs of his jeans. Everything went into a plastic laundry bag, which I'd throw away in the morning. I had a long hot shower and washed my hair. Then I got dressed, checked the door lock and lay on the bed.

I woke up at about five thirty in the morning, after a terrible night's sleep. I wasn't sure if all the bad stuff was a dream.

I thought again about money. I definitely couldn't use credit cards because I had to assume they'd either been frozen or would be used as a trace. It was cash or nothing – not easy in the West nowadays. Pat, if I got to him, would fund me, but I knew I'd have to take advantage of any spare time to get hold of more. Kelly was snoring big-time. I picked up the key card, gently closed the door behind me, checked the sign was up and went looking for a fire extinguisher.

12

As I passed the open door to the cleaners' store room I spotted half a dozen wedge-shaped doorstops on a shelf. I helped myself to a couple.

I found the fire extinguisher on the wall by the elevators. I quickly unscrewed the top of it and removed the carbon dioxide cylinder, a 9-inch black steel tube. I put it in my jacket and walked back to the room.

I put the three spare magazines for the Sig .45 in the left-hand pocket of Kev's jacket and decided I was going to keep the USP in the room. I hid it in the cistern. A weapon can stand getting wet in the short term. I just didn't want Kelly to find it and start putting holes in herself.

I dozed some more, woke up and dozed again. By 7 a.m. I was bored and hungry. Breakfast was included in the room price, but to get it I'd have to go downstairs to reception.

Kelly started to stir. I said, 'Good morning. Do you fancy something to eat?'

She was all yawny, sitting up and looking like a scarecrow because she'd gone to sleep with wet hair. Straight away I put on the TV for her because I didn't really know what to say. She looked down at her clothes, trying to work it out.

'You fell asleep,' I laughed. 'I couldn't even undress you last night. Hey, it's like camping, isn't it?'

She liked that. 'Yeah,' she smiled, still sleepy.

'Shall I go and get you some breakfast?'

She didn't look up, just nodded at the television.

'Remember, you must do this every time; you never, ever open the door. I'll come back using the key. Don't even open the curtains, because the cleaning ladies will think it's OK to come in, and we don't want to talk to anyone, do we? I'll leave the Do Not Disturb sign, OK?'

She nodded. I wasn't sure how much of it had gone in. I picked up the tray the ice bucket was on, put on my glasses and went down to reception.

It was already fairly packed: people with camper vans, who couldn't be arsed to sleep in them, and salesmen looking clean, fresh and straight out of the 'appearance counts' section of the manual.

The breakfast area was made up of two or three tables by the coffee flasks under the TV. I took three packets of cereal, bagels and muffins, some apples, then two cups of coffee and an orange juice.

The corn child had just finished her shift and came over. 'I hope everything goes well with your passports and all,' she smiled, helping herself to a bagel.

'I'm sure it'll be fine. We're just going to concentrate on having a good holiday.'

'If you need any help, you just come and ask.'

'Thanks.' I walked over to the desk and picked up a complimentary *USA Today*. I also helped myself to a Roadies Inn book of matches from a whole bowl of them and a paper clip that was in an ashtray full of elastic bands and office bits, and went back to the room.

Ten minutes later Kelly was munching on her cereal and glued to Nickelodeon.

I said, 'I'm going out for about an hour. I've got stuff to do. While I'm away I want you to have a wash and be all nice and clean for when I get back, and have your hair brushed. Are you going to be all right on your own, with your big-girl haircut?'

She shrugged. 'Whatever.'

'What are your favourite colours?'

'My favourite colours are pink and blue.'

'Well, we've got the pink.' I pointed at the coat hanging up with her shoes sticking out of the pockets. That had been a bit of luck. 'Now I've got to get you something blue.'

I gave my glasses a quick clean with toilet paper, put them back in their case and into Kev's jacket, then put my long black rain-coat over the top, checking the pocket for the cylinder. I emptied my pockets of loose change – I wanted to cut down on noise and always felt better anyway with as little as possible dragging around my clothes.

I had my Kangol hat in my hand and was all ready to go.

'I won't be long. Remember, let no-one in. I'll be back before you know it.'

It had stopped raining, but the sky was still grey and the ground wet. The road was choked with cars heading into downtown DC. It's a people town and the sidewalks were busy, too.

I walked briskly to keep pace with the office workers, all with their 'got to get up, got to get on' expressions, all the time look-ing for the ideal place to make some money quickly and get back to the hotel before Kelly started panicking.

It was too early for a shopping mall, since they didn't open until tenish, and I wasn't in an area with a lot of hotels – they were all further downtown. There were fast-food outlets, but they normally had just one way in and out, and too much toilet traffic, so they wouldn't be a good choice. A service station would do, so long as it had an outside rest room that could only be opened by a key obtained from the pay desk.

I'd been walking around for maybe twenty minutes. I walked through a couple of filling stations that were busy enough, but they were modern, with inside toilets.

Eventually I found what I was looking for, an outdoor toilet with a sign on the door that said, 'Key At Paydesk'. I checked to ensure that the door was locked, then I walked on.

I was looking for two things now: for somewhere natural to watch the forecourt from, and for my escape route. Further up, on the other side of the road, was a run of lawyers' offices, credit unions and insurance brokers, in wonderful 1930s detached brick houses; in between were what looked like well-used alleyways. I crossed over, walked down one and came out onto the parallel road; turning right, I followed the road to a junction, turned left, then right again up another alleyway. The whole area was perfect for angles and distance. I made my way back to the filling station by a different route.

There was a bus stop across the street about 100 metres away. I strolled along to it, stood in a doorway and waited; it had to look natural, I had to have a reason to be doing what I was doing. There were two or three people waiting, then the queue gradually got longer, a bus came and we were back to two or three again. I looked at the destination board of each bus as it approached, looked fed up that it wasn't the one I wanted and got back in the doorway.

People don't carry much cash with them nowadays, especially here in the land of the credit card. The ideal target is always a tourist – they tend to carry more cash and traveller's cheques – but there weren't likely to be many in this part of town.

Over a period of about thirty minutes there'd been four or five possibles going in to fill up their cars, but unfortunately it seemed that none of them was in need of a shit. I thought about Kelly; I hoped she was sticking to the script.

A white guy in his twenties drove onto the forecourt in a new Camaro. It carried thirty-day plates while waiting for the new registration. He was wearing a baggy shell suit that was red, blue, green, orange and six other colours, and basketball shoes to match. His hair was shaved at the sides with the rest pointing skywards. The sound system was booming out bass that I could feel vibrating from across the street.

He filled up with fuel and went in to pay. When he came out he was carrying what looked like a small lump of wood. He turned left towards the toilet. This was my boy.

I stepped out of the doorway, turned up my collar and headed across the road. He was putting his wallet into his shell-suit top and doing up the zip. I'd already checked the garage surveillance cameras and they wouldn't be a problem: they were focused on the forecourt to catch drive-aways, not on the gable end of the building to catch toilet-paper thieves.

As I left the doorway I was a man who needed a piss and couldn't wait any longer for his bus to arrive. It was unlikely to register with anybody at the bus stop; first thing in the morning people are brooding about the day's work ahead, or about their mortgages or kids or the wife's headache the night before; they're not going to worry too much about a guy going into a toilet. I walked towards the door with just enough spring in my step to look like the man with the world's fullest bladder, and went in.

The room was about 12 feet by 12, fairly clean and reeking of bleach blocks. Dead ahead were two urinals, with a basin and a wall-mounted paper-towel dispenser. My boy was in one of the two cubicles to the right.

I could hear the sound of zips being undone, the rustle of a general sorting out and a little cough. I closed the door behind me and jammed in the two door stops with my shoe. No-one would be getting in or out of here unless I wanted them to.

I stood at the urinal and made it look as if I was taking a leak. My hands were in front of me, but holding the steel cylinder. I'd keep my back to him until he came out to wash his hands.

I stood there for three or four minutes. I heard him pissing. It stopped, then nothing. This character was taking too long. I swung my head to the right, as if to look out of the small barred window, but carried on with the motions of pissing in case he could see me and, for some reason, was being hesitant about leaving the cubicle.

Then, casually looking right behind me, I saw something really bizarre. American public toilets have saloon-type doors with a bigger gap at the top and bottom than in the UK. Through the bottom gap I could see one foot, which looked as if it was his right foot, on the ground and facing the toilet, and his tracksuit bottoms weren't bunched around his ankles. I thought, Weird position, but there you go. Then I noticed that the door was open an inch. He hadn't locked it.

I wasn't going to stop and puzzle it out. Clenching my right fist around the cylinder, and with my left hand out to protect myself, I started quickly but quietly towards the door. At the last minute I took a deep breath, dropped my shoulder and barged into it.

He banged up against the wall, screaming, 'What the fuck! What the fuck!' His hands went out to try to stop himself falling and the door held; his bulk was stopping the door from opening.

I had to barge it again. The hard and fast rule of mugging is to be exactly that: hard and fast. Putting all my weight behind the door I had him pinned up against the wall. He was a big boy; I had to be careful, I could get fucked over here. I grabbed a hand-ful of his gelled hair with my left hand and pulled his head over to the left, exposing the right side of his neck.

You don't just use your arm to hit somebody. I needed to get as much weight as I could behind the cylinder, like a boxer using his hips and the top half of his body to power the swing. Still push-ing the door with my left hand, I brought the cylinder up in my right and swung my whole body round, as if throwing a down-ward right hook, and cracked him just below the ear. The idea was just to take him down, not kill him or give him brain damage for the rest of his days; if I'd wanted to do that I'd have cracked him over the head a few times. As it was, it wouldn't be his best day out, but tough shit – wrong place, wrong time.

It had been a good hit. He groaned and went down. He was fucked and, without a doubt, he would have had starbursts in the eyes, that crackling and popping sensation you get when you go down semi-conscious. He'd just want to curl up and get under the duvet and hide. That was why I'd used the cylinder instead of a gun. You can't predict people's reactions to a pistol. He might have been an undercover cop with a gun himself, he might have been some kind of a heroic have-a-go citizen. Not that it mattered now. The old ways are the best.

He'd banged his head on the cistern and smashed his nose, and blood was pouring down his chin. There was a high-pitched, childlike moan coming from him. He was in shit state but he'd live. I gave him another one for good measure; I wanted him down and well out. He stopped making a noise.

I put my left hand on his head and held it facing away from me. I didn't want him to be able to ID me. With my right hand I felt under his belly and twisted his shell-suit top round towards me, unzipped it and pulled out his wallet. Then I started to feel down his pockets in case he had another big wad stashed away there. My fingers closed around a plastic bag that filled the ball of my hand. I pulled out what looked like enough white powder to send the guy's entire neighbourhood into orbit, all in neat little plastic wallets, ready for sale. No good to me; I left it on the floor.

It was then that I realized what he'd been up to while I was at the urinal. Wrapped tight around his left arm was a rubber tube and there was blood dripping from a small puncture wound. He must have had his left leg up on the toilet seat to support his arm while he was shooting up. I saw the hypodermic on the floor.

As I stood up my trousers felt wet and I looked down. He'd had the last laugh. I'd made him lose control of his bodily functions and he'd pissed himself. And I'd been kneeling in it.

I picked up the key from the floor. That, too, was covered in piss. He was starting to come round a bit and there were a few moans and groans. I got hold of his head and banged it against the toilet to give him the message to stay where he was for a while.

I stepped back from the cubicle. There was no time to try to clean my coat. I went to the main door, retrieved the wedges, put them in my pocket, came out and locked the door behind me. I tossed the key into some shrubbery.

I was out of breath and had a bit of sweat coming down the side of my face, but I had to make myself look calm and casual. If another customer happened to come round the corner to use the toilet I'd say it was out of order.

As I crossed the road I glanced left and behind me. Nothing. I wouldn't look back again. I'd soon know if something was going on because I'd hear all the screaming and shouting, or the sound of people running towards me. Then I'd have to react – but at the end of the day I was the one with the big fucking gun.

I passed the bus stop and carried on towards the first alleyway. After two more turns I took off my coat, wrapped it round the cylinder and folded the whole lot up. I took off the hat and folded that into the coat as well. I carried on walking, found a bin and got rid of my bundle. That was me sorted; a new man, or I would be as soon as I put on my glasses.

Once out on the road again I got out the wallet, as if I was checking whether I had my credit card. I opened it up and found that I was a family man; there was a very nice picture of me, my wife and two kids, the family of Lance White. I didn't think Mrs White would be too pleased with the state of me when I got home.

There was about $240 in the billfold; White had either just been to an ATM or done some early-morning deals. There were also a couple of credit cards, but I wouldn't keep them; it would be time-consuming to sell them, and if I tried to use them for cash back it could only be in the next hour or so – but why run the risk of the police doing a trace and ending up with my description from a sales assistant? The rest of the stuff was shit, bits of paper with phone numbers on. Probably his client list. As I passed another bin I jacked everything except the cash.

I now had just under $400 in my pocket, enough for the next few days if I couldn't contact Pat or he didn't come up with the goods.

The piss on my trousers was starting to dry up a bit as I walked, but it was stinking good-style. It was time for a change of clothes.

I reached the Burger King and all the other shops near the hotel. I was in and out of a discount shop in about a quarter of an hour, with a holdall containing new jeans, sweatshirt and underwear, all bought with cash. Kelly had also got a complete new set of clothes, down to knickers and vests.

I had a quick look at my watch on the way up to the room. I'd been gone about two and a quarter hours, a bit longer than I'd said I'd be.

Before I even got to the door I could see it was ajar. I looked down and saw a pillow keeping it open. I could hear the TV.

Pulling my pistol I went against the wall, the weapon pointing towards the gap. I felt disbelief, then shock. I felt emptiness in my stomach and then I felt sick.

13

I moved into the room. Nothing.

I checked on the other side of the bed, in case she might be hiding there. Maybe she was playing some game on me.

'Kelly! Are you in there?' My voice was serious and she'd have known it.

No reply. My heart was pumping so hard my chest hurt. If they had her, why hadn't they jumped me by now?

I felt sweat slide down the side of my face. I started to panic, thinking about her in her house, seeing her father being beaten, screaming for her mummy. I understood that feeling of desperation when you want someone to take all the scary things away.

I forced myself to stop, calm down, think about what I was going to do. I came out onto the verandah again and broke into a run, calling, 'Kelly! Kelly!' in a loud semi-shout. I turned the corner and there she was.

Pleased as Punch, she was just leaving the Coke machine, wrestling with the ringpull on a can. The 'look at me, aren't I a big girl?' smile soon changed when she saw me, weapon in hand, looking as serious as cancer.

For a moment I was going to read her her horoscope, but I bit my lip.

She was suddenly looking sad and sorry for herself. Getting herself a can of Coke was the first thing she'd done on her own in many days and I'd ruined it by coming back so soon. Leading her back to the room, I kept looking round the open square to check we hadn't been seen.

There were empty crisp bags and all sorts on her bed; it looked like a scene out of *Animal House*.

I sat her down while I went and ran a bath. When I came back she still had a long face. I sat beside her. 'I'm not cross with you, Kelly, it's just that I worry if I don't know where you are. Will you promise not to do it again?'

'Only if you promise not to leave me again.'

'I promise. Now get undressed for a bath.' I picked her up and basically threw her in the bath before she had time to think.

'Do you wash your own hair or do you get somebody to do it?' I asked; I didn't have a clue.

She looked like she was going to cry.

I said, 'Do you want me to wash it for you?'

'Yes, please.' I wondered what was going on in that little mind of hers.

I got out the shampoo and got stuck in; she moaned about the soap in her eyes and that the suds were tickling her ears, but I could tell she loved the attention. I couldn't blame her; she hadn't had much lately. Her world had been turned upside down and she didn't even know it yet.

'You stink!' Kelly made a face as she caught the smell of Lance White's bladder on my clothes.

'These clothes are a bit old,' I said. 'Make sure you get all the shampoo out of your hair and wash yourself with the soap.'

She looked as if she was having fun. I was glad somebody was. Walking into the bedroom I called behind me, 'Then I want you to put on some clean clothes. There's knickers and a vest on the bed.'

'What're knickers?'

'These.' I picked them up and walked back to show her.

'They're not, they're panties!'

Kelly was a water baby. That was great for me; the longer she was in the bath the less time I had to spend dealing with her. I was finding it quite knackering having to clean, dress, talk and answer questions. I left her splashing around for another half an hour, then dragged her out and told her to go and dry herself.

I got in the shower, had a shave and got changed, bundling all my old clothes and Kelly's into a plastic laundry bag and stowing it inside the holdall. I'd get rid of it at the first opportunity.

We were both in the bedroom and she was dressed. Her shirt buttons were in the wrong holes; while I was undoing them and sorting them out, I realized she was looking disapprovingly at me.

'What's the problem?'

'Those jeans. They're sad. You should get 501s like Daddy.'

On top of everything else, I had the fashion police after me. She went on, 'You can't get 501s in my size. That's what Mommy says anyway. She doesn't wear jeans; she's like Aida, she likes dresses and skirts.'

In my mind's eye I saw Marsha kneeling by her bed. I turned away for a moment so Kelly couldn't see my face.

I got to grips with her hair. It was another new skill I hadn't mastered and the brush kept snagging and pulling. Kelly kept crying out and grabbing at my hand. In the end I gave her the brush and let her get on with it.

While she was doing that I sat on the bed and said, 'Kelly, do you know your dad's special code for his phone? I don't; I've tried it loads of times. I've pressed 1111, 2222, I've pressed them all and I still don't know. Have you got any idea?'

She stopped brushing, stared at me for a few moments, then nodded.

'Right! What are the numbers, then?'

She didn't say anything. She seemed to be working something out in her mind. Maybe she was wondering if she'd be betraying her daddy by telling me.

I pulled the phone from my pocket, turned it on and said, 'Look! What does it say? Enter PIN number! Do you know what numbers your daddy puts in?'

She nodded and I said, 'Come on, you show me, then.' She pressed the buttons and I watched her fingers.

'1990?' I said.

'The year I was born,' she beamed, going back to brushing.

We were in business. I fetched the Yellow Pages from one of the drawers and went back.

'What are you looking for?' she asked, brushing smoothly and expertly.

'A restaurant called Good Fellas,' I said. I found the address. 'We're going to go there and look for Pat.'

I thought about phoning the place and asking about him, but they'd probably just fuck me off. In any case, that could trigger off a series of events I'd know nothing about until we were both suddenly lifted. It would be better to go there.

I put on my glasses and she giggled. I got her coat and held it for her to put on. As she turned round I noticed she still had the label dangling off her jeans; I ripped that off, then checked that nothing else looked out of place – just like any other unfashionable dad taking his daughter out for the day.

I put on my jacket, checked for the mags and phone, and said, 'Do you remember Pat?'

'No. Who is she?'

'It's a him; he's a man called Patrick. Maybe you've seen him with Daddy?'

'Is Pat going to take me home?'

'You will be going soon, Kelly. But only when Daddy is better and if you're a good girl and do what I say.'

Her face fell. 'Will I be home for Saturday? That's Melissa's party and she's having a sleepover and I must be there.'

I carried on. There was nothing else I could do. I didn't have the skills to coax her out of her mood.

'Pat came round to your house. Surely you remember Pat?'

'And I've got to buy her a present. I've made her some friend-ship bracelets, but I want something else.'

'Well, we're going to try to find Pat today because he's going to help us get you home. Maybe we'll have time to do your shopping, OK?'

'Where is Pat?'

'I think he might be in the restaurant. But you've got to be really quiet when we get there, OK, and not talk to anyone. If anybody talks to you, I want you just to nod your head or shake it, OK? We've got to be really careful, otherwise they won't tell me where Pat is and then we might get into trouble.'

I knew she'd be all right on the dumb act. She'd done what I'd said by the bins. I felt bad talking about her going home, but I couldn't think of a better way of controlling her behaviour; and anyway, with any luck I wouldn't be there when she was finally told the truth.

There were a couple of other jobs to do before we left the room. I took the bottom left hand corner of the blanket on my bed and folded it in a neat, diagonal pleat. Then I took a matchstick from the book I'd picked up in reception and wedged it between the wall and the long low chest of drawers that the TV rested on. I put a pen mark the size of a pinhead on the wall and covered it with the match head. Finally I placed the paper clip in one of the drawers under the TV, and turned the volume up a shade.

I had a quick look round the room to make sure we hadn't left anything compromising lying around; I even put the Yellow Pages back in the drawer. The pistol was still in the cistern, but there were no problems with that; there was no reason for a cleaner to come in, let alone the police with a search warrant.

I picked up a couple of apples and chocolate bars and put them in the pocket of my brand-new three-quarter-length blue coat. Then I closed the door, checked the sign and off we went.

We took a taxi to Georgetown. It would have conserved funds if we'd taken a bus or the Metro, but this way meant less exposure to commuters or pedestrians. The driver was a Nigerian.

The map of the city on the front passenger seat didn't instil much confidence, and he could only just about speak English. He used what few words he had to ask me where Georgetown was. It was like a London taxi driver not knowing Chelsea. I patiently pointed on the map. By my guess it was about thirty minutes away.

It was spitting with rain, not enough to keep the wipers on, but enough to make him give them a flick every minute or so. Kelly munched on an apple and looked out of the window. I kept an eye out for other motels. We'd have to move again soon.

We sat in silence for a few minutes, until it occurred to me that the driver would expect to hear us talking. 'When I was your age I hadn't been in a taxi,' I said. 'I don't think I went in one until I was about fifteen.'

Kelly looked at me, still chewing on the candy. 'Didn't you like taxis?'

'No, it's just we didn't have much money. My stepfather couldn't find a job.'

She looked puzzled. She looked at me for a long time, then turned her head and looked out of the window.

The traffic was queueing for Key Bridge. Georgetown was just the other side of the Potomac and it would have been quicker to get out and walk, but it made sense to stay out of sight. By now Kelly's face would be in the newspapers, maybe even on posters. The police would be putting in a lot of time and effort to find her abductor.

I leaned over the front seat, picked up the map and directed the driver to the river end of Wisconsin Avenue, the main north–south drag. I remembered Georgetown as almost self-contained, with a genteel, quaint feel to the town houses that reminded me of San Francisco. The sidewalks were red brick and uneven, and every car seemed to be a BMW, Volvo, Mercedes, Golf GTi or Discovery. Every house and shop had a prominent sign warning that the property was guarded by a security firm. Try breaking in and you'd have a rapid-response team climbing aboard you before you even had time to rip the leads from the back of the video.

Wisconsin is a wide road with shops and houses on either side. We found Good Fellas about half a mile up the hill on the right-hand side. As restaurants go it looked one of the moody, designer-type places; the whole front was black, even down to the smoked-glass windows; the only relief was the gold lettering above the door. It was now nearly lunchtime; all the staff would have clocked in.

We entered through two blackened glass swing doors and were hit by the frosty blast of air-conditioning. We were at one end of a semi-lit hallway that ran the length of the frontage. Halfway down was a young receptionist sitting at her desk, looking very upmarket and friendly. I was impressed with Pat's taste. The girl smiled as we walked towards her, Kelly's hand in mine.

As we got closer I realized that the smile was a quizzical one. By now she was standing up, and I could see she was dressed very smartly in white shirt and black trousers. 'Excuse me, sir,' she said, 'we don't . . .'

I held up my hand and smiled. 'That's fine, we haven't come for lunch. I'm trying to find a friend of mine called Patrick. He used to come here a lot, maybe six or seven months ago. Does that ring any bells? As far as I know he was going out with one of your staff. He's an Englishman, speaks like me.'

'I don't know, sir, I've only been here since the beginning of the semester.'

Semester? Of course, we were in Georgetown, the university area. Every student was also a waiter or waitress.

'Could you maybe call somebody, because it's really important that I make contact with him.' I winked conspiratorially and said, 'I've brought a friend of his – it's a surprise.'

She looked down and smiled warmly. 'Hi. Do you want a mint?' Kelly took a small handful.

I went on, 'Maybe one of the people in the back might know him?'

While she was thinking about it a couple of boys in suits came in behind us. Kelly was looking up at them, lumps in her cheeks. 'Hi, little lady,' one of them laughed. 'You're a bit young for this, aren't you?'

Kelly shrugged. Not a word.

The receptionist said, 'Excuse me a moment,' and went off to do her hostess bit, opening the door beyond the desk for somebody else to meet the two guests and show them to their table.

She came back and picked up the phone. 'I'll call.'

I looked down and winked at Kelly.

'We've got somebody here with a child, and they're after an Englishman called Patrick?' she said with that upward inflection at the end that had started in Ramsay Street and taken over the world.

She put down the phone and said, 'There'll be somebody here in a minute.'

It rang again almost immediately and she took a booking.

Kelly and I just stood there. In a minute or two a waitress appeared from the dining room. 'Hi. Follow me.'

Things were looking up. I got hold of Kelly's hand and we went through the door to the dining room.

People here obviously liked eating in semi-darkness because all the tables were lit only by candles. Looking around, I noticed that all the waitresses seemed to wear small white T-shirts that exposed their midriffs, with tight shorts and sneakers with little ankle socks.

On the right-hand side, against the wall, was a bar with overhead lighting. The two suits were the only two customers. In the middle of the room I noticed a small raised stage with spotlights above.

I laughed to myself; good stitch, Pat!

Arse or no arse, Slack had always been successful with women. At the time of Gibraltar he was single like me and rented the house next door. For about a year he'd been having what he called a 'relationship', but we all knew better. They'd met at a

Medieval Night fancy-dress party; at four o'clock the next morning I was woken by the sound of a vehicle screeching up outside his house, then doors slamming and lots of giggling and laughing. We lived in a small estate, the sort of houses they threw up in about five minutes all through the Eighties, so I could hear his front door crashing and thought, Here we go. Then I heard a bit of music and the toilet flushing, which is always nice at four in the morning. Then lots more laughing and giggling and they were away. At noon the next day I was in the kitchen, mincing around with the washing-up, when a taxi drew up, and that was when Queen Elizabeth I and one of her young ladies-in-waiting came scuttling out of Pat's front door, hair all over the place, looking incredibly embarrassed as they jumped into the cab, hoping no-one would see them. When we grilled him, it turned out he was doing it with a mother-and-daughter combo. We hadn't let him hear the end of it ever since. Now it looked like he'd got his own back.

One of the girls waved to Kelly. 'Hi, honey!' Beneath her T-shirt was what looked like a dead heat in a Zeppelin race.

Kelly was loving it. I held her hand tight. As we followed the girl, Kelly looked up at me and said, 'What is this place?'

'It's a kind of bar where people go to relax after work.'

'Like TGI Friday's?'

'Sort of.'

We came to another set of double doors and went through into a world of bright light and clatter. There were the kitchens on the right, full of noisy chaos; on the left, offices. The walls were dirty-white plaster with gouge marks from where they'd been knocked by furniture – or maybe by runaway Zeppelins.

Further down the corridor we came to another room. Our friend led us in and announced, 'Here he is!'

This was obviously where all the girls hung out – in some cases, literally. If I'd had to imagine a changing room in a lap-dancing bar I'd have thought of semi-naked girls in front of mirrors with big bulbs around the edges, but this didn't fit the bill at all; it was much more like somebody's sitting room. It was clean, with three or four settees, a couple of chairs, a few mirrors. There was a No Smoking sign, which I could smell was observed, and noticeboards full of university meetings and goings-on.

Everybody went, 'Hi. How are you!' to Kelly.

I looked at a policewoman wearing a skirt that was very non-regulation length. 'I'm trying to find an Englishman called Pat. He told me he came here a lot.'

Kelly was getting dragged away by two of the girls. 'What's your name, honey?' There was nothing I could do to stop it.

I said, 'Her name's Josie.'

They were all in their fantasy rigs. One held out an Indian outfit, with fringed buckskin sleeves, feathers, the lot. She said to Kelly, 'Do you like this?' and started to dress her. Kelly's eyes widened with excitement.

I carried on talking with Washington's finest. 'It's just that there's been a big mess-up on the dates. We were supposed to have met Pat so Josie and him can go on vacation. It's no problem, I'll look after her, but she really wants to see him.'

'We haven't seen Pat for ages, but Sherry'll know, she used to go out with him. She's late but she'll be here soon. If you want to stay, that's fine. Help yourself to some coffee.'

I went over, poured myself a cup and sat down. I watched Kelly giggling. For me, this should have been like dying and going to heaven, but I was tense about Kelly letting something slip.

I could see textbooks lying around. There was one girl on a settee who looked as if she'd come out of a Turkish harem, and she was there with her laptop, tapping away at her dissertation.

Twenty minutes later the door burst open and a girl carrying a black sports bag ran in like a thing possessed, out of breath, hair everywhere.

'Sorry I'm late, girls. I wasn't on first, was I?'

She started to take off her shoes, catching her breath.

The police sergeant called over, 'Sherry, this guy wants to know where Pat is. Have you seen him lately?'

I stood up. 'I've been trying to find him for ages; you know what he's like, he's all over the place.'

'Tell me about it.' She started to take off her jeans in front of me as casually as if we'd been married ten years. 'He's been away for a while. I saw him about a month ago when he came back.' She shot a glance at Kelly and back at me. 'You a friend of his?'

'We go way back.'

'I guess he won't mind. I've got his number here, if I can find it.'

Dressed now only in her bra and pants, she rummaged through her bag as she talked. She looked up at one of the other girls and said, 'What number am I?'

'Four.'

'Christ! Can somebody go ahead of me? Can I go number six? I've got no make-up on yet.'

There was a grunt from behind the laptop. It seemed the Turkish harem girl was going on fourth now.

Sherry tipped out an Aladdin's cave of a handbag. 'Here we are.'

She handed me a restaurant card with an address and telephone number scribbled on the back. I recognized the writing.

'Is this local?' I asked.

'Riverwood? About a quarter of an hour by car, over the bridge.'

'I'll give him a ring. Thank you!'

'Remind him I'm alive, will you?' she smiled with weary hope.

I went over to Kelly and said, 'We've got to go now, Josie!'

She stuck out her lower lip. 'Ohhh . . .' Maybe it was being in the company of other females, but she looked more relaxed than at any point since we'd driven away from the house. 'Do we?' she pleaded with big round eyes that were covered in make-up. So were her lips.

'I'm afraid we must,' I said, starting to wipe it off.

The policewoman said, 'Can't we keep her here? We'll look after her. We'll show her how to dance.'

'I'd like that, Nick!'

'Sorry, Josie, you have to be much older to work here, isn't that right, girls?'

They helped Kelly to get all her feathers off. One of them said, 'You work real hard at school, honey. Then you can work here with us.'

They pointed to a quicker way out, through the service exit at the back. As we were leaving, Kelly looked up and said, 'What do they do, then?'

'They're dancers.'

'Why do they put on bikinis, and all those feathers?'

'I don't know,' I said. 'Some people like watching that sort of thing.'

Just as we got to the exit I heard Sherry shout, 'His daughter? The lying bastard!'

14

We walked back down the hill, looking for somewhere to sit out
of the rain. A place that looked more like a house than a restaurant had a sign calling itself the Georgetown Diner. We went in.

We sat in the three-quarters-empty café, me with a coffee, Kelly
with a Coke, both deep in thought – me about how to make contact with Pat, she most probably about growing up and going to
college dressed like Pocahontas. Our table was by a rack of greet-
ings cards and local drawings for sale. It was more like an art
gallery than a coffee shop.

'We can't just turn up at Pat's address because we might compromise him,' I thought aloud to her. 'And I can't phone him
because they might have made the connection between us and
there could be a device on his phone and a trigger on the house.'

Kelly nodded knowingly, not understanding a word I was on
about, but pleased to be part of grown-up stuff instead of being
abandoned or dragged around.

'It's so annoying because he's only fifteen minutes away,' I
went on. 'What can I do?'

She gave a little shrug, then pointed at the rack behind me and
said, 'Send him a card.'

'Good idea, but it would take too long.'

Then I had a brainwave. 'Well done, Kelly!'

She grinned from ear to ear as I got up and bought a birthday card showing a velvet rabbit holding a rose. I asked for a pen and went back to the table. I wrote, 'Pat, I'm in the shit. Kev is dead and Kelly is with me. I need help. IT WAS NOT ME. Call 181-322-8665 from a public landline ASAP. Nick.'

I sealed the envelope and wrote Pat's address, then asked to borrow their Yellow Pages. I found what I was looking for, and it was on the same road, seemingly within walking distance. We did up our coats and left. It had stopped raining, but the sidewalk was still wet. I checked the street numbers; we had to go down-hill towards the river.

The courier firm's office was next door to a weird and wonder-ful New Age shop with a window full of healing crystals that could change your life. I wondered which one they'd prescribe if I went in and told them my circumstances. Kelly wanted to stay outside and look in the window, but I wanted her with me; people might look twice at a child on her own outside a shop and something might register. There was a risk of someone in the shop identifying her, but it was a question of balance between exposing her and making the best use of her as cover.

'Can you get this to my friend after four o'clock today?' I said to the guy at the desk. 'We're in real big trouble because we for-got to post his birthday card, aren't we, Josie?'

I paid the $15 fee in cash, and they promised to bike it round at 4 p.m. I needed the intervening two hours to prepare the ground for a meet.

We went into the Latham hotel. I'd guessed my accent wouldn't stick out in there and I was right; the large reception area was full of foreign tourists. I sat Kelly in a corner and went to the information desk.

'I'm looking for a mall that would have a Fun Zone or Kids Have Fun,' I said.

It turned out there were about half a dozen of them in and around the DC area; it was just a matter of looking up all the different addresses in the city guide she'd kindly lent me. There was one at the Landside Mall, not far from the Roadies Inn. I hailed a taxi, and this time the driver knew where he was going.

Kids Have Fun is a franchised playcentre operation. The idea is that you drop your kids off for a few hours while you go off on your big shopping frenzy. I'd once gone with Marsha to pick up Kelly and Aida from one. The child gets a name tag on their wrist that they can't remove, and the adult is given an ID card that means they're the only person who can collect the child. The girls had been playing up the morning I went, and I remembered that, as we approached the centre, Marsha had grinned at the travel agent's opposite and said, 'I always think that's brilliant positioning; the number of times I've been tempted to drop off the kids and pop in for a one-way ticket to Rio!'

The mall was shaped like a large cross, with a different department store – Sears, Hecht's, JCPenney, Nordstrom – at the end of each spur. There were three storeys, with escalators moving people up and down from the central hub. The food hall was on the third floor. It was as busy as it was massive, and the heat was nearly tropical – probably on purpose, to send you to the drinks counters.

I spotted Kids Have Fun on the Hecht's spur. I turned to Kelly. 'Hey, do you want to go in there later on? There's videos and all sorts of stuff.'

'I know. But I want to stay with you.'

'Let's go in and have a look anyway.' I didn't want to put her in there yet because I didn't even know if we were going to get the phone call or not, but I'd still have to do the recce and prepare the ground.

I went up to the desk. 'Do we have to book to come in?'

Apparently not, we just turned up and filled in a form. I worked out that, if I did get a phone call at 4 p.m., I'd only have half an hour at the most to hide her. I had to assume the worst-case scenario, which was that they knew Kev's mobile number and were waiting to intercept it and listen to me giving Pat directions. I wanted her away from that area and safe. Also, I couldn't be sure about Pat. He might be part of a trap. I had to be careful, but at the same time I was desperate to see him.

I could see her looking round. It didn't look that bad. We walked out.

'You can come with me now, but I have to go on my own later, OK?'

She looked pissed off. 'Whyyy?'

'Because I have to do stuff, OK? You can help me now, though.'

At last I got a smile. 'Oh, OK, but you won't be long, will you?'

'I'll be back before you know it.'

Kelly and I started walking around, doing recces without her realizing it.

'What are we looking for, Nick?'

'A shop with cameras and telephones.'

We walked the whole mall, eventually finding one on the ground floor. I bought a battery charger for the mobile phone. She decided not to buy another present for Melissa after all, announcing that she'd just pick up the friendship bracelets from home. I didn't comment.

At five minutes to four I took the phone from my pocket and turned on the power. The battery and signal strength were fine. I was ready.

At ten past four it started ringing. I pressed receive. 'Hello?'

'It's me.'

'Where are you?'

'In a call box.'

'At five o'clock, I want you to come to the Landside Mall in Alexandria. I want you to enter via JCPenney, go to the centre hub, take the escalator to the third floor, go straight towards Sears. OK so far?'

There was a pause as it was sinking in. 'OK.'

'On the left-hand side there's a restaurant called the Roadhouse. Go into the Roadhouse and get two coffees. I'll see you there.'

'See yer.'

I turned the power off.

Kelly said, 'Who was that?'

'Remember I talked about Pat? I'm going to see him later on – that's good, isn't it? Anyway, are you ready for Kids Have Fun?'

She was going whether she liked it or not. If Pat stitched me up, this place would soon be swamped with police.

I filled in the form with the names we were using at the hotel. Kelly was studying the assault course with padding and plastic balls to break your fall. There were video areas where a huge variety of films were being shown, a juice dispenser, toilets. It looked really well organized and the place was packed. I could see the hosts, who were playing games with the kids and doing magic tricks. Seeing as she'd been doing nothing but watch children's TV for the last two days, Kelly should be into all that. The downside was the danger of her talking, but I had no choice. I paid my money, plus $20 deposit for the magic key to reclaim my child.

I asked her, 'Do you want me to stay for a while?'

She was dismissive. 'You can't stay, this is just for children.' She pointed at a warning sign that said. 'Be careful, parents, don't go near the playthings because you might trip over and hurt your-selves.'

I squatted, looking into her eyes. 'Remember, your name's Josie today, not Kelly. It's a big secret, OK?'

'Yeah, OK.' She was too busy looking into the play area.

'I'll be back soon. You know I'll always be back, don't you?'

'Yeah, yeah,' she was dragging herself away. Her face was towards me, but her eyes were looking the other way. A good sign, I thought as I headed off.

I took the escalator to the third floor. I got myself tucked into the corner table of a café and ordered an espresso and a Danish.

I knew that, if he was late, he wouldn't move into the RV. The SOP was that he'd wait an hour. If that didn't happen, it would be the same routine tomorrow. That's the great thing about working with people you know.

I looked at my watch. It was two minutes to five – or two minutes to eight in the morning in Baghdad. Looking down the escalators I could see the JCPenney spur joining the hub. On my floor I could also see the entrance to Sears and the Roadhouse.

At about two minutes past I saw Pat below me, walking in from the direction of JCPenney. He was sauntering along, casual and unhurried, wearing a brown leather bomber jacket, jeans and trainers. From this distance he looked unchanged, just a bit thinner on top. I looked forward to taking the piss out of him for that.

I knew he'd be at JCPenney dead on five; I knew he would have been putting in his own anti-surveillance drills *en route*, driving into the car park early to check it out, even sitting in his car to time it right. Pat might have his head in the clouds, but when he had to perform he was shit-hot. At the moment, however, my only worry was not so much about what was in his head as about what might be up his nose.

He walked onto the escalator and I looked away. I wasn't interested in him now, I was watching everywhere else, checking to see if he was being followed. By covering his back I was protecting my own. I had the easy part, being the third party and aware. The biggest problem would be for the surveillance operators who were following him and trying not to get pinged by people like me.

In an urban environment it's always best to meet people where there's a lot of pedestrian traffic. It looks normal, people meeting people. The downside is that, if there is any surveillance on you, they can blend in a lot easier too. However, it is chaos for them, because you can walk in and out of shops, stop at a counter, then move on, then turn round and go back to another counter; so, if you're going to RV with somebody to talk, go shopping.

Pat came up the last escalator, standing ahead of a group of teenage girls. They got off and turned left to the Baskin Robbins.

Pat went right. There were only four escalators, two up, two down. I couldn't see anyone who looked like an operator.

I watched him go into the Roadhouse. I gave it another five minutes, checked again, made sure the girl saw me throw my couple of dollars on the table, and left. Once on the Sears spur I got on the right-hand side of the walkway, which gave me a better view of the Roadhouse on the left, and that in turn gave me more time to tune in and look about to see if there were any men in Victoria's Secret looking out of place as they flicked through the ladies' lingerie.

I still couldn't be sure about Pat. But I didn't get nervous about that sort of thing; it was a drill, I'd done it so many times. I looked at it technically, in terms of what-ifs? What if they lift me from the direction of Sears? What if they come out from the shops each side of me? 'What if' stops you freezing like a rabbit in the middle of the road when the headlights hit you. It gets you out of that initial danger. In this particular case, I'd draw my weapon, move out of the danger area, through Sears or the escalators, and make a run for it.

I entered the Roadhouse and saw Pat closer up. Age was getting to him. He was only forty, but he looked eligible for some kind of pension.

He was sitting at a twin table on the far left-hand side, with two cappuccinos in front of him. There were about a dozen other people talking, eating and telling off their kids. I went over, pulled out the $5 bill that I had ready in my pocket, put it on the table and said, with a big flashy smile of greeting, 'Follow me, mate.'

If he was intending to stitch me up, I was just about to find out.

I was sponsoring the RV, so he didn't say anything, he just came with me. We went over to the far wall, where the toilet sign was; as we went through the door we came into a long corridor, with the toilets down the bottom on the left-hand side. I'd recce'd this on the walkabout with Kelly. To the right was another door, which led into Sears. These were shared toilets and that was why

I'd chosen them. I opened the door, let Pat through and followed him into the babywear department. We took the escalators to the ground, putting in angles and distance. It might not work all the time, but it was the best I could do.

From the perfume counter on the ground floor it was straight out into the car park, and we started to walk along the sidewalk towards a run of smaller shops and snack bars.

Not a word had been said. No need; Pat knew what was happening.

We walked into a SubZone, a very clinical, spotlessly clean franchise place selling baguettes with the world's supply of hot fillings. I told Pat to order me a drink and a cheese and meat special. The place was full. That was good; it made life more complicated for anybody looking.

I said, 'Sit over there at that table, mate, facing the toilets, and I'll be back in a minute.'

He stood in line to order.

I went through the door to the toilets and on to the far end, where there was a fire escape. I wanted to be sure it hadn't been obstructed by a rubbish bin or anything since I'd last checked. The fire-escape door was alarmed, so I wasn't going to test it to make sure it would open. I'd done my recce, so I knew what was on the other side and where to run.

Pat was already sitting down with two coffees and an order ticket. I was getting caffeine overload. I was also starting to feel like shit; the heat of the shopping mall and now this place, and the energy expended in this last two days were taking their toll. But I had to keep on top of that because this was an operation.

I sat down opposite him in the booth, looking beyond him at the glass frontage of the shop. I could see everybody coming in and out, and had a pillar and Pat as cover. I wanted to dominate the area because I needed to see what was going on.

I looked at Pat and decided not to take the piss out of his hair. He looked wrecked and wasted. His eyes were no longer clear and sharp, but red and clouded. He'd put on weight and there was an overhang pulling at his T-shirt and flopping over his belt. His face looked puffy and I could only just make out his Adam's apple.

I said, 'The reason we're here is that I've come over to see you on holiday and we're shopping.'

'Fine.'

I still had to test him, in case he was rigged up with a listening device.

'If there's a drama, I'm going to go through there.' I pointed towards the toilets. I was waiting for him to say, 'Oh what, you're going to go to the toilets?' for the benefit of anybody who might be listening in. But he didn't. He just said, 'OK.' I was as sure as I could be that I was safe. There was no more time to mess around.

I said, 'You OK, mate?'

'So so. Put it this way, a bit fucking better than you. How did you find me?'

'Sherry, at Good Fellas.' I looked at him and he smiled. 'Yeah, good stitch, Pat!'

His smile got bigger. 'Anyway, what's the score?'

'I've got every man and his dog after me.'

'So it seems.' His red eyes twinkled.

I started explaining and was still in full flow when the girl brought over the subs. They were huge, big enough to feed a family.

'What the fuck did you order?' I said. 'We're going to be here all day!'

Pat was hungry, fighting with the hot cheese as it stranded between his mouth and the sub. It made me wonder when he'd last eaten.

I was too busy gobbing off to eat. I said, 'Look, mate, to tell you the truth, all I want to do is fuck off and get back to the UK – but that's going to be a pain in the arse. I need to know what's going on, I need to know why this is happening. Do you remember Simmonds?'

'Yeah. He still in?'

138

'Yes. I've been in contact with him. I've even said that, if the Firm doesn't help me, I'll open up my security blanket.'

Pat's eyes widened. 'Wow, that's big boys' stuff! You really are in the shit. What did Simmonds have to say to that?' His shoulders went into a slow roll as he laughed through a mouthful.

I carried on for another quarter of an hour. At the end of it Pat said, 'Do you think that PIRA might have dropped Kev?' He was now picking at my sub. He made it clear he wanted a few bites. I pushed it over.

'Fuck knows. I can't see it myself. Can you make any sense of it?'

'The buzz around DC was that there was some American involvement in Gibraltar in '88.' He was picking the gherkins and tomatoes out of my baguette.

'What sort of involvement?'

'I don't know. It's something to do with the Irish-American vote, all that sort of shit. And PIRA gearing up funds from Noraid by getting into the drugs market.'

I wondered how Pat knew. Maybe that was where he got his supply. The thought made me sad.

My mind ticked over a bit more. Pat just kept on attacking my sub. 'Maybe that's where the connection with Kev comes in,' I said. 'DEA, drugs, what do you think?'

'Maybe. The Brits have been giving the Americans a hard time for years over Noraid giving money to PIRA, but the Yanks can't fuck about with all those millions of Irish-American votes.'

I sat back and studied his face. 'Can I ask how you know all this?'

'I don't. All I've heard is that PIRA buys cocaine and gears it up once they get it out of the US. It's been doing the rounds for donkey's years; there's nothing new in that. But maybe it's a starting point for you. I mean, fucking hell, you're the brainy one, not me.'

It made sense; if you've got some money and you're a terrorist organization, of course you're going to buy drugs, flog them and make a profit. And there was no way the American government was going to attack Noraid, it would be political suicide. But if Noraid could be shown to be linked with drug trafficking, that was something else. Maybe Kev was working against PIRA and got killed by them.

I said, 'Do you reckon Kev might have come across some shit? Or maybe he was even part of it and got fucked over?'

'I haven't got a clue, mate. Stuff like that gives me a headache.' He paused. 'So tell me, what do you need?'

I shrugged. 'Cash.'

He stopped eating my sub and got out his wallet. He handed me an ATM card. 'There's about three thousand dollars in there,' he said. 'It's a savings account, so you can draw out as much as you need. What about the girl? What's the score?'

'She's all right, mate. I've got her.'

If Pat was stitching me up, at least I was sending a message that I was aware of that possibility and taking precautions.

I said, 'Thanks very much for this, mate – for the card, and just for being here.' I'd known that he would help me out, but I didn't want him to think I was taking him for granted.

I said, 'Look, I'm not going to get you in the shit. I won't compromise you, but there is something else I need. Is there any chance of you phoning me some time tonight? I need to sit down and think about what I've got to do.'

'About nine-thirty?'

I smiled. Then all of a sudden I had my second brainwave of the day. 'You don't know any Sinn Féin or PIRA locations in Washington?'

'No, but I can find out. What are you thinking?'

'I need to find out if there's a connection between PIRA and the people who are trying to zap me – and who maybe dropped Kev. If I can check who comes in and out of a location, well, it's a start. If it came to anything, maybe I'd go in and have a look around.'

Pat demolished the last of my sub. 'Be careful, mate, don't get fucked over.'

'I won't. Right, I'll stay here – I'll give you ten minutes and then I'll leave. The mobile will be switched on from nine twenty-five.'

'No drama, we'll talk. Be lucky.'

He got up, picking at the fragments of cheese and meat at the bottom of the basket.

'Sherry, huh?' he said. 'How's she looking? She missing me?' Then he walked away, shoulders rolling as he laughed.

15

I went back into the mall via Sears, found an ATM machine and drew out $300.

It was dark outside, but the shopping mall was packed. There was still a possibility that I had surveillance on, waiting for me to RV with Kelly, so I stood off and waited before picking her up. Nothing looked unusual; the only thing I had to be aware of was the security cameras. The quicker I got in and out, the better.

I watched the area for ten minutes, then moved in closer. Opposite the play centre was a sports shop; I went in and became an instant basketball fan, studying all the shirts that were part of the display near the window. Kids Have Fun was crammed with kids, but I couldn't see her.

I mooched around the shop a bit, went back to the rack, had another look and caught sight of her. She was sitting on the floor watching a home-cinema-type TV. She was there with about a dozen other kids, each with a small carton of juice. It dawned on me that the girl did nothing but eat, drink and watch TV. It was a wonder she didn't look more like Slack Pat.

I went in, presented my identification card and asked for my daughter. They went through their process of verification and, a few minutes later, Kelly appeared with an escort.

I started to put her shoes on. 'Hi, Josie, how's it going?'

She sat there sulking that I'd arrived halfway through a film. I took that as a good sign; it showed there was a slight trace of normality coming back. It had been a relief not having her with me for a short while, but at the same time it felt good to have her back. I didn't know quite what to make of that.

We got a taxi, but dropped off about four blocks short of the hotel and walked in. It was our only secure area.

I opened the door. The TV was still on, telling us how great Nissan cars were. I flicked the light switch, told Kelly to stay where she was and looked inside.

The beds weren't made and the curtains were closed, so it looked as if the maid had obeyed the sign on the door. She wouldn't have given a damn; it was less for her to clean and she still got the same money.

More tellingly, the small pleat was still in the blanket. If I'd seen from the doorway that it had been disturbed, I'd have needed to make a very quick decision on whether or not just to walk away.

We went inside. Using the TV for support, I leaned to the rear of the drawer cabinet, looking into the gap between it and the wall. The match was still in place, covering the pinhead-sized pen mark. Even if they'd noticed that they'd dislodged it when checking under the cabinet, it was very unlikely that they'd have put it back in exactly the same position. Looking good so far.

'What are you doing, Nick?'

'I'm just checking to see if the plug is in properly. It looked like it was going to fall out.'

She didn't say anything, just stared at me as if I had a stupidity leak. Still not looking at her, I got on my knees ready to look at the drawer.

'Can I help you, Nick?'

'I'd like to hear what's on the TV.'

She sat down on the bed and started to tuck into a packet of Oreos. This kid was really eating healthily.

There were three drawers in the low chest and I'd slipped the paper clip in the front left-hand side of the middle one. I got the table lamp and shone it up and down, trying to catch the reflection of the paper clip. I did; the drawer hadn't been opened.

I got Kelly sorted out – took her coat off, put her shoes in the pockets and hung it by the door. I cleaned her bed up a bit, gathering up the food wrappers and brushing away the crumbs.

'Are you hungry?' I said.

She looked at the half-empty packet of Oreos. 'I'm not sure. Do you think I am?'

'Without a doubt. I'll go and get some food. You can stay here and I'll let you stay up late. But don't tell anybody; it's our little secret!'

She laughed. 'I won't!'

I realized that I was hungry too. Pat hadn't left me much at SubZone.

'You know the score, don't you?' I went through it all over again. 'I'll put up the Do Not Disturb sign, and you don't open the door for anyone. Do you understand?'

'Without a doubt.'

I did a double take. 'You taking the micky?'

'Without a doubt.'

It wasn't that busy on the street and the rain had eased. I got a job lot of clothes for us both – jackets and coats, jeans and shirts – enough to see us through the next two appearance-changes at least.

Once done, I walked over to the burger bar. As I stood in the queue I thought how weird this all was. One minute I'm at Vauxhall being briefed for a job, the next I'm trying to remember what flavour milk shake to buy for a child. I wondered if she'd approve of the shirts I'd got her.

On the way back I checked my watch. It was nine twenty; I'd been longer than I'd expected. Time to turn on the phone. I waited in a shop doorway out of the drizzle.

Dead on nine thirty, it rang. I was excited, but at the same time nervous. It might be for Kev. I hit the receive button. 'Hello?'

'Hi. It's me. I've got something for you.'

'Great. Wait . . .' I put my finger in my other ear. I didn't want to mishear this. 'Go ahead.'

'It's 126 Ball Street. It's in the old part of Crystal City by the river – between the Pentagon and Washington National. Got that?'

'Yeah.' I let it sink into my head. I'd been to the Pentagon before, and had used the domestic airport a couple of times. I had a rough memory of the area. 'Are you going to phone me to-morrow?'

'Yeah.'

'Same time?'

'Same time. Stay lucky, mate.'

'Cheers.'

And that was it. I turned off the power and repeated the address to myself to keep it in my head. I wasn't going to write it down. If I got lifted, I needed to be sterile.

On the way back to the hotel I was feeling quite upbeat. Up until now I'd been in the wilderness. I didn't exactly know what I was going to do with this new information, but it was a start. I felt more in the driving seat.

We ate and I watched some telly with her, but she seemed more interested in talking.

'Do you watch television at home, Nick?'

'Some.'

'What's your favourite programme?'

'I don't know. The news, I suppose. We have different programmes from you. What's your favourite?'

'*Clueless*.'

'What's that? A detective?'

'Loser, moron, double moron! It's about a girl.' She did a very good impression of a Valley girl.

'What does she do?'

'She goes shopping.'

* * *

By ten forty-five she'd fallen asleep. I got out the city guide I'd forgotten to give back at the Latham hotel and looked for Ball Street.

I followed the river south until I saw Washington National airport. The target was between that and the Pentagon, on the west bank. I had a little laugh to myself. If it was a PIRA location, they had a lot of bollocks; they probably drank at the same bars as the boys from the National Security Council.

There was not a lot I could do at the moment. Kelly was lying on her back imitating a starfish. I covered her with the eiderdown, moved all the shit off the other bed and got my head down. A saying from my infantry days, a lifetime ago, roared in my ears: 'Whenever there is a lull in battle, sleep. You never know when you are going to get another chance.' At last I was doing as I'd been told.

When I woke up it seemed like the same cartoon was running. I must have left the TV on all night. I was gagging for a brew.

I got up, wet my hair, made myself look semi-presentable and looked out of the window. The rain had got a bit more intense. I went downstairs and collected enough food and drink for three people – which was just as well, seeing the amount that Kelly ate.

'Wakey wakey!' I said.

Kelly still wanted to be marine life, but she woke up, yawning, stretching, then curling up into a ball. I went into the bathroom and started to run a bath.

She appeared in the doorway with a towel. She was starting to catch on.

While she was splashing around I sat on the bed flicking through the news channels. There was nothing about us. There had been so many other murders in the homicide capital of the USA that we were old hat.

She came out, got dressed and combed her hair, all without a single reminder from me. I opened an eat-from-the-pack carton of cereal for her and poured in some milk, then headed for the shower.

When I reappeared, all clean and presentable, I said, 'We've got to move from here today.'

Her face lit up. 'Can we go home now? You said Pat was going to help us go home.'

I picked her coat off the hanger and helped her put her shoes on. 'Really soon, yes, we will. But Daddy needs more time to rest. Pat will find out when it's OK,' I said. 'But, first, we've got to do stuff. It's really difficult for me to explain to you what's going on just now, Kelly, but it won't be long. I promise you will be home soon.'

'Good, because Jenny and Ricky are missing me.'

My heart missed a beat. Had I fucked up? Had there been other people in the house?

She must have read my mind. 'They're my teddies.' She laughed, then her face went serious. 'I miss them. And I want to go to Melissa's party.'

I started patting the top of her head. She looked at me; she knew she was being patronized. I changed the subject.

'Look, I'll show you where we're going.'

I got out the map. 'This is where we are now and that's where we're heading – just by the river. We'll get a taxi, find a nice hotel, and we'll make sure they've got cable so we can watch films. If they haven't, maybe we could go see a movie.'

'Can we see *Jungle Jungle*?'

'Sure we can!'

What the fuck was that? Never mind, at least we'd got off the subject of family.

After checking out and, to my surprise, being offered a one-night rebate, I went upstairs to collect Kelly and the blue nylon sports bag. I left the USP in the cistern. It only had one magazine of 9mm and I was carrying three of .45 with the Sig.

Leaving the hotel, we turned left and immediately left again. I wanted to get out of line of sight of reception before somebody thought of asking, 'Where's the wife?'

We hailed a cab and I asked for Pentagon City. The driver was an Asian in his sixties. He had a map on his seat but didn't bother to look at it. We seemed to be heading in the right direction. Kelly had her hat on. I thought of teasing her that she looked like Paddington Bear, but it would have taken too long to explain.

The driver asked where exactly I wanted to be dropped.

'The Metro stop, please.' I didn't have a clue where that was, but it sounded as good a place as any.

I paid the old boy his cash and off he drove. The whole area looked new and high-rent, both shopping and residential. There was a Ritz Carlton hotel and, a few minutes away, the Pentagon. I got my bearings and led Kelly towards the mall. I wanted to visit an ATM to celebrate the start of a new financial day.

We exited and walked across the supermarket car park, then on towards the river. It was strange because, for the first time, I felt like I was really responsible for her. I still held her hand when we were crossing roads, but now it seemed natural to keep holding it on the sidewalks, too. I had to admit, it felt good to have her with me, but maybe that was only because I knew it looked natural and therefore provided ideal cover.

We walked under the concrete freeway bridge that led to downtown DC. It was very busy and the movement of traffic sounded like muffled thunder. I told Kelly about the scene in *Cabaret* where Sally Bowles goes under the railway bridge to scream when things get too much for her. I didn't tell her that was what I'd been feeling like doing for the past forty-eight hours.

Once past the bridge the landscape changed. It was easy to imagine what this area must have looked like maybe fifty or sixty years earlier, because it hadn't been fully developed yet. It was full of derelict railway-siding buildings, some of which had been taken over as offices, though much of the area was just fenced off into lots or used as car pounds.

I looked left and saw the elevated section of the highway

disappear into the distance towards downtown DC. A concrete wall hid all the supports and a road ran alongside. There was no sidewalk, just a thin strip of hard ground, littered with drinks cans and cigarette packets. It looked as if people parked up on the verges here to avoid the parking charges further in. There were old, broken-down buildings everywhere, but the place was still being used. On the right was a fringe theatre in what had once been a railway warehouse. The tracks were still there, but they were now rusty and weeds were growing through. From above us came the continuous roar of traffic on the elevated highway.

We passed a scrap-metal merchant's, then a disused cement-distribution plant, where the boats used to come up the Potomac and dump their loads. I then saw something that was so totally out of place it was almost surreal. A late 1960s hotel, the Calypso, was still standing in defiance of progress. It was marooned in the middle of an ocean of chrome, smoked glass and shiny brick, as if the owners had decided to lift a finger to the property developers who were slowly taking over this dying area.

It was a very basic, four-storey building, built in the shape of an open square; in the middle was a car park crammed with cars and pick-ups. There were no windows on the outer walls, just air-conditioners sticking out of the breeze-block. I turned left; with the highway thundering away above me, I walked past the hotel on my right-hand side. I was now parallel with Ball Street, which lay behind it. Kelly hadn't said a word. I was in work mode anyway, and if it weren't for the fact that I had hold of her hand I would probably have forgotten she was with me.

As we got level with the Calypso I wiped the drizzle from my face and peered up into the gloom. On its roof was a massive satellite dish, easily 3 metres across. It wouldn't have looked out of place on top of the Pentagon. We turned right and right again. We were on Ball Street.

From street numbers on the map I knew that the target was going to be on my left. I kept to the right side for a better perspective.

It was still incredibly noisy; if it wasn't an aircraft taking off from the airport just the other side of the tree line, it was the continuous roar from Highway 1.

'Where are we going?' Kelly had to shout to be heard above it all.

'Down there,' I nodded. 'I want to see if we can find a friend's office. And then we can find a nice new hotel to stay in.'

'Why do we have to change hotels all the time?'

I was stumped on that one. I was still looking at the street numbers, not at her. 'Because I get bored easily, especially if the food's no good. That one last night was crap, wasn't it?'

There was a pause, then, 'What's crap?'

'It means that it's not very nice.'

'It was all right.'

'It was dirty. Let's go to a decent hotel, that's what I want to do.'

'But we can stay at my house.'

A jet had just left the runway and was banking hard at what appeared to be rooftop level. We watched for a while, transfixed; even Kelly was impressed.

As the roar of its engines died down I said, 'Come on, let's find that office.'

I kept looking forward and left, trying to judge which building it was going to be. There was a hotchpotch of styles: old factories and storage units, new, purpose-built two-storey office blocks rubbed shoulders with car parks and truck container dumps. In between the buildings I could just glimpse the trees that lined the Potomac, maybe 300 metres beyond.

We were in the high 90s, so I knew the PIRA office block wouldn't be far away. We walked on until we got to a new-looking two-storey office block, all steel frames and exposed pipework. All the fluorescent lights were on inside. I tried to read the name plates, but couldn't make them out in the gloom without squinting hard or going closer, neither of which I wanted to do. One said Unicom, but I couldn't make out the others.

It didn't look much like the sort of Sinn Féin or PIRA offices I was used to. Cable Street in Londonderry, for example, was a two-up, two-down in a 1920s terrace, and the places in west Belfast were much the same. They certainly weren't high-tech office blocks that looked like miniatures of the Pompidou Centre. Had Pat got this right? In my mind I'd been expecting some old tenement. Chances were this was just a front – it would be a commercial business and the people working there would be legit.

I focused on the target as we completed a walk-past, but didn't look back. You have to take in all the information first time around.

'Nick?'

'What?'

'I'm wet.'

I looked down. Her feet were soaked; I'd been concentrating so much on what to do next that I hadn't noticed the puddles we were walking through. I should have bought her a pair of wellies at the mall.

We got to a T-junction. Looking left, I could see that the road led down towards the river. More cars parked up on verges, and even more scrapyards.

I looked right. At the end of the street was the elevated highway and, just before that, above the rooftops, I could see the dish on top of the Calypso hotel. I was feeling good. A target walk-past and somewhere to stay, and all before 11 a.m.

16

We walked into the hotel car park. I pointed between a pick-up truck and a UPS van. 'Wait under the landing, keep out of the rain. I'll be back soon.'

'I want to come with you, Nick.'

I started my puppy training act. 'No . . . wait . . . there. I won't be long.' I disappeared before she could argue.

The hotel reception was just one of the ground-floor rooms turned into an office, and checking in was as casual as the layout. The poor Brit family story was understood a lot quicker here; they obviously didn't grow too much corn around these parts.

I went outside, collected Kelly and, as we walked along the concrete and breeze-block towards our new room on the second floor, I was busy thinking about what I'd have to do next. She suddenly tugged my hand. 'Double crap!'

'What?'

'You know, not nice. You said the other one was crap. This is double crap.'

I had to agree. I even thought I could smell vomit. 'No, no, wait till you get in. You see that satellite dish? We can probably get every single programme in the world on that. It's not going to be crap at all.'

There were two king-sized beds in the room, a big TV and the usual dark lacquered surfaces and a few bits of furniture – a long sideboard that had seen better days, a wardrobe that was just a rail inside an open cupboard in the corner and one of those things that you rest your suitcase on.

I checked the bathroom and saw a little bottle of shampoo. 'See that?' I said. 'Always the sign of good hotel. I think we're in the Ritz.'

I plugged in the telephone and recharger, then it was straight on with the telly, flicking through the channels for a kids' programme. It was part of the SOPs now.

I pulled her coat off, gave it a shake out and hung it up, then went over to the air-conditioner and pressed a few buttons. I held my coat out, testing the air flow; I wanted the room to get hot. Still waiting for some reaction from the machine I said, 'What's on?'

'*Power Rangers.*'

'Who are they?'

I knew very well what it was all about, but there was no harm in a bit of conversation. I didn't want us to be best mates, go on holidays together and share toothbrushes and all that sort of shit – far from it, the sooner this was sorted out, the better. But for the relationship to look normal it had to be normal, and I didn't want to get lifted because some busybody thought we didn't belong together.

I said, 'Which one do you like?'

'I like Katherine; she's the pink one.'

'Why's that, because of the colour?'

'Because she's not a geek, she's really cool.' Then she told me all about Katherine and how she was a Brit. 'I like that because Daddy comes from England.'

I made her change into a pair of jeans and a sweatshirt. It took a lifetime. I thought, Fuck parenting, it's not for me. Every moment of your time is taken up. What was the point, if you just spent all day on butler duty?

She was finally dry and sorted out. Next to the TV was a coffee percolator and packets of milk and sugar, and I got that on the go. As the machine started to purr and bubble I went to the window. As I looked out of the net curtain, left and right of me were the other two sides of the drab, grey concrete square; below was the car park, and across the road and higher up was the highway. I realized that my mood matched the view.

Rain was still falling. I could see the plumes of spray behind the trucks as they rolled along the highway. It wasn't heavy, but continuous, the kind that seeps into everything. I was suddenly aware of Kelly standing next to me.

'I hate this type of weather,' I said. 'Always have, ever since I was a teenager and joined the Army. Even now, on a really wet and windy winter's day, I'll make myself a mug of tea and sit on a chair by the window, and just look out and think of all the poor soldiers sitting in a hole in the middle of nowhere, freezing, soaking wet, wondering what they're doing there.'

A wry smile came to my face as the percolator stopped bubbling and I looked down at Kelly. What wouldn't I give to be back on Salisbury Plain, just sitting in a soaking-wet trench, my only worry in the world how to stop being wet, cold and hungry?

I went and lay on the bed, working out my options. Not that there were that many. Why didn't I just make a run for it? I could steal passports and try my luck at an airport, but the chances of getting away with it were slim. There were less conventional routes back. I'd heard that you could get all the way from Canada to the UK by ferry and land-hopping, a route popular with students. Or I could go south, getting into Belize or Guatemala; I'd spent years in the jungle on that border and I knew how to get out. I could go to an island off Belize called San Pedro, a staging post for drug runners on their way to the east coast of Florida. From there I could get further into the Caribbean, where I'd pick up passage on a boat.

More bizarre still, one of the blokes in the Regiment had flown a single-engined Cessna from Canada to the UK. The tiny fixed-wing aircraft had no special equipment apart from an extra fuel bladder in the back. The radio wasn't the right kind and he had to work out the antenna lengths with wire hanging from the aircraft on a brick. He wore a parachute, so that if anything went wrong he'd open the door and leap out. How I'd sort that out I didn't know, but at least I knew it could be done.

However, there was too much risk involved in all of these schemes. I didn't want to spend the rest of my days in a state penitentiary, but at the same time I didn't want Kelly and me to be killed in the process of escaping. Simmonds had presented me with the best option. If I turned up in London with what he wanted, I wouldn't exactly be home and dry, but at least I'd be home. I had to stay and tough it out.

It all boiled down to the fact that I needed to see who and what was going into and out of the building on Ball Street.

'Kelly? You know what I'm going to say, don't you?'

'Without a doubt,' she smiled. I'd obviously been forgiven for drying her hair and putting her into nice dry clothes.

'Ten minutes, all right?'

I closed the door, listened, heard her put it on the latch, and hung the sign on the door. Further to my left was a small open area that housed the Coke and snack machines. I bought a can, then walked back past our room towards the lift. To the left was the fire escape, a concrete staircase leading up and down. I knew the safety regulations meant that there had to be an exit on to the roof; in the event of a fire down below, the rescue would be by helicopter.

I went upstairs as far as I could. Double fire doors led to the roof; push the bar and they'd open. There was no sign warning that the doors were alarmed, but I had to check. I looked around the door frame, but couldn't see a circuit-break alarm. I pushed the bar and the door opened. No bells.

The roof was flat, its surface covered with 2-inch diameter lumps of gravel. I picked up a handful and used it to jam the doors open.

An aircraft was landing at Washington National and I could just see its lights through the drizzle. The satellite dish was on the far corner of the roof. There was also a green aluminium shed, which I guessed was the lift housing. A metre-high wall ran around the edge of the roof, hiding me from the ground, but not from the highway.

I walked across the gravel to the side facing the river. Looking down at the target building from this angle I could see the flat roof and its air ducts. It was rectangular and looked quite large. Behind it was an area of waste ground and fences that seemed to divide the area into new building plots waiting to be sold. I could just make out the Potomac beyond the tree line and the end of the runway.

I walked back, stepping over a series of thick electricity cables. I stopped at the lift housing. What I wanted now was a power source. I could use batteries to power the surveillance equipment I'd be using, but I couldn't guarantee their life. I tried the door of the lift housing, but it was locked. I had a quick look at the lock: a pin tumbler. I'd be able to defeat that easily.

Back in the room, I got out the Yellow Pages and looked for addresses of pawnshops.

Then I went into the bathroom, sat on the edge of the bath and unloaded the .45 ammunition from the magazines into my pocket, easing the springs. It's not something that you have to do every day, but it needs to be done. The majority of weapon stoppages are magazine-connected. I didn't know how long it had been left loaded; I might squeeze off the first round and the second one wouldn't feed into the chamber because the magazine spring had stuck. That's why a revolver is sometimes far better, especially if you're going to have a pistol lying about for ages and don't want to service it. A revolver is just a cylinder with six rounds in it, so you could keep it loaded all year and it wouldn't matter – as soon as you pick it up you know the thing will work. I emptied the magazines into my pocket so that I then had the ammunition, magazines and pistol all on me.

156

I came out of the bathroom and wrote myself a shopping list of kit that I was going to be needing, and checked how much money I had. There was enough for today. I could always get more out tomorrow.

I wasn't worried about Kelly. She had loads of food and was half asleep anyway. I turned up the temperature dial even higher on the air-conditioner. She'd soon be drowsy.

I said, 'I'm going to go and get you some colouring books and pencils and all that sort of stuff. Shall I bring back a Micky D's?'

'Can I have sweet and sour sauce with the fries? Can I come with you?'

'The weather's terrible. I don't want you catching cold.'

She got up and walked to the door, ready to drop the latch without me having to ask.

I went downstairs and walked to the Metro station.

17

The Washington Metro is fast and quiet, clean and efficient, everything an underground should be. The tunnels are vast and dimly lit, somehow soothing, which is maybe why passengers seem more relaxed than in London or New York and some even exchange eye contact. It's also about the only part of the capital where you won't be asked by a seventeen- or seventy-seven-year-old Vietnam vet if you can spare some change.

I got out after seven or eight stops and one platform-change. The place I was looking for was just a few blocks away, but it was in a neighbourhood I bet didn't feature in anybody's holiday brochure. I was used to the Washington where those who had really had. This was the part of town where those who didn't have had absolutely fuck all.

The single-storey building was set back from the road and looked more like a supermarket than a pawnshop, with frontage that was at least 50 metres long. The whole façade was glass, with bars running vertically. The window displays were piled high with everything from drum kits to surfboards and bedding. Fluorescent yellow posters promised everything from 0 per cent interest to the best gold price in town. Three armed guards controlled the doors and watched me enter.

Looking along one of the aisles to the rear, I saw a long glass showcase that also formed the counter. Behind it were more than a dozen assistants, all wearing a similar red polo shirt. It seemed to be the busiest department in the shop. Then I saw all the handguns and rifles behind the glass. A sign announced that customers were welcome to test fire any weapon on the range out back.

I carried on towards the camera department. In an ideal world, what I was looking for would be something like a security camera, with a long lead connecting the camera itself to a separate control box that also housed the video tape. I could put the camera in position on the roof, leave it where it was and hide the control box elsewhere, maybe inside the lift housing. That way it would be easier for me to get to it to change the tape and, if I couldn't find mains power, the batteries, and all without having to disturb the camera.

Unfortunately I couldn't find anything like that. But I did find something that was almost as good, and that was a Hi-8 video camera, the type favoured by a lot of freelance TV journalists. Certainly I'd be able to change the lens to give me more distance. I remembered working in Bosnia and seeing guys running around with Hi-8s glued to their eyes. They all thought they were destined for fortunes by selling the networks 'bang bang' footage.

I caught the eye of one of the assistants.

'How much for the Hi-8?' I said in my usual bad American accent.

'It's nearly new, hardly out of the packaging. Five hundred dollars.'

I smirked.

'So make me an offer,' he said.

'Has it got a spare battery and all the attachments for external power?'

'Of course. It's got it all. It's even got its own bag.'

'Can I see it working?'

'Of course, of course.'

'All right – four hundred, cash.'

He did what every plumber and builder throughout the world does when discussing prices: started sucking air through his teeth. 'I'll tell you what, four hundred and fifty.'

'Done. I also want a playback machine, but it mustn't be a VCR.'

'I have exactly what you want. Follow me.'

The machine he retrieved from the back of a shelf had a $100 price tag. It looked about a hundred years old, complete with dust. He said, 'I'll tell you what, save the trouble, ninety dollars and it's yours.'

I nodded. 'I also want some lenses.'

'What sort are you after?'

'At least a two hundred millimetre to go on this, preferably Nikon.'

I worked on the basis of one millimetre of lens for every metre of distance to target. For years I had been stuck in people's roof spaces after breaking into their houses and removing one of the tiles so I could take pictures of a target, and I'd learned the hard way that it's wasted effort unless the result is good ID-able images.

He showed me a 250mm lens.

'How much?'

'One hundred and fifty dollars.' He was waiting for me to say it was too much.

'All right, done – if you throw in two four-hour tapes and an extension lead.'

He seemed almost upset at the lack of fight. 'What length?'

More haggling. He was gagging for it.

'The longest one you've got.'

'Twenty foot?'

'Done.' He was happy now. He no doubt had a 40-foot.

I came across a Walmart a couple of blocks short of the Metro. I ducked inside and wandered around looking for the items I'd need to help me set up the camera.

As I moved down the aisles I found myself doing something I

always did, no matter where in the world I was: looking at cooking ingredients and cans of domestic cleaner, and working out which would go with what to make chaos. Mix this stuff and that stuff, then boil it up and stir in a bit of this, and I'd have an incendiary device. Or boil all that down and scrape off the scum from around the edge of the pot, then add some of this stuff from the bake-a-cake counter and boil that up some more until I just got a sediment at the bottom, and I'd have low explosive. Twenty minutes in Sainsbury's would be enough to buy all the ingredients for a bomb powerful enough to blow a car in half, and you'd still have change from a tenner.

I didn't need any of that today, however. What I was after was a 2-litre plastic bottle of Coke, a pair of scissors, a roll of bin liners, a mini Maglite torch with a range of filters, a roll of gaffer tape and a selection pack of screwdrivers and pliers – twenty-one pieces for $5, and an absolute rip-off; they'd last about five minutes, but that was all I'd need. That done, I grabbed a book of adventure stories for Kelly, some colouring books, pencils and other bits and pieces to keep her entertained. I also put a few more dollars in Mr Oreo's pocket.

I entered the Metro and found a bench. Lights at the edge of the platform flash when a train's approaching; until then most locals sit chatting or reading. There was nothing else to do, so I opened the Coke, had a biscuit, started a dot-to-dot picture in one of the colouring books and waited for the lights.

The rain had stopped at Pentagon City, though it was still overcast and the ground was wet. I decided to do a quick walk-past of the target while I didn't have Kelly.

Cutting across the supermarket car park, I headed for the highway tunnel and Ball Street. I was soon on the same side of the road and level with the building. A small concrete staircase surrounded by dense shrubbery led up to the glass doors at the front. They opened into a reception area, and then another set of doors that probably led into the office complex itself. A security camera was trained on the front doors. The windows were sealed, double-glazed units. Inside, the building on both floors seemed full of PCs and noticeboards, the normal office environment.

I couldn't see any external alarm signs, nor any signs saying that the property was guarded. Maybe the alarm was at the rear. If not, whatever detectors existed were probably connected to a telephone line linked directly to the police or a security firm.

I got to the end of the road, turned right and headed back to the hotel.

The room was like a sauna. Kelly's hair was sticking up all over the place and she had sleep in her eyes. Her face was creased and had some crumbs stuck on it. By the looks of things she'd been halfway through a biscuit and fallen asleep.

As I dumped all the kit on the side she said, 'Where have you been?'

'I've bought loads of stuff.' I started diving into the bags and dragging things out. 'I've got you some books, some colouring books, some crayons . . .'

I laid them on the bed and stepped back, waiting for some form of appreciation. Instead, she looked at me as if I was some sort of madman.

'I've done those.'

I hadn't known, I thought a colouring book was a colouring book. I'd quite enjoyed doing my dot to dot. 'Never mind, I've got you some sandwiches and some Coke, and you're to drink as much as you can because I need the bottle for something.'

'Aren't we going out for something to eat?'

'There's some biscuits in there . . .' I pointed into the bag.

'I don't want any more cookies. I hate it in here all the time.'

'We've got to stay in the hotel today. Remember, we've got people who are looking for us at the moment, and I don't want them to find us. It won't be for long.'

I suddenly thought, Shit, what if she knows her home number and starts using the phone? While she was pouring out some Coke, with both hands around the bottle that seemed as big as she was, I stretched around the back of the small cupboard between the two beds and pulled out the telephone jack.

I looked at my watch. It was four thirty; the best part of five hours to go until Pat made contact again.

I wanted to get the camera sorted out. I wanted it working at first light; I might even be able to get in an hour of filming before last light today.

Kelly got up and looked out of the window, a bored, caged-up kid.

I poured myself some Coke and said, 'Do you want some more of this before I tip it away? I need the bottle.'

She shook her head. I went into the bathroom and tipped the remainder down the sink. I ripped the wrapper off and, with the scissors I'd just bought, I made a cut at the top, where the bottle started to curve into the neck. I also cut at the base, so I was left with a cylinder. I cut a straight line up it and pushed the resulting rectangle of plastic down flat to get rid of the curve. I cut a circle, by first trimming off the corners of the rectangle, then developing the shape. That was me, ready to burgle.

I came back into the room and checked the leads and made the camera ready for use, by battery or mains.

'What are you doing, Nick?'

I'd been hoping she wasn't going to ask, but I should have known better by now. I had a lie all prepared. 'I'm going to make a film so you can say hello to Mummy, Daddy and Aida because you said you were bored. Here, say hello.'

I got the camera to my eye.

'Hello, Mommy, Daddy and Aida,' she said into the camera. 'We are in a hotel room waiting to come home. I hope you get well soon, Daddy.'

'Tell them about your new clothes,' I said.

'Oh yes.' She walked over to the wall. 'This is my new blue coat. Nick got me a pink one also. He knows my favourite colours are pink and blue.'

'I'm running out of tape, Kelly. Say goodbye.'

She waved. 'Bye, Mommy; bye, Daddy; bye, Aida. I love you.'

She came skipping over to me. 'Can I see it now?'

Another lie. 'I haven't got the leads to plug in the TV. But I'm seeing Pat soon, maybe he'll get some for me.'

She went back to her glass of Coke a very happy bunny. She picked up a crayon, opened the colouring book and was soon engrossed. Good; it meant I was able to put a tape into the camera without her seeing.

I picked up two plastic coffee cups, got the rest of the kit together, put it all in the video bag, and said, 'Sorry about this, but . . .'

She looked at me and shrugged.

I made my way up to the roof. The rain was holding off – the aircraft and traffic noise wasn't.

The first thing I wanted to do was get into the lift housing; I needed to know whether or not I could get mains power.

I got out my circle of plastic and put it in the crease of the green door. I pushed and turned it, making it work its way through the twists and turns of the door frame until it hit against the lock itself. The door was there to keep people out for safety reasons, not to protect something of value, so it was a simple lock to defeat.

Once inside I turned on my mini Maglite torch, and the first thing I saw was a bank of four power points.

I looked up at the ceiling. The shed was made up of panels of quarter-inch mild steel bolted onto a frame. I got the pliers and undid two of the bolts just enough to lift up a bit of the roof. Then I got the power lead from the camera, pushed it through the gap and ran it down against the wall. It didn't look out of place amongst all the other shit. I plugged the lead into one of the power points.

I kept the door open to give me some light while I prepared the camera. I got two bin liners and put one inside the other, then put the camera inside, pushing it against the plastic at the bottom until the lens just burst through. I then took the two plastic coffee cups, split them both down the sides, cut the bottoms off both, put them into one another, and fed them over the lens as a hood. That was going to keep off the rain, but at the same time let enough light into the lens so the thing could work. I used gaffer tape to keep everything in position.

I got on the roof with the camera and plugged it in. I lay flat and looked through the viewfinder, waiting for it to spark up and show me what the lens could see. I wanted a reasonable close-up of the staircase leading up to the main door.

Once it had jumped into life I focused the lens, got it bang on target and pressed Play. I tested Stop and Rewind, then Play again. It worked. I tucked in the plastic, making sure not to dislodge the camera, pressed Record and walked away.

18

I went and bought a dustbin-sized pizza, which we sat down and ate in front of the television, with the telephone plugged in and on charge.

Then it was just a matter of hanging around with indigestion, waiting for Pat to call and the four-hour tape to finish. It was dark now, but I wanted it to run the full four hours: one, to check that the system worked and, two, to see what the quality was like at night.

Both of us were bored. Kelly had endured death by TV, death by pizza, death by Mountain Dew and Coke. She wearily picked up the adventure book and said, 'Can you read me some of this?'

I thought, All right, it's just a collection of stories, it won't take that long to read a couple. I soon discovered it was one continuous adventure, with optional endings to each chapter. I was reading to her about three kids in a museum. One had gone missing – no-one knew where – when the story just stopped. At the bottom of the page it said, 'Do you want to go to page 16 and follow him through the magic tunnel, or do you want to go and see Madame Edie on page 56, who might tell you where he is? It's your choice.'

'Where do you want to go?' I said.

'Through the tunnel.'

Off we went. After about three-quarters of an hour and changing tack about eight times, I thought we must be getting to the end soon. It took nearly two hours to get through it. At least she had fun.

The room was warm and I still had all my kit on, ready to go. I kept dozing off, waking up every half-hour or so to the sound of *The Simpsons* or *Loony Tunes*. One time, I woke up and looked down at my jacket. It had come undone and my pistol was exposed. I looked across at Kelly, but she didn't even give it a second glance; maybe she was used to her dad wearing one.

I opened up a can of Mountain Dew and looked at my watch. It was only eight fifteen; I'd go and get the first video in about a quarter of an hour's time, put in a new tape, and then wait for Pat's call.

When the time came I said, 'I'm just popping out for five minutes to get some drink. Do you want some?'

She looked quizzical and said, 'We've got loads here.'

'Yeah, but they're warm. I'll bring some cold ones.'

I went up to the roof. It was damp and drizzling now. I opened up the back of the plastic bag, pressed the eject button and quickly exchanged tapes ready for the morning.

I came downstairs, passed our room and got another couple of cans of drink. Coca-Cola shares had probably rocketed over the last few days.

Clueless came on, the TV series she'd told me she loved. I was amazed as I listened to her reciting all the catchphrases off pat: 'Loser . . . double loser, moron . . . whatever!' Now I knew where a lot of her sayings came from.

At last it was just three minutes to go before Pat was due to check in. I went into the bathroom, closed the door and listened for *Clueless*. Nothing.

Dead on time the phone rang.

'Hello?'

'All right, mate? Thanks for the sub!'

We both had a quiet laugh.

'Do you know what floor they're occupying?'

There was a short pause, then, 'Second floor.'

'OK. Any chance of more money? I need a big wad, mate.'

'I could get you about ten grand, but not until tomorrow, or possibly the day after. You're welcome to it until you're sorted – and I take it you've got a way out?'

'Yeah,' I lied. It was for the best. If he got lifted he could only give false information, and they'd start looking at airports and docks instead of mincing around Washington.

Then I said, 'I need more contact in case I manage to find out anything about the building and things start changing rapidly. What about 1200, 1800 and 2300 – is that OK?'

'All right, mate. Your little friend and her family have been in the media a lot lately. Is there anything else?'

'No, mate. Be careful.'

'And you. See yer!'

I turned off the telephone, went back into the bedroom and put it back on the charger. I didn't know if Kelly had heard anything or not, but she was quiet and seemed uneasy.

I got the video player set up, pushed in the tape, and tuned in the television.

Kelly was watching intently.

'Do you fancy playing a game?' I said. 'If not, I'll just do it on my own.'

'OK.' It beat counting cars on the highway. 'But you said you didn't have any leads to put into the TV.'

She'd got me on that one. 'I bought some when I went out.'

'So why can't we see the video for my mommy?'

'Because I've already posted it. Sorry.'

She looked at me a little confused.

'We're going to watch this tape of a building,' I went on. 'It's got people going in and out of it. Now, there's going to be some famous people going in there, and people that you know, like friends of Daddy's and Mummy's and people that I know. We've got to see how many people we can each recognize. Whoever sees the most is the winner. You want to play?'

'Yeah!'

'You've got to be really quick, because I'm going to fast-forward it. Every time you see somebody moving, you've got to tell me, then I'll stop and rewind, and we'll have a look at it.'

I took some of the hotel stationery and a pencil and off we went. I had to use the button on the machine to fast-forward because there was no remote. I sat on the floor, under the player by the TV. Kelly's eyes didn't leave the screen. I was quite pleased with the tape. The quality wasn't bad at all; you could tell the difference between this and a home video, and I'd managed to get full-length pictures of the people covering about two-thirds of the screen.

'Stop, stop, stop!' she shrieked.

I rewound and had a look. Kelly had made me stop at the first hint of movement. There were a few people entering. I didn't recognize any of them. Kelly was sure that man number three was from a pop group called Back Street Boys.

She got into the game more and more. Everyone seemed to be famous. I logged them all, using the counter.

298: two men, one with a long light coat, one with a blue coat.

People think that being a baby spy is all James Bond, sports cars and casinos. I'd always wished the fuck it was. The reality is sheer hard graft to get information, then sitting down and working out what it is you've gathered. The fact that two people walk up a set of stairs means fuck all. It's interpreting what's going on that's important – identifying them, their body language, what happened before, what you think is going to happen later on. So you have to log everything, just in case, at a later date, it might be important. Give me a sports car any day.

The screen was slowly getting darker. The ambient street light was helping, but it was quite hard to see faces and we were losing colour; I could tell the difference between a man and a woman and their ages but only just.

It came to the end of the working day and everything began to close down; people going home were throwing switches and the light dwindled. In the end there were lights only in the hallway, reception area and corridors.

I left the tape running at normal speed. What I now wanted to know was whether there was a night watchman around, but I couldn't see anyone.

Kelly was loving it. She'd seen four actors, two of the Spice Girls and one of her schoolteachers. Not bad at all. But what if she did recognize somebody? I couldn't be entirely sure of what she said, I'd have to take it with a pinch of salt; after all, she was only seven. But I'd have nothing to lose by believing her.

'Do you want to do this again tomorrow?'

'Yes, I like it. I have more points than you.'

'So you do. I tell you what, after all that winning I think you should lie down on the bed and have a rest.'

If Kelly or I recognized anybody on the tape tomorrow it would be a bonus for me to take to Simmonds and prove a link. It would also mean that I'd definitely have to CTR the building and find out why they were there. I decided to go and have a closer look at the outside, and then I could plan how to make entry.

By 11 p.m. Kelly was sound asleep, still fully clothed. I put the eiderdown over her, picked up the key card and left.

To avoid the office I came out of the hotel via the emergency stairs. I got on the road by the highway, turned right and walked past the playhouse towards the target. The traffic was quieter now, just groups of noise instead of a constant roar. I turned right, then right again. I was on Ball Street.

19

It was the back I really needed to take a look at, but first I wanted to recce the front again. I wanted to see if there was a night watchman in there and get a better mental picture of what it looked like inside.

I moved into a doorway opposite. If I was pinged, I'd pretend I was drunk and having a piss. I was in deep shadow as I looked over at the target. I could see through the two sets of doors into the reception area; the lights were still on, giving a sheen to the wet concrete steps and the leaves of the bushes. I looked upstairs and saw light shining through the windows directly above the main entrance. That meant the corridor lights were on upstairs as well.

I waited around for a quarter of an hour, watching for signs of movement. Was there security sitting downstairs watching the telly? Was he upstairs, doing his rounds? I didn't see anything. Time to look at the rear.

I went back the way I'd come, but, instead of turning left, went right towards the river. It was just a single-track road with muddy slush on the sides and potholes filled with oily water that glistened in the ambient light. Using the shadows, I passed the scrap-metal merchant's and crossed over the railway tracks that led to the old cement depot. My footsteps made more noise than the highway now. Fences divided all the plots, secured with old chains and padlocks. I followed the road further, looking for a point to turn and get behind the target.

The highway lights weren't strong enough to have any effect at this distance, but I could make out the mist coming from the river. I'd reached a dead end. A fence blocked the old road and a large muddy turning circle had been made by cars looking for a parking space and discovering what I just had. I could also see lights from the airport, beyond the woods that sloped down to the Potomac.

There was no alternative but to walk back to the disused railway tracks, which years ago would have been a branch of the main line. I looked left, following the tracks; they ran about 200 metres to the rear of the target, and to their left were some old, rusted corrugated-iron buildings.

I started climbing over the wire gates, where the trains would have gone through to the depot; the padlocked chains rattled under the strain. I got into some shadow and waited. There were no dogs barking, and the airport was probably closed down this late at night because it was so close to the city; all I could hear was a distant siren.

I carried on along the tracks, and soon the only noises were of my feet and breath.

To my right was the scrapyard, enclosed by a fence, with old cars piled on top of each other seven or eight high. After about 100 metres the ground started to open up and I could see buildings. Fences made it clear what belonged to whom. The area had been cleared and flattened ready for developers. One of those buildings beyond it was the rear of my target; on the other side I could see street lights on Ball Street and the highway. The drizzle gave them a misty, faded look.

I slowed down, had a quick look at the target, then started to walk across the 150 metres of newly levelled ground to a fence that was about 50 metres short of the target building.

Near the fence I found some bushes, stopped and squatted

down. The things that always give you away are shape, shine, shadow, silhouette, spacing and movement. Forget about them and they'll get you killed.

Still on my haunches, I did nothing but sit and watch for the next few minutes. You have to give your senses a chance to adjust to a new environment. After a while my eyes began to adapt to the light and I could start to make things out. I could see that there were no windows in the back of the building, just a solid brick wall. There was, however, a four-flight steel staircase, the fire-escape route for both the ground and first floors. To the right of it, at ground level, were the junction boxes for the building's utilities.

I looked at the fire exits. If I had to make entry at some stage to find out what PIRA were up to, that was probably the way I'd go in. It depended whether or not they had external locks, and there was only one way to find out.

I scanned along the line of the 6-foot chain link fence, looking for a break. I couldn't see one. Grabbing the top edge of the wire, I pulled myself up, got a foot on the top and clambered over. I crouched down again and stayed still, watching and listening for any reaction.

There was no need to rush; slow movement meant that, not only did I reduce noise and the risk of being detected, but I could also control my breath and hear more around me. I used the shadows created by the building and trees, moving from one pool of darkness to the next, all the time keeping eyes on the target and the surrounding area.

Once I got close enough, I stopped at the base of two trees and stood against one of the trunks. Looking at the rear wall, I noticed a motion detector that had been fixed at a height and angle to cover people walking up the fire escape. I had no way of knowing what the detector triggered, whether it was an alarm, a light, or a camera, or maybe all three. I couldn't see any cameras, but I could see two light fittings, one above each fire exit. They weren't on. Were they what the motion detector triggered? Probably, but why wasn't there also a camera covering the rear, so that security could see what had triggered the light? It didn't matter, I'd treat the detector as if it triggered everything.

I noticed three wooden pallets to the right of the building by the fence. I could use those.

I looked at the doors. They had sheet steel covering them, together with an extra strip that went over the frame to prevent anyone tampering with the gap. Close up, I could see that the locks were pin tumbler type, similar to British Yales, but bigger. Piece of piss; I could defeat them.

A quick check of the utilities boxes and dials showed me that gas, electricity, water and telephone were all exposed and ready to be played with. I was feeling better about this all the time.

I was still worried about the possibility of a night watchman. In some circumstances, it can actually be a bonus. You can try to get him to come and open the door – and, hey presto, you've got an unalarmed entry. However, if I had to go in it would be covertly.

The car park was empty, which could be another indication that there was no-one inside. I had to confirm it one way or another. I decided to be slightly pissed, walk up to the main entrance and take a leak; while I was doing that I could get a better look inside. If there was anyone in the foyer he might come out and fuck me off, or I might see him watching telly in the back somewhere.

I followed the same route all the way back and walked onto Ball Street. I was quite damp now; the drizzle and wet rusty fences had done their work on my clothes.

I walked on the opposite side of the road towards the target. As I got nearer, I started to cross at an angle that gave me more time with eyes on. Head down, conscious of the camera covering the door, I started to stumble up the steps, and about three-quarters of the way up, as soon as I was able to see into the right-hand window, I turned, opened my flies and started pissing down onto the bushes.

Almost instantly, a male voice roared, 'Fuck you! Fuck you!

Fuck you!' and there was an explosion of movement in the shrubbery. I nearly jumped out of my skin.

I took my hand straight off my cock and onto the Sig. I tried to stop pissing, but I was in full flow. My jeans took the brunt.

I went for the pistol, then realized that maybe I didn't need to pull it yet. He might be security. Maybe I could talk my way out of this.

'Fuck you! Who do you think you are? You fucker!'

I could hear him, but still couldn't see anything. There was rustling and all sorts going on, then more 'Fuck you! Fuck you!' and I saw him appearing through the bushes.

'Fucking asshole, piss on me, you fuck. I'll show you! Look at me! You've pissed on me!'

He was in his early twenties, wearing old army boots without laces, and dirty, greasy black jeans. He had a hooded parka-type jacket that was in shit state, grimed with muck and with the elbows hanging out. When he was about 10 metres away I could also see he had a bum-fluff beard, a big earring in one ear and long, greasy dreadlocks. He was soaked.

The moment he saw me, his face lit up. To him I was the accidental tourist, Mr Hush Puppy lost at the wrong end of town. I could almost see the cogs turning; he thought he'd cracked it here, he was going to get some easy money out of this punter.

'Fuck you, asshole, you owe me a new sleeping bag! Look at my clothes, you've pissed all over me, fucking animal! Give me some money, man!'

He was certainly going for an Oscar. 'Do you know who I am? Fucking piss on me, man, I'll fucking kick your ass!'

I needed to take advantage of this. I went up to the window and started banging hard. If there was security he should come to investigate. I'd just play Hush Puppy man needing protection from this madman.

I banged so hard I thought the glass would break, making sure all the time that I had my back to the camera. It sparked up New Age man even more because he thought I was flapping.

He started to come up the stairs. I carried on looking inside the building. There were no used ashtrays in sight, no magazines lying open on chairs, no TV on, no evening paper; the furniture was well arranged, the chair by reception was neatly under the desk, there was nothing to show that anyone was there.

Nearly on top of me now, I heard 'Fucking asshole!'

I turned, opened my jacket and put my hand on the pistol.

He saw it and stopped in his tracks. 'Ah, for fuck's sake! Fucking hell!' He backed off and started to walk backwards down the stairs, his eyes fixed on the pistol. 'Fucking cops,' he muttered.

I had to try hard not to laugh.

'Fucking cops, piss on me every fucking which way!'

I waited for him to disappear. New Age man thought *he* had problems – this was the second time in two days that I'd had piss all over me. All the same, I felt sorry for him; I thought about all the time he'd probably spent finding himself a snug little basha, well concealed from predators and nicely warmed by the air-conditioning outlets and other machinery tucked underneath. Then some dickhead comes and empties his bladder all over the show.

It took me a quarter of an hour to get back to the hotel. I opened the door nice and quietly. Kelly was in child heaven, not having had to clean herself or tidy her mess, just falling asleep surrounded by candy and cookies.

I got undressed, had a shower and a shave, then binned the clothes in the hotel laundry bag. The holdall was now getting pretty full of dirty and bloodstained clothes. I was down to my last change. I got dressed again, tucked the pistol into my waistband, put on my coat, and set the alarm for five thirty.

20

I was half awake anyway when the alarm went. I'd been tossing and turning all night and now I couldn't really be arsed to get up. People must feel like this when they go to a job they really hate.

I finally got myself to my feet, went over to the window and opened the curtains. We were just below eye level with the highway and almost in its shadow. Headlights lumbered silently towards me from out of the gloom; in the other lanes, tail lights disappeared back into the darkness like slow-moving tracer. It wasn't time yet.

I let the curtain fall and turned down the heating, got the coffee machine gurgling and went into the bathroom.

As I took a leak I looked at myself in the mirror. I looked like a scarecrow, with creases on my face where I'd been lying on some crayons. I took off my jacket, turned in the collar on my polo shirt and splashed my face in a basin of water.

I went back into the bedroom. The brew wasn't ready yet and my mouth felt as if a gorilla had dumped in it. He'd certainly been in the room while we were both asleep, throwing food and drink cans everywhere. I picked up an already opened can of Mountain Dew and took a couple of flat, warm sips.

Until first light, there wasn't that much to do. I was used to this; so much of my life had been hurry up and wait. I pulled up the chair by the window and opened the curtains. Looking at the highway, I couldn't make out whether it was still raining or if it was just vehicle spray in the headlights that made it look that way.

By the end of a quarter of an hour I could begin to make out the shape of the cars as well as their headlights. It was time. There was no need to wake Kelly; the more she slept, the easier my life would be. I checked I had the key card and moved up to the roof.

Rain danced on the metal roof of the lift housing. I pulled myself up and lay there, getting soaked front and back as I pressed the play button on the camera. I checked that I still had the correct site picture and that the lens hadn't misted up. It had. I honked at myself because I should have put on another plastic bag to stop the moisture getting in overnight. I started to wipe the moisture off with my cuff and suddenly had the feeling that I was between two worlds. Behind me roared the early morning traffic, yet in front, towards the river, I could just about hear birds giving it their early morning song. I was almost enjoying it. The moment was soon shattered when the first aircraft of the day took off and disappeared into low cloud.

Lens dry, I rechecked the camera position, made sure it was recording and closed the bin liners.

It was now nearly 6 a.m. I went back to the room and my chair by the window, coffee in hand. I smiled as I watched a couple come out of the room next door, hand in hand. Something about them didn't quite match up. I made a bet with myself that they'd leave in separate cars.

For the hundredth time, my mind drifted to the telephone call I'd had with Kev. Pat had said that, if it was PIRA, there could be a connection with drugs, Gibraltar and the Americans. My hard drive went into freewheel, because something about the Gibraltar job had always puzzled me.

1987 had been PIRA's annus horribilis, and, as Det operators in

178

the province, Euan and I had done our fair share to fuck them over. At the beginning of the year they'd made a promise to their faithful of 'tangible success in the war of national liberation', but it hadn't taken long for that to turn to rat shit. In February PIRA fielded twenty-seven Sinn Féin candidates in the Irish general election, but they only managed to scrape about 1,000 votes each. Few people in the South gave a toss about reunification with Northern Ireland; they were far more concerned with other issues, like unemployment and the crippling level of taxation. It showed how out of touch PIRA were and how successful the Anglo-Irish accord was proving. Ordinary people really did believe that London and Dublin could work together to bring about a long-term solution to the troubles.

PIRA couldn't take that lying down and must have decided they needed a morale-booster. Their knee-jerk reaction was the murder, on Saturday, 25 April, of Lord Justice Maurice Gibson, one of the province's most senior judges. Euan and I saw, at first-hand, the celebrations in some of PIRA's illegal drinking dens that weekend. We even had a few drinks ourselves as we hung around. The players loved what had happened. Not only had they got rid of one of their worst enemies, but recriminations were flying left, right and centre between London and Dublin. The Anglo-Irish accord, which had done so much to undermine PIRA's power base, was itself now in question.

However, barely had the hangovers gone away, when PIRA had another disaster. Two weeks later, at Loughall in County Armagh, blokes from the Regiment ambushed PIRA's East Tyrone Brigade while they were attempting to bomb a police station. From a force of 1,000 hardcore players in 1980, PIRA's strength had already dwindled to less than 250, of which maybe fifty were members of active service units. Our successes had further cut this to forty, which meant that the operation at Loughall wiped out one fifth of PIRA's hardliners at a stroke. It was the IRA's biggest loss in a single action since 1921. If this carried on, all of PIRA would soon be riding around in the same taxi.

The massive defeat of Loughall was followed soon afterwards by a disastrous showing by Gerry Adams in the British general election. Sinn Féin's vote plummeted, with the Catholic vote switching to the moderate SDLP. Then, on 31 October, during Sinn Féin's annual conference in Dublin, French customs seized a small freighter called the *Eksund* off the coast of Brittany. On board was an early Christmas present to PIRA from Colonel Gaddafi – hundreds of AK47s, tons of Semtex, several ground-to-air missiles and so much ammunition it was a miracle that the ship stayed afloat.

The humiliation was complete. No wonder Gerry Adams and PIRA wanted revenge, and some sort of publicity coup to show people like Gaddafi and those Irish-Americans who contributed to Noraid that they hadn't completely lost their grip.

On 8 November, Remembrance Day, they planted a 30-pound bomb, with a timer device, at the town memorial in Enniskillen in County Fermanagh. Eleven civilians were killed in the explosion and more than sixty were seriously injured. Outrage at the atrocity was instant and worldwide. In Dublin, thousands lined up to sign a book of condolence. In Moscow, not a place well known for its community care, the Tass news agency denounced what it called 'barbaric murders'. But, worst of all for PIRA, even the Irish-Americans appeared to have had enough. PIRA had fucked up big-time. They'd thought the bombing would be hailed as a victory in their struggle against an occupying power, but all it had done was to show them up for what they really were. It might be one thing to kill 'legitimate' targets, like judges, policemen and members of the security forces, but murdering innocent civilians while they were honouring their dead at a Remembrance Day service?

That was why Gibraltar had been such a puzzle to me. I could see why Adams and co would be desperate to show their diminishing group of sympathizers that they were still in business, but why risk a repeat of the international backlash they'd suffered after Enniskillen? If they bombed Gibraltar, it wouldn't be only British civilians who might end up killed. At that time of the year, hundreds of foreign tourists pack the squares and streets of the colony, many from the cruise liners that regularly dock in the harbour. And many of those, PIRA would have known full well, are American. I'd never been able to see a method in their madness.

It suddenly hit me that maybe I'd been looking down the wrong end of the telescope. PIRA were terrorists, but their presence here in Washington proved that they were also businessmen. There was no sectarian divide when it came to money, just normal competition and greed. I knew that they got together with Protestant paramilitaries on a regular basis, to talk about their drug, prostitution and extortion rackets, even to discuss demarcation lines for different taxi firms and sites for gaming machines back in the province. They had the infrastructure, the knowledge and the weapons to be major players in the world of crime. With co-operation from other terror organizations throughout the world, the possibilities were endless. If so, this was serious shit.

Down in the car park the couple were having a long, lingering embrace. What was going on there was serious shit, too. Then one final kiss and, yep, separate cars.

I wasn't expecting a phone call from Pat until midday and there were still about three hours to wait for the tape to finish recording, so there wasn't much to do apart from watch invaders from Mars and talking shoes who lived in dustbins. I felt uneasy. I needed to do something.

I shook Kelly. She moaned and pulled the covers back over her. I spoke gently in her ear. 'I'm going downstairs to buy some stuff, OK?'

I got a very weak 'Yes.' She couldn't have cared less. I was beginning to realize she wasn't a morning person.

I used the emergency stairs again and crossed under the highway to the 7-Eleven. Inside, it looked like Fort Knox. There was a

181

grating in the wall with a cubby hole behind, and a Korean face glowering out and then turning back to watch a portable TV. The shop was too hot and it stank of cigarettes and overbrewed coffee. Every inch of wall space was plastered with signs informing the local villains, 'Cash Register Holds Only $50, Everything Else Deposited'.

I didn't really need to buy anything; we had more stuff in the room than we could shake a stick at, certainly more biscuits than Mr Oreo. But I wanted some time to myself, away from Kelly. I found it tiring just being around her. There was always something that needed doing, checking or washing, and, in any time that was left over, I seemed to be nagging her to hurry up and get dressed.

At the magazine rack another friendly sign said, 'No Spitting Or Reading The Merchandise'. I picked up a *Washington Post* and a handful of magazines, some for me and some for Kelly, I didn't even bother looking at what they were, and went and put my money through the small hole in the grille. The Korean looked disappointed he hadn't been forced to use the machete I was sure he had under the till.

I strolled into reception to collect breakfast. The room was full. There was a TV mounted on a wall bracket above the food and drink collection point. As I started to load up three paper plates, I could hear the anchorman talking about George Mitchell and his part in the Irish peace process. I listened to a couple of sound bites from Sinn Féin and the British government, both pouring scorn on the other side's statements, both claiming that they were the ones who truly wanted peace.

A woman's voice interrupted my thoughts. She was presenting the local news and, as I poured an orange juice for Kelly, I could feel my skin tingle all over. She was talking about the Browns.

I didn't dare turn round. One of the barbecue pictures could be appearing on screen any moment.

The woman told viewers that police had not come up with any new leads, but that the investigation of the kidnapping of seven-year-old Kelly had moved forward with a computer image of the man seen leaving with her. She gave my height, build and hair colour.

There wasn't room to pour any more coffee or juice, and the tray was overflowing with food. But I didn't dare move. I felt as if every pair of eyes in the room was fixed on me. I put a bagel into the toaster and waited, drinking coffee, not looking up or round. I felt I was in a cocoon of silence, apart from the voice of the newsreader. I prayed for her to turn to a new subject. The bagel popped up. Shit. I put some spread on it. I knew people were looking at me; they must be. I'd run out of things to do.

I took a deep breath, picked up my tray and turned round. The noise of the room came back. No-one was looking. They were too busy eating, talking and reading the papers.

Kelly was still asleep. Good. I put her food on the side and started to munch my Cheerios. I switched on the TV, muted it and flicked through the other channels, looking for local news. There was nothing more about the situation in Hunting Bear Path.

I attacked the newspaper. We were famous – well, sort of. A small piece on page five. No pictures. A police spokesman was reported as saying that they were reluctant to come up with any theories until they had more concrete evidence, but, yes, the murders were being treated as drug-related. Luther and co would be pleased about that. Other than that, there were no new leads. I wasn't the only one in the dark.

I had to try to cut all the conjecture from my mind because it was getting far too confusing. As the policeman said, without information it was pointless spending time and effort trying to think of different scenarios. I determined to focus all my effort into: one, protecting Kelly and myself; two, keeping the video on target to discover if there was a connection between PIRA and Kev's death; three, getting some money from Pat, so that I could arrange my return to the UK and, four, getting hold of Euan for

183

help in dealing with Simmonds – or, if I had nothing for him, to help me negotiate with him.

I looked over at Kelly. She was on her back, with her arms out in a star shape, dreaming she was Katherine, the pink one. I felt sorry for her. She hadn't a clue what had happened to her family. Some poor bastard was going to have to tell her one day, and, after that, someone would have to look after her. I just hoped it was someone nice; maybe her grandparents, wherever they might be.

At least she was alive. Those boys must be flapping now. They'd have to assume that Kelly had given me their descriptions and that she'd overheard what all the shouting was about. They must be desperate to get their hands on us.

I started to wonder how I could get more information out of her, but gave up on that one. I was no psychologist; if anything, I was a candidate for seeing one.

I picked up a bike mag and, by the end, had changed loyalties from Ducati to BMW. Then I read in a fishing magazine how wonderful Lake Tahoe was for men with long wellington boots, and was lost in a whole new world of hook sizes and rod materials, when all of a sudden there was a knock on the door.

No time to think. I pulled the Sig, checked chamber and looked at Kelly. I thought, We both might be dead soon.

I put my hand over her mouth and gave her a shake. She woke up scared. I put my fingers to my mouth. It wasn't in a nice manner; it was saying, Shut the fuck up. Don't say a fucking thing.

I called out, 'One minute, one minute!' I went through and turned on the shower, came back out, then went up to the door sounding disorganized. 'Hello, who is it?'

A pause. 'Housekeeping.'

I looked through the spyhole and saw a woman, black, in her fifties; she had a cleaner's uniform on and a trolley behind her.

I couldn't see anything else, but then, if she had the police or Luther's boys either side of her, they weren't going to be show-ing their faces.

I looked at her and tried to interpret from her eyes what was going on. They would soon tell me if there were ten policemen around the corner bristling with body armour and firepower.

I said, 'It's OK, not today thank you, we're sleeping.'

I saw her look down and heard, 'Sorry, sir, you didn't have your sign on.'

'Oh, OK.'

'Would you like some towels?'

'One minute, I'm just coming out of the shower, I'll get some clothes on.'

It would be natural to be wanting towels.

I put the weapon in my left hand, undid the lock and opened the door just a fraction. The weapon was pointing through the door on the left-hand side; if any fucker pushed past her to get in, it would be the last thing he did.

I opened the door a little more, held it with my leg and put my head in the gap. I smiled. 'Ah, hiya.' The gun was pointing at her behind the door. I didn't put my hand out to get the towels, I didn't want someone grabbing it. All I did was put my hand up and say, 'I'll put the others out later on. I just need two big towels; that'll be fine – and have you got some more shampoo?'

She gave me what I wanted. I said, 'Thank you,' and she smiled back. I closed the door.

Kelly was lying on the bed open-mouthed, watching my every move.

I shrugged. 'Don't you just hate it when people do that?'

She started laughing. So did I. 'They nearly had us that time!' I said.

Her expression changed and she slowly shook her head. 'I know you won't ever let them get me.'

It was ten thirty, another twenty minutes to go before I went up and changed the tapes. I picked up the one we'd been watching the night before, slapped it back into the player and rewound it ready for its next session.

I only had to smile at her and she jumped up and went to the door, ready to drop the latch.

'While I'm out I want you to have a shower. Will you do that?'

She shrugged. 'I get all the good jobs.'

I went upstairs to the roof.

The weather was still crap.

21

There was still an hour to go before the midday call. We sat down together to watch the latest footage.

I said, 'It's really important, we might see somebody we know. Then we can give the tape to Daddy and he can find out who was shouting at him. Anybody that you think you might know, like Melissa's dad or the man at the grocery store, or even the men who came to see Daddy, tell me and we can have a closer look, OK?'

I started to fast-forward, stopping the tape whenever there was traffic. I logged what they looked like: male, female, black, white, Asian; and what they were wearing: black on blue, red on blue.

The game wasn't as much fun for Kelly the second time round.

'What about him?' I enthused.

'No.'

'That lady?'

'No.'

'You sure you've never seen this man?'

'Never!'

At last she spotted somebody she knew. I rewound the tape. 'Who is he?'

'Mr Mooner on *Fox Kids*.'

'OK, I'll write that down.'

Another guy started to walk up the stairs. I stopped the tape and rewound. 'Do you know him?'

She shook her head.

I said, 'Well, I know somebody who looks exactly like him. I used to work with a man who could never remember where he left things, and one day we hid his false teeth and he had to eat soup all week!' She had a little laugh and it kept her going a bit longer.

At eleven forty-five we were still going through the tape and logging. I stopped at two men who were going in together.

'Do you know either of them, because I don't, I can't think of anybody who looks like them.' I was racking my brains trying to think of another story to keep her interested.

'No, I don't know them.'

'Oh all right then. Just a couple more, then we'll do something else.' I started to fast-forward, saw a figure coming out of the building, rewound and played it.

She moved to the edge of the bed. 'I know that man,' she said.

I pressed freeze-frame. I was looking at a black guy in his mid-thirties.

'Who is he?'

'He came to see Daddy with the other men.'

I tried to sound calm. 'What's his name? Do you know any of their names?'

'Can I go home and see Mommy now? You said I could go home tomorrow and now it's tomorrow.'

'We have to sort this out first, Kelly. Daddy needs to know their names. He can't remember.'

I was trying to do the psychology bit, but I knew more about fly-fishing now than I did about child psychology.

She shook her head.

'Daddy knew them, though, didn't he?'

'Yes, he knew them. They came to see Daddy.'

'Can you remember anything else about them? Were they smoking?'

'I don't know. I don't think so.'

'Did any of them have glasses?'

'I think this man had glasses.'

I looked closer at the screen. He wore thin wire frames.

'OK, were they wearing rings or anything?'

'I don't know.'

I tried the colour of the car, their shoes, their coats. Did they talk to each other using different names? Were they American?

She was starting to get upset, but I had to know.

I said, 'Kelly, are you sure this man came to see Daddy the day I found you?'

Her eyes were welling up. I'd gone too far.

'Don't cry.' I put my arm around her. 'It's OK. This man came with the other men, yes?'

I felt her nod.

'That's very good because I can give this information to Daddy when I see him and that will help catch them. You see, you've helped him!'

She looked up at me. There was a slight smile under the tears.

If she was right, then what we had was one of the people who'd killed Kev coming out of an office that was fronting for PIRA.

There was still more tape to run. I tried to sound upbeat. 'OK, then, let's have a look and see if we can see the other men. They were black too, weren't they?'

'No, white.'

'Oh yes, of course.'

We carried on through the tape. I came out with a possible ID of Nelson Mandela, and she saw Michael Jackson. Apart from that, jack shit.

'Can we go home now and show this to Daddy? He must be better now. You said so, if we saw anyone.'

I was digging myself deeper. 'No, not yet. I have to make sure that he is the man who came to see Daddy. But not long now, not long.'

I lay on the bed pretending to read the fishing mag. My heart was beating loud and slow. I was trying to keep to my game plan of only concentrating on the matter in hand, but I couldn't. Why would Kev be killed by people who knew him? Were Luther and co the same group? They must be. What did Kev know, or what was he involved in? Why would he tell me about his problem if he was corrupt? Were the DEA investigating PIRA and drug dealing? Maybe Kev was, and the murders were carried out by PIRA or the drug dealers because of something he had done or was about to do? But why did they know him?

Conjecture would get me nowhere. It was just a waste of time and effort. Kelly was stretched out beside me and was looking at the magazine. It was a strange feeling having her head on my chest. I moved my arm around her to look at my watch. She thought I was going to cuddle her.

It was nearly time for Pat to call. I got up and switched on the mobile phone, then stood by the window, pulling a gap in the curtain, looking at the highway through the rain, deciding my next phase. I tried to think of a good RV. It wouldn't be secure to meet again at the shopping mall.

Dead on time the phone rang.

'Hello?'

'Hello, mate.' I could hear the traffic going past a call box.

'Things are happening,' I said. 'I need an RV.'

'In two hours, is that OK?'

'Two hours. Union Station all right for you?'

'Er ... Union ... yep, no problems.' He sounded spaced out.

I'd travelled through the terminus a few times before and could remember its layout. 'Come in through the main entrance,' I said. 'Go up to the top floor, to the coffee bar facing the stairs. Buy a cup of coffee, sit down and wait. I'll pick you up there, OK?'

There was a long, worrying pause. 'Is that OK, Pat?'

'I'll be there. See yer.' The line went dead.

Union Station is the main Amtrak station in Washington, DC. It is so grand and elegant that it should be in Paris, not here in the home of the breeze-block and dark-wood veneer. At most major railway stations in the world you expect to find the seedier side of life, but not so at Union. The ticketing, check-in and baggage-handling areas look like part of a modern airport. There's even a first-class lounge. You don't see the trains because they're behind screens and, in any case, you'd be much too distracted by the shopping mall, the food hall, the coffee shops, even a five-screen cinema. More importantly for me, however, I remembered it as a big, busy location, and, because of the Easter holiday, I knew there'd be a big transient population of people from out of town, who would know nothing of the events at Hunting Bear Path.

A cab got us to the station early. There was just under an hour to kill, so I made the most of it shopping for items I'd be needing for the CTR of the PIRA office, besides the stuff I'd already bought at Walmart. Now that Kelly had confirmed the black guy, the only option was to get in there and have a look around.

I bought a Polaroid camera and six packs of film; a pair of cheap and nasty fibre coveralls; more rolls of gaffer tape and Sellotape; heavy-duty scissors that promised I could cut through a shiny new penny with them; a Leatherman, a tool that's a bit like a Swiss Army knife; trainers; rubber gloves; batteries; cling-film; a plastic bottle of orange juice with a large spout; a box of large drawing pins; a box of twelve eggs; and a quartz kitchen clock, 9 inches in diameter. Kelly looked at it all and raised an eyebrow, but didn't ask.

By one forty I had a couple of carrier bags full of gear, as well as the books and time-wasters I'd had to put in her basket to keep her involved.

I remembered the beautiful tiled flooring in the entrance hall, but I'd forgotten the cathedral-high ceilings. In the middle was a rotunda shape with a news-stand and groups of tables outside. Above it, reached by a flight of stairs, was a restaurant. It was absolutely perfect for what I needed.

We were greeted at the top by a waitress.

I smiled. 'Table for two, please.'

'Smoking or non-smoking?'

I pointed at a table right at the back. 'Can we have that one?'

We sat down and I put the bags under the table. I couldn't see the main entrance, but I'd be able to see Pat heading towards the coffee shop because that was further into the main part of the station and up a level.

The waitress came to take the drinks order. I asked for two Cokes and said, 'I'm ready to order now, if that's all right? We'll take a nine-inch pizza.'

Kelly looked up. 'Can we have extra mushrooms, please?'

I nodded at the waitress and she left.

Kelly smiled. 'I am just like my mommy. We both like extra mushrooms. Daddy says we must be forest pixies!' She smiled again, wanting a reaction.

'That's nice,' I said. This was a conversation that needed nipping in the bud.

Kelly got stuck into her Coke, obviously enjoying being able to watch real people for a change.

Pat was early and wore the same clothes as a VDM (visual distinguishing mark). Either that or the fucker simply hadn't changed. As he walked past and below me, something about him didn't seem right. There was a very slight stagger in his stride, and I knew it wouldn't have come from drinking too much beer. I feared the worst.

I carried on doing my checks, covering his arse to protect my own.

I gave it about five minutes, got up and said to Kelly, 'I have to go to the toilet. I won't be long.' On the way out, I asked the waitress to keep an eye on Kelly and our bags.

Another set of doors took me into the main ticketing and train area. The place was heaving; half of the USA must have been on the move. Even the air-conditioning was finding it too much: the combination of heat and wet from the people made it feel like a greenhouse. I joined the packed crowds slowly shuffling up to the top floor.

He was in the queue at the coffee shop, with about three or four people ahead of him. Very hale and hearty, I went over and slapped him on the back. 'Pat! What are you doing here?'

Reciprocating my big smile, he said, 'I'm here to meet some-body.' His pupils were as big as saucers.

'Me too. You got time for a Micky D's?'

'Yeah, yeah, why not?'

We started to walk beyond the coffee shop, following exit signs through automatic doors, and took the escalator up to the multi-storey car park.

Pat was a step or two above. He looked down at me, puzzled. 'What the fuck's a Micky D?'

'McDonald's,' I said, as if he should have known. But, then, he didn't have a seven-year-old on his case day and night. 'Come on, mate, get with the programme!'

He started to do a Michael Jackson moondance.

By now we were nearly at the bus station level. I said, 'If there's a drama I'm going to the bus station area, turning right and out of an exit.'

'Fine. No problems!' He sounded OK, but looked shit.

The cars were on the two levels above. We walked up the bare concrete stairs, stopped at the first level and got into a position that looked back the way we had come.

I didn't have time to fuck about. 'Two things, mate. I've got a list here I didn't fancy reading to you over a landline.' I passed it over. 'I need all that kit. And the other thing, what's the score on the money?'

He was already looking at the small notebook I'd handed him. Either he was amazed at the contents or he couldn't focus. Without looking up he said, 'I got some money for you today.

But, fucking hell, most of it's going to be used up on this gear. I'll be able to get you some more, probably tomorrow or the day after. Fuck me,' he shook his head, 'when do you want all this by?' Then he started to giggle as if he'd just had a funny in his head and wasn't going to share it with me.

'Actually, tonight, mate. You reckon you can do it, or what?' I moved my head to get eye-to-eye.

The giggle became a laugh, until he saw me looking serious. He cleared his throat and tried to switch on. 'I'll do my best, mate. I'll see what I can get on this list.'

'I'd really fucking appreciate it,' I said. 'Don't let me down, Pat. I really need your help.' I hoped the urgency was going to register with him. I was still checking down the stairs. 'Also at the back there' – I opened the page for him to make sure he saw it – 'I've put a casual pick-up. I need that to happen at twenty-three hundred tonight.'

Pat was looking at the RV notes. I bent my knees to lower myself and moved his face over so I could get eye-to-eye again. 'Eleven o'clock tonight, mate. Eleven o'clock, OK?'

I knew Pat well enough to tell he knew it was serious. He knew he was fucked up, and was trying hard to understand everything I said.

I was glad now that I'd put the details down on paper for him. He looked as if he needed all the help he could get.

'What car do you drive?' I asked.

'A red Mustang.' He pushed his face closer to mine. 'Redder than Satan's bollocks!' He enjoyed the joke so much he couldn't help laughing.

'Leave via H Street.' I pointed away from the rear of the station.

'See you tonight, then,' he smiled, moving off. From behind I could see a slight veer to the left as he walked.

I waited and checked he wasn't being followed, then carried on up towards the car park level, making it look as if I was off to my car. From there, I took the lift back down to the coffee shop level.

I went back towards the restaurant, stood off and watched. Kelly was still fighting with the pizza.

'You were ages!' she said through a mouthful of mushrooms.

'Yes, they ran out of toilet paper,' I laughed as I rejoined her.

She thought about it for a moment and did the same.

22

As soon as we got back I put the TV on for Kelly and tipped out the carrier bags on my bed. She asked me what I was doing.

'I'm just helping Pat. He's asked me to do some stuff. You can watch the TV if you want. You hungry?'

'No.' She was right, after a pizza the size of a tank mine it was a stupid question.

I picked up the big red-and-white-framed quartz kitchen clock and went and sat on the chair by the window. I broke off the frame until I was left with just the hands and clock face, with the quartz mechanics behind it. By bending it very gently, I now started to break off the plastic face. When there was just about an inch of jagged remains around the centre of the hands I finally snapped off the hour and second hands. Only the minute hand was left. I put in a new battery.

Kelly was watching. 'Now what are you doing, Nick?'

'It's a trick. Once I've finished I'll show you, OK?'

'OK.' She turned back to the TV, but with one eye on me.

I took the egg box over to the bin and tipped out its contents. I ripped off the top and half of the bottom so that there were just six compartments left. With Sellotape, I fashioned a small sleeve running all the way up the side of the egg box, and just big enough to accommodate the minute hand. I called over to Kelly, who was mouthing the signature tune to a soap. 'Do you want to see what this does?'

She looked intrigued as I slotted the egg box onto the minute hand.

The bedside cabinet was about 4 inches below the level of the TV's controls. I positioned the clock on it, so that it was directly below the infra-red sensor on the set, and secured it in place with gaffer tape.

Kelly was taking even more interest. 'What are you doing?'

'See the remote control? Use it to turn the sound up.'

She did.

'Now turn it down. OK, I bet you that, in about fifteen minutes' time, you can't turn the sound up.' I went and joined her on the bed. 'Both of us must sit here and not move, OK?'

'OK.' She thought I was going to do something to the remote control, and smiled as she hid it under the pillow.

It was quite nice really, watching TV during some downtime, apart from every minute hearing 'Is it fifteen minutes yet?'

'No, only seven.' By now the egg box, attached to the minute hand, was working its way up towards the base of the TV.

When the egg box was upright and obscuring the sensor I said, 'Go on then, try to turn the sound up.'

She did and nothing happened.

'Maybe it's the battery?' I teased.

We put a fresh battery into the remote control. Still nothing. She couldn't work it out and I wasn't going to explain my trick.

'Magic!' I grinned.

I got out the rest of the stuff, drank some of the orange juice and rinsed out the container, then made sure that all the electrical kit had fresh batteries, and prepared everything ready to be packed.

It was about twenty past ten and Kelly was asleep. I'd have to wake her up and tell her I was going out, because I didn't want her to wake on her own and start flapping. At times I thought she was just a pain in the arse, but I wanted to protect her. She looked so innocent playing starfish again. What would happen to her after all this, I wondered – presuming she lived.

I checked and tested everything again, unplugged the mobile and put it in my pocket, and finally checked my weapon and that I had some cash. I picked up a half-empty packet of biscuits to eat on the way.

Close to her ear, I whispered, 'Kelly!'

I got no response. I shook her a bit. She stirred and I said, 'I've put the TV on low so you can watch it if you want. I've just got to go out for a little while.'

'Yeah.'

I didn't know if she understood or not. I preferred telling her this when she was half asleep.

'Don't put the lock on this time because I'll take the key. I don't want to wake you when I come in, OK?'

I left, went down in the lift and onto the road. The highway traffic rumbled above me. At last, no rain, just air that smelled damp. It was just cold enough for me to see my breath.

I turned left and walked in the opposite direction to normal, just for one last check. I munched the biscuits as I walked past the target. All the same lights were on, nothing had changed. I wondered if the homeless bloke was underneath, waiting with a machete for somebody else to have a piss on him. I quickened my pace to meet Pat on time. I got to the highway and turned right, following the road with the roar of traffic above me.

The road swung right and I started to leave the highway behind. Soon there was waste ground on both sides and the sound of traffic receded. I could hear my footsteps again. To my right were more car pounds. How could Washington be in such a financial mess when the city must be making a fortune on towed-away vehicles? To my left were the new, jerry-built office-cum-workshops. I got to the first one, moved off the road into its shadow and waited.

It was bizarre to be only hundreds of metres away from the Pentagon and possibly right under the nose of the very people who'd like to see me dead. It was also quite a thrill. It always had been. Pat had a term for it; he called it 'the juice'.

I heard an engine coming towards me. I looked round the corner of the building. Just one vehicle. It must be him. I pulled my pistol.

The red Mustang drew up. I was in a semi-crouch fire position, aiming at the driver with my Sig until it stopped. It was Pat. I could see his Roman nose silhouetted in the ambient light from the airport.

Pistol still in hand, I walked over to the passenger door, opened it and the interior light didn't come on. I got in and closed the door gently, on to its first click only.

Pat had his hand on the handbrake and slowly released it to move off. From a distance, it's very difficult to tell whether a car is stopping if you can't see brake lights – that was why Pat was using the handbrake – and with no interior light coming on and no noise of a car door shutting the pick-up would have been very hard to detect.

Checking the road behind us, I said, 'Turn right at the next junction.'

There was no time to fuck about; he knew it and I knew it. Pat said, 'Everything's in the back, in that holdall.' He'd come down from whatever high he'd been on and sounded quite embarrassed.

I leaned over and lifted out the laptop. I said, 'Is the sound turned off?' When Windows 95 came up I didn't want the Microsoft sound playing.

He made a face that let me know I was a dickhead for even asking. We both laughed and it broke the ice.

We came up to the concrete wall and, as we passed the hotel, I was careful not to turn my head. We turned right under the highway and stopped at traffic lights on the other side.

I said, 'Go straight and turn right on Penn.'

'No problem.'

The area was urban and now well lit. He kept checking in his rear-view mirror that we weren't being followed. My eyes were fixed on the wing mirror. I didn't turn and look now; neither of us wanted to look aware.

There were a few cars behind us, but they had come from other directions. That wasn't to say they weren't following us.

I looked at Pat. His 9mm semi was snug under his right thigh, and in the footwell under his legs he had a 9mm MP5K, an excellent in-car weapon because of its compact size and rate of fire, but a bit over the top for this job. He'd clipped on double thirty-round magazines.

'What the fuck did you bring that thing along for?'

'I didn't like the sound of your new best mate, Luther. I didn't want him and his buddies dragging me in for a little chat.'

We approached another set of lights.

'Do a right to left switch here, mate. Let's see if we have any groupies.'

There were one or two cars behind us. The shape of a vehicle's headlights, once it is up close, helps a lot to ID it. If the same shape is up your arse on three turns in the same direction it's time to get out the worry beads.

Pat indicated and started to move to the right. All the other cars seemed to want to go straight ahead or to turn right with us; nobody was in the left-turn lane. At the last moment Pat indicated left and moved over – nothing that was aggressive or would provoke a bout of road rage, just a change of mind.

We were all held at the lights. I looked at each car in turn. Just couples or kids cruising – or so it appeared. I'd soon know if I saw them again.

We turned on green and nothing followed. It was now time to talk.

Pat started it off. 'Your instructions were shit. You said three buildings; there were four. It's a good job I'm switched on.' He was waiting for praise.

'The fact is I couldn't remember how many. The taxi was driving too fast. I can't count anyway.'

We were now just cruising. Pat said, 'I've been thinking. Do you want me to go in as your number two?'

That would be good. It would get the job done quicker and would mean better security and firepower if we were in the shit. But I decided against; Pat was my only link with the outside world and I didn't want to compromise that.

'No fucking way. I remember what happened the last time.'

We both started to laugh. 'That device swap?'

PIRA had concealed a car bomb in a hide, ready to be used two days after. It consisted of 4 pounds of shaped high explosive on a Parkway timer device, a sixty-minute reminder on a keyring that told you when your parking meter had run out. They were PIRA's toy of the month.

We drove into the Shantello estate, a nationalist stronghold in Derry, parked up and made entry into a council house. The hide was a hole dug out of the concrete foundations in the kitchen, with a plug over it and a gas cooker on top of that. We stole the bomb, Pat carrying it in an old canvas holdall.

We'd parked up by the small shopping and social club area. All we had to do now was get back to the car, then go and put the bomb under the vehicle of an INLA major player on the other side of town near the Creggan estate. They would find it – we'd make sure of that – identify it as a PIRA device, and then there would be shit on. Great. They could then direct their time and resources into killing each other instead of the security forces and the local population.

I looked at Pat. He, too, was lost in his thoughts. 'Did the car ever get recovered?'

'Don't know, don't care.'

We'd turned the corner to walk across the car park, only to find that our car was missing. Some fucker had nicked it. Yet we had to get this device in place that night. The whole INLA leadership had been lifted for questioning by the police to guarantee that the target vehicle would be there, but there was a limit to how long they could be held. There was only one thing for it. We ran.

I checked the wing mirror again, then looked at Pat, his shoulders rolling as he laughed inside. I smiled at the memory of coming across two army foot patrols and bluffing our way through. It wouldn't have been easy trying to explain away a holdall full of high explosive to eight very wet and pissed-off soldiers pointing their SA80s at your head, each of them itching for a kill so they'd get the reward of extra leave.

It was great to have some light relief. It was even better seeing Pat back on planet earth.

'Take us back to the Pentagon City Metro stop, will you, mate?'

I started to prepare for the drop-off and got into acting mode again. He put his indicators on, everything correct, nothing untoward, nice slow approach and into the kerb outside the Metro. I got out and put my head back in through the open window. 'Thanks a lot, mate, see you later on.' I retrieved the black nylon bag from the back seat. My mindset was that I'd been playing softball with him all night, and now I was going home; he'd just dropped me off after a drink. I closed the door and tapped the roof a couple of times and off he drove. I suddenly felt very alone. Had I made the right decision about Pat not coming on target with me? I made distance and angles before doing a circuit back to the hotel, arriving at about eleven fifty.

I quickly sorted out and double-checked all the stuff that Pat had given me and packed what I needed into the bag. I emptied my pockets of change and anything else that might rattle or fall out. Then I cut off most of the top end of a bin liner, put in my passport and wallet, wrapped it into a small bundle and put it into my coat pocket.

Once I'd done that, I jumped up and down one more time to check for noise, picking up the bag and shaking that as well. 'Guess what, Kelly? I'm going to go out again in a minute, but I'll be back very soon. Will you be OK?'

But she was out of it. I left the hotel and walked towards the target.

23

The bag had two handles and a long shoulder strap. I walked towards the river with it slung over my shoulder, following the same route as last night. The rain was holding off and I could now see the stars and my own breath. Nothing had changed, except that the lights from the highway were a bit brighter tonight without the mist.

At the fenced gate I used the handles of the holdall to put it on my back like a bergen and climbed over. I'd keep it on my back now; if I was confronted I could run and still keep the kit, or, as a last resort, draw down on them with the Sig.

I got level with the target building, with the waste ground and fence in between. There was no sound apart from the hum of the highway. I started to pick my way through the clutter of the waste ground. It was muddy; not deep squelching mud, because the earth was quite hard, but I still needed to take my time to get through; I didn't want to slip over and make noise, because my wet friend in the shrubbery might not be the only homeless person around here.

I got to the fence near the PIRA building. Using the bush as cover, I eased the bag off my shoulders and sat on it. The first bound was completed; it was time to stop, look, listen and take everything in. I needed to be extra careful because I was on my own. Really this was a job for two people, one watching, one doing. I spent a few minutes more just tuning in. Visibility was a bit better tonight because of the stars. Looking left, the car park was still empty; to the right, the pallets were still where I'd seen them.

From my coat pocket I pulled out the bin liner protecting my docs. At the base of a bush I dug a shallow hole in the mud with my hands, threw in the bundle and covered it over. This was my emergency cache, my 'hidey-hole' as Kelly would say. If I got lifted I would be sterile, and if I got away there would always be the chance of coming back and retrieving it.

I wiped the mud off my hands onto a small tuft of grass and started to get myself ready for the job. I gently unzipped the holdall and got out the pair of cheap and nasty navy-blue coveralls, probably just like the ones Kev's friends had worn.

I was set for the next bound, although 'bound' wasn't the right word for it. The problem with getting over a high fence with a 40-pound bag is that you can spend more time getting stuck and making noise than actually crossing it.

I pulled the draw cord from the centre of my coat and put it between my teeth. Moving as near to the steel stake support as I could without breaking cover, I then lifted the bag up to shoulder height. Using my shoulders to support its weight, I tied the handles as near to the top of the fence as I could with a quick-release knot, throwing the free end of the cord over the top.

Checking that my weapon was secure, I reached up, put my fingers through the chain link and started to climb. Once on the other side I again stopped, looked and listened; only then did I climb back up and lift the bag over the chain link. I climbed down once more and then got hold of the free end of the cord and pulled. The bag came free from the fence and I took its weight. Then, squatting, I watched and listened again.

Working alone on a job takes a lot of concentration, because you can't look and work at the same time, yet both have to be done. So you do one or the other; you either get on with the job or you get on with looking. Try to do both and you'll fuck up.

I stood up, put the bag on my left shoulder and gently pulled apart the Velcro of the coveralls so that, if necessary, I could get to my weapon. Taking my time, I moved to the left-hand side of the building.

Before I did anything, I had to defeat the motion detector. I was to the left of it, with my back against the wall. Putting the bag in my left hand, I kept my eyes on the detector high above me and started slowly edging towards it. When I got more or less as far as I estimated I could without getting pinged, I bent down and placed the bag by my feet. Everything I did from now on would happen on the near side of the bag.

Security lights that respond to movement make life much harder for people like me, but only if they cover the whole of the building. I found it strange that there was only one detector, rather than two or three overlapping each other to eliminate dead spots. I was expecting, at any moment, to be pinged by one I hadn't noticed. But whoever had installed the security system had obviously worked on the premise that only the lower fire-escape door had to be covered and not the approach routes to it.

It was nearly 1 a.m., which left me just over five hours before first light. Time was against me, but I wasn't going to rush. I went the long way round to go and collect one of the pallets. I got both hands in between the slats of wood, heaved it up against my chest and started to walk slowly. The ground still had a top layer of slush and my shoes squelched as they made contact. I finally reached the wall, placed the pallet against the brickwork on my side of the bag, and went back for the second one.

I wedged the two pallets together, the bottom of the second jammed into the gap about three rungs down from the top of the first to make a ladder. I stopped, looked and listened. The pallets had been heavy and I heard nothing apart from the sound of my lungs gasping for air through my dry throat.

I climbed up on the first pallet, and that was fine. I got up onto the second pallet, and it, too, seemed stable enough. I started to climb. I'd moved just two rungs when the whole structure buckled and collapsed. I hit the ground like a bag of shit and the two pallets slammed down onto each other with a resounding thud and clatter. *Shit. Shit. Shit.*

I was lying on my back with one of the pallets across my legs. No-one came running to investigate, no dogs started barking, no lights came on. Nothing but the noise of the traffic and me swallowing hard, trying to moisten my mouth.

Luckily everything had happened on my side of the bag. I lifted the pallet and crawled from under it, quietly cursing. This was shit. But what else could I have done – bought a ladder at the mall and carried it to the target? I moved to the corner of the building, got down on the tips of my toes and fingers, as if I was going to do a press-up, and stuck my head round towards Ball Street.

I was still annoyed with myself. I could spend all night improvising before I even got into a position to attack this motion detector. Maybe a ladder wasn't such a stupid idea; I should have got one and somehow tried to dump it off earlier on, then picked it up *en route*. But it was too late now.

I stood against the wall and re-evaluated. I decided to 'react as the situation dictated', which was the Firm's favourite get-out clause. It simply meant they didn't know what to do. A bit like me really.

Fuck it, I was going to get Kelly. All she'd have to do was lean against the pallets; she only had to be there for about fifteen minutes and I'd be done. After that she could stay with me, or I could dump her back at the hotel. I'd cross that bridge when I came to it.

I picked up the bag, retraced the route to the high fence and, staying on the target side, dumped the bag and coveralls. Then I followed the fence along, looking for an opening to get onto Ball Street. There wasn't time to do the job properly and go back all the way round. I finally found a service alley between two buildings that belonged in some film about the Mafia in 1950s

New York. I was straight down it to the road and walked briskly to the hotel, no more than two minutes away. It was only then that I realized I didn't have the room key because I'd left it in the bin liner. I'd have to wake Kelly.

I knocked gently at first, then a bit harder. Just when I was starting to flap, I heard 'Hi, Nick.' A moment or two later, the door opened.

I gave her a look of concern. 'How did you know it was me? You should have waited until I answered.' Then I saw the chair and the drag marks on the carpet. I smiled and gave her a pat on the head. 'You looked through the spyhole, didn't you, clever clogs? Hey, because you're so clever, I've got a job for you. I really, really need your help. Would you like to help me?'

She looked sleepy. 'What do you want me to do?'

'I'll show you when we get there. Will you come with me?'

'I suppose so.'

I had a brainwave. 'Do you want to do what your dad does? Because this is what Daddy does for the good guys. You can tell him all about it soon.'

Her face brightened. She was a happy bunny again.

She had to more or less run to keep up with me. We got to the alleyway and headed down towards the waste ground. It was dark; she wasn't too keen. She started dragging her feet. 'Where are we going, Nick?'

'You want to play spies, don't you?' I said in an excited whisper. 'Imagine you are a Power Ranger and you're going on a secret mission.'

We reached the waste ground and took the same route towards the chain link fence. I held her hand and she kept pace; I guessed she was getting into it.

We got to the bag. I picked up the coveralls and said, 'I've got to put these on because they're special spy coveralls.' Her face changed when she saw them. I suddenly realized she must have made the connection with the men who'd come to see Kev. 'Your

Daddy wears them too. You'd better be a spy as well; undo your coat.' I turned it inside out and told her to put it back on. She liked that.

I picked up the bag and put it over my shoulder. I pointed. 'Now we'll walk really slowly over there.'

We reached the pallets and I put the bag down in the same place as before. 'OK?' I asked, giving her a thumbs up.

'OK.' Thumbs up.

'See that thing up there? If that sees you, it'll go *whoa-whoa* and there'll be lights and all sorts, and then we've lost. So you must never go the other side of that bag, OK?' I pointed.

'OK.' We gave each other another thumbs up.

I repositioned the pallets and showed her what I wanted her to do. I could hear her making little grunts. She had started leaning as I'd shown her and probably thought she had to make noises, doing manual work and all.

I unzipped the bag, pulled out the clock and egg box and slipped the minute hand into its Sellotape sleeve. I gently squeezed the tape and it held nice and firm.

Kelly was still pushing and I told her to rest. At least she was keen. She was watching me as I put the clock and egg box on the floor and placed two elastic bands around my wrist.

'It's magic. Watch me!'

She nodded, probably still trying to work out how I'd stopped the remote control from operating the TV.

'You ready, Kelly?'

'Ready.'

'Let's go!'

I climbed up slowly, trying to give the least weight and move-ment for Kelly to have to handle.

Once up, and about an arm's length from one side of the detector, I got my wrist resting on my chest so that I had a good firm support. I turned the egg box so that its long edge was horizontal with the ground. Then I moved it gently towards and about 6 inches below the motion detector, but not going any further than its front. Once there, I rested my back against the wall and my wrists on my chest. I'd have to stay like that for about fifteen minutes.

I was waiting for the egg box to move up slowly and gently against the face of the motion detector, the movement so imperceptible that the detector wasn't sensitive enough to register it – otherwise it would have triggered every time a spider walked across its face. I just hoped Kelly didn't give up. I would find out soon.

Now and again I looked down and winked at her. 'Good this, isn't it?' She looked back at me with a big smile – or so I assumed, because all I could see was an inside-out coat, a hood and a cloud of breath.

As we both waited for the minute hand to become vertical, all of a sudden there was a single *whoa!* of a dying police siren.

Shit! Shit!

It was on the road on the other side of the building. It couldn't have anything to do with us. Otherwise why just one unit, and why use the siren anyway?

I couldn't move. If I did it would trip the device – and what for? I hadn't even seen torchlight yet.

'Nick, Nick, did you hear that?'

'It's OK, Kelly. Just keep on pushing. It's OK, I can hear them.'

What could I do? I told myself not to flap, to stay calm and think.

A shout echoed around the car park. It had come from Ball Street, but a bit of a distance away. Other voices joined in. An argument had broken out. I couldn't make out what was being said, but there were car doors being slammed and words exchanged, then the sound of a car starting up. All I could think of was that someone had parked up while I fetched Kelly – possibly one of the couples I'd seen from Pat's car – they'd been busy getting the windows steamed up and had got caught by the police. It sounded plausible; I just made myself believe it.

The egg box was close to vertical. I held my breath. This wasn't a science; we had a fifty–fifty chance of success, no more. If it pinged us, we'd have to fuck off quick-style and take our chances.

At last the box obscured the detector. No lights came on. With my teeth, I pulled the two thin elastic bands off my wrist; I got the first one over the top of the egg box and around the motion detector, then pulled the back of it tight, twisted it and wound round another loop of the band. I put the other band round to make it even tighter. The motion detector was defeated.

I slipped the clock off the box and put it in one of the deep pockets at the front of my coveralls. I clambered down and rubbed Kelly's shoulders. 'Good work!'

She gave me a huge smile, still not too sure what it was all about – but, hey, this was what Daddy did.

24

The next thing to attack was the alarms, which would mean neutralizing the telephone lines. One of Pat's presents was a disruption device, a black box of computer technology about 8 inches by 6 inches; coming out of it were six different-coloured leads with crocodile grips at the end, a combination of which I'd attach to the telephone line. When the intruder alarm inside the building was tripped, a signal should, in theory, be sent to the monitor station or the police; however, it wouldn't get there because the disruption device would have engaged all the lines.

I got close to Kelly's ear and said, 'You can help me even more now.' I put the clock back into the bag, picked it up and walked past the fire-exit doors to the utilities bank.

From the bag I pulled out another item from Pat's shopping list, a 2-metre square of thick blackout material, the sort photographers use.

I winked at Kelly. 'More magic,' I said, 'and I'll need you to tell me if it works.' I was talking in a very low tone; at night, whispering can sometimes be heard as far away as normal speech. I came right up to her ear again and said, 'We've got to be really quiet, OK? If you want to talk to me, just tap me on the shoulder, and then I'll look at you and you can talk in my ear. Do you understand?'

She spoke into my ear. 'Yes.'

'That's great, because that's what spies do.' I put on my rubber gloves.

She stood there with an earnest expression on her face, but looking quite stupid with her coat inside out and the hood up.

I said, 'If you see any of the light coming out, I also want you to tap me on the shoulder, OK?'

'Yeah.'

'OK, stand there against the wall.' I moved her into position, looking out towards the fences and bushes.

'I want you to stand very still. If you see or hear anything, you tap me on the shoulder. OK?'

'Yeah.'

'Even if there's only a little bit of light coming from me, tap me on the shoulder. OK?'

'Yeah.'

I went over to the bank of utilities, put the material over my shoulders, turned on the Maglite with a red filter and got to work.

I'd used disruption devices many times. I worked with the torch in my mouth and was soon dribbling. I attached the clips to the telephone line in a variety of combinations; as they bit in, a row of lights came on, and the aim was to get all six red lights up. When that happened, the lines were engaged. Ten minutes was all it took.

I rested the box in between the electricity and the gas meters. I only hoped there wasn't an audio alarm as well as a telephoned warning. I doubted it somehow, seeing as the budget had only stretched to one external detector.

I took off the blanket, wrapped it up into a bundle and handed it to Kelly. 'You've got to hold that for me, because I'm going to need it again in a minute. This is fun, isn't it?'

'Yes. But I'm cold.'

'We'll be inside in a minute and it'll be all nice and warm. Don't you worry about that.'

I stopped, looked, listened, then moved over to the door. The next thing was making entry.

The Americans are into pin tumbler locks in a big way. There are three main ways to defeat them. The first, and easiest, is just to get a duplicate key. The second is called hard keying. You get a titanium key the size of the lock, and the key has a bolthead that you whack with a mallet; the titanium key hammers in and gouges out all the soft steel. You then fit a special bar onto the bolthead, pull down and it rips out the whole of the cylinder. Hard keying was no good for me tonight because I wanted to be in and out without anybody knowing. I'd have to use the third option.

A lock-pick gun is a metal lock-picking device in the configuration of a small pistol. It has both straight and offset pick options to accommodate different locks and keyways. The 'trigger' of the gun is spring-loaded; you squeeze it rapidly, and this trigger movement causes the pick to snap upwards within the lock and transfers the striking force to the pins that work the lock mechanism. When the pins are properly aligned, you use a separate tension wrench to turn the lock cylinder. Bad news for people with pin tumblers, but a lock-pick gun can open most of them in under a minute.

With the blanket over me I turned on the Maglite and put it in my mouth. I inserted the tension wrench into the bottom of the keyway opposite the pins, and applied light pressure anticlockwise, in the direction I expected the lock to turn. I then inserted the pick that protruded from the front of the lock-pick gun. Once the gun and tension wrench were in place, I started squeezing the trigger rapidly. I gave it five shots, but the lock didn't open, so I increased the tension adjustment and tried again. I could hear it go *clink, clink, clink* as I squeezed; again I turned the tension adjustment so that the needle would strike the pins with just enough force. One by one I heard the pins drop and eventually the tumbler turned. I held the small tension wrench in the lock and pulled the door to take the pressure off the lock itself, because I didn't want to have too much torque on the wrench and bust it, leaving the tell-tale bit of metal stuck inside. I pulled the door and felt it give.

I opened it a fraction, half-expecting the sound of an alarm. Nothing. I grinned at Kelly, who was right up against the wall with me, very excited. I closed the door again to keep the light in. 'When we get in you mustn't touch anything unless I tell you, OK?' She nodded.

There's a world outside which is full of mud and shit, and there's a world inside which is clean, and if you don't want to be compromised you don't combine the two. I took off the coveralls, turned them inside out and put them in the bag. I then took off my shoes and they also went in the bag. I put on a pair of trainers, which meant that, not only could I move quickly and silently inside, but also I wouldn't be leaving a trail of mud everywhere.

We were nearly compromised 'withdrawing' documents from the offices of BCCI in London in 1991. We'd been sent into the bank ten hours before the Serious Fraud Office were due to arrive to close the bank down and Price Waterhouse came to sort out the books. The job was so rushed that the 'expert', a small, bald weasel of a man, had to come with us to look at the documents. He turned up totally unprepared. We had him walking in his socks. He left a trail of sweat stains along the polished floors that even Kelly could have interpreted. The four of us had spent more time clearing up after him than stopping the information becoming public.

No problem tonight: the floor was carpeted. I took off her coat, put it on the right way round, and got her to take off her shoes and put them in the bag.

I had one last check around the area to make sure I hadn't left anything. 'We're going to go inside now, Kelly. This is the first time a little girl has done spying like this – ever, ever, ever. But you must do what I say, OK?'

She accepted the mission.

I picked up the bag and we moved over to the left-hand side of the door. 'When I open this just walk in a couple of steps and give me enough room to come in behind you, OK?'

'OK.'

I didn't want to tell her what to do if anything went wrong, because I didn't want to get her frightened. I wanted to make it sound as if everything I did was going to work.

'After three – one, two, three.' I opened the door halfway and she was straight in. I followed, closed the door and put the lock back on. Done. We were inside.

We followed the corridor, looking now for the staircase to the second floor. I had the bag on my left shoulder. Through glass doors at the end of the corridor I could see the front part of the building. It was a large, open-plan office area with everything I'd have expected to see. Desks, filing cabinets and rubber plants with name tags. To the left and right of us there were other offices and a photocopy room. The air-conditioning was still on.

I found the stairs, behind unlocked swing doors on the left of the corridor. Gently, so that it didn't squeak, I pulled one of the doors open and let Kelly through. There was no light in the stair-well. I switched on the Maglite and played the beam on to the stairs. We climbed slowly.

Quiet as we were, the stairwell was an echo chamber, and to Kelly the red light must have made everything look scary. She said, 'Nick, I don't like this!'

'Shhh! It's OK, don't worry about it; me and your dad used to do this all the time.' I grabbed her hand and we carried on.

We got to the door. It would open towards us because it was a fire exit. I put down the bag, put my lips to Kelly's ear and went, 'Shhh,' trying to make it all exciting.

I slowly eased the door open an inch and looked out into the corridor. Same as downstairs, the lights were on and everything seemed deserted. I listened, opened the door a little more to let Kelly through, and pointed where I wanted her to go and stand. She was a lot happier to be in the light.

I put the bag down next to her. 'Wait there a minute.' I turned right, past the toilets and a room without a door that housed the Coke, water and coffee machines. Next was a photocopy room. I went to the fire-escape door, pulled it towards me, undid the latch and checked that it would open. I already knew there was nothing the other side to obstruct it, because I'd just been fucking about below it. If there was a drama, we had an escape route.

I picked up the bag again and we started to walk along the corridor towards the front of the building. We came to the same sort of glass doors as on the floor below, which opened up into the open-plan area. I could see all the workstations, and around the edge there were other offices, all glass-fronted. Obviously the managers liked to keep an eye on everyone.

The windows that fronted the office block were maybe 50 feet away. Light from the street and the corridor gave the whole area an eerie glow. To the right there was another glass door that led into another corridor.

I knew what I was looking for, but I didn't know where I'd find it; all I knew was that it certainly wouldn't be in this part of the building.

I looked down and smiled at Kelly. She was happy as Larry, just as her dad would have been. Keeping well away from the windows, we walked to the other side of the open-plan area towards the glass door.

There was all the normal office stuff, a noticeboard with targets to be reached, pictures of salesman of the year and a thank-you card from somebody who'd just had a baby. Most desks had a small frame with pictures of the family, and everywhere I looked there were motivation posters, shit like 'Winners never quit, Quitters never win' or 'You cannot discover new oceans until you have the courage to lose sight of the shore'. I had to stop and read them. The only one I'd ever seen was of a big pen of sheep all closed up together, and it said, 'Either lead, follow, or get out of the way'. It was on the wall of the HQ of the SAS and had been there for years. It seemed to me to be the only one you needed.

We went through the glass doors. The corridor was about 10 feet wide, with plain white walls and not a poster or pot plant in sight, just a large fire extinguisher near the door. The sudden brightness of the strip lighting made me close my eyes until they adjusted. There were no more doors, but about 30 feet further down was a T-junction. I could see offices. As we walked towards them, I put the bag down and motioned Kelly to stay with it. 'Remember, don't touch a thing!'

The handle on the door of each office was a large metal knob with a pin tumbler lock in the middle. I tested each one in turn, pulling the handle towards me so as not to make any noise, then gently trying to turn it. There were seven offices in this corridor area and all of them were locked. That was nothing special in itself, it just meant that I'd have to use the lock-pick gun on each one in turn.

I went back to the bag. Kelly was standing beside it, desperate for a job. I said, 'Kelly, you've really got to help me now. I want you to stand where I tell you, and you've got to tell me if any-one's coming, all right? I've got to do exactly what I did outside, and I still need your help, OK?'

I was getting nod after nod. I carried on, 'It's really important; it's the most important job tonight. And we've both got to be really, really quiet, OK?'

Another nod. I moved her into position. 'Your job is also to look after that bag, because there's a lot of important stuff in it. If you see anything, just tap me on the shoulder like before.'

She nodded and I got out the lock-pick gun.

I got to the first door and started to squeeze. I opened it with the tension wrench and popped my head in, made sure I couldn't see any windows and turned on the light. It was basically just one office, quite large, about 20 feet by 15 feet, a couple of telephones, a picture of the worker's wife, a couple of filing cabinets, very basic furniture. Nothing resembling what I was looking for. I didn't check the filing cabinets; the first look is nothing more than a once-over; you don't want to spend ages in one location only to find out that what you want is sitting on a desk in the room next door.

I didn't relock the door because I might have to go back in. Leaving it ajar, I looked at Kelly, still at her post; I put my thumb up and she grinned. She had a big job to do.

I made entry into office number two. Exactly the same normal office shit: the year planner with different-coloured bits of tape on, signs stating that there was a strict no-smoking policy and individual mugs for coffee. People's offices are a reflection of themselves; that's why on a job like this it's so important that nothing is left out of place. They would notice.

I carried on down the corridor and went to number three. The same. Four: the same. I was starting to feel like I was on a wild-goose chase.

Now for the other three offices; I crossed over the T, and as I passed Kelly she tried to look even more hard-working. I gave her another thumbs up and went to number five.

It was a much bigger office. There were two settees facing each other, with a coffee table in between and a neat scattering of magazines; a wooden drinks cabinet, smart wooden filing cabinets, framed diplomas and all sorts on the wall. But nothing that resembled the sort of thing I was looking for.

However, behind a large desk and leather swing chair, there was another door. I got the lock-pick gun working, and inside found filing cabinets, a fantastically expensive-looking leather-topped desk and a swivel chair. On the desk was a PC. It wasn't connected to another computer and it wasn't connected to a land-line. There wasn't even a telephone in the room. This could be where the key point was.

It could be a fibre-optic cable that's controlling fixed Scud-launching sites in northern Iraq, or it could be just one small component in the control room of a nuclear power station, but a key point has to be protected. If it's damaged, everything else is inoperable. It might not take a hundred pounds of explosives to destroy a target; if you can identify the key point, then sometimes one blow from a two-pound ball hammer will do the trick. I quickly checked the remaining two offices and confirmed that this was the one I should be concentrating on.

I went back to the bag and got out the Polaroid camera. Kelly was still working for her gold star for best spy. I smiled. 'I think I've found it, Kelly!'

She smiled back. She didn't have a clue what I was talking about.

I took pictures of the outer office, of what the desktop looked like, a couple of panoramic shots of the area, the coffee table in detail, including the way the magazines were lying; the way that the stuff was set on the table, a picture of all the drawers. I took eight shots in all of the inside of the first office. I now knew exactly what it had looked like when I entered, so when we left I could make sure it looked exactly the same.

I laid the Polaroids in a row on the floor against the wall, just inside the office by the door. The rubbish from the prints went straight into my pockets.

Waiting for the photographs to come into focus, I put my head round the door to check on Kelly.

I went and picked up the bag and brought her with me into the bigger office. I said, 'I want you to tell me when those pictures are all developed. Make sure you don't touch a thing, but it's really important that I know when those pictures are ready. Your daddy used to do this job.'

'Did he?'

I closed the door behind us and jammed two wedges in place, then I moved into the second office and started taking more pictures. The contract cleaners hadn't been in here. The other offices had empty bins, but these two offices hadn't been touched; they obviously did those themselves, but not every day. Even more indication that this was a secure area. As I moved around this small room I saw a shredder beside the filing cabinet, and that confirmed it. What was being kept secure, however, I didn't yet know. I put the second-room pictures on the floor and went back into the main office.

Looking over her shoulder I asked, 'How's it going?'

'One's nearly ready, look!'

'Great. What Daddy does also is collect the other pictures.' I pointed to the ones next door on the carpet. 'But one at a time, and put them in a nice long line just here.' I showed her that I wanted them against the wall. 'Can you manage that?'

'Yeah, OK.' She walked off.

I went back next door and had a quick look at the PC. It was already on but asleep. Kelly was walking in and out, carrying one picture at a time as if it was a bomb.

I pressed the return key on the keyboard; I didn't want to touch the mouse because maybe it was positioned as a tell-tale. The screen came alive with Windows 95 and the Microsoft sound – which pleased me, because I'd have been struggling with anything else.

I went back to Kelly, who was still staring at the pictures in the other office.

'Look,' she said, 'some more are ready!'

I nodded as I delved into the bag for the disk with the sniffer program. I wasn't as good with computers as sixteen-year-olds in London who hack into the USAF computer defence system, but I knew how to use one of these. All you have to do is insert a floppy and off it goes, rooting into passwords, infiltrating programs. There's nothing they can't get into.

I got up and turned towards the back office. 'Won't be long,' I smiled. 'Come and tell me when they're ready to look at.'

Eyes glued to the pictures, she just nodded. As I walked back in I looked at the tracks our feet had brushed in the carpet. I'd smooth it out again once we had finished.

I put the disk in and started it. The wonderful thing about this particular program was that you had to answer just two questions. There was a *wup!* sound and the first one came up.

'Do you want to proceed with X1222? Yes – Y or No – N.'

I pressed the Y key. Off it went again, disk whirring and clicking.

A progress bar came up as the machine clicked away. The next stage would take a few minutes.

I looked at the filing cabinet; it was going to be a piece of piss to get into.

I went to the bag and retrieved what was officially called the 'surreptitious entry kit', but which to me was just the pick and rakes wallet. It was a small, black leather case that contained a general assortment of tools designed for the efficient opening of most pin tumbler, wafer, lever and double-sided locks. Among the sixty bits and pieces were full, half and three-quarter rakes, diamond-tip picks, single, double and half-double ball picks; light, medium and heavyweight tension wrenches of various lengths and styles; hook- and saw-type broken-key extractors, probes, feeler pick, needle pick and double-ball rake. Don't leave home without it!

The progress bar was showing the program was just halfway through a process, so I started on the filing cabinets with a feeler pick. It was a standard lock and opened easily. The contents meant nothing to me. They seemed to be spreadsheets and documents with itemized bills and invoices.

I looked at the screen. Nearly at the end of the progress bar.

The bloke who'd produced the sniffer program was a rave-attending, Ecstasy-taking eighteen-year-old whizz-kid who was so into body piercing he had half of British Steel hanging out of his face. He dressed as if he was homeless and had a shaven head – but that was only after we'd been taking the piss out of his close-cropped effort with a star dyed on the top. The government had been spending hundreds of thousands of pounds trying to develop ways to get into computer programs, only to discover, after he had got arrested on some unrelated charge, that this eighteen-year-old had come up with the greatest sniffer program ever written. His weekly Giro suddenly started looking like a cheque from the National Lottery, and he spent a lot of time at GCHQ.

Wup! The progress bar was complete. Up came a little box which said, 'Password: So0}Ssh1time!' Full marks to them for originality; normally it was something like a spouse's nickname, a family member's date of birth, or a number plate. Then up came, 'Do you want to proceed? Yes – Y, No – N'.

Fucking right I did! I hit the Y key and was into the machine. I went to the bag and I got out the portable back-up drive and cables and a handful of high-capacity back-up disks.

I went to the back of the machine and had a good look at the state of play. I connected the drive leads and plugged it into the mains. I was going to copy everything: programs, system files, applications, the lot.

I now had to move the mouse. I took a Polaroid of its position on the mousepad but still studied it before moving it.

I clicked the box to select the back-up of all files, and it whirred into action, sucking information on to the back-up disks. I went back to the filing cabinets and had another mooch around, not really knowing what I was looking at, just trying to see if there was anything I recognized.

Wup! The prompt came up, telling me the sniffer software needed another instruction. It had been working out another password and wanted to know whether to proceed.

I hit the Y key.

The machines whirred again. I looked at Kelly. She was still standing by the photos, but playing a game with an imaginary companion. Just like her dad; give her a job to do and she'd forget it.

'Kelly, I want you to come with me. If that machine asks me a question again I might not see it – will you look out for it?'

'OK.' It wasn't as exciting a job as she'd been hoping for.

As she sat on the floor with her back against the wall, she looked up at me and said, 'Nick, I need the bathroom.'

'Yeah, in a minute, we'll be finished soon.' It was exactly as I remembered as a kid, sitting in the car and adults not taking me seriously: 'We'll be there soon, Nick, just around the corner.'

She'd be all right. I said, 'I'll take you in a minute.'

Wup! I pressed the Y key.

Kelly said again, 'I really have, I've got to go to the bathroom.'

I couldn't think of the right words for a seven-year-old. In the end I said, 'Do you want to go big toilet or little toilet?'

She looked at me blankly. What could I do? Using the toilet at a location like this is always a big no-no, because of the compromise factor from noise and visible remains. What you enter with must come out with you, which was why I'd bought an orange-juice bottle to piss into and cling film for anything else. I couldn't imagine getting Kelly to piss in the bottle while I held the film under her bum. That was one thing her dad could do that she couldn't tonight.

She said, 'I wanna go, I wanna go,' and started crossing and uncrossing her legs. Then she stood up and was bouncing up and down on the balls of her feet.

I said, 'OK, we'll go. Come on, come with me.'

I didn't need this, but I had to do it. I couldn't have her shitting all over the carpet.

I got hold of her hand. I took the doorstops from the outer office door, gently opened it and checked the corridor.

We moved across the open-plan office, through the glass door and into the fire-escape corridor. We went into the toilet and turned on the toilet light. Poor girl, she was pulling down her trousers in such a hurry she was fumbling with her buttons. I helped her, but, even so, she nearly missed the toilet altogether in her rush.

I was wasting time. I had to go back to the machine and she might be there for five minutes or more. Backing away, I said, 'Don't move, and don't flush the toilet afterwards; I'll do all that for you. I just have to go back one minute and get the computer working. I'll be right back. Remember, shhh, be quiet!'

At that particular moment she didn't really care where I went or what I did. She was in her own heaven.

Wup! I left her and quietly ran towards the office. Once I'd got the disk copying again I'd come back to Kelly, clean the shit out with my hand, and put it in the cling film. Then I'd keep pushing the toilet brush down the pan to lower the level of the water by pushing it through the U bend, and get some fresh water from the drinking fountain to bring the level back up again.

I got back to the office and pressed the Y key. Then I went to the bag to fetch the cling film.

And it was then that I heard the scream.

Instinctively, I pulled out my pistol and went against the wall. I checked chamber and took off the safety catch with my thumb.

I could feel my heart beating faster and the familiar sensation of cold sweat breaking out over my body. My body was getting ready for fight or flight. The screaming was from the area of the fire escape, my only way out. It looked as if I would have to fight.

25

My heart was pumping so hard it was nearly in my mouth. I'd learned long ago that fear is a good thing. If you aren't scared you're lying – or you're mentally unstable. Everyone has fear, but as a professional you use training, experience and knowledge to block out the emotion and help you overcome the problem.

I was still thinking it out when I heard a longer, more pitiful scream of 'Nick! Help me!' The sound went through me like a knife. Images flashed through my mind of her curled up in a ball in the hidey-hole, of brushing her hair and playing that stupid video-watching game.

I was by the office door leading out into the corridor.

I heard a man's voice shout, 'I've got her! I'll fucking kill her! Think about it. Don't make me do it!'

It was not an American voice. Or Hispanic. Or anything else I might have expected. But I knew it straight away. West Belfast.

It sounded as if they were now in the main office area. He started to shout more threats at me above Kelly's screams. I couldn't make out every word and I didn't have to. I got the message.

'OK, OK! I'm going to come into your view in a minute.' My voice echoed in the semi-darkness.

'Fuck you! Throw your weapon into the corridor. Do it!'

Then I could hear him shouting at Kelly, 'Shut the fuck up! Shut up!'

I came out of the office and stopped just short of the corridor junction. I slid my pistol out into the main corridor.

'Put your hands on your head, walk out to the middle of the corridor. If you do anything else, I'll fucking kill her – do you understand?'

The voice was controlled; he didn't sound like a madman.

'Yes, I'm coming out, my hands are on my head,' I said. 'Tell me when to move.'

'Now, you fucker!'

Kelly's screams were deafening, even through the glass door.

I started to walk and, in four paces, came to the corridor junction. I knew that, if I looked left, I'd be able to see them through the door, but that wasn't the game just now. I didn't want eye-to-eye; he might overreact.

'Stop where you are, you fucker!'

I stopped. I could still hear the whimpering. I didn't say a word or turn my head.

In films you always hear the good guy give encouragement to the hostage. In real life it doesn't work like that; you just shut up and do what you're told.

He said, 'Turn left.'

I could now see them both in the shadows. Kelly had her back to me as he dragged her towards me with a weapon stuck in her shoulder area. He pushed the glass door open with his foot and came out into the light of the corridor.

As I saw him my heart dropped from beating in quick time to a slow thud. I felt as if a 10-ton weight had just been dropped on my shoulder.

It was Morgan McGear.

He was dressed very smartly in a dark-blue two-piece suit and a crisp, clean white shirt; even his shoes looked expensive. It was a far cry from the Falls Road uniform of jeans, bomber jacket and trainers. I couldn't see exactly what sort of weapon he was carrying; it looked like some sort of semi-automatic.

He was watching me, working me out. What was I doing here with a small child? He knew he had control, he knew there was fuck all I was going to do. He now had his left hand wrapped around her hair – what a pity I hadn't cut off more in the motel room – and he had the weapon stuck into her neck. This was not a meaningless gesture; he was capable of killing her.

She looked hysterical, poor kid, she was panicking big-time.

He called out, 'Walk towards me – slowly. Walk now. C'mon, don't fuck with me, you shite.'

Every noise in the corridor seemed to be amplified tenfold; McGear shouting with spit flying out of his mouth, Kelly screaming. It seemed to reverberate round the whole building.

I did as he said. As I got nearer I looked at her and tried to get eye-to-eye; I wanted to comfort her, but it didn't work. Her eyes were swollen with tears, her face was soaking wet and red. Her jeans weren't even done up yet.

He got me within about 10 feet of him and now I looked into his eyes, and I could see that he knew he was in a position of power, but flapping a bit. His voice might have sounded confident, but his eyes gave it away. If his job was to kill us, now was his moment. With my eyes I said to him, Just get it over and done with. There are times when, after using plans A, B and C, you must accept you're in the shit – or shite as this boy would say.

He snapped, 'Stop!' and the echo round the corridor seemed to reinforce the threat.

I looked at Kelly, still trying to get that eye-to-eye contact to say, Everything's all right, everything's OK. You asked me to help you and I'm here.

McGear told me to turn round and now I knew it was time to flap.

He said, 'On your knees, you fucker.'

Facing away from him, I went down so I was sitting back on

my heels; if I had the chance to react, at least from here I had some sort of springboard.

'Up!' he shouted. 'Get up, get your arse up!' He knew what I was doing; this boy was good. 'Kneel upright. More, more. Stay there, fuck you. Think you're some fucking hard guy . . .'

He moved behind me, dragging Kelly with him. I could still hear her cries, but there was another noise now. Something else was moving; it wasn't just their movements and Kelly's moans. I didn't know what it was, just that something unhealthy was going to happen. All I could do was close my eyes, grit my teeth and wait for it.

He took a couple of laboured steps towards me. I could hear Kelly getting nearer, obviously still in tow.

'Keep looking straight ahead,' he said, 'or I will be hurting the wee one. Do what I say or—'

Either he didn't finish his sentence or I didn't hear it. The bang on the top of my shoulders and head sent me straight down.

I went into a semi-conscious state. I was awake, but I knew I was fucked, like a boxer who goes down and is trying to get up to show the referee that he's all right, but he's not, he's all over the place.

I felt nailed to the floor; as I looked up, I couldn't see what had done the damage. It hadn't been a pistol. It takes a decent weight to knock a person over. Whatever it was, it took me down good-style.

The strange thing about the next bit was that I knew what was happening, but I couldn't do anything about it. I was aware of him pulling me over onto my back and jumping astride me, and I felt cold metal being pushed against my face and finally into my mouth. Slowly, slowly, it dawned on me that it was the pistol, and the jumble of words he was screaming became clearer and clearer. 'Don't fuck with me! Don't fuck with me! Don't fuck with me!' He sounded out of control.

I could smell the fucker. He'd been drinking; there was alcohol on his breath. He reeked of aftershave and cigarettes.

He was sitting astride me with his knees on my shoulders and the pistol stuck in my mouth. He still had his left hand around Kelly's hair and had pulled her onto the floor; he was tugging her from side to side like a rag doll, either for the sheer hell of it, or perhaps just to keep her screaming and make me more compliant.

All I could hear was scream, scream, scream; 'Don't fuck with me!'; scream, scream, scream; 'Don't fuck with me! Think you're a fucking hard guy, do you, think you're a fucking tough guy, huh?'

Not good. I knew what they did to 'hard guys'. McGear once got an informer into a flat in the Divis estate for questioning; his kneecaps were drilled with a Black & Decker, he was burned by an electric fire, then electrocuted in the bath. He managed to jump out of a window naked, but broke his back. They dragged him back into the lift and shot him.

I felt as if I was drunk. I was aware of what was happening, but it was taking too long for the message to reach my brain.

Then the software started to kick in. I tried to see if the hammer was back on the pistol, but all I could still see was bubbles of red light in front of my eyes and starbursts of white. All I could make out was a blur of screaming and ranting from him, 'You bastard! I'm gonna fuck you up! Who are you?' and the screaming from Kelly. It was total confusion.

I tried again to focus my eyes and this time it worked – and I could see the position of the hammer.

The hammer was back. It was a 9-milly. But what about the safety catch? It was off.

There was nothing I could do. He'd got his finger on the trigger; if I struggled, I was dead, whether he intended it or not.

He said, 'You think you're fucking hard? Do you? Do you? We'll soon see who is the hard man.' Then he jumped his weight up and down to crush my chest, forcing the pistol harder into my mouth.

To add to the confusion, Kelly was still screaming with terror and pain. I didn't have a clue what was expected of me; all I knew was that I had a pistol stuck in my gob and this guy was in charge.

He started to regain his composure. The pistol was still shoved hard into my mouth, but he was beginning to ease himself to his feet. He did it by putting weight on the pistol and hand and then against my face, and, as the pistol turned in my mouth, it twisted painfully up against my cheek and teeth, scraping them with the foresight. And all the time he kept a grip on Kelly's hair, pulling her round all over the place.

He moved back, keeping the pistol aimed at my chest.

'Get back up on your knees!'

'All right, mate, OK. You got me, OK.'

As I moved I saw the fire extinguisher that had taken me down. The skin at the back of my head was split open. There was blood oozing out all over the place and matting all the way down the back of my head. There was fuck all I could do; you just can't stop capillary bleeding.

I got back on my knees, my arse up in the air again so I wasn't resting on the back of my feet, and I was looking at him, trying to sort myself out. He started to walk backwards towards the office and kept the weapon pointing at me.

'Come on, hard man, on your knees.'

I got the hint he wanted me to follow him.

By now Kelly was in shit state. There was a small trail of my blood being wiped along the floor. Kelly must have been kneeling in it before she was moved. She had her hands on his wrist, trying to support herself. She kept on tripping up, walking on her knees, trying to pick herself up, as if she was getting dragged behind a horse. All he was interested in was moving backwards with the weapon pointing at me.

He said, 'Stay where you are!' and then shuffled backwards past the door to the large office.

I was trying to compose myself; I knew I didn't have long to live unless I took some action.

'In there!'

I started to shuffle in.

'Walk!'

I got up and walked into the room, my back still towards him. I walked slowly towards the coffee table and was just about to move off to the side to go round it when he said, 'Stop! Turn round!'

I did as I was told. It was an unusual command because, normally, you want the person you're holding to face away from you so they don't know what's going on. If you can't see, it's difficult to react.

As I turned I saw Kelly sitting on the leather swivel chair that had now been dragged to the left of the desk. He was standing behind her. He still had his left hand wrapped around her hair and was pulling her back onto the seat and pointing the 9-milly at me.

The top half of a semi-automatic, the part of the weapon on which the fore and rear sights are mounted, is called the topslide. It moves back when you've fired to eject the empty case, then picks up a round on its return. If it's moved back by as little as an eighth of an inch, the weapon can't fire, which means that, if you're quick enough, you can shove your hand hard onto the front of the muzzle, push the topslide back, and the trigger won't work – as long as you can keep it there. It's got to be really quick, really aggressive, but I had nothing to lose.

Nothing seemed to be happening; there was a lull. Was he trying to make a decision about what to do? It was less than twenty seconds, but it seemed like for ever.

Kelly kept crying and whimpering; there were friction burns on her knees where she had been dragged earlier on. With his left hand he hoiked her upright and said, 'Shut the fuck up!' And just as he did that we stopped having eye-to-eye contact and I knew it was time.

I leaped forward, shouting at the top of my voice to disorient him, got my right hand and pushed it as hard as I could against the muzzle, pressing down on the topslide so it moved back maybe half an inch.

He shouted a loud, drawn-out 'Fuck!' half in anger, half in pain.

I got hold of his wrist, pulled it towards me and pushed away with my right hand against the topslide. He tried, but it was too late for him; it didn't fire. I needed to grip my hand around the muzzle now to keep the topslide back.

As this was happening I was pushing towards the wall – just push, push, push; he still had hold of Kelly, and she was being dragged around, screaming at the top of her voice. I shut her out of my mind, keeping my eyes on the pistol, my body bent down, pushing and pushing. I felt the air leave his body as he hit the wall. Kelly was getting in the way and I was stepping on her, he was stepping on her and she was screaming out in pain. He must have decided he needed two hands to sort me out because, the next thing I knew, Kelly was running.

I started to head-butt in earnest. I was hitting him with my head, I was hitting him with my nose, with the side of my face. My nose was hurting and bleeding as much as his must have been, but I just kept on butting, butting and butting, trying to do as much damage to him as possible and, at the same time, keeping him against the wall.

He was screaming, 'You fucker! You fucker! You fucker! You're dead!'

And I was doing exactly the same back, screaming, 'Fuck you! Fuck you! Fuck! Fuck!'

I still had him pushed right against the wall. As I butted him, his teeth cut into my face, opening up my forehead and just below my eye. You don't notice pain when the adrenalin is pumping. I head-butted him again and again; it wasn't going to do him much lasting damage, but that was the best I could do at the moment. My hands were on the weapon and I was shouting all sorts of shit at the top of my voice to scare him and, even more, to keep me psyched up.

As his head came down, I bit the first thing that came into range. I felt my teeth on the taut skin of his cheek. There was that initial resistance and then my teeth broke into what felt like warm squid and I was ripping his face open. He screamed out even louder, but I was focused totally on what I was doing; all other thoughts went out of the window as I bit, gouged and did whatever damage I could.

My teeth sank in and in. He squealed like a pig. I had a mouthful of his cheek and was ripping and tearing. I saw terror in his eyes.

By now there was blood all over the two of us. I could taste the iron tang of it and my whole face was drenched from the cuts on my face and his, all getting mixed in with our sweat. Trying to clear my mouth, I choked some of it up into the back of my nose.

All the time, I was twisting the weapon away from me and trying to keep the topslide back. He was still pretty switched on and was squeezing the trigger, but fuck all was happening – for now. His other hand was pulling at my fingers, trying to prise them off the weapon. As long as I kept my hand gripped around that topslide, I'd be all right. I kept on pushing and pushing, keeping him up against something firm so I could lean against him, because all I wanted to do was move that pistol around.

I was still biting and gnawing. I'd gone through the first part of his cheek and kept on going. I felt my teeth on his face bones; it gave me the same feeling as the gun metal did before. By now I was biting the top of his eyelid, I was biting his nose, everywhere I was ripping through the skin onto the bone of his jaw and skull.

I was running out of breath because the adrenalin was leaving me, and pushing him against the wall had taken a lot of physical strength out of me. Then I started to choke, and I realized I had some of his skin at the back of my throat. I could hear air being sucked into the hole in his cheek as he was breathing; I could hear my own throat rattling, blocked by chunks of his skin.

I was fighting him by feel not by sight. Our blood was burning into my eyes. Everything was blurred. I didn't know where Kelly was, and at this stage I didn't care. I couldn't help her until I'd helped myself.

I was still trying to get the pistol in to him somewhere. I didn't care where it went; it could go into his leg, into his stomach, I didn't give a fuck, so long as I could start shooting him.

His screams increased as my finger wrapped around his on the trigger.

I turned it round, let go of the topslide and squeezed.

The first two missed, but I kept on firing. I moved it round again and got him in the hip and then the thigh. He went down.

Everything stopped. The sudden silence was absolutely deafening.

After two or three seconds I could hear Kelly's screams resounding off the walls. At least she was still in the building. She sounded as though she was throwing a fit. All I could hear was a high-pitched continuous scream. I was too fucked to do anything about it. I was too busy trying to cough up his skin.

I'd find her later. I pulled myself up. I was in pain. The back of my neck felt as though it could no longer hold my head.

He writhed on the ground, bleeding and begging, 'Don't kill me, man! Don't kill me! Don't kill me!'

I got hold of the pistol and did to him as he had done to me, jumping astride him, ramming it deep into his mouth.

For several seconds I just sat there trying to catch my breath. McGear's body might be dying, but his eyes were alive.

'Why did you kill the family?' I said, pulling the pistol from his mouth so he could speak. 'Tell me and you'll live.'

He was looking at me as if he wanted to say something but didn't know what.

'Just tell me why. I need to know.'

'I don't know what the fuck you mean.'

I looked into his eyes and knew he was telling the truth.

'What is on that computer?'

There was no slow reaction this time. His lip curled and he said, 'Fuck you.'

234

I jammed the weapon back into his mouth and said quietly, firmly, almost sort of fatherly, 'Look at me! Look at me!'

I looked back into his eyes. No point carrying this on. He wouldn't say anything. He was too good for that.

Fuck it. I pulled the trigger.

26

I took a deep breath and wiped away the blood that had splattered onto my eyes when he took the round. I tried to regain some form of composure. Stop, just take that couple of seconds, take another deep breath and try to work out what the fuck to do next.

The shots would have been heard and reported – or I had to plan as if they were. I could still hear Kelly screaming in the distance somewhere.

First priority was the equipment. I pushed myself up off his chest and staggered back into the small office. I ripped the cable and mains lead from the PC, took the sniffer software out of the floppy drive and put it in my top pocket. I packed everything in the bag and moved back into the large office.

I went over to McGear. He looked like Kelly when she was sleeping, except this starfish had a face like a pizza and a large exit wound in the back of his head, oozing grey stuff onto the office carpet.

I picked up the bag, slung it over my left shoulder and moved into the corridor to pick up my pistol. I had to find Kelly. Easy, I just had to follow the screams.

She was fighting with the fire-escape door, the back of her coat marked with blood – probably mine from when McGear took me down. She was right up against the door trying to manipulate the handle, but in such a state that her fingers couldn't do it. She was jumping from foot to foot, screaming and beating her fists against the door in frustration and terror. I came up behind her, got hold of her arm and shook her.

'Stop it! Stop it!'

It wasn't the right thing to do. She was hysterical.

I looked into her eyes under the tears and said, 'Look, people are trying to kill you. Do you understand that? Do you want to die?'

She tried to shake me off. I put my hand over her mouth and listened to her blocked-up nose fighting for oxygen. I got her face right up against mine. 'These people are trying to kill you. Stop crying, do you understand me? Stop crying.'

She went quiet and limp and I let go of her. 'Give me your hand, Kelly.'

It was like holding lettuce. I said, 'Be quiet and just listen to me. You've got to listen to me, OK?' I was looking at her eyes and nodding away.

She just stared through me, tears still running down her cheeks, but trying to hold back.

I pushed the fire-exit bar and cold, damp air hit my face. I couldn't see anything, but that might be because my night vision was fucked. I dragged Kelly by the hand and the clunks of our footsteps echoed down the metal stairs. I didn't care about the noise; we'd made enough already.

Running towards the fence, I slipped on the mud. When she saw me fall, Kelly let out a cry and burst into tears again. I shook her and told her to shut up.

As we got to the fence I could already hear sirens on the highway. I had to assume they were coming for us. After a moment I could hear more noise coming from the car park area.

'Wait here!'

I climbed up the chain link fence with the equipment, dropped it over the other side and jumped. They were getting closer, but I couldn't see them yet. Kelly was looking at me from the other side of the fence, bobbing up and down, hands on the wire.

'Nick . . . Nick . . . Please, I want to come with you!'

I didn't even look where I was digging. My eyes were fixed on the gap between the two buildings. Coming from my right to left, flashing blue lights on the highway lit up the sky.

Kelly's whimpers turned to sobs.

I said, 'We'll be all right, we'll be all right. Just stay where you are. Look at me! Look at me!' I got eye-to-eye. 'Stay where you are!'

The lights and noise were now on Ball Street. I got hold of my documents and put them in my pocket.

All the vehicles had stopped, their sirens dying. The blue lights were still flashing, reflecting on Kelly's face that was wet with tears.

I looked at her through the chain link and whispered, 'Kelly! Kelly!'

She was in a daze of fear.

'Kelly, follow me now. Do you understand? Come on!'

I started moving along the fence. She was whining and wanting her mummy. She sounded more and more desperate. I said, 'You've got to keep up, Kelly, you've got to keep up. Come on!'

I was moving fast and she slipped and fell into the mud. I wasn't there to pick her up this time. She lay there sobbing. 'I want to go home, I want to go home. Please take me home.'

By now there were three police cars on target. We weren't even 200 metres away yet. Very soon they would start using their searchlights and ping us.

'Get up, Kelly, get up!'

The target now seemed surrounded by a haze of blue and red lights. Torchlights were jerking in the darkness at the rear.

We carried on until we got level with the alleyway. The sound of sirens filled the night.

I climbed over the fence, the bag nearly landing on top of her as I let it fall. I grabbed her right hand with my left and started towards the alley.

I needed to find a car that was parked in shadow and of the right age to have no alarms.

We emerged from the alley and turned left, following a line of parked cars. I found an early-Nineties Chevy. I put down the bag and ordered Kelly, 'Sit by this.'

I opened the bag and got out the picks. Minutes later I was in. I wired up the ignition and the engine fired. The digital clock said 03:33.

I let the engine run and put the windscreen wipers and heater on full blast to clear the morning dew. I got hold of Kelly and the bag and threw them both in the back. 'Lie down, Kelly, go to sleep.' No argument from her on the lying down. She might have trouble sleeping, though. Perhaps for the rest of her life.

I drove to the road and turned left, nice and slow. After just a quarter of a mile I spotted flashing lights coming towards me. I got out my pistol and put it under my right thigh. There was no way I was going to let the fuckers take us.

I shouted back at Kelly, 'Stay down, do not get up, do you understand?'

There was no reply.

'Kelly?'

I got a weak 'Yes.'

If I had to kill these policemen it would be unfortunate, but at the end of the day this was the sort of thing they got paid for. I made my plan. If they stopped me I'd wait until one or both came within range. The pistol was where my hand would naturally go and I'd draw down on them.

The flashing blue and red came closer. I just drove on towards them. My mindset was that I was a shift worker, on my way to earn my living. Now their lights were making me screw up my eyes so I could see beyond.

I wasn't worried. I felt very calm. Just wait and see. They went past at over 60 m.p.h.

I looked in the rear-view mirror. They hit the brakes and now I was flapping. I watched and made distance at the same time. The brake lights went off. Either they'd just been slowing down or they'd changed their minds.

I needed to dump this car before first light, which was probably the earliest the owner would discover it missing. I also had to get both of us a change of clothes and into another hotel.

Kelly started yelling, 'I want to go home! I want to go home! I want my—'

'Kelly, we are going home! But not yet!' I had to shout to cut in.

I couldn't see her and tilted the mirror. She was curled up with her thumb in her mouth. My mind flashed back to the two other times I'd found her like that, and I said quietly, 'We will, don't worry.'

We were following a road that seemed to parallel the Potomac, on its west side. After about half an hour I found a twenty-four-hour mart and parked up. There were maybe twenty or thirty vehicles outside; at that time of the morning most of them probably belonged to employees.

Kelly didn't ask why we were stopping. I turned round and said, 'I'm going to go and get us some more clothes. Do you want anything? Shall I see if they've got a deli and we'll get some sandwiches?'

She whimpered, 'Don't go, don't leave me!' She looked as if she'd been slapped. Her face was bright red, with puffy eyes and wet hair stuck to her face. You don't take a beaten-up seven-year-old with blood on her clothes into a supermarket at just after four in the morning.

I leaned over into the back, unzipped the bag and took out the coveralls. I said, 'I've got to leave you here. I need somebody to look after everything.' I pointed to the bag. 'Can you do that for me? You're a big girl now, a great spy.'

She nodded reluctantly.

I started to get the coveralls on while still sitting in the car seat. 'Nick?'

240

'What?' I was busy fighting with a leg.

'I heard a gun. Is that man dead?'

'Which man is that?' I didn't want to turn round, didn't want to face her. 'No, he's not. I think he made a mistake and thought we were someone else. He'll be OK.'

I was now arching my back to get the top half on. 'The police will take him to hospital.'

That was enough of that. I got out of the car quickly and poked my head back in. Before I even started to say the routine, she said, 'You will come back, won't you? I want to go home and see Mommy.'

'Definitely, I will come back, no problems, and you will see Mummy soon.'

I turned the interior light on and moved the rear-view mirror so I could see my face. The deep cuts on my forehead and under my eye were still wet, the plasma trying hard to get a scab going. I spat on my hand and used the cuff of the coveralls to wipe the rest of the blood off, but there wasn't much more I could do. Industrial accident.

I signalled to Kelly to lock the door and lie down. She nodded and complied.

I picked up a trolley and went through the electric swing gate. I got money from the ATM, then two sets of everything for Kelly and me, plus washing and shaving kit and a box of wipes, and some painkillers for my neck. It was hurting badly now. I could only look left or right by turning my whole body. I must have looked like a robot. I threw in some Coke, crisps and biscuits.

There weren't many shoppers. My cuts drew the odd glance, but no stares.

I got back to the car and tapped on the window. Kelly looked up; the windows were now covered in condensation, and she had to wipe it with her sleeve. Through the circle she'd created I could see she'd been crying, and she was rubbing her eyes. I pointed at the lock and she opened it.

I was all big smiles. 'Hiya! How's it going?'

There wasn't much of a reply. As I dumped the bags onto the passenger seat I said, 'Look, I've got a present for you.' I showed her a Dime bar. There was a reluctant smile. She took it and opened it.

I looked at the car clock. It was nearly 5 a.m. We started driving towards the Beltway, then headed west.

I saw the sign for Dulles International and slowed down for the off-ramp. We had to dump the car soon; I had to assume that its owner was an early riser.

Kelly was lying in the back, staring at the door. It seemed she was in a dream world. If not, she was damaged mentally by what she had seen. At the moment I didn't really care which.

We were about 8 miles from Dulles and I started to keep a look-out for hotels. I saw the sign for an Economy Inn. Absolutely perfect; but, first, we had to get ourselves cleaned up.

As we carried on towards the airport I could see the wing lights of what was probably the first of the day's aircraft making its approach about 4 miles away. I followed the signs to the economy parking, having stopped just short to check for cameras at the entry point. There weren't any; they must register on the way out. I took my ticket and parked up among thousands of other cars.

'Kelly, we're going to get you dressed in some new clothes,' I said.

I showed her what I'd bought and, as she was getting undressed, I got out the baby wipes and cleaned her face. 'Here, let's get rid of all those tears. Here you are, here's a brush.' I brushed her hair – too quickly, and it hurt her. 'OK, let's get this sweatshirt on you. Here you go. There, you're looking good. Here's another wipe – blow your nose.'

While she was doing that I got myself changed as well and dumped all the clothes in the passenger footwell. Kelly was still looking miserable as the shuttle took us to the terminal.

27

We walked into the departures area. The terminal was busier than I'd been expecting for this time of the morning. People were checking in all along the lines of desks, mooching around in the shops, or sitting in the cafés reading newspapers.

I wasn't saying much to Kelly, just holding her hand as I moved along, bag on my left shoulder, looking for the sign to arrivals, then to the taxi rank. An escalator showed me the way down. We were nearly at the bottom when Kelly announced, 'I need the bathroom, Nick.'

'You sure?' I just wanted to get out of here.

'Really, I need to go.'

'OK.' After the last time I'd learned my lesson.

I followed signs to the rest rooms. They were to the left, near the large exit doors from international arrivals. You went in through one of two large openings in the wall, and immediately came across a run of seven or eight disabled toilets, all unisex, and either side of this were the entrances to the single-sex toilets. I stayed outside in the main concourse, watching all the people who were waiting for the automatic doors to open and their loved ones to be disgorged.

You always know when you're being stared at. I'd been standing there a minute or two when I became aware. I looked up. It was an old woman, standing against the rail facing me on the opposite side of the channel made by the barriers, obviously waiting for somebody to come through. There was a silver-haired man with her, but her eyes were fixed on my face.

She looked away, turning her back to the exit doors, even though people were streaming out with their trolleys. Every few seconds I heard a scream of joy as people were reunited. Then there were camera flashes.

What had she been looking at? The cuts on my face? I hoped it was just that. There was nothing I could do about it. I would have to bluff it out, but keep an eye on her all the same.

Then I saw her start talking to her husband. Her body language looked urgent and agitated; she wasn't passing the time of day. He looked over in my direction, then back at her; he gave her a shrug that said, 'What the hell are you talking about, woman?' She must have seen Kelly and me going into the toilets and said to herself, 'Now, why do I know those two?'

I wasn't going to move. I wanted to see what she was doing. The moment she started to walk away, I'd have to take action.

I could tell she was still trying to work it out. I felt my heart pumping. I avoided eye contact, but I knew she was staring. Any minute now she'd remember the news report where she'd seen Kelly's face.

The seconds ticked by. At last Kelly came out and stood by me. 'Shall we go now?' I said, grabbing her hand before she could answer.

As I turned with her for the exit I could clearly see the woman tugging her husband's arm. However, he had now seen whoever it was they were meeting and was looking the other way.

She pulled his arm more urgently.

I wanted to run, but that would have just confirmed it for her. We walked and I talked crap to Kelly with the actions of a happy dad. 'Look at those lights, aren't they nice? This is the airport I fly into every time I come here. Have you been here before?' Kelly didn't have time to answer any of them.

I had to fight the urge to turn round and look. I started to think, What if? If I got the police onto me here, I was fucked. There was nowhere to go, just more of the airport, with more security than you could shake a nightstick at. My eyes were darting around. We had about 30 or 40 metres to go to the exit sign. With each step I expected to hear a cop shouting for me to freeze. All I could hear was the general hubbub and the occasional squeal of greeting.

We reached the exit, turned left and started walking downhill on a wide ramp that led to the pick-up points and taxi ranks. The moment we'd made that angle I started to move faster and chanced a look behind.

Kelly said, 'What's up?'

I said, 'There's the taxis, let's go.'

We had to wait for three other people in the queue before it was our turn. I felt like a child who desperately wants something and cannot wait any longer. *Come on, come on!*

At last we bundled into a cab and drove off, and I turned and looked behind me. Nothing. I still couldn't relax. Kelly could obviously sense the drama but didn't say another word.

I tried to block it out of my mind. Look hard enough and you'll find a positive in even the worst situation – that was what I'd always told myself. But I couldn't get a silver lining out of what had just happened. If the old woman did make the connection and told the police she had seen us heading for the taxi rank, it was negatives all the way.

I looked at Kelly and yawned. 'I'm sleepy,' I said, 'what about you?'

She nodded and put her head in my lap.

I gave the driver directions. Once off the freeway we drove a few blocks, then I got him to pull in. I watched him drive away as we stood in the car park of the Marriott. We would walk to the Economy Inn from there.

'We're going to a hotel now,' I said. 'Usual story. I'll be saying a lot of things that aren't true, and all you've got to do is be quiet and look really tired, OK? If you do what you're told and it works out, we can all go home.' We walked towards the reception.

There was a young black guy on the desk, his head buried in a textbook. We went through all the same routine, only this time I'd been beaten up during the robbery. He looked embarrassed. 'All of America's not like this, you know. It's beautiful.' He started talking about the Grand Canyon; after making a promise that I'd make a point of visiting it this trip I turned and walked out.

We got to the room and I started helping her off with her coat. As she turned so that her other arm came away out of the sleeve, she questioned me without warning. 'Are we going to see Mommy and Daddy now?'

'Not yet, we've still got stuff to do.'

'I want my mommy, Nick. I want to go home. You promised.'

'We will go soon, don't worry.'

'Are you sure Mommy and Daddy and Aida will be there?'

'Of course they will be.'

She didn't look convinced. It was crunch time. I couldn't carry this on any more. If we got out of this mess, I couldn't bring myself to let her be dumped on her grandparents or whoever, and for her to find out what a lying bastard I'd been all this time.

'Kelly . . .'

I sat next to her and started stroking her hair as she lay with her head on my lap.

'Kelly, when you get home, Mummy, Daddy and Aida will not be there. They never will now. They've gone to heaven. Do you know what that means?'

I said it almost as a throwaway, not really wanting to get into it any deeper. I wanted her to say, 'Oh, I see,' and then ask me if we could have a Micky D's.

There was a gap while she thought about it. All I could hear was the hum of the air-conditioning.

Her face creased into a frown. 'Is it because I was a bad girl and didn't help Daddy?'

246

I felt as if somebody was stabbing me. But it wasn't too hard a question; I felt OK answering that one. 'Kelly, even if you had tried to help Daddy, they would still have died.'

She was crying quietly into my leg. I rubbed her back and tried to think of something to say.

I heard, 'I don't want them to be dead. I want to be with them.'

'But you are.' I was fumbling for words.

She lifted her face and looked at me.

'You are with them. Every time you do something that you did with them means they are with you.'

She was trying to work this one out. So was I.

'Every time I eat a pizza with mushrooms I think of your mummy and daddy, because I know Mummy liked them. That's why they are never far away from me – and why Mummy, Daddy and Aida will be with you all the time.'

She looked at me, waiting for more. 'What do you mean?'

I was struggling. 'I mean, every time you put plates on a table, Mummy will be with you because she showed you how. Every time you shoot hoops, Daddy is with you because he taught you. Every time you show someone how to do something, Aida is with you – that's because you used to do it with her. You see, they are always with you!'

I didn't know how good it was, but it was the best I could come up with. She was back on my leg and I could feel the heat of her tears and breath.

'But I want to *see* them. When will I see them, Nick?'

I hadn't got through. I didn't know who was more upset, me or Kelly. A large lump was swelling in my throat. I had got into something I couldn't get out of.

'They aren't coming back, Kelly. They are dead. It's not because of anything you did or didn't do. They didn't want to leave you. Sometimes things happen that even grown-ups can't avoid or fix.'

She lay there listening. I looked down. Her eyes were open, staring at the wall. I stopped stroking her and put my arm around her.

People need to show sadness and loss. Maybe this was the time for Kelly to do that. If so, I wanted to reach out, not cross the street. I just didn't know if this was how you did it.

'You will be with them one day, but not for a long time. You will have children first, just like Mummy. Then your children will be sad when you die, just like you are now. They all loved you very much, Kelly. I only knew your mummy and daddy for a few years. Just think – you knew them all your life!'

I saw a small smile moving the sides of her face. She pressed her body closer into my legs.

'I want to stay with you, Nick.'

'That would be nice, but it wouldn't work. You have to go to school and learn how to be a grown-up.'

'You can help me do that.'

If only she knew. I didn't even have a garage to keep a bike in, let alone somewhere to look after a child.

Your weapon, your kit, and only then yourself – that's the order of things. I wanted to ease my magazine springs; it wasn't strictly necessary, but I felt that I needed to do it to mark the end of one phase and the beginning of a new one.

By now Kelly was sound asleep.

I plugged in the telephone to keep it recharged. It was my lifeline. Then I tipped all the kit from the bag and sorted it out. The new clothes were put to one side and I packed the CTR stuff back into the holdall. I was pissed off about having to leave the video camera on the roof; it would be found and a connection inevitably made between us and the shooting. Plus, the videotape was lost, and that might have been of use to Simmonds – it might even have been enough to guarantee me a future.

I repacked the kit and lay back on the bed, hands behind my head. Listening to the low drone of the air-conditioning, I started to think about this whole fucking game and how people like me and McGear were the ones that got used time and time again. When I realized I was starting to feel sorry for myself, I cut it.

248

McGear and I both had a choice and this was what we chose to do.

There were a few good things that had come out of last night's drama. At least I didn't have to worry about dumping all the blood- and piss-stained clothes that were in the blue holdall. The police would no doubt match the blood to the Browns', but that was nothing compared with the trouble I was already in. And, best of all, I had confirmed a definite connection between Kev, PIRA, the building and whatever it was that I'd copied from that computer.

I wasn't going to attempt to get the laptop out and start faffing about with it. I was too tired, I'd make mistakes and miss things. Besides, the adrenalin had gone now and the pain across my back and neck was even more intense.

I had a hot shower and tried to shave. McGear's bite marks on my face were scabbing nicely. I left them to sort themselves out.

I dressed in jeans, sweatshirt and trainers, and reloaded my mags. I needed rest, but I had to be ready for a quick move. The plan was to have a couple of hours' sleep and something to eat, and then sit down and see what was on the laptop, but it wasn't working out. I was tossing and turning, snatching a bit of sleep, waking up.

I turned on the TV and flicked through the channels to see if McGear was news yet, and he was.

The cameras panned the front of the PIRA building, with the obligatory backdrop of police and ambulance crews, then a man fronted to camera and started gobbing off. I didn't bother turning up the volume, I knew the gist of what he'd be saying. I was half expecting to see my piss-covered, homeless friend describing what he had seen and heard.

Kelly was starting to toss and turn, probably with pictures of McGear in her head.

I lay there looking at her. The girl had done well, without a doubt. The last few days had been chaos for her and I started to worry about it. Seven-year-old kids shouldn't be exposed to this sort of shit. Nobody should. What would become of her? It suddenly occurred to me that I was worrying more about her than I was about myself.

I woke with the TV still on. I looked at my watch. Nine thirty-five. At midday Pat would be calling me. I hit the off button. I wanted to start mincing about with the laptop. I started to get up and found I could hardly move. I felt like an OAP as I lifted myself off the bed, my neck as stiff as a board.

I made a racket getting the laptop out of the holdall and plugging everything in, and Kelly started to wriggle around. By the time I'd got it up and running and connected to the back-up drive she was propped up on one elbow watching me. Her hair looked like an explosion. She listened for a while as I cursed at the laptop for not accessing the back-up drive, then said, 'Why don't you just reboot and then look at the program?'

I looked at her as if to say, You fucking smart arse! Instead, I said, 'Mmm, maybe.' I rebooted and it worked. I turned round and smiled at her and got one in return.

I started to scroll through the files. Instead of the businesslike file names I'd been expecting, the documents had code words like Weasel, Boy, Guru. A lot of them turned out to be spreadsheets or invoices – I could see what they were, but I didn't know what they meant. To me, the whole forty or so pages might just as well have been in Japanese.

I then opened up another file called Dad. It was just dots and numbers across the screen. I turned to Kelly, 'What's that, then, smart guy?'

She looked. 'I don't know. I'm only seven; I don't know everything.'

It was five minutes to noon. I turned on the phone and carried on flicking through the files, trying to make sense of them.

Twelve o'clock came and went.

By quarter past, the call still hadn't happened. I was flapping. Come on, Pat, I need to get out of the US and back to Simmonds.

I have enough information – maybe. The longer I stay now, the higher the risk. Pat, I need you!

For Slack to miss an RV there must be a major drama; even when he was high, he'd come up with the goods. I tried to block dark thoughts out of my head by telling myself that he'd call at the next arranged window. But as I carried on half-heartedly on the laptop I started to feel almost physically sick. My only way out had been lost. I had that awful sinking feeling that everything was going to go horribly wrong. I needed to do something.

I closed down the laptop and put the back-up disk in my pocket. Kelly was half buried under the covers, watching TV.

I joked, 'Well, you know what I'm going to do in a minute, don't you?'

She jumped out of bed and threw her arms around me, frowning. 'Don't go! Don't go! We'll watch the TV together, or I can come with you?'

'You can't do that, I want you to stay here.'

'Please!'

What could I do? I felt her pain at being scared and alone. 'OK, come with me – but you've got to do what I say.'

'OK, OK!' She jumped up and went to get her coat.

'No, not yet!' I pointed to the bathroom. 'First things first. Get in that bath, wash your hair, come out and I'll dry it, then you can get changed into your new clothes, and then we'll go out. OK?'

She was trembling with excitement, like a dog about to go for walkies. 'Yeah, OK!' She skipped to the bathroom.

I sat down on the bed and shouted into the bathroom as I flicked through the news channels, 'Kelly, make sure you brush your teeth or they'll all fall out and you won't be able to eat when you're older.'

I heard 'Yeah, yeah, OK.'

There was nothing more about McGear on the TV. After a while I walked into the bathroom. The toothpaste tube hadn't been opened. 'Have you brushed your teeth?'

She nodded, looking guilty.

I said, 'Well, let's have a smell.' I bent down and put my nose near her mouth. 'You haven't. Come on, do you know how to brush your teeth?'

'I know how to brush my teeth.'

'Show me, then.'

She picked up the toothbrush. It was way too big for her mouth and she was brushing from side to side.

I said, 'That's not the way you've been taught, is it?'

She said, 'Yes, it is!'

I shook my head slowly. I knew that she would have been taught properly. I said, 'All right, we'll do it together.' I put some toothpaste on the brush and made her stand in front of the mirror. I stood beside her and she watched as I pretended to brush. Looking after kids was easy after all. It was all down to EDI: explanation, demonstration, imitation. Just that, instead of doing it with a weapon to a room full of recruits, I was doing it with a seven-year-old girl. 'Now with me, like this, then brush round in little circles. And let's make sure we do the backs.'

And then it got stupid. She started to laugh at the sight of me pretending to brush my teeth and, as she laughed, all the tooth-paste sprayed from her mouth and onto the mirror. I laughed with her.

She finished her bath and changed into her new jeans and sweatshirt. I'd also bought us matching baseball hats at the mart, black denim with the words, Washington, DC.

I wet my hair and washed, and we both looked sparkly clean. She put on her new blue coat and trainers and we were ready to go. My plan was to get to the vicinity of Pat's apartment. When he rang at six o'clock, we'd be able to meet straight away.

What was I going to do with the back-up disk? I decided to hide it in the room, because I was going to split my gold: if the back-up stayed here, and Kelly came with me and we were lifted, at least they wouldn't have the job lot. The long, dark-wood side-board with the TV on top covered a third of the room; it was about 2 feet high and rested on little half-inch legs. I lifted one corner, gaffer-taped the disk to the underside and positioned a couple of tell-tales. One last look around the room and we left.

It was still drizzling and was slightly colder than earlier in the morning. Kelly was on cloud nine; I reciprocated her smiles and happy noises, but underneath I was flapping about Pat. As we crossed the grass to avoid reception I wondered about phoning Euan. I decided not to. Not yet anyway. I might need him later. He was a card to keep up my sleeve.

The whole area was dotted with hotels. We walked across the road to one about 400 metres away, and I went into the lobby and ordered a taxi. Kelly waited outside under the awning.

As I came out again I said, 'When we get into this taxi I'm going to put your hood up and I want you to rest against me as if you're sleepy. Remember, you promised you'd do exactly what I said.'

The taxi turned up and took us to Georgetown. Kelly leaned against me and I got her nuzzled in on my lap with her hood up so it hid her.

We got out on Wisconsin. It was four o'clock and everybody around us looked so normal as they chatted, strolled and enjoyed their shopping. We spent the next hour or so walking and snacking. By five thirty the Georgetown mall where we were sitting was quite warm and we were both feeling sleepy.

I was having a coffee, she was having a milkshake, which she wasn't touching because by now she was full of burger. I looked at the display of my watch every half-minute until it was five fifty-five. Then I switched on the phone. Good battery level, good signal strength.

Six o'clock came.

Nothing.

A minute past.

Two minutes past.

I sat there almost paralysed with disbelief. Kelly was absorbed in a comic she'd picked out for herself.

Four minutes past. This was desperate. Pat wouldn't let me

down unless he couldn't help it. He knew as well as I did that, on operations, if you're a minute late you might as well be an hour or a day late, because people's lives might depend on it. The attack might have had to go in, unsupported by your covering fire.

There must be a problem. A major problem.

I kept the phone switched on. Finally, at six twenty, I said, 'Come on, Kelly, we're going to visit Pat.'

Now the normality stopped. There was shit on. All hope had evaporated.

28

We came out of the mall and I flagged down a cab.

Riverwood turned out to be a well-established, upmarket area, rows of weatherboarded houses with neat lawns and a couple of European cars in the drive, and smart apartment blocks with underground parking. The shops reflected its wealth, with good bookshops, expensive-looking clothes boutiques and small art galleries.

I stopped the cab a block past Pat's street. I paid him off and he left us in the light rain. It was getting dark, a bit earlier than it should have done, but the cloud cover made everything gloomy. Some cars already had their headlights on.

'Let's hope Pat's in,' I said, 'otherwise we'll have to go all the way back to the hotel without saying hello!'

She looked excited about meeting him. After all, this was the man I'd said would help her go back home. I couldn't be sure if what I had said about her family had sunk in. I didn't even know if kids of that age understood what death was and, if they did, that it was irreversible.

Looking up the hill, I could see that Pat's street was pure Riverwood, broad and elegant, with houses and shops that had been there for years. Above the skyline one or two new apartment blocks seemed to be taking over, but even they looked very ordered, clean and wealthy. I wasn't entirely sure which one he lived in, but it was easy enough to count the numbers and work it out. We walked past, and I had a clear view into the rear secure car park. I saw the red Mustang, redder than Satan's bollocks. It was seven fifteen. If he was there, why the fuck hadn't he phoned?

We went into a coffee shop opposite. The waft of newly ground beans and the blare of rumba music inside La Colombina took me straight back to Bogotá; maybe that was why Pat had chosen to live here. We wanted a window seat, which wasn't a problem. The glass was misted up; I cleared a circle with a paper napkin and sat and watched.

Kelly was doing what she had been told, keeping quiet until I told her not to be. Anyway, *Girl!* magazine seemed the thing to shut kids up with. I checked the phone. Good signal, plenty of power.

A waitress came over to take our order. I was going to ask for food, even though I didn't really want it, because it would take time to prepare it, and then it would take time to eat it, and that way we could spend more time here without it looking un-natural.

'I'll take a club and a large cappuccino,' I said. 'And what do you want, Josie?'

Kelly beamed at the waitress. 'Do you do Shirley Temples?'

'Sure we do, honey!'

It sounded like a cocktail to me, but the waitress went away quite happily to order it. Kelly went back to her magazine and I just kept looking out of the window.

The drinks arrived. When we were alone again I said, 'What is that?'

'Cherries and strawberries, mixed with Sprite.'

'Sounds disgusting. I'd better try some.'

It tasted like bubble gum to me, but it was obviously what kids liked. She was slugging it down good-style.

The sandwich mountain arrived. I didn't need it, but I ate it anyway. In my days in the Regiment and since, I'd learned to think of food the way an infantryman thinks of sleep. Get it down you whenever you get the chance.

Things were running their natural course in the coffee shop; it was now coming up for three-quarters of an hour that we'd been sitting there, and you can only stay in a place for so long without arousing suspicion or drowning in coffee.

Kelly made the decision for me as she spoke. 'What are we going to do now?'

I put some cash down on the table. 'Let's zip you up and see if Pat is at home.'

We went out and walked past Pat's apartment once more. The car was still there. I was desperate to know one way or another what was going on. If it was just that he didn't want to play any more, fair one. But I couldn't really see that; I knew that he wanted to help. There was a problem, without a doubt. But I needed it confirmed; then I could reassess and make a plan without him in it.

As we walked back down the hill Kelly said, 'Do you actually know where Pat lives?'

'Yes, I do, but I know he's not there yet. We've just walked past his place and I couldn't see him.'

'Can't you phone him?'

I couldn't contact him directly; if the phone was tapped I didn't want anyone to make the connection between us. I'd promised not to compromise him. But she'd just given me an idea all the same.

'Kelly, do you want to help me play a trick on Pat?'

'Oh yeah!'

'OK, this is what I want you to do.'

We carried on walking and started to do a circuit around the area. We practised and practised, until she said she was ready to go. We got to a phone box about three blocks away, a half-sized booth attached to the wall. I brought the receiver down to Kelly's level. 'Ready?'

She gave me a thumbs up. She was excited; she thought this was great.

I dialled 911, and about three seconds later Kelly was shouting, 'Yes, I've just seen a man! I've just seen a man on the second floor, 1121 Twenty-seventh Street and . . . and . . . he's got a gun and the man's shot, and . . . and . . . and he's got a gun – please help!'

I put my hand on the hook.

'Good one! Now, shall we go and see what happens next?'

I picked a different route back. This time we were going to approach from the top of the hill and walk down towards the apartment block. By now it was properly dark and still very wet. Heads bent in the rain, we made it to Twenty-seventh Street, turned right and started walking slowly down the hill.

I heard the siren first, louder and louder, then the flash of its emergency lights as a blue-and-white sped past us. Then I saw other blue and red lights, all flashing in the darkness in the area of the apartment block.

As we got closer I made out three police cars. An unmarked car also turned up, a portable light flashing on the roof, just above the driver.

We walked further down and stopped at a bus stop. All I was doing was watching and waiting – much like everybody else, as a small crowd had gathered.

'Are they all coming for Pat?' Kelly asked.

I was too busy feeling depressed to answer; the sight of an ambulance arriving had pole-axed me. I stroked her head over her coat hood.

'I'll tell you about it in a minute. Just let me watch what's happening.'

We waited, like everyone else. A quarter of an hour went by. By now local TV news crews were turning up. Then I saw them come out – two boys with a trolley, and on top was a corpse in a body bag. I didn't have to see the face to know who was inside. I only hoped it had been quick for him, but, judging by the condition of the Browns, I had a terrible feeling that it hadn't.

I said quietly, 'We're going to go now, Kelly. Pat's not there tonight.'

I felt as if one of my most treasured possessions had been stolen from under my nose and I knew that I'd never get it back. Our friendship had been rekindled after all these years and this was the price he had paid for it. I felt lost and desperate, as if I'd got detached from the rest of my patrol in hostile territory, without a map or a weapon, and no hint of which way to go. He had been a true friend. Even after all these years of not seeing each other I would miss the man with no arse.

As Pat was being loaded into the ambulance I forced myself to cut away from the emotion. I turned and started to walk back down the way we'd come, to avoid the police. One of the cars had now left with its siren going and the ambulance was just about to. I imagined the scene-of-the-crime people inside the apartment, putting on their coveralls and unpacking their gear. Again I tried to cut away, make myself look at the situation logically: Pat was gone, now all I had left was Euan. But it was much harder to do than it normally was.

We took the first left to get off the main drag and I listened as the ambulance siren twice went off to manoeuvre in the traffic. We carried on along the road. It wasn't a main thoroughfare and was residential on both sides, large houses with wide stone staircases leading up to the front doors.

I had Kelly's hand and we were walking without talking.

Feelings about Pat had no place in my mind at the moment. What mattered was what information he could have given about us to whoever had zapped him. PIRA or Luther and co, who could tell? It had to be one or the other. Assuming his death was connected with me, of course. Fuck knows what else he could have been up to. However, I had to work on the basis that whoever killed him wanted to know where we were. All Pat knew was the phone number and that I was planning on going into the PIRA office. OPSEC might have saved our lives.

I was thinking so hard that at first the voice didn't really register. Then I thought it was Kelly, and I was going to give her hand a bit of a squeeze and tell her to be quiet and let me think. But then it spoke again, a man's voice, low and resolute, and this time there was no mistaking the words.

'Freeze. If you move, I'll kill you. Stay exactly where you are. Do not move.'

It wasn't a druggy voice; it wasn't a young nervous voice; it was a voice that was in total control.

29

I kept my hands where they were.

Kelly flung her arms around my waist.

'It's OK, it's all right. They aren't going to hurt you,' I lied like a cheap watch.

His footsteps moved from behind me and to the left. He must have come from the service alley that ran behind the houses we'd just passed.

He said, 'You have two choices. Get smart by keeping still. Get dead by moving.' The voice was late twenties, early thirties, precise, well drilled.

It was pointless trying to draw down on him. He would kill me the instant I made a move.

I decided to take choice one.

More footsteps came from the other side and somebody was tugging Kelly away. She cried out, 'Nick! Nick!' but I could do nothing to help and her grip was no match for theirs. She was dragged behind me and out of sight. I still couldn't see anything of the guys who'd caught us. I made myself calm down and accept what was happening.

The voice started to give me commands in the same no-nonsense, almost pleasant voice. He said, 'I want you to raise your hands slowly and put them on top of your head. Do that now.'

When I'd complied he said, 'Now turn around.'

I turned slowly and saw a short, dark-haired man aiming a pistol at me in a very professional manner. He was standing about 10 metres from me at the entrance to the alleyway. He was breathing heavily, probably after running round the streets to find us both. He was wearing a suit and I saw Velcro. I now knew who had got to Pat.

'Walk towards me. Do it now.'

I couldn't see Kelly. She must already have been taken down the alleyway. They had got her at last. I pictured Aida's savaged little body as I came towards him.

'Stop. Turn left.' Very low, very calm and confident. As he said it I heard a car pull up to my right, and out of the corner of my eye I could see it was the Caprice from the first motel.

'Walk.'

I moved into the alleyway. Still no sign of Kelly.

I heard 'Get on your knees.'

I knelt down. I'd never been particularly worried about dying; we've all got to check out some time. When it did happen I just wanted it to be nice and quick. I'd always hoped there was an afterlife, but not as reincarnation back on Earth. I'd hate to find myself back here as something low down the food chain. But I wouldn't mind a spiritual thing, where you just become aware of everything, from the truth about the creation of mankind to the recipe for Coca-Cola. I'd always had the feeling that I was going to die young, but this was just a bit too early.

Nothing was happening and nothing was said. Then what must have been that Caprice drove into the alley behind me, its headlights illuminating the backs of the houses. Each had facing garages and three or four cars parked along the sides of the alley. I could see my kneeling shadow cast against the wet tarmac.

The engine was still running and I heard the doors being opened. There was radio traffic from a different voice; this one had an accent that should have been selling hot dogs in New

York. He was giving a location. 'Affirmative, we're in the service road for Dent and Avon. We are on the south side. You'll see our lights. Affirmative, we have both of them.'

I stayed on my knees with my hands on my head in the rain while we waited for the others to arrive. I heard footsteps coming towards me from the car. I clenched my teeth and closed my eyes, expecting to be given the good news. They walked slightly past me to my right and stopped.

I didn't hear the second one come up behind me. I just felt a heavy hand grip my own firmly on my head as the other felt for my weapon. The hand pulled out the Sig and I watched him check the safety catch in front of my face. Then he released his grip on my hands and, in the same movement, produced a clear plastic bag. I could smell coffee on his slightly laboured breath.

Nothing happened for a moment or two, apart from the rustling of the bag behind me. Into view on my right came a man who looked a bit of a fashion seeker, dressed in a black suit with a mandarin jacket. Fuck me, it was Mr Armani. He was maybe late twenties, very clean-cut, and dark and smooth. He probably glided over the ground so his shoes never got wet. He was covering me.

I heard Kelly crying in the background. She must be in the car. Fuck knows how she got there, but at least I knew where she was. The man behind me carried on the search and placed my stuff in the bag.

The hot-dog seller was being quite good with her, he didn't sound too aggressive or rough. Maybe he had kids of his own. 'It's OK, it's OK,' he said. 'What's your name?'

I couldn't hear her reply, but I heard him say, 'No, little lady, I don't think your name's Josie, I think your name is Kelly.'

Good one, mate, at least you tried!

Car lights stopped on the main drag about 150 metres further down, at the end of the alleyway. Then reversing lights were coming towards me.

By now all my stuff was in the plastic bag and being held by whoever was behind me. I was still on my knees, hands on head, with Mr Armani hovering to my right.

There were noises of more people behind me. I was hoping that it was passers-by who would report it. But to whom? My hopes collapsed as I heard the driver get out of the car and start to speak.

'That's OK, folks, all under control. There's nothing to see here.'

I was confused. How could they just move people on – unless they were law enforcement. Maybe there was a glimmer of hope; maybe I'd be able to talk my way out of this one. I still had the back-up disk hidden. Maybe I could bargain with it.

The reversing car stopped about 5 metres away and three people got out – the driver from the left-hand side and two out of the back. At first they were in shadow and I couldn't see their faces, but then one walked into the glare of the other car's head-lights. And then I knew I was really in the shit.

Luther was looking a little the worse for wear and he wasn't blowing me kisses. Caught in the headlights he looked like a pissed-off devil with a large boil dressing. He still had a suit on, but he wouldn't be wearing a tie for a while. I could tell by the smile on his face that he had a few tricks saved up for me. Fair one.

He walked towards me and I thought he was going to make a point. I closed my eyes and got ready to take the hit, but he walked straight past. That scared me even more.

Luther started to talk as he got to the car. 'Hi, Kelly, remember me? My name's Luther.'

There were some mumblings in reply. I was straining to hear the conversation, but only the adult voice was audible.

'Don't you remember me? I came to pick up your daddy for work a couple of times. You have to come with me now because I've been sent to look after you.'

I could hear protests from the car.

'No, he's not dead. He wants me to collect you. Now, come on, move it, you little bitch!'

Kelly screamed, 'Nick, Nick! I don't want to go!' She sounded terrified.

Luther walked back to his car with her. He had his arm around her tight to stop her from bucking and kicking with fright. It was all over in a few seconds. Once Kelly was secure in the back of the car all three drove off. I felt as if I'd been taken down by the fire extinguisher again.

'Get up.' My hands were still on my head and I felt someone's hand grip onto my right tricep and lift me up. I heard the car behind me move.

I looked to my right. The short guy had hold of me with his left hand; in his right he had the plastic bag with Kev's mobile, my weapon, wallet, passport, ATM card and loose change. He turned me round to face the car, which had just finished moving side-on in the road, pointing towards the right, and pushed me towards it. Mr Armani had me covered.

I'd stayed calm so far. But I had to get out of this shit now. I was going to be killed, it was as easy as that. The engine was running and I had about 10 metres in which to do something. Whatever I did, there would have to be a lot of speed, aggression and surprise. And it must work first time; if not, I was dead.

The guy who was holding me was right-handed, or he wouldn't be dragging me along with his left, and therefore, if I started fucking about, he would have to drop the bag and draw his pistol. If I was wrong about that, I would soon be dying. But I was dead anyway, so fuck it – why not go for it?

There were about 3 metres left between me and the car. By now Mr Armani had glided to the rear door to open it and, as his eyes glanced down for the door handle, I knew it was time.

YAAAAAAHHHHHH!!!

Screaming at the top of my voice, I brought my right hand down hard, half turned my hips and hit his left shoulder as hard as I could.

I'd got surprise. All three now had to take in what was going on and make an assessment. It would take them little more than a second to turn that assessment into reaction.

As I hit him, I started to push in an attempt to spin him to his left so that his right-hand side would come towards me. We were both screaming now. He'd already made his assessment. He dropped the bag and was going for his weapon.

I knew that, for him, too, it was happening in slow time. I could see the saliva spray out of his mouth as he shouted a warning to the others. There was nothing to worry about with the other two at the moment; if they were quicker than me, knowing about it wouldn't make it any better.

Looking down at his belt I could see the pistol moving slowly towards me as he spun round. Nothing else mattered. I kept my eyes on it. I heard the other two screaming. We were all at it.

The Colt .45 is a single-action weapon, which means that all the trigger does is release the hammer. To cock the hammer in the first place and chamber the first round, you must rack back the top-slide by pinching in with the fingers and thumb of the left hand against its serrations, pulling it back firmly to the rear and releasing. The pistol can be carried 'cocked and locked' – hammer back and safety on – with a round in the breech. The Colt also has both a manual safety and a grip safety. Even if the manual safety is off, your hand must be firm enough on the grip to keep the grip safety depressed, or the weapon won't fire.

I grabbed the pistol with my left hand, I didn't care where. At the same time I brought my right hand down, with four fingers together and my thumb stretched out to present a big recess for the weapon. I pushed onto it with the web of my hand, taking the manual safety catch off with my thumb and using the web of my hand to release the grip safety by holding the weapon correctly. I couldn't see if the hammer was back or not. And I had no way of knowing if the weapon had a round in the chamber. With my left hand, I racked the topslide back to cock it. It had already been cocked. A brass round spun out of the ejection port, glinting as it tumbled in the street lights. It didn't matter losing one round; at least I wouldn't get a dead man's click.

I knew the first threat was Mr Armani. He had a weapon in his hand.

I carried on turning in the direction the shoulder hit had taken me and, as I did, I came up into the aim, firing low because these fuckers wore armour. Armani went down. I didn't know if he was dead or not.

I carried on spinning and dropped the short guy, moved forward and looked at the driver. He was still in his seat, but in a crouched position, screaming and writhing.

I ran to his side of the car, pointing the pistol. 'Move over! Move over! Move over!'

I pulled the door open and, keeping the pistol at the aim, kicked him with my right leg. I wasn't going to start dragging him out, it would take too long. I just wanted to get in the car and go. I shoved the muzzle into his cheek and pulled out his weapon, kept it and threw mine out – I didn't know how many rounds were left.

The injury was to his upper right arm. There was a small entry hole in the material, but not much blood around the site. He must have taken one of the rounds aimed at Armani as I spun round. His hand, however, was red and dripping from where blood was coursing down his arm. The .45 round is big and heavy and doesn't fuck around. The massive exit wound would have blown away most of the underside of his arm. I would be having no problems from this boy.

As I drove off I screamed at him, 'Where are they going? Where are they going?'

His answer was half a cry, half a shout. 'Fuck you! Fuck you!' His dark-grey suit was turning brown with blood.

I jabbed his leg hard with the pistol. 'Where are they going?'

We were in a narrow residential road. I took off both wing mirrors in the process of turning to question him. He told me to fuck off again, so I fired. I could feel the air pressure change as the gases left the barrel, and then the smell of cordite filled the air. There was an explosion of material and flesh as the round ploughed a 12-inch furrow along and down into his leg. He howled like a stuck pig.

I didn't know where I was heading. The driver's screams quickly subsided, but he kept thrashing about. His convulsions left him on his knees in the footwell, with his head on the seat. He was starting to go into shock. He was probably wishing he did sell hot dogs in New York.

'Where are they going?' I demanded again. I didn't want him to pass out before I got the information.

'They're heading south,' he moaned. 'I-95 south.'

We were speeding on the elevated section of highway that took us to the interstate.

I looked across. 'Who are you?'

His face screwed up in pain as he fought for breath. He didn't reply. I hit him on the temple with the pistol. He gave a low moan and moved his fingers sluggishly from his leg to his head. We passed the Pentagon, then I saw the sign for the Calypso hotel. It seemed like a bad dream.

'Who are you? Tell me why you're after me!'

I could barely hear his reply. His mouth was dribbling blood and he was finding it hard to breathe.

'Let me go, man. Just leave me here and I'll tell you.'

No way was I falling for that one.

'You're going to die soon. Tell me and I'll help you. Why are you trying to kill us? Who are you?'

His head lolled. He didn't reply because he couldn't.

I found them just short of the Beltway, in the middle of the three lanes. It was easy to pick them out in my headlights and I could see it was still three up; one in the front, two in the back. No sign of Kelly, but there was enough space between the two boys in the back to have another body between them. She was only a little fucker; her head wouldn't be showing.

I couldn't do anything on the freeway, so now was the time to calm down and get my head round the next plan. What was I going to do? Whatever it was, it had to be soon, because I didn't know their destination, and I-95 goes all the way to Florida. Much nearer, however, about thirty minutes away, was Quantico, the FBI and DEA academy. It was starting to make sense. Luther and the black guy coming to the house, both knowing Kev; they were all the same group. But why would they kill Kev? And if they were the killers, what connection then did 'bad DEA' have with my 'friends over the water'? Was there something happening here between these two groups that Kev had discovered and got fucked over for?

I thought again of Florida and it gave me an idea. I tucked it away for later.

I looked down at the driver. He was in shit state, still losing blood. He was sitting in a pool of it because the rubber mat in the footwell stopped the carpet from soaking it up. I could see his face as the lights from the opposite side of the freeway hit us now and again; all the agitation had drained from it and he looked ashen, like an old fish; life was slowly going out of his eyes, which were staring into space. He was going to die soon. Tough shit.

I reached over, flipped open his jacket and took the two magazines that were in a holder on his shoulder holster. He was oblivious to what I was doing; he was in his own place now, perhaps reflecting on his life before he died.

I had surveillance on the target car. My wipers were on quick time as the trucks and cars splashed more water onto the windscreen than the rain itself. I put the demister on full blast. The driver's leaking blood and my own sweating body were misting up the car big-time.

A freeway was perfect for my purposes; I could just drive along and even allow a bit of distance to develop, to the point of letting another car get in between me and the target. As an exit came up I'd just get a little bit closer; if he was going to turn off I could then filter in naturally and come up behind him.

After about another five minutes I saw a sign saying 'Lorton 1 mile'. They started to indicate that they were getting into the filter lane to take the off-ramp. They weren't going to Quantico after all. There was no time to think about that; this was the time to hit them. I glanced down, changed mags and checked chamber.

As I came across to get in lane, I realized for the first time that we were driving through heavily wooded terrain. The tyres throbbed rhythmically as they hit the joints in the concrete freeway.

By now the driver had slumped completely into the footwell, with his back against the door. It was only the body armour under his shirt that gave him posture. He was dead.

I was now in the filter lane and just 20 metres behind their vehicle, close enough to be on top of them, but far enough so that, if they looked behind, they'd just see headlights. I saw no heads turning round; they weren't looking aware. I started to take deep breaths and spark myself up.

The Lorton exit ramp was a slight uphill with a gentle right-hand bend. The tall trees each side gave the impression of a tunnel. I planned to do it at the first junction. My brain was in overdrive, getting me into a mindset, trying to take the fear away.

I could see traffic lights in the middle distance and put my foot on the gas to close up even more. Their brake lights came on, then their right-hand indicator. A truck thundered past from left to right. It looked like it was a wide major road ahead. The car started its right turn. Pushing myself back into the seat, I put my foot down hard on the accelerator and braced my arms on the wheel.

I must have been doing about 45 m.p.h. and was still accelerating as I drew level and yanked the wheel hard right. My right wing hit the front of theirs. There was a massive jolt. My air bag exploded as the car slewed round into the main drag. The other car spun sideways. I heard glass shattering and the screech of tortured rubber.

The moment the vehicle came to a halt I stabbed at the seat belt release and opened the door. The air felt freezing. At first all I could hear was the hiss of the radiator and the *ping ping ping* warning that the door was open and the lights on; then came the sound of muffled shouts from inside the other vehicle.

The first priority was the driver. The car had to be immobilized. He was still fighting his seat belt. I fired through the windscreen. I didn't know where I hit him, but he was down. As I looked into the back I could see Kelly, or at least her shape. She was low down in the footwell, hands over her ears.

Luther was getting his first rounds down on me. His door was half open and he was starting to roll out. I'd have been doing the same because a car draws fire – so get out of the way. As he rolled I kept on firing, just below the level of the door. He screamed. I'd got him. I couldn't tell whether it was a direct hit or the splash of the round off the tarmac, but it didn't matter, the effect was the same.

I moved from behind the bonnet of my car to take on the third guy. He was out now but had had a change of heart. He put his hands up and yelled, 'Don't do it, don't do it!' His eyes were like saucers. I double-tapped him in the head.

Kelly was still curled up in a ball in the footwell. She wasn't going anywhere.

I searched the two bodies for wallets and magazines. I left Luther for last.

He was on the ground behind his car, hands clutched to his chest. 'Help me . . . help me . . . please . . .'

He'd taken a round in the armpit as he rolled on the floor and it must have carried on into his chest cavity. I thought of Kev, Marsha and Aida, and kicked. He opened his mouth to scream, but all that came out was a gurgle. He was on his way out. Good. Let it happen slowly.

I ran back for Kelly and lifted her out of her hiding place. I had to shout at her above her screams. 'It's OK, Kelly. I'm here, it's OK.'

I held her tight in my arms. She was nearly deafening me.

'It's all over now! It's OK!'

It wasn't.

The police would be here soon. I looked around me. The junction was with a trunk road, two lanes in each direction. To my left and downhill was the I-95, crossing the road by a bridge, with a Texaco gas station about 400 metres away on the other side of it on the right. Uphill and about the same distance away was a Best Western hotel cutting the skyline.

Lights were coming from the exit road towards us. Luther was lying there softly moaning to himself. He wasn't dead, but it wouldn't be long. The lights came closer.

Kelly was still hysterical. Grabbing her to conceal my pistol, I went behind the two cars. The lights were nearly level with us. I moved out and waved the vehicle down.

The good Samaritans were in a Toyota Previa, man and wife in the front, two kids in the back. I played the traumatized victim for all I was worth, shouting, 'Help! Help!' as I rushed to the driver's side. The woman was at the wheel; she opened her door. 'Oh my gosh, oh my gosh!' Her husband already had his mobile out for an ambulance.

I put the safety catch on and held the gun against her face. 'Everybody out now! Get out, get out now!' My other arm was windmilling like a madman's. Hopefully they'd think I was one. 'Get out! I'll fucking kill you! Get out!'

The one thing I did know about families is that no-one will risk theirs. The husband started to lose it. 'Please don't,' he whimpered, 'please don't!' Then he started to cry.

Kelly had quietened down, listening to my act.

It was the mother who kept her cool. 'OK, we are getting out. Dean, get the kids out. Out!'

Dean got his act together. I yelled at him, 'Throw your wallet back inside!'

I bundled Kelly through the sliding door, slammed it shut, ran round to the driver's side, climbed up and we were off.

I wanted to get away from the initial danger area, then sort myself out. The freeway was out because it would be too easy for the police to pick me up. I drove up onto the junction and turned left under the freeway bridge, past the garage. The road became a normal two-lane carriageway and I put my foot down.

This was no time to explain stuff to Kelly. She was curled up on the back seat, sobbing. My adrenalin rush was slowing down, but my face was soaked with sweat and I was lathering up. I took deep breaths, trying to get more oxygen into my body and calm everything down. I felt unbelievably angry with myself for losing control back there. I should have killed Luther straight away, not fucked about.

I realized we were heading south, away from the airport. I'd have to stop and sort myself out instead of just running in a blind panic. I pulled over and checked the map book. Kelly didn't look good, but I didn't have too much of a clue what to say to comfort her. 'I told you I was going to look after you,' I tried. 'Are you OK?'

She looked up at me and nodded, her bottom lip quivering.

I made a decision. Fuck it, let's just go straight to the hotel, get the back-up disk and clear off. I swung the Previa around in a U-turn, heading for the freeway. We stayed on it until we hit the Beltway.

Blue lights flickered towards us. There must have been ten of them. I wasn't worried. Even if they did ID me they'd have to get across the central reservation.

It took us just under an hour to get to the Economy Inn. We drove straight into the car park and I told Kelly to wait where she was. If she did hear me, there was no reaction. I tried again and got a nod.

I went upstairs, got out my pistol and made entry. I pulled the cabinet onto its side, the TV crashing onto the floor, and ripped the disk away from the tape. If Luther and co were connected with PIRA, they must know I had a disk – they had to assume it anyway. Retrieving the black bag, I went into the bathroom and threw two hand towels into the bath and ran the water. While that was happening I got the plastic laundry bag from the drawer. I put in the wet towels and some soap. I walked out of the room and kept the Do Not Disturb sign on the handle.

Kelly was still curled up on the back seat. We drove straight down the road to the Marriott.

30

I parked up alongside a line of cars and pick-up trucks and moved round to the back to dig out the towels. The moment I opened the door Kelly ambushed me, throwing her arms around my neck and clinging on hard. Her whole body was shaking.

I lifted her head off my shoulder. Blood from the boy I'd head-jobbed had gone over my jacket, and now some of it was on her face, too, mixing with her tears. I whispered in her ear, 'It's OK now, Kelly, really it is. It's all over.'

She held on even harder. Her tears were warm and wet on my neck.

I said, 'I've got to go and get another car, so I want you to stay here. I won't be long.'

I started to lift her away from me to put her back on the seat, but she resisted, burying her face in my shoulder. I could feel the heat of her breath through the material of my jacket.

I put my hand on the back of her head and rocked gently. For a moment I didn't know who was clinging to whom. The idea of what was happening and who might be behind it scared me shit-less. I had to confirm with Kelly what Luther had said, and now was as bad a time as any. 'Kelly, do you know Luther? Was it true what he said about him coming to pick up Daddy?'

I felt her head nod slowly against my shoulder.

'I'll never leave you alone again, Kelly. Let's just clean our-selves up a bit, shall we?'

I tried to sound happy as I used one of the wet hand towels to wipe her face. 'If you're going to come with me I'd better give you a really important job. I want you to look after the bag while I go and get a car, OK?'

'OK.'

As she dried herself I checked the wallets. Just over $200 in all.

The car park surrounded the whole hotel and was lit only by borrowed light from the street. The area dividers that made it easier for people to find their cars were waist-high bushes and shrubs, with small trees around the main perimeter. There was plenty of shadow.

I positioned Kelly in a clump of shrubbery with the bag. 'Stay hiding until I stop the car and get out to fetch the bag, OK?'

'Will I be able to see you?' she whispered as she put up her hood. Her coat was already wet from the leaves. 'I want to see you.'

I had my eye on a family Dodge in the long lines of cars. I said, 'See that big blue car over there? That's the one I'm going to pick up.' I didn't actually want to tell her I was going to steal it, which seemed mad after what had just happened.

It took about five minutes to break in, but the vehicle started first time. I put the windscreen wipers and demister on full, wiping the inside of the screen with my sleeve. I reversed back to the bushes, stopped and got out. She climbed into the front with a big smile and we started driving off. I stopped. 'Seat belt!'

She put it on.

We headed south on I-95. About 20 miles before the Lorton exit we came across temporary traffic signs warning us that the junction was closed off. As we crossed the bridge I looked down to my right and got a bird's eye view of the shooting. Police cars were dotted all over the area, red and blue lights flashing. I didn't slow down with the rest of the traffic to take a closer look.

The fuel gauge showed three-quarters full, so we'd be able to gain a decent distance before refuelling. I turned on the radio, surfing the channels to find some news.

There was quite a lot of traffic, which was good because it made us just one of many, but the highway itself was mesmerizingly boring. The only variant was that sometimes it was two lanes, then three, then back to two. At least it had stopped raining.

After 100 miles or so I was knackered and my eyes were starting to sting. I stopped for fuel just over the Virginia/North Carolina border and carried on south. Kelly was asleep in the back.

By 1 a.m. we had travelled about 170 miles, but at least the speed limit was higher, up from 60 m.p.h. to 70. I kept seeing large billboards featuring a cartoon of a Mexican, advertising a place called South of the Border. That would be our next stop – in 200 miles' time.

We crossed the South Carolina border at about 5 a.m. South of the Border was just a mile or two further down the road and turned out to be a mixture of a service area and funfair. It was probably a great hit with families going to and from the beaches of North and South Carolina, covering a huge area and including beachwear shops, grocery stores, drugstores, even a bar with dancing. It looked as if it was still open, going by the number of cars parked outside.

I started to refuel. The weather was only a little bit warmer than in DC, but I could hear crickets; I definitely knew I was going south. I was still standing there watching the numbers spin on the pump when a brand-new four-wheel-drive Cherokee rolled onto the forecourt. Rap music blasted out as the doors opened. Inside were four white kids of college age, two boys and two girls.

Kelly had already been woken by the strong white light under the filling station's canopy and now took an interest in the mobile disco. I motioned with my hand through the window to ask her if she wanted a drink. She nodded, rubbing her eyes.

I went inside, picked up some drinks and sandwiches, and went up to the pay desk. The cashier, a black guy in his late fifties, started totalling up my stuff.

The two girls came in, followed by one of the boys. Both girls had dyed-blond, shoulder-length hair. The lad was skinny, spotty, and had a bum-fluff goatee beard.

The cashier winked and said quietly, 'Love is blind.' I smiled in agreement.

The girls were talking to each other and their noise was louder than the music system's. Maybe they'd blown their eardrums. I looked outside at the other boy filling up. All were in the same uniform: baggy T-shirts and shorts. They looked as if they'd been to the beach. You could tell they had money, Daddy's money.

They lined up behind me. One of the girls was going to pay. 'That was a most totally cool day,' she shouted. I was meeting a real-life member of the cast of *Clueless*. By the sound of the conversation, their parents were total arseholes who never gave them enough money, even though they were loaded and could easily afford it.

The black guy gave me my change and leaned over to me. 'Maybe getting a job would help!' His eyes twinkled.

I smiled back and started to pick up my stuff from the counter. The girl came level with me to pay and opened up her purse. Clueless Two, still behind me with the boy, was pissed off with the cashier's comment and with me for agreeing. 'Look at that face, guys!' she stage-whispered behind my back. 'What's bitten you, mister?' The lad guffawed.

Daddy was very generous by the look of it, no matter what she said. I saw a wad of cash and enough cards for a hand of whist. The others behind me were holding the beers they'd got from the fridge and giggling. I left.

Our vehicles were facing each other on the forecourt. Sitting in the front of the Cherokee was the fourth member of the group, who'd finished filling up and was now air-drumming along to whatever the shit was on the CD.

Kelly was lying on the back seat. I went over to her window, hiding just below it, then tapped. Kelly sat up, startled, and I held up her Coke.

The other three were now coming out of the shop. Clueless Two was still pissed off. As they got in their car I heard one of the girls shriek, 'Fucking asshole.' 'Is that the black asshole or the white asshole?' her friend replied, and they closed the doors to gales of laughter.

I got into the Dodge and drove over to the air point. The story was now being told to the driver and I could see them all getting worked up about it. The boys had to show how hard they were and the girls didn't like being shown up in front of their beaus. There was a lot of chemistry driving out of the garage.

As the Cherokee rolled off the forecourt it caught me in its headlights, chatting away with Kelly as I checked the tyres. They slowed right down and looked at us. Clueless One must have made a funny about my appearance, because they all laughed and the driver gave me the finger to make himself look good and then zoomed off into the night.

I gave it about a minute, backed out and followed.

I didn't want to do it on the highway unless I had to. Sooner or later, I guessed, they'd turn off the main drag so they could drink those beers out of sight of highway cops and maybe spread a couple of blankets on the ground.

After just 5 miles we followed the big jeep onto a potholed tarmac road that seemed to go through the middle of nowhere.

'Kelly, see that car ahead? I have to stop and ask them something. I want you to stay in the car, OK?'

'OK.' She was more interested in the Coke.

I didn't want to force them off the road or anything drastic. It had to look natural in case another car drove past.

We passed a roadside shop that was closed, then a large truck park, then a trailer- home site and a big stretch of dark nothingness, then an isolated house. I was beginning to think I'd fucked up when at last it happened. I saw a stop sign 400 yards ahead; accelerating, I got a bit closer and checked for other car lights.

I drove up level on their left-hand side. Bipping my horn, I waved at them with the map book and gave a big smile. They all looked over and, as I turned the interior light on, they saw first me, then Kelly in the back half asleep. They looked worried, then obviously recognized me as the white asshole. Funnies were exchanged and their beer cans came back up to their mouths from their hiding places.

I got out. The crickets were louder out here than at the filling station. I kept looking at them, smiling. The map book was for Washington, DC, but they weren't to know that, and by the time they did it would be too late.

The driver was making a comment to the rest, probably joking about driving off as soon as I got to the door.

I said, 'Hiya! Can you help me? I'm trying to get to Raleigh,' which was a place I'd seen signposted on the freeway, way back in North Carolina.

As the electric window rolled down further I could hear whispered giggles from the back seat for the driver to fuck me off. I could see he had other ideas, maybe to send me anywhere but Raleigh. 'Sure, man, I'll show you.'

I put the map book through the open window and into his hands. 'I don't know how I got lost. I must have taken the wrong turning after I got some gas.'

He didn't need the map book. He started to give directions, pointing down the road. 'Hey, man, just turn left and go for about twenty miles until you see . . .' The girls were liking this one, working hard to stifle their sniggers.

I got hold of his head with my left hand, pulled my pistol up, and stuck it into the young flesh of his cheek.

'Oh shit, he's got a gun, he's got a gun!'

The other three fell silent, but the driver's mouth went into freewheel. 'I'm sorry, man, it was a joke, just a joke. We're drunk, man. It's the bitch in the back who started it, I've got nothing against you, man.'

I couldn't even be bothered to answer him. I shouted into the back, 'Throw your purses out! Now!'

My American accent was quite good, I thought. I just hoped I was looking scary enough. The girls passed over their handbags. By now the driver was trembling and quiet tears rolled down his cheeks. The girls cuddled each other.

I looked at the front passenger. 'You.'

He looked at me as if he was one of a hundred I could be talking to. 'Yes, you. Give me your money, out of this window.' It took all of two seconds for him to comply.

Now it was the driver's turn, and he beat his pal's record. I reached in, took the keys and put them in my pocket. He didn't look too clever now. I had another look around for lights. All clear. The pistol was still against his skin. I said quietly into his ear, 'I'm going to kill you now.'

Everyone else heard it and wanted nothing to do with him. I said, 'Say whatever prayer you need to say and be quick.'

He didn't pray, he begged. 'Please don't kill me, man, please don't.'

I looked down and saw that his shorts, made of grey sweatshirt material, were rather darker now. Daddy would not be impressed with the stains on his nice beige leather.

I was quite enjoying it, but knew I had to get going. I stepped back and picked everything off the road. I glanced at Clueless Two. She looked like she'd swallowed a wasp. 'What's bitten you?' I said.

I got in the car, did a 180, and drove off.

Kelly said, 'Why did you make those people give you their things?' She sounded confused.

'Because we need loads of money, and we're much nicer than they are, so they wanted us to have it.'

I looked at her in the rear-view mirror. She knew damned well I was lying.

281

I said, 'You want a job?'

'What?'

'Count this money.'

She opened up the bags and wallets and piled all the notes in her lap.

'More than a million dollars,' she said at length.

'Maybe count it once more to check.'

Five minutes later I got the more realistic figure of $336. The *Clueless* girls were wrong. Daddy was a diamond.

We started seeing signs for Florence. That would do me fine. The town was 60 miles away, and it was about five twenty in the morning. It would be getting light by sevenish and, if possible, I wanted to be in a town before dawn. I'd dump the Dodge, and we'd have to find some other transport. Whatever, we needed to get to Florida.

About 10 miles short, I saw a sign for a lay-by picnic area with toilets and an information kiosk. I pulled in and took a free map of the town and surrounding area. Kelly was semi-awake as we parked up. I opened the door and got out. The birds were singing and I could just make out the pre-dawn. There was a little nip in the air, but you could tell it was going to be a nice warm day. It felt great to have a stretch; I stank of sweat and had a layer of grease on my skin; my eyes were stinging and no doubt were bloodshot and swollen from lack of sleep. The pain in my neck still made me walk as if I had a plank of wood strapped to my back.

The map showed a train station in the town; not necessarily helpful, but it was a start. I got back into the car and started to get the bags and wallets together to dump. All were expensive leather. A couple were even monogrammed. Inside one of them I found heroin and a lump of pot in tin foil. The spoiled brats had obviously been Easter 'breakers', college kids using up all their hormones before the next term. Mummy and Daddy worked their arses off and provided for these kids and they thought the world owed them a living. Fuck 'em, I was glad I'd robbed them. I laughed; there was a good chance they'd be too embarrassed even to report it. They were probably still sitting there blaming each other and trying to think of a way of getting piss stains off leather upholstery. I dumped everything in the bins.

We drove towards the station. It looked as if the town centre was terminally ill but big efforts had been made to keep the patient alive; the old historical centre had been rejuvenated, but it seemed that every shop sold scented candles, guest soap and pot pourri. There was nothing there for real people, no life in it at all.

We got to the station, and it could have been any station in any American town, full of the homeless who stayed there because it was warm. It reeked of bodies and decay. Drunks were sprawled on benches that nobody in their right mind would go near in case they got their head bitten off.

I looked at the destination boards. It seemed we could get to De Land by train, with a bus transfer to Daytona. It was just before 6 a.m.; the train would be arriving at seven.

The ticket office was already open and looked as if it had been modelled on a Korean 7-Eleven, wire mesh everywhere, painted white but chipped. I could just about see the large black face behind it that was demanding to know where I wanted to go.

An hour later we got on the train, found our seats and collapsed. Our carriage was no more than half full. Kelly cuddled into me, dog-tired.

'Nick?'

'What?'

I was busy looking at the other passengers. They all looked like me, frazzled grown-ups looking after kids.

'Where are we going?'

'To see a friend.'

'Who's that?' She sounded happy at the idea. Probably she was fed up with my company.

'He lives near the beach. His name is Frankie.'

283

'Are we going on vacation with him?'

'No, Frankie's not that kind of friend.'

I decided to keep the conversation going as she would be asleep in no time at all. The rhythmic sounds and motion of the train would soon send her off.

'Who is your best friend? Is it Melissa?'

'Yes. We tell each other things that we promise not to tell any-one else.' After declaring her undying love for Melissa she started to tell me all her bad points, which mostly involved her playing with a girl Kelly didn't like.

'Who is your best friend, Nick?'

That was easy, but I wasn't going to say his name. If we were lifted again, I would hate it if he was mentioned and put in danger. The sun was starting to burn through the windows; I leaned across her and pulled down the blind.

'My best friend is called . . . David.' It was about as far away from Euan as I could think of. 'Just like you and Melissa, we tell each other things that no-one else knows. In fact, he has a daughter who's just a little bit older than you. No-one else knows about her apart from David and me – and now you!'

There was no reply. It seemed she was starting to doze off. I carried on anyway, I didn't know why. 'We've known each other since we were seventeen and we've been friends ever since.' I started to stroke her hair. I was going to talk more, but found it really hard to tell her. I couldn't put it into words. Euan and I were just there for each other and always had been. That was it really. I just didn't have the tools to describe it.

31

Frank de Sabatino had been crossed off the Christmas-card list of LCN – La Cosa Nostra – in Miami and, for his own protection, had been sent over to the UK on a Federal witness protection scheme. I had been one of the team tasked with looking after him for the three months he spent in Abergavenny before returning to the US. I remembered Frankie as about 5 feet 5 inches and seedy; he had very black, tight, curly hair, which looked as if it had been permed in the style of a 1980s football player. The rest of him looked like the football itself.

The FBI had been investigating LCN in south Florida – they don't use the word Mafia – and had discovered that de Sabatino, a thirty-four-year-old computer nerd who worked for one of the major players, had been skimming off hundreds of thousands of dollars from their drug operations. The government agents coerced de Sabatino into gathering evidence for their prosecution; he had no choice because otherwise he would have been arrested and LCN told what he'd been up to. LCN members in prison would have done the rest. Pat had had a good relationship with him during the job, and we'd later joked that maybe that was why he'd got out straight afterwards. I now knew that Pat had liked to sample the goods a bit too much.

Frankie's clothing had been anything but low profile; to him, subdued meant a pale orange shirt with purple trousers and alligator-skin cowboy boots. Whatever he was wearing, his fat would push up against his shirt. It didn't take much imagination to see him as a bit of a pervie. The last I'd heard of him, he'd been given a new identity after the trial and, very surprisingly, had voted to stay in the United States – and, even more weird, in Florida. Maybe the shirt selection wasn't so good elsewhere.

I'd thought again about calling Euan, but what could he do for me at the moment? I decided against; better not use up all my resources at once. Frankie would help decrypt the PIRA stuff, then Euan could help me once I was back in the UK.

We got to De Land station just before 2 p.m. and the transfer bus was waiting to take us to the coast. After so many hours of air-conditioning on the train, the heat of the Florida afternoon hit us as if I'd opened the door of a blast furnace. Both of us were blinking like bats under the clear, oppressive sky, surrounded by people with tans and summer clothes. The electronic information scroll at the station told us it was 78 degrees. We boarded the hot bus, sat down and waited for the PVC to stick to our backs as we chugged along the highway to Daytona bus depot.

It was an uneventful trip. Occasionally from behind us would come the sound of rolling thunder, and a blur of chrome, leather and sawn-off denim would flash past with the distinctive, explosive bubbling gurgle of a Harley-Davidson. I'd forgotten Daytona was a Mecca for bikers. From the bus window, the roadside diners looked black with them.

Two hours later we trundled across the bridge over the inland waterway into downtown Daytona. We prised ourselves off the seats and I reclaimed our bag. The first thing I did was buy us two freshly squeezed orange juices. As we walked from the shelter of the bus depot, I could feel the sunlight burning through my shirt.

At the taxi rank I asked the driver to take us to an ordinary hotel.

'What kind of ordinary?' he asked.

'The cheap sort.'

286

The driver was Latino. Gloria Estefan blasted out of the cassette player, he had a little statue of the Virgin Mary on the dashboard, a picture of his kids hanging off the mirror, and he was wearing a big, loud, flowery shirt de Sabatino would have died for. I wound down my window and let the breeze hit my face. We turned onto Atlantic Avenue and I found myself staring at a massive white ribbon of hard-packed sand that stretched to infinity. We drove past diners, beachwear and biker shops, Chinese restaurants, oyster houses, 7-Elevens, parking lots, tacky hotels, then yet more diners and beachwear shops.

This whole place was built for holidays. Everywhere I turned I saw hotels with brightly coloured murals. Nearly all had signs that said 'Breakers welcome'. There was even a cheerleaders' convention going on; I could see scores of girls in skimpy outfits strutting their stuff on a playing field outside the convention centre. Maybe Frankie was there, sitting in a corner, ogling.

'Are we there yet?' Kelly asked.

The driver said, 'Two blocks more on the left.'

I saw all the usual chain hotels, and then ours – the Castaway Hotel.

Standing on the sidewalk outside, listening to Gloria's singing disappearing into the distance, I looked at Kelly and said, 'Yeah, I know – crap.'

She grinned. 'Triple-decker crap with cheese.'

Maybe, but it looked perfect for us. What was more, it was only $24 a night, though I could already tell from the outside that we'd only get $24 worth.

I came out with the same old story, plus us being determined still to have our Disney holiday. I didn't think the woman at the desk believed a word I was saying, but she just didn't care, so long as I gave her the cash that went into the front pocket of her dirty black jeans.

The landing our room was on was filled with boys who didn't look college material on vacation. Maybe they were in town because they'd heard about the cheerleaders.

Our room was a small box with a pane of glass in one wall. The floor had a layer of dust that it would have been a shame to clean, and the heat bouncing off the breeze-block made it feel like the black hole of Calcutta.

'Once the air-conditioning is on it'll be OK,' I said.

'What air-conditioning?' Kelly asked, looking at the bare walls.

She flopped onto the bed and I could have sworn I heard a thousand bedbugs scream. 'Can we go to the beach?'

I was thinking the same, but the first priority, as ever, was the kit.

'We'll go out soon. Do you want to help me sort everything out first?'

She seemed happy at the suggestion. I gave her the .45 magazines from the Lorton turn-off shooting. 'Can you take the bullets out and put them in there?' I pointed to the side pocket of the bag. The mags didn't fit into my Sig but the rounds were the same.

'Sure.' She looked really pleased.

I didn't show her how to do it because I wanted to keep her busy. I hid the back-up disk inside the bed, using one of the screwdrivers to rip the lining. Then I got the washing kit out and had a shower and a shave. The scabs were a dark colour now and hard. I got dressed in my new jeans and grey T-shirt. Then I got Kelly cleaned up too.

It was four forty-five. She was still getting dressed in black trousers and a green sweatshirt as I leaned over to the cabinet between the two beds and pulled out the telephone book.

'What's this when it's at home?' I pointed a thumb at the TV.

'*The Big Bad Beetleborgs.*'

'The who?'

She started to explain, but I wasn't really listening; I just nodded and agreed and read the phone book.

I was looking for the surname De Niro. It was a crazy name for him to have chosen, but I remembered that was what he'd renamed himself: Al De Niro. For somebody who was supposed to spend his life in low profile it wasn't exactly the most secure, but he was Al and Bob's biggest fan. The only reason he'd got involved in the drug scene in the first place was that he'd seen Al Pacino in *Scarface*. His whole life had been a fantasy. He knew all the dialogue from their films, he'd even entertained us in Abergavenny with passable impressions. Sad, but true.

Needless to say, there was no listing under A. De Niro. I tried directory enquiries. They couldn't help, either. The next step would be to start phoning all around the State or to get a private eye on to it with some story, but that was going to take a lot of time and money.

I got up and walked over to the curtains, scratching my arse until I realized Kelly was watching, and pulled them back. We were two bats in the bat cave again, exposed to the deadly sunlight. Craning my neck round to the left I could just about see the ocean view I'd paid an extra $5 for. People were strewn all over the beach; there was a young couple who couldn't keep their hands off each other, and families, some with tans and others like us, the lily-white ones, who looked like uncooked chips. Maybe they'd come on the same train.

The boys from the room three along had obviously finished wiring in the sound system from hell because heavy bass music began banging through the walls. I could picture the dust dancing. They came onto the landing; all four of them had loud vests on and shorts that went down to their knees. They looked drunk and were putting cream on their new, still scabby, tribal armband tattoos.

I turned to Kelly. She was happy enough that the Beetleborgs had saved the world again, but looked bored. 'What are we going to do now?' she said.

'I've got to find my friend, but I'm not sure where he lives. I'm just thinking about how to go about it.'

'The computer geek you told me about?'

I nodded.

All very nonchalant, she said, 'Why don't you try the Net?' She wasn't even looking at me; she was now back to watching the shit on the TV. Of course – the bloke is a computer freak; there's no way he's not going to be on the Internet, probably surfing the porn pages for pictures of naked teenagers. It was as good a starting point as any. Better than my private-eye idea anyway.

I walked over to the bag. 'You can use the Net, can you?'

'Of course. We do it at pre-school.'

'Pre-school?'

'Where you go before school starts so parents can go to work. And we use the Net every morning; they teach us how to use it.'

I started to get the laptop out, feeling quite excited about this girl's genius. The grunge brigade outside were now shouting stuff from the landing. It was hormone time.

I suddenly realized that, even if there was an internal modem and Internet software on the laptop, it would be no good to me. I didn't have any credit cards I could use to register with and I couldn't use the stolen ones because they'd need a billing address. I put the laptop on the bed.

'Good idea,' I said, 'but I can't do it on this machine.'

Still looking at the TV, she was now drinking a warm Minute Maid that had been in the bag, using both hands on the carton so she didn't have to tilt her head and miss anything. She said, 'We'll just go to a cyber café – when Melissa's house didn't have a telephone for weeks, her mommy used to go to the cyber café for her e-mail.'

'Oh, did she?'

Cybercino was a coffee shop with croissants, sticky buns and sandwiches, with the addition of office dividers to create small cubicles. In each was a PC with a little recess for food and drink. Pinned on the dividers were notices about session times, how to log on, and little business cards advertising various sites.

I bought coffee, Danish pastries and Coke and tried to log on. In the end I handed the controls to a more skilled pilot. Kelly zoomed off into cyberspace as if it was her own backyard.

'Is he AOL, msn, CompuServe or what?' she demanded.

I didn't have a clue.

She shrugged. 'We'll use a search engine.'

Less than a minute later we were visiting a site called InfoSpace. She hit the e-mail icon and a dialogue box appeared.

'Surname?'

I spelled out De Niro.

'First name?'

'Al.'

'City?'

'Better leave that blank. Just put Florida. He might have moved.'

She hit Search and, moments later, up came his e-mail address. I couldn't believe it. There was even a Send Mail icon, which she hit.

I sent him a message saying I wanted to contact Al De Niro – or anyone who was a Pacino/De Niro fan and knew 'Nicky Two' from the UK. That was the nickname de Sabatino had given me. There were three Nicks on the team. I was the second one he'd come into contact with. When we met he would do his Godfather thing, holding out his arms, saying, 'Heyyy, Nicky Two,' as he gave me a kiss and a hug. Thankfully he did that to everyone.

The café would open the next day at 10 a.m. Our session fee included the use of the Cybercino address, so I signed off by saying that I would log on at ten fifteen tomorrow to retrieve any messages. The risk was small that his e-mail was being monitored and somebody could make a connection between me and 'Nicky Two'.

By now I was hungry and so was Kelly, and for more than sticky buns. We walked back towards the main strip and stopped at our favourite restaurant. We ordered to go and ate our Big Macs on the walk back. The temperature was still in the 70s, even at this time of the evening.

'Can't we play minigolf?' Kelly said. She pointed to what looked like a cross between Disneyland and Gleneagles, with trees, waterfalls and a pirate ship, all made to look like a floodlit Treasure Island.

I actually enjoyed it. There was no danger and the pressure release was tremendous, even if Kelly was cheating. She started to putt on the 11th hole. A dragon behind us was blowing out water rather than fire from its cave.

'Nick?'

'What?' I was busy working out how to negotiate the 90-degree angle I needed to hole the ball.

'Will we see your friend, you know – David?'

'Maybe some day.' I putted and it didn't work. I was stuck on the water obstacle.

'Have you got any sisters or brothers?'

It felt like Twenty Questions. 'Yes, I have.'

'How many?'

I marked my card after six attempts on a par 3 hole.

'Three brothers.' I decided to cut the interrogation. 'They are called . . . John, Joe and Jim.'

'Oh. How old are they?'

She got me on that one. I didn't even know where they lived, let alone how old they were. 'I don't know really.'

'Why not?'

I found it hard to explain because I didn't really know the answer.

'Because.' I positioned the ball for her to putt. 'Come on, or we'll hold everyone up.'

On the way back I felt strangely close to her and that worried me. She seemed to have latched on to me as a stand-in parent and we'd only been together six days. I couldn't take the place of Kev and Marsha, even if I wanted to. The prospect was too scary.

It was ice cream for breakfast, then we logged on at ten fifteen. There was a message waiting for us, telling us to visit a chat room. Kelly hit a few keys and there we were. De Sabatino was waiting for us; or at least someone called Big Al was. A dialogue box invited us to a private room for a one-on-one; thank goodness Kelly was there to do the navigating.

I got straight down to it. Kelly typed, 'I need your help.'

'What do you want?'

'I've got something here that I need you to decode or translate – I'm not entirely sure what it is, but I know you'll be able to do it.'

'What is it? Work?'

I needed to get him hooked. For him, half the point of nicking all that money had been the sheer kick of doing it – the 'juice'. Thinking about it now, Pat had probably got the term from Big Al in the first place. This guy enjoyed getting one over on the big boys; he needed to be involved, to be part of something, and I knew that, if I used the right bait, he'd come and see me.

I spoke and she typed, 'I'm not going to tell you! Believe me, it's good. If you want to look, you'll have to see me. I'm in Daytona.' And then I started to lie. 'Other people say it's impossible. I thought of you.'

I'd got him. Straight away he came back. 'What format?'

I told him all the details.

He said, 'Can't see you until 9 p.m. tonight. Outside Boot Hill Saloon, Main Street.'

'I'll be there.'

Big Al came back. 'Yeehah! Yeehah!'

There was fuck all changed about him, then. Kelly logged off and we paid the $12. About a hundredth of what a private eye would have cost me.

Now we had hours to kill. We bought sunglasses, and I also got Kelly a fashionable pair of shorts, a T-shirt and sandals. I had to stay as I was, wearing my shirt over my trousers to cover my pistol. The only addition was a bandana to cover the cut on my forehead. Chrome aviators covered the lower one.

With the wind on our faces, we mooched along the beach. It was that time of day when the restaurants were starting to fill up with people wanting early lunches.

Back at the hotel I made some calls to check flights out of the country. If the stuff Big Al decrypted for me seemed to be what Simmonds wanted, Kelly and I were out of here. I knew Big Al would have the contacts and resources to get passports for our exit, even money. Then it was lunch, followed by eighteen holes with the pirates – I let her win – and then it was time to start getting ready for the meet.

At about seven thirty the sun started to go down and the street neon came on. Suddenly it was another world, with music pumping out of the shops and the kids now driving faster up and down the strip than the legal 10 m.p.h.

I didn't know what it was, the weather maybe, but I felt detached from the situation I was in. It was just the two of us; we were having fun, eating ice creams and walking around looking in shops. She was doing normal kid things, even to the point of looking at something in a shop window and giving it the 'Look at that!' act, as in, hint, hint, are you going to buy it for me? I found myself acting the parent, saying, 'No, I think we've had enough today.'

I did worry about her. I felt she should be more upset, shouldn't really be taking it so well. Maybe she hadn't understood what I'd said to her about her family; maybe her subconscious was putting a lid on it. At the moment, however, that was exactly what I needed: a child looking and behaving normally.

We stopped outside a toy shop. She asked for a ring in the window that glowed in the dark. I lied and said I had no money left.

'Can't you steal it for me?' she said.

We had a serious talk about right and wrong. She was getting along too well with this on-the-run thing.

It was round about a quarter to nine by now; we'd had a pizza and, at that time of night on holiday, the next thing you should always have is Häagen Dazs. Afterwards, we started to wander to the RV with Big Al. We squeezed past ranks of parked motorcycles and jostling crowds, most wearing T-shirts with bike slogans.

I got us into a position from where I could see both approaches to the Boot Hill Saloon, in the old graveyard on the other side of the road. It was all that remained of the original town that was there in the 1920s, the only thing that couldn't be ripped apart and have a hotel built on it. As bikers parked up and opened the doors, loud rock and roll thundered from the bar. It collided head-on with the Latin and rap that were blaring from the vehicles cruising up and down; it was that body-fluid time of night, and groups of breakers were hanging out of Jeeps and pick-ups with banks of six or seven speakers in the back. Some even had electric-blue lights fitted under the car; as they drove past they looked like hovering spaceships playing music from Mars. I thought about our friends in the Cherokee. I wondered if they'd got home yet.

Kelly and I just waited, eating our ice creams and sitting on a bank next to Mrs J. Mostyn, who went to Our Saviour on 16 July 1924, God rest her soul.

32

Main Street wasn't in fact the main drag but a road that led from the sea to a bridge over the inland waterway. Daytona has a bike week each year and this was the street on which the thousands of bikers descended. It was a one-theme street, and that theme was Harleys. If it wasn't a bike bar, it seemed to be a shop selling spare parts, helmets or leathers. And, even when the convention wasn't on, bikes with helmets on the seats were lined up by the dozen outside bars with names like the Boot Hill Saloon, Dirty Harry's, or Froggie's, where there was even a bike made of dusty bones in the window.

I could spot Big Al a mile off as he shambled towards us from the direction of the bridge. He was wearing a blue, white and yellow Hawaiian shirt and pale-pink trousers, both straining against a body that was even fatter than I remembered it; his outfit was set off by white shoes and the same shaggy hairstyle, looking like an out-of-work extra from *Miami Vice*. In his left hand he carried a briefcase, which was a good sign; he'd brought with him the tools of his trade. I watched him duck into the Main Street Cigar Store and emerge chomping on a huge corona.

He stopped outside the saloon, Harleys all around him. He put down his briefcase between his feet and stood there sucking his cigar as if he owned the place. Behind him was an enormous mural of a biker on the beach, which covered one entire wall of the saloon. A board announced, 'No Colors, Club Patches or Insignias'.

I nudged Kelly. 'See that man over there?'

'Which one?'

'The one with that really big flowery shirt on, the big fat man.'

'You mean the geekazoid?'

'What?'

'Next one up from geek.'

'Whatever,' I grinned. 'He's the man we're going to see.'

A Metro bus passed between us. Splashed along its side was an ad for SeaWorld, showing a giant orca leaping out of the pool. Kelly and I looked at the bus, then at each other, and burst out laughing.

She said, 'Why didn't we wait over there for him?'

'No, no, what you do is stand off and watch. See what I'm doing? I'm looking up and down the road, just to make sure there's no bad guys following him. Then I know we're safe. What do you think? Reckon it's OK?'

Suddenly she'd become all-important. She looked up and down and said, 'All clear.' She didn't have a clue what she was looking for.

'Come on, then, give me your hand. We've got to be careful with these cars driving so fast.'

We left Mrs Mostyn and stopped at the edge of the kerb. I said, 'When we go and meet him, I might have to do stuff that looks horrible, but actually it's not – it's stuff that we do all the time; he understands it.'

As we dodged through the traffic she said, 'OK.' After what she had been seeing lately this would be kindergarten stuff.

We got closer and he was certainly looking older. He recognized me from 20 yards away and was suddenly starring in *The Godfather* again. Cigar into his right hand, arms thrown out wide, head cocked to one side, he growled, 'Aaaggghh! It's Nicky Two!' He had a smile on his face the size of half a watermelon; it was probably shit living in hiding, and at last he had somebody from the past he could talk freely with.

He jammed the cigar back into his mouth, picked up his brief-case in his right hand and walked towards us, his fat thighs rubbing together. 'Hey! how's it going?' he beamed and started pumping my hand, at the same time studying Kelly. He stank of flowery aftershave.

'And who's this pretty little lady, then?' He bent down to greet her and I felt a slight twinge of wariness. Maybe the charm was genuine, but for some reason it made me feel a bit revolted.

I said, 'This is Kelly, she's one of my friend's daughters and I'm looking after her for a while.'

I very much doubted he knew what had been going on up North. He certainly didn't know Kev.

Still bending down and shaking her hand for a bit too long, he said, 'It's great here – we've got SeaWorld, Disney World, every-thing to make a little lady happy. This is the Sunshine State!'

He stood up and said, slightly out of breath, 'Where are we going?' He pointed hopefully and said, 'Main Street Pier? Shrimp?'

I shook my head. 'No, we'll go back to the hotel. I've got all the stuff there I want you to have a look at. Follow me.'

I held Kelly's hand in my left and got him on the right. As we walked we made small talk about how wonderful it was to see each other again, but he knew very well that this meeting wasn't casual – and he liked it. He got off on this sort of stuff, just like Al and Bob.

We turned right and took the first turning left, which was into a parking area behind the shops. I looked at Kelly and nodded to show everything was fine, then let go of her hand. Big Al was still jabbering away. I grabbed his left arm with both hands and used his own momentum to turn him against the wall. He hit it with quite a bounce. I pushed him into the doorway of a restaurant's fire exit.

'It's cool, I'm cool.' Big Al was keeping a low voice. He knew the score.

Just looking at him it was obvious he couldn't conceal so much as a playing card under his clothes, let alone a weapon, the material was stretched so tight against his skin. However, I ran my hand down the back of his spine in case he had something concealed in the lumbar region; the natural curve makes it a wonderful place to hide odds and ends, and Big Al's was curvier than most. I carried on screening him.

He looked down at Kelly, who was watching everything. He winked. 'I suppose you've seen him do this lots of times?'

'My daddy does it as well, in heaven.'

'Ah, OK, yeah, smart kid, smart kid.' He looked at her and tried to work that one out.

Then came the bit that he probably enjoyed most – me running my hand up his trouser legs. I checked thoroughly at the top. I said, 'You know I need to look in your briefcase now, don't you?'

'Yeah, sure.' He opened it up; I found two cigars in tubes and all his work bits and pieces – floppy disks, a back-up drive and disks, leads, wires, all sorts of shit. I had a quick feel around to make sure there wasn't a secret panel.

I was happy. He was also. In fact, he probably had a hard-on.

I said, 'Right, let's go.'

'Let's get some ice cream on the way,' he suggested.

We waved down a cab. Kelly and I got in the back and he squeezed into the front, resting a two-pint tub of Ben & Jerry's on his briefcase.

We got to the hotel and went to the room. His body language was excited, probably because he thought it was like the old days, all spies and sneaky-beaky, and the cheapness of the room only made it all the more exhilarating for him. He put his briefcase on one of the beds, opened it up and started taking out all his gizmos. He fished, 'So what do you get up to these days?'

I didn't reply.

Kelly and I were sitting on the bed, not really doing much except watch what was going on. Kelly started to take quite an interest.

'You got any games?' she said.

I thought de Sabatino would look at her in disgust: I'm a technician, I don't have games. But he went, 'Yeah, loads! Maybe, if we get time, we can sit down and play a few. What ones do you like?'

They went off at a tangent about Quake and Third Dimension. I cut in and said, 'So what do you do with yourself nowadays? What do you get up to?'

'I just teach people how to work these things.' He pointed at the laptop. 'Also I do a bit of work for a couple of private eyes down here, getting into bank accounts, that sort of thing. Pretty low-key stuff but it's all right – I have to keep my head down.'

Almost choking on Kouros and looking at his choice of clothes, I hated to think what his idea of high profile would be.

Not having got a reply to his original question, he seemed to feel compelled to fill the silence. He started sniggering and said, 'Still managed to tuck away a few hundred thou! So, plus the resettlement, things ain't too bad.'

He was fiddling about, attaching bits and pieces to the laptop. I let him get on with it. He tried again. 'What about you? Same old thing?'

'Yeah, same old sort of stuff. Bits and pieces.'

Now sitting at the table, with his back to me, he was concentrating on what he was doing with the laptop. 'What bits and pieces would those be? You still being a – what did you call it – a baby spy?'

'I do that a bit.'

'You working now, are you?'

'Yeah, I'm working.'

He laughed. 'You lying fucker!' He looked at Kelly and said, 'Oops! Do you do French at school?' He turned back to me and said, 'You wouldn't need me if you were, you'd be getting somebody else to do it. You can't bullshit Big Al!' He looked at Kelly and said, '*Français!*' Then he looked back at me and said, 'You still married?'

The Microsoft sound chimed as Windows 95 opened on his machine.

'Divorced about three years ago,' I said. 'Work and stuff. I haven't heard from her for about two years. I think she's living up in Scotland or somewhere; I don't know.'

I suddenly realized that Kelly was hanging on every word.

He winked at her. 'Just like me – young, free and single! Yeah!' Big Al was one of life's really sad fucks; I was probably the nearest thing he had to a friend.

The heavy bass rap started up along the landing. I could hear the boys singing along flatly, accompanied by female voices. It sounded as if they'd found the cheerleaders.

I handed him the back-up disk and it was soon humming in the drive. It wouldn't be long before I got a few answers. By now there was a pall of cigar smoke filling the top quarter of the room. Between that, the Kouros and the lack of air-conditioning, the room was close to unbearable. It was just as well we'd be moving from here the moment Big Al had left.

I checked outside by moving the curtain, then opened the window. The boys were in full swing, empty beer cans all over the landing, entertaining a group of adoring girls. Maybe Big Al should invest in an armband tattoo and a pair of cut-offs.

The first lot of documents came up onto the screen and I looked over his shoulder as he tapped away in the semi-darkness. I pointed at one of the spreadsheets. 'This is where I've got a problem. I haven't got a clue what that means. Any idea?'

'I'll tell you what we have here.' His eyes never left the screen. 'These are shipment and payment records – of what, I don't know.' As he pointed to the screen his finger touched it and squidged the liquid underneath. 'Never touch the screen!' he scolded himself as if he was telling off one of his students. He was loving it; he was really getting into this.

'See these here?' His voice had changed from that of a no-hoper to that of someone who knew his stuff.

I looked at columns headed by groups of initials like UM, JC,

PJS. He said, 'They refer to shipments. They're telling you what's going where, and to whom.'

He started to scroll down the pages, confirming it to himself. As he was looking through he nodded emphatically. 'These are definitely shipments and payments. How did you get into this anyway? You're not exactly the world's most computer-literate person and there's no way this stuff wasn't passworded.'

'I had a sniffer program.'

'Wow! Which one do you have?' The computer nerd was coming back.

'Mexy Twenty-one,' I lied.

'That's shit! Oops, garbage! There's stuff now that does it at three times the speed.' He looked down at Kelly. 'That's the problem with the Brits; they're still in the steam age.'

He was now out of the spreadsheets and looking at more file names.

I said, 'This is another lot of files I was having problems with. Can you decrypt them?'

'I don't understand,' he said. 'Which files are you having trouble with?'

'Well, they're in code, or something – just a lot of random letters and numbers. Any chance of you sorting it out?' He made me feel like a ten-year-old child having to ask for his shoelaces to be tied.

He scrolled down the file names. 'You mean these GIFs?' he said. 'They're graphics files, that's all. You just need a graphics program to read them.'

He tapped a few keys, found what he was looking for and selected one of the files. 'They're scans of photographs,' he said.

He leaned over and pulled open the tub of ice cream, got one of the plastic spoons and started to tuck in. He threw a spoon to Kelly and said, 'You'd better get in here before Uncle Al finishes it all.'

The first picture was now on the screen. It was a grainy black-and-white of two people standing at the top of a flight of steps that led to a grand old building. I knew both men very well. Seamus Macauley and Liam Fernahan were 'businessmen' who fronted a lot of fund-raising and other operations for PIRA. They were good at the game, once even getting a scheme backed by the British government to finance regeneration in Northern Ireland cities. The whole scheme was designed to provide local employment. It was sold to the government that, if a community was responsible for its own rebuilding, there would be less chance of them then wanting to go and blow it up. But what the government didn't know was that the contractors could only employ people that PIRA wanted to work; those people were still claiming unemployment and social benefits, and PIRA were getting a kickback for letting them work on the sites illegally, so it was costing the government twice over – and, of course, the businessmen got their cut as well. And, if the government were paying, why not blow more up and rebuild?

Without a doubt, PIRA had come a long way from the days of rattling collecting tins in west Belfast, Kilburn and Boston. So much so that the Northern Ireland Office had established a Terrorist Finance Unit as a counter-measure in 1988, staffed by specialists in accountancy, law, tax and computing. Euan and I had done a lot of work with them.

Big Al now opened and viewed a series of shots of Macauley and Fernahan shaking hands with two other men, then walking down the steps and getting into a Merc. One of them was the late Mr Morgan McGear, looking very smart in a suit I recognized. I quickly looked at Kelly, but it was clear his face meant nothing to her. The fourth man I had no idea about. That didn't matter too much at the moment.

The photography was covert: I could see the darkness around the edge of the frames where they hadn't got the aperture right, but it was good enough for me to tell, by the cars parked in the background, that they were in Europe.

I said, 'Let's see the next one.'

De Sabatino knew that I'd recognized something or someone;

he was looking at me, gagging to know what it was, wanting to get in on the act. He'd had five years on the back burner and now was the chance for a comeback.

I was going to tell him jack shit. 'Let's push on.'

There was another group of pictures that he opened and viewed, but these ones meant nothing at all to me.

Big Al looked at them. The big half-watermelon was back on his face. 'I know what all those spreadsheets refer to now.'

'What's that?'

'*Está es la coca, señor!* Hey, I know this guy. He works for the cartels.'

I was looking at an early-forties, really smart-looking Latino getting out of a car. I could tell by the background it was in the United States. 'That's Raoul Martinez,' he said. 'He's part of the Colombian trade delegation.'

This was getting more interesting by the minute. PIRA always claimed no association with drug trafficking, but the profits were too great for them to ignore. What I had in front of me now was close to submissible evidence of their direct involvement with the cartels. But that still didn't help me with my problem.

He looked through the pictures. 'You'll see Raoul with some-body else in a minute, I guarantee it.' He flicked through a couple more. 'There you are – big bad Sal.'

This other character was about the same age but much taller; he'd probably been a weightlifter at some stage, then ballooned out to maybe 16 or 17 stones. Sal was a big old boy, and very bald.

De Sabatino said, 'Martinez is never without him. We used to do a lot of business with them in the old days. A nice man, a family man. We used to run cocaine up the east coast, all the way to the Canadian border. Basically we needed things sorted out to ease the route; these boys did the necessary and everybody was making money. Yeah, these boys, they're all right.'

As we went through viewing more picture files, I saw both men eating in a restaurant with another guy, a caucasian.

Big Al said, 'I haven't got a clue who he is.'

I was looking over de Sabatino's shoulder, concentrating hard on the screen.

Kelly sparked up. 'Nick?'

'In a minute.' I turned my head to Big Al. 'Absolutely no idea?'

'Not a clue.'

'Nick?'

I cut in. 'Not now, Kelly.'

Kelly butted in again. 'Nick, Nick!'

'Go back to the—'

'Nick, Nick! I know who that man is.'

I looked at her. 'Which man?'

'The man in the photograph.' She grinned. 'You said you don't know who he is, but I do.'

'This one?' I pointed at Martinez.

'No, the one before.'

Big Al closed a few more windows, scrolling back. 'Him! That one there!'

It was the white guy who was sitting with Raoul and big bad Sal.

I said, 'You're sure?'

'Yes.'

'Who is he?' After our experience with the video I expected her to nominate anyone from Clint Eastwood to Brad Pitt.

'It's Daddy's boss.'

There was a long, palpable silence as I let it sink in. Big Al was sucking air through his teeth. I said, 'What do you mean, Daddy's boss?'

'He came to our house with a lady once for supper.'

'Do you remember his name?'

'No, I came down for some water and they were eating with Mommy and Daddy. Daddy let me say hello and he said, "Big smile, Kelly, this is my boss!"' It was a good imitation of Kev, and I saw a flicker of sadness in her eyes.

Big Al joined the conversation in nerd mode. 'Whoa! There you go! Who's your daddy, then?'

I swung around. 'Shut up!'

305

I pushed him off his seat and sat down, with Kelly on my knee so she had a better view of the screen. 'Are you definitely sure he's Daddy's boss?'

'Yes, I know it's his boss; Daddy told me. The next day Mommy and me, we made jokes about his moustache because he looked like a cowboy.'

He did, he looked as if he belonged in a Marlboro ad. As she pointed, her finger touched the screen and Daddy's boss was distorted. Having Kelly in my arms and seeing someone who might have been responsible for her father's death made me want to do the same to him in person.

I looked at Big Al. 'Let's go back through all the photos.'

The party along the landing was in full swing. Big Al sat down and scrolled back through the files to the pictures of Macauley and Fernahan with McGear. 'Do you know these people?' Kelly answered my question with a 'No', but I wasn't really listening to her now. I was in my own world. I'd noticed two other cars parked up on the other side of the road. I looked hard at the number plates and then I knew where the pictures had been taken.

'Gibraltar.' I couldn't help mouthing it aloud.

Big Al pointed to Macauley and co. 'Are these terrorists from Ireland?'

'Sort of.'

There was a gap while I tried to work this one out.

Big Al sparked up. 'It's obvious to me what's going on.'

'What's that?'

'I knew the Irish terrorist boys were buying cocaine from the Colombians. It came by the normal route to the Florida Keys, then the Caribbean and North Africa. They then used Gibraltar as the jump-off point for the rest of Europe. They made fortunes, and at the same time we took our cut for letting them move it through South Florida. All of a sudden, though, at the end of '87, it stopped going through Gibraltar.'

'Why was that?' I was finding it hard to stay calm.

Big Al shrugged. 'Some big drama with the locals. I think they now run it from South Africa instead, into the west coast of Spain, something like that. They're linked in with some other terrorists up there.'

'ETA?'

'Search me. Some bunch of terrorists or freedom fighters. Call them what you like, to me they're all just dealers. Anyway, they help the Irish now. No doubt old Raoul sorted things out Stateside with Daddy's boss to ensure that the route to Florida stayed open for the Irish, because otherwise the Colombians would have given it to someone else.'

'You make it sound like allocating air routes or something.'

Big Al shrugged again. 'Of course. It's business.' He spoke as if all this stuff was common knowledge. It was news to me.

So who the fuck were PIRA talking to in Gibraltar? Were they there in an attempt to keep the drug trafficking going? It came back to me that, in September 1988, Sir Peter Terry, who'd been instrumental in pressing for a crackdown on drug smuggling, and who'd been governor of Gibraltar until earlier that year, had narrowly survived an assassination attempt at his home in Staffordshire. A gunman, who'd never been caught, had given him the good news with twenty rounds from an AK47 – something, as it happened, that Mr McGear was not unaccustomed to doing. Maybe the fourth man in the photograph was getting a similar warning? And was there some sort of connection between the ending of the drug runs and the shooting of PIRA players there just a few months later?

Whatever, it confirmed that there were some strange things going on with some members of the DEA, including Kev's boss. Maybe they were getting a cut of the action from PIRA and Kev found out?

Big Al sucked through his teeth once more. 'You've got a brilliant package here, my man. So which one are you going to blackmail?'

'Blackmail?'

'Nicky – you've got a senior figure in the DEA, talking with big-cheese cartel members, your terrorist boys and Gibraltar government, law enforcement, whatever. You're not trying to tell me these pictures aren't for the purposes of blackmail? Get real. If you're not going to use them, then whoever took these photographs certainly is.'

33

We went through all the pictures one more time. Kelly didn't recognize any more of the people.

I asked de Sabatino if there was any way we could enhance the photography.

'What's the point? You seem to know everybody.' He was right. I just wanted Kelly to look at 'Daddy's boss' more closely.

There was silence for about three minutes as we just kept on flicking through.

'What else do you know about Gibraltar?' I asked.

'Not much. What more do you want?' His second cigar was well on its way, and Kelly was waving away the smoke. 'It's common sense – if you've got enough money, do a deal with the Colombians and get the stuff into Europe. Every other bunch of badasses is doing it, so why not your Irish boys?'

Big Al was looking at me as if what we'd stumbled across was very mundane. And I had to admit it didn't seem enough for Kev and his family to have been murdered for.

There was too much silence; Big Al had to inject something. 'Whatever, someone is definitely in the blackmail biz.'

I wasn't so sure. Maybe it was some kind of insurance for PIRA. If Kev's boss or the Gibraltarians decided not to play any more, maybe this was what would keep them in the game.

I looked at Kelly. 'Can you do us a favour? Will you go and get some cans of drink?'

She looked happy to get out of the smoke. I followed her to the door and pulled the curtain so I could see the machines. The landing was clear; the boys' door was closed, but the music still hammered through the thin plaster walls; inside, no doubt, the cheerleaders were running through a few routines. I watched Kelly until she reached the machines, then sat down on the bed. Big Al was still playing with the laptop.

'I turned up at her parents' house a week ago,' I said. 'Everybody was dead. He was in the DEA, killed by people he knew.' I pointed at the screen. 'Now we've got Daddy's boss mixing with the cartels. It's reasonable to assume that what we've got here is corruption within the DEA, involving drug movements via Florida to Irish terrorists, who've been getting it into Europe via Gibraltar. Only now it seems there were some problems for them in late '87.'

Big Al wasn't really listening. The thought of a corrupt DEA officer had taken him to another planet. 'Way to go! You gonna stitch the bastard?'

'I don't know what I'm going to do.'

'Fucking stitch him, Nicky! I hate cops! I hate the DEA! I hate every fucker who's ruined my life. I have to live like a fucking hermit. Federal Witness Programme, kiss my ass!'

I was worried that five years of frustration were about to explode out of him. I had no time for that. 'Frankie, I need a car.'

He wasn't listening. 'They used me, then they just fucked me over . . .'

'I need a car.'

He slowly came back to earth. 'Sure, OK, for how long?'

'Two days, maybe three. And I need some money.'

'When do you want it by?'

'Now.'

Big Al was weird and a sad fuck, too soft and stupid to be in this sort of world, but I felt sorry for him. Me turning up must have been the best thing that had happened to him in years. Life must be shit with no friends, and always worrying about being hit. But that was how mine was going to be if I didn't get this stuff back to Simmonds.

Big Al used the room phone to call a car hire company. It would take about an hour to deliver a vehicle, so the three of us strolled to an ATM. He drew out $1,200 from four different accounts. 'You never know when you're going to need *mucho dinero* in a hurry!' he grinned. Maybe he wasn't so stupid after all.

Back in the room, waiting for the car, I could sense there was more to come from him. He'd definitely been brooding on something for the last half-hour.

'Would you like to make some money, Nicky – real money?'

I was checking my bag to make sure I hadn't left anything.

'Why's that? Are you going to give me some?'

'Sort of.' He came and stood by me as I zipped the bag closed. 'On those files there are some account numbers stuffed with lovely narco-dollars. Give me two minutes to access the stuff I need and then I can hack in. I can do that shit in my sleep.' He put an arm around me. 'Nick, two minutes on my laptop and we could be talking serious enrichment. What do you think?' His head was nodding at 1000 r.p.m., his eyes never leaving mine.

I let him sweat a bit. 'How do I know that you'll pay me my half?' I thought I'd let him know how much I wanted.

'I can transfer it anywhere you want. And don't worry, once I've moved it, they'll never know where it's gone.'

I had to smile. The one thing Frank de Sabatino was good at was hiding money. 'C'mon, Nicky Two, what do you say!' He had his arms wide open and was looking at me like a child who'd done wrong.

I gave him the time he needed with the laptop and wrote down the account number for him to transfer my share to. Fuck it, Kelly was going to need money for school and stuff, and I wanted a payback for working against these people for so many years. It felt good and, anyway, it was just business.

He finished. There was a serious, down-to-work look on his face. 'Where are you going now?' he asked.

'I'm not going to tell you; you know the score. People that I've been in contact with are now dead and I don't want that to happen to you.'

'Bullshit!' He looked at Kelly and shrugged his shoulders. 'You just don't want me to know in case I go blurting off to somebody.'

'That's not the case,' I said, though in fact it was. 'If you did that, or didn't send the money, you know what I'd do.'

He raised an eyebrow.

I looked at him and smiled. 'I'd make sure the right people know where you are.'

The colour drained from his face for a while, then back came the watermelon. He shook his head. 'I may have been out of the loop for a while, but I see nothing has changed.'

The telephone rang. The blue Nissan was waiting outside reception. Big Al signed for it and gave me the customer copy of the agreement for when I dropped it off. Kelly and I got in, Big Al stayed on the sidewalk with his briefcase. I pressed the switch to open the windows. The bass rap still played in the background.

'Listen, Al, I'll e-mail you to make sure you know where the car's been dropped off, OK?'

He nodded slowly. It was sinking in that he was about to lose us.

'Do you want a lift anywhere?'

'No, I've got work to do. By the morning we could be rich.'

We shook hands through the open window. Al smiled at Kelly and said, 'Make sure you come and visit Uncle Al in about ten years' time, little lady. I'll buy the ice cream!'

We set off slowly down the strip. It was still packed. There was so much neon the street lighting was superfluous.

Kelly was in the back, staring out of the window, then gazing into space, lost in her own little world. I didn't tell her that ahead of us lay a 700-mile drive.

Soon Daytona was behind us and we were back on the long, open road. As I drove, I mulled over Kev's words again: 'You won't believe the stuff I've got here. Your friends over the water are busy.' And he'd also said, 'I've just started the ball rolling on something, but I'd be interested to know what you think.' Did that mean he'd spoken to his boss? Had his boss then got him zapped? But there was no way Kev would have been talking to anyone in the DEA if he suspected corruption. So who the fuck did he call?

I had some valuable stuff from the PIRA office, a lot of which I didn't understand, but maybe Kev had more. The more information I got hold of, the better it was going to be for me when I got it to Simmonds, and that was why we were going back to Washington.

Once on the interstate I put the car on to cruise control and my mind into neutral.

We drove through the night, stopping only to refuel and for a caffeine fix to keep me awake at the wheel. I bought cans of Coke to keep the levels topped up as we drove and in case Kelly woke up.

At first light I could begin to make out changes in the terrain, proof that we were moving north into a more temperate climate. Then the sun came up, a big burning ball in my half-right position, and my eyes started to sting.

We stopped at another gas station to fill up. This time Kelly stirred. 'Where are we?' she yawned.

'I don't know.'

'Well, where are we going?'

'It's a surprise.'

'Tell me about your wife,' she said.

'It seems so long ago I can hardly remember.'

I looked in the mirror. She'd slumped back down, too tired to pursue it. Or maybe she was suffering from terminal boredom, and who could blame her?

I wanted to have one hit on Kev's to see what he had, and I wanted to make entry at last light tonight. I knew there'd be a secure area somewhere in the house – exactly where, we'd have to find out. After that I wanted to be out of the Washington area again before first light. Big Al didn't know it yet, but he was going to get his ass into gear and help us out of the US. If he didn't do it voluntarily, I'd be giving him a bump start.

By mid-morning Kelly was wide awake, reading a magazine I'd got her at the last stop. She was lying in the back, shoes off, totally absorbed. We hadn't talked. We were in a world of empty sweet wrappers, polystyrene coffee cups, crisp packets and bottles of Coke with bits of crisp floating in them.

'Kelly?'

'Mm?'

'You know in your house Daddy had a hidey-hole for you and Aida?'

'Yeah?'

'Well, do you know if Daddy had any hidey-holes for important things like money, or where Mummy would keep her rings? Did he have a special place where they'd put stuff?'

'Sure, yeah, Daddy's got his own special place.'

Busying myself with the cruise control, I said, 'Oh, and where is that, then?'

'In his den.'

Which made sense. But that was the room that had been well fucked over.

'Where is it exactly?'

'In the wall.'

'Whereabouts?'

'In the wall! I saw Daddy doing it once. We're not allowed in there, but the door was open and we'd just come in from school and we saw Daddy putting something in there. We were standing right by the door and he didn't know.'

'Is it behind the picture?' I asked, though there was no way he'd be that bone.

'No, it's behind the wood.'

'The wood?'

'The wood.'

'Could you show me?'

'Is that where we're going?' She suddenly sat bolt upright. 'I want Jenny and Ricky!'

'We can't see them when we get there because they'll be busy.'

She looked at me as if I was mad. 'They're my teddies, I've told you! They're in my bedroom. Can't I get them? They need me.'

I felt a right dickhead. 'Of course you can. So long as you're quiet.' I knew there was more to come.

'Can I see Melissa and tell her sorry that I missed the sleep-over?'

'We won't have time.'

She sat back into her seat, brooding.

'But you're going to phone her mommy?'

I nodded.

I started to see signs for Washington. We'd been on the road for nearly eighteen hours. My eyes were smarting worse than ever, despite the air-conditioner being on full blast. We'd get there in two hours, but there'd still be a few hours to kill before last light. I pulled in at a rest area and tried to sleep. It would be a busy night.

Kelly was in the back doing her own thing in a sea of stale food, sweat and my farts.

It was about six in the evening as we approached the Lorton turn-off. For once it wasn't raining, just overcast. Only about forty-five minutes to go.

I couldn't see Kelly in the mirror. She was hunkered down in the seat again.

'Are you awake?'

315

'Ahh, I'm tired, Nick. Are we there yet?'

'I'm not going to tell you. It's going to be a surprise. Just keep down; I don't want you to sit up.'

I drove into the estate and onto Hunting Bear Path, negotiating the speed bumps ultra cautiously so I could have a good look around. Everything looked quite normal. I could see the back of Kev's garage, but I couldn't see the front of the house yet.

When I got up level, the driveway was finally exposed. Parked up outside the front door was a blue-and-white. No problem, just look ahead, act normal.

I drove on, checking in the rear-view mirror. The sidelights were on and it was two up. They were basically just on stag. The house hadn't been boarded up yet, but it was still cordoned off with yellow tape.

I drove straight on; I couldn't tell if they were looking at me. Even if they did a plate check as I drove past, it wouldn't matter. They'd only come up with Big Al. If I was compromised, I'd run for it and leave Kelly here. Maybe the uniformed police would be good guys and look after her. At least, that would be the logical thing to do, but there was a conflict. I'd promised that I wouldn't leave her; that promise shouldn't mean much, but it did.

I went down to the bottom of the road and turned right, to get out of sight as quickly as possible, then drove a big square to get back in behind them. I reached the small parade of shops. The car park was about a quarter full, so we could pull in without attracting attention.

Kelly shrieked, 'We're at the stores!'

'That's right, but we can't buy anything because I haven't much money left. But we can go to the house.'

'Yesss! Can I get my Pollypockets and Yak-backs from my bedroom too?'

'Of course you can.' I didn't have a clue what she was on about.

I went round to the back, opened up the boot and got out the bag, then opened her door. I threw the bag in beside her and leaned in.

'Are we going to my house now?'

I started to sort out the kit I'd be needing.

'Yes. I want you to help me because I want you to show me Daddy's hidey-hole. Can you do that? It's important; he wanted me to check something. We've got to sneak in because there's police outside. Are you going to do everything that I say?'

'Yeah, I'll do that! Can I get Pocahontas as well?'

'Yep.'

I didn't give a fuck, I'd have nodded and agreed to anything so long as she showed me the cache.

'You ready? Let's put your hood up.' It was dark and cloudy, and thankfully the road wasn't exactly built for pedestrians. We shouldn't encounter any Melissas *en route*.

With the bag slung over my shoulder, I held her hand and we set off towards the house. It was nearly seven o'clock and the street lights were on. My plan was to work our way to the back of the house, so I could stand off, have a look at it and prepare to make entry.

We started to walk over the waste ground to the rear of the house, past Portakabins and stockpiles of girders and building materials. The mud was so treacherous in places I thought we'd lose our shoes.

She was almost beside herself with excitement, but fighting it hard. 'That's where my friend Candice lives!' She pointed to a house. 'I helped her with their yard sale. We got twenty dollars.'

'Shhh!' Smiling, I said slowly, 'We've got to be very very quiet or the policemen will get us.' It didn't take long for that to register.

Finally we were standing in the shadow of the neighbour's garage. I put the bag down and watched and listened. The engine of the blue-and-white was ticking over. They were less than 20 metres away on the other side of the target. I could hear a little of their radio traffic, but couldn't make out what was being said. Now and again a car drove past, braked for the speed bumps, rattled over and accelerated away.

Lights were on in some of the houses and I could see into the rooms. It had always given me a strange sort of kick doing this, like my own private viewing of a David Attenborough documentary: human beings in their natural habitat. As a young soldier in the late seventies in Northern Ireland, part of our job was to 'lurk' – hang around in the shadows, watching and listening, hoping to catch a glimpse of someone with a weapon. It was amazing what you'd see people doing in their cars or front rooms, and slightly less amazing what they'd be up to in their bedrooms. Sometimes we'd watch for hours on end, all in the line of duty. I really enjoyed it. Here, people were just doing their washing-up or watching TV, and probably worrying about the effect of multiple murders on real-estate prices.

There were no proximity lights at the back of the house, just standard ones with an on/off by the patio doors. I remembered switching them on for a barbecue.

I stroked Kelly's hair and looked down and smiled. Then, slowly and quietly, I unzipped the bag and got out what I needed. I put my mouth right to her ear and whispered, 'I want you to stay here. It's really important that you look after this kit. You'll see me over there, OK?'

She nodded. Off I went.

I reached the patio doors. First things first: make sure they're locked. They were. I got my Maglite and checked to see if there were any bolts at the top and bottom of the frame. It's no good defeating a lock if there are also bolts across, and that's one of the reasons why you try to attack a building at the point of last exit, because you know they can't have bolted up again from the outside.

Normally the next thing to do would be to look for the spare key – why spend an hour with the lock-picking kit if there's one hidden only feet away? Some people still leave theirs dangling on a string just the other side of the letter box, or on the inside of a cat flap. Others leave it under a dustbin or just behind a little pile of rocks by the door. If there's a lamp-post in the garden, it always pays to feel around the base because it's a natural marker. If a key is going to be left, it will nearly always be somewhere on the normal approach to the door. But this was Kev's house: I wouldn't find spare keys lying around. I put the photographer's blanket over my head and shoulders and, with the Maglite in my mouth, got to work with the lock-pick gun. It didn't take long.

I opened the doors gently, moved the curtain aside and looked inside the living room. The first thing I noticed was that all the other curtains and shutters were closed, which was good for me because, once inside, we'd have cover. The second thing that hit me was an overpowering smell of chemicals.

34

I tiptoed back to Kelly and whispered, 'Come on, then!'

Our shoes were caked with mud, so we took them off on the concrete terrace and put them in the bag. Then we stepped inside and I pulled the doors closed.

I held the Maglite with my middle finger and forefinger over the lens to contain most of the light, and kept it close to the floor so we could see our way through the living room. The carpet and underlay had been taken up and all the furniture was pushed to one side. All that was left were the chipboard sheets that the builders had used instead of floorboards. Someone had done a good job of scrubbing the bloodstains where Kev had been lying, which explained the chemical smell. The Murder Mop people had been in; once forensics finished it was up to the commercial companies to clear away the mess.

We reached the door that led into the front hall. Kelly stood still, an old hand at this stuff now. I got on my knees, eased it ajar and looked through. The front door was closed, but light from the street lamps shone through the stained-glass flower set into the window above it. I switched off the torch and stationed Kelly by the bag in the hallway.

I stopped and listened and generally tuned in. The engine was still idling.

I felt Kelly pulling my jacket.

'Nick?'

'Shhh!'

'Where's the carpet gone – and what's that horrible smell?'

I turned round and half crouched down. I put my finger on her lips again and said, 'We'll talk about it later.'

There was a *beep beep beep* from the blue-and-white's radio. The guys inside were probably drinking coffee, pissed off to be on stag all night. Some radio traffic came on the net. Whoever was Control sounded like Hitler with a dress on. She was giving somebody a bollocking.

Indicating that Kelly should stay where she was, I moved across to the study and gently opened the door. I went back, picked up the bag and guided Kelly into the room, propping the door open with the bag to let the light come through from the hall.

Everything looked very much the same as before, except that the stuff that had been strewn all over the place had now been arranged in a neat line along one wall. The PC was still on its side on the desk, the printer and scanner in position on the floor. They had all been dusted for prints.

I took the photographer's material and a box of board pins from the bag, and lifted the chair near to the window. Taking my time, I climbed up and pinned the fabric along the top and down the sides of the entire wooden window frame.

I could now close the door and put on the torch, taking care not to shine it in my face – I didn't want to scare her. I'd done a job once which involved getting a mother and her child out of the Yemen, and the child went apeshit because we were working with torches in our mouths and it made us look like the devil at work. I felt quite pleased with myself for remembering this and sparing Kelly; maybe I knew something about kids after all.

I went over to her. Even above the reek of solvents and cleaners I got a waft of greasy hair, Coca-Cola, bubble gum and chocolate. I whispered into her ear, 'Where is it? Just point.'

I shone the torch all around the walls and she pointed at the skirting board behind the door. This was good shit; nothing seemed to have been disturbed.

I immediately started prising the wooden strip away from the wall with a screwdriver. A vehicle passed the house and I heard laughter from the police car – probably at Control's expense. They'd be there solely to deter people from coming round and being nosy. Chances were, the place would be pulled down soon. Who'd want to buy a house a family had been murdered in? Maybe it would be turned into a memorial park or something.

I kept Kelly right next to me; I wanted to keep her reassured. She was interested in what was happening, and I smiled at her now and again to show that everything was fine.

With a small creak the section of board started to give way. I pulled it right off and put it to one side. Then I bent down again and shone the torch inside. The beam glinted on metal. What looked like a gun safety box, about 18 inches square, was recessed into the wall. The lock was a lever, very similar to a UK Chubb. It was going to need decoding. It could take hours.

I got out the black wallet and set to work, trying to remember to grin at her and let her know it wouldn't be long, but I could see she was getting restless. Ten minutes went by. Fifteen. Twenty. Finally it was all too much for her. In a loud whisper she said crossly, 'What about my teddies?'

'Shhh!' I put my finger to her lips. 'The police!' What I meant was, 'Fuck the teddies; we'll get them when I'm ready.' I carried on decoding.

There was a pause, then, no longer a whisper, 'But you said!'

It had to be cut. Obviously being Mr Smiley wasn't working. I turned on her and hissed, 'We'll do it in a minute! Now, shut up!'

She was taken aback, but it worked.

I was luckier than I might have been with the decoding. I'd just finished, had put the tools away and was opening the box, when I heard a low moan from her. 'I don't like it here, Nick. It's all changed.'

I turned round, grabbed her and covered her mouth with my

hand. 'For fuck's sake shut up!' It wasn't what she expected, but I didn't have time to explain.

With my hand still clamped hard over mouth, I picked her up and slowly walked over to the window. I listened, waited, but there was nothing. Just a bit of banter and laughing, and the crackle of their radio.

As I turned back, however, there was a short, sharp metallic dragging sound.

Then, for a split second, nothing.

Then, as Kev's pewter tankard of pens and pencils fell from the desk and hit the bare flooring, there was a resounding crash. The noise went on as bits and pieces scattered in all directions. As I'd turned, Kelly's coat must have caught on the sharp points of the pencils and dragged the tankard off the table.

I knew the noise was magnified twenty times in my head, but I also knew they would have heard it.

Kelly chose that moment to start to lose it, but there was no time to worry about that. I just left her where she was, went to the doorway, and listened to the sound of car doors opening and a sudden increase in radio traffic.

Pulling the pistol from my jeans and checking chamber, I moved out of the study. Three strides got me across the hall and into the kitchen. I closed the door behind me, took a couple of deep breaths and waited.

The front door opened and I could hear both of them in the hallway. There was a click and light spilled under the kitchen door.

Then footsteps, and I could hear nervous breathing from the other side of the four-ply, and the jangle of keys on a belt.

I heard the study door opening. Then a half-shouted, half-whispered, 'Melvin, Melvin – in here!'

'Yo!'

I knew it was my time. I brought the pistol up into the fire position, put my hand on the doorknob and gently twisted. I moved into the hall.

Melvin was in the study doorway, his back towards me. He was young and of medium build. I took a couple of big strides, grabbed him across the forehead with my left hand, yanked his head back and rammed the pistol muzzle into his neck. In a very controlled voice that had nothing to do with the way I was feeling, I said, 'Drop your weapon, Melvin. Don't fuck me about. Drop it now.'

Melvin's arm came down to his side and he let the pistol fall to the floor.

I couldn't see whether or not the other one had his pistol out. It was still dark in the study. Their torchlight was no help. Melvin and I blocked out most of the hallway light. I was hoping that he'd already reholstered, because part of their training would be not to scare kids. As far as he was concerned, it was just a kid there on her own.

I shouted, 'Put the lights on, Kelly – do it now!'

Nothing happened.

'Kelly, turn the lights on.' I heard small footsteps coming towards us. There was a click and the lights came on.

'Now wait there.' I could see her eyes were swollen and red.

Inside the room stood Michelin Man. He must have weighed 15 stones and, by the looks of the boy, he had only a couple of years to go before retirement. He was holstered, but his hand was down by his pistol.

I said, 'Don't do it! Tell him, Melvin.' I prodded his neck.

Melvin went, 'I'm fucked, Ron.'

'Ron, don't start messing about. This is not the one to do it for. It's not worth it, not just for this.'

I could see that Ron was quite switched on. He was thinking about his wife, his mortgage and the chances of ever seeing another bag of doughnuts.

Melvin's radio sparked up. Control snapped, 'Unit Sixty-two, Unit Sixty-two. Do you copy?' It sounded like a demand, not a request. It must have been great to be married to her.

'That's you, isn't it, Melvin?' I said.

'Yes, sir, that's us.'

'Melvin, tell them you're OK.' I jabbed the pistol a little harder into his neck to underline the point. 'The safety catch is off, Melvin, I've got my finger on the trigger. Just tell them everything's OK. It ain't worth it, mate.'

Ron blurted, 'I'll do it.'

Another demand: 'Unit Sixty-two, respond.'

I said, 'Put your right hand up and answer with your left. Kelly, be very quiet, OK?'

She nodded. Ron pressed his radio. 'Hello, Control. We've checked. Everything's fine.'

'Roger, Unit Sixty-two, your report timed at 2213.'

Ron clicked off.

Kelly immediately went back into crying mode and sank to the floor. I was stuck in the doorway with a pistol to Melvin's neck, and Ron, who still had a weapon in his holster, was facing me from the middle of the room.

'At the end of the day, Ron, if you don't play the game, Melvin's going to die – and then you're going to die. Do you understand me?'

Ron nodded.

'OK, Ron, let's see you turn round.'

He did.

'Get on your knees.'

He did. He was about 4 feet from Kelly, but as long as she stayed still she wasn't in the line of fire.

Melvin was sweating good-style. My hand was slipping on his forehead. There were even droplets running down the topslide. His shirt was so wet I could make out the shape of his body armour underneath.

I said, 'With your left hand, Ron, I want you to lift out your pistol. Very slow, and use just your thumb and forefinger. Then I want you to move it to your left-hand side and drop it. Do you understand me, Ron?'

Ron nodded.

I said, 'Tell him, Melvin, tell him not to fuck about.'

'Don't fuck around, Ron.'

Ron gently removed his pistol from its holster and dropped it on the floor.

'What I want you to do now, with your left hand, is get hold of your handcuffs, and I want you to drop them just behind you. Understand?'

Ron complied. I turned my attention to Melvin, who was starting to tremble. I spoke quietly in his ear. 'Don't worry about it, you're going to live. You'll be talking to your grandchildren about this. Just do exactly what I say. Understand?'

He nodded.

I turned to Ron and said, 'Now lie down, Ron. Face-down on the floor.'

Ron spreadeagled himself and was now under control. I said, 'What I'm going to do next, Melvin, is take one step back, and this pistol is going to leave your neck, but it's still going to be pointing at your head, so don't get any ideas. Once I've stepped back, I'm then going to tell you to kneel down. Do you understand me?'

He nodded and I took a swift step backwards. I wanted to be out of arm's length from him straight away; I didn't want him doing some kind of heroic pirouette to grab the pistol or knock it out of the way.

'OK, now kneel down, then lie down. Just like Ron. Now put your hand next to Ron.'

I now had both of them lying face down, forearms together. I moved behind them, picked up the handcuffs and, with the pistol stuck in Melvin's ear, I locked his left wrist to Ron's right. I then took Melvin's handcuffs from their holster, stepped back and said, 'I want you to arch your bodies and move your free hands round so they're together as well. Both understand me? Believe me, boys, I want to get this over and done with. I just want out of here.'

I finished the job. At last they were both totally under control.

I took their wallets and threw them into the bag. I took Melvin's radio and kept it with me, and I took the battery out of Ron's and threw it into the bag. At the same time, I took out the roll of gaffer tape. I started with their legs, then used it to bind their heads together as well. I put a final strip around their necks and another around their mouths. I checked that both were breathing through their noses, then dragged them into the hallway – no small job, but I didn't want them to see what I was going to do next.

I looked at Kelly, pressed against the study wall. She looked pathetic. This must have been terrible for her. She'd been looking forward so much to coming home, only to find it wasn't the place she'd been expecting. It wasn't only her family that was missing; everything that was familiar to her was drenched in chemicals, shoved to one side or simply not there.

I heard myself saying, 'Go and see if your teddies are there.'

She turned and ran and I heard her rattling up the stairs.

I went into the study, crouched down by the skirting board and, at last, was able to open the gun box. There was nothing inside but a lone floppy disk.

I put the chair back by the desk and lifted up the PC. I soon had it working. There was no password protection, probably deliberately. If anything happened to Kev, he'd want the whole world to read what was on it.

I clicked various files but found nothing interesting. Then I found a file called Flavius and I knew I'd hit pay dirt. It was the codename of the Gibraltar operation.

I started reading. Kev had found out much the same as Big Al had told me – that PIRA's connection with the cartels originated when they started running drugs for the Colombians up through North Africa and into Gibraltar, for distribution in Spain and the rest of Europe. PIRA were good at the job and the cartels paid well.

After a while, PIRA had also begun to use the drugs trade to gear up some of their own money, funds collected by Noraid in the USA. Big sums were involved; Kev's figures showed that Sinn Féin had been netting more than £500,000 a year.

These donations had been invested in narcotics, transported to Europe and then bartered for arms and explosives in the old Eastern-bloc countries. It was a business marriage made in heaven; PIRA had the drugs, the East had the weapons. The downfall of the USSR and the rise of the Russian Mafia couldn't have been better-timed.

I had to get back into work mode. I couldn't just sit here reading. I was in a house with two policemen and one pissed-off little girl. I ejected the floppy disk and put it in my coat pocket.

The controller from hell came back on the net. 'Unit Sixty-two, do you copy?'

Shit.

I went into the hall. 'Ron, time to speak up.'

Ron looked at me, and I knew he was going to fuck me off. His face was a picture of defiance. I moved over to them and pulled the tape off their mouths. Ron was the first to talk. 'You answer it because we can't. You won't kill us, not for that.'

Control went up an octave. 'Unit Sixty-two!'

Ron had a point.

'Kelly! Kelly! Where are you?'

'Coming – just found Ricky.'

I stepped back over my two new friends towards Kelly coming down the stairs. There was no time to be sympathetic or nice. 'Get your coat and shoes on – quick!'

I got all the kit together, put on my trainers, and checked Ron and Melvin weren't choking to death on the gaffer tape. Both looked quite happy with themselves, but still thinking of a good excuse for why they were in this state in the first place.

We left the same way we'd come. I was gripping her hand, more or less dragging her along, and keeping an eagle eye on Jenny and Ricky. I didn't want the neighbours hearing screams for lost teddies.

As we drove, bursts of light from the street lamps strobed into the back of the car and I could see her in the rear-view mirror. She was looking miserable, her eyes puffy and wet. She had every right to be sad. She was bright enough to realize that this was probably the last time she'd be here. This wasn't her home any more. Now she was the same as me. Neither of us had one.

I saw the signs for Dulles airport and pushed my foot down. I was not going to take the risk of driving back to Florida.

35

I hit the airport approach road and headed for economy parking. I allowed myself a wry smile; if this carried on, it would soon be full of my stolen cars. I got one or two spots of rain on my arm as I took a ticket from the machine, and by the time we'd parked there was a light patter on the roof.

Ron and Melvin might have made a connection between me and the car because of the drive-past. They might have been rescued and circulated the registration. There was not a lot I could do about that but just sit tight and hope that the mass of cars and the rain would conceal us, because it was far too early for a child to be moving around an airport with an adult man with scabs on his face.

I turned round in the seat and said, 'Are you all right, Kelly? I'm sorry I had to shout, but sometimes adults have to be really firm with kids.'

She was looking down at one of the teddies, picking the fur, pouting.

I said, 'You're not a bad girl and I'm sorry that I told you off. I didn't really mean it, I was just getting all excited.'

She nodded slowly, still playing with her furry friend.

'Do you want to come to England?'

She looked up. She didn't say anything, but I took it as a yes.

'That's good, because I would like you to come too. You've been a really good girl, you always do what I say. Do you want to help me again?'

She shrugged. I leaned over and picked up the other teddy and rubbed its face against her cheek. 'We'll get Jenny and Ricky to help me as well. How about that?'

She gave a reluctant nod.

'First of all, we've got to sort out the bag.'

I got into the back seat and put the holdall between us, opening it up. 'What do you think we should take out, then?'

I knew exactly what we were going to take out: everything apart from the blanket and washing kit, because they were the only things I needed now. I said, 'What do you reckon? Is that all?' She nodded and agreed, as if she'd packed it herself.

Everything I was not going to take I put into the boot. The rain was now coming down more heavily. I sat with her again and pulled out the blanket. 'We have to wait here for the next couple of hours. It's too early to go to the airport yet. You can have a sleep if you like.'

I folded up the bag and made a pillow. 'There, that's better – cuddle Jenny and Ricky.'

She looked at me and smiled. We were mates again.

'You aren't going away again, are you, Nick?'

For once I told the truth. 'No, I'm going to do some work. You just go to sleep. I'm not going anywhere.' I got out and sat in the front again. I rested the laptop on my knees and lifted the screen. I checked that the keys were in the ignition and I could easily grab the steering wheel. I had to be ready to move at once if we got pinged.

I pressed the on switch, and as the screen lit up it cast a glow inside the car. I inserted Kev's floppy disk. I was desperate to read the rest of his report, but, first, as an extra back-up, I downloaded everything onto the laptop. As I waited, I said quietly, 'Kelly?' There was no reply. The gentle rhythm of the rain had done its job.

I began reading where I'd left off. I knew that Gibraltar had always been a centre for international drug trafficking, money laundering and smuggling, but it seemed that, in 1987, Spain not only still wanted Gib back, it also wanted the Brits to crack down on drug trafficking as well. Thatcher's government told the Gibraltarians to sort it out, but the high-powered speedboats still ran drugs over from North Africa. The Brits threatened direct control of the colony if the trafficking didn't stop, and, at the same time, ordered a highly illegal operation against police and government officials they suspected of involvement. The boys taking the backhanders got the hint and suddenly stopped co-operating with PIRA and everyone else.

My eyes were racing ahead of my brain.

The closure of the Gibraltar route was all well and good for the war against corruption, but the Colombians were very pissed off. A major trade artery had been clamped off, and they wanted it reopened. According to Kev's findings, they'd decided a show of strength was required. They wanted Gibraltar bombed as a warning that the officials should start co-operating again, and they ordered PIRA to carry it out.

PIRA had a problem with this. They wanted the route reopened as much as the Colombians did, but, after the débâcle of Enniskillen, they couldn't run the risk of killing non-UK civilians and invoking even greater international condemnation. They'd refused to do it.

From evidence that Kev had gathered, the cartels' reply to PIRA was blunt: either you bomb Gibraltar or we shift our drugs business to the Protestant UVF. For PIRA, not a good day out.

PIRA's head shed came up with a solution and, as I read on, I couldn't help but admire it. 'Mad Danny' McCann had already been kicked out of PIRA and reinstated against Gerry Adams's wishes. Mairead Farrell, after the death of her boyfriend, had become too fanatical for her own good – 'a bit of a social hand grenade', Simmonds had said of her. PIRA's plan was to send to Gibraltar two players they'd be happy to see the back of, together with Sean Savage, who just had the misfortune to be part of the same ASU.

The team were issued with the technology and Semtex for the bomb, but were told it was to stay behind in Spain until they had done their recces and rehearsals. They were told only to take it in once the blocking car was in position, to guarantee the correct placement of the bomb. PIRA then gave the three players bad passports and leaked information to London. They wanted the Brits to react and stop the bombing so that, when the three were arrested, they could claim to the cartels that they'd given it their best shot.

We'd duly been told about the ASU, but, as I remembered, we'd also been briefed that there would be no blocking car and that the bomb would be detonated by a hand-held device. These last two pieces of intelligence meant that McCann, Farrell and Savage had never stood a chance. They were dead from the moment we thought the bomb was in position and armed, because one of them was bound to make a hand movement at some stage that would be construed as an attempt to detonate the device. I certainly wouldn't have taken the chance that Savage was only going for his packet of mints, and Euan obviously didn't when he initiated the contact with McCann and Farrell. There is an old saying in the Regiment: Better to be tried by twelve than carried by six.

A dialogue box came up on the screen telling me that I was running short of power and needed to plug into another power source. Fuck! I wanted to read more. I got back to the screen and read as fast as I could to get the drift.

Even though there hadn't been a bomb, the cartels had accepted that their Irish lackeys were playing ball. After all, three of their people had been killed in the process. PIRA kept the trade with the Colombians, even though, as Big Al had said, it was thereafter routed through South Africa and Spain.

PIRA were in raptures. They'd got rid of two troublemakers, not quite in the way that they'd intended, but three martyrs had been created, with the result that their cause at home was strengthened, and even more dollars rolled into the coffers from the Irish-Americans. It was only the Brits who appeared to have been left with egg on their faces, but, even so, no matter how much the international community publicly condemned the shootings, in secret most heads of state admired Thatcher's muscular stand against terrorism.

Fuck it. Another box came up and told me to plug into an external power source. I switched the laptop off and packed it away, full of frustration. I wanted to know more. At the same time I was on a high. If we made it back to the UK with this stuff, I'd have cracked it with Simmonds.

It was 3.30 a.m. There was nothing to do but wait for the next couple of hours or so, until the first wave of aircraft started to arrive and depart, creating enough activity for a man with a scabby face and a seven-year-old in tow to blend in.

I let the backrest down a bit and tried to get my neck into a comfortable position, but I couldn't relax. My mind was racing. The whole operation in Gibraltar had been a set-up so that PIRA and the Colombians could keep making money. Fair one, but where did Kev and I fit into the scheme of things? I lay there and listened to the beat of rain on the roof.

For Euan and me it had all started on 3 March, less than a week before the shootings. We were both on different jobs over the water and had got lifted off and sent to Lisburn, HQ of the British army in Northern Ireland. From there it was a quick move by Puma to Stirling Lines in Hereford, England, the home of the Special Air Service.

One of the slime was waiting to take us straight to RHQ, and the moment I saw the china cups and biscuits outside the briefing room I knew that something big was in the offing. Last time that had happened, the prime minister had been here.

The room was in semi-darkness and packed. There was a large screen at the back of a stage and tiered seats so that everyone got a good view.

We were looking for somewhere to sit when I heard, 'Oi, over here, dickspot!'

Kev and Slack Pat were sitting drinking tea. With them were the other two members of their four-man team, Geoff and Steve. All were from A Squadron and were doing their six months on the counter-terrorist team.

Euan turned to Kev and said, 'Know what this job is about?'

'We're off to Gib, mate. PIRA's planning a bomb.'

The CO got up on the stage and the room fell silent. 'Two problems,' he said. 'Number one, a shortage of time. You leave immediately after this briefing. Number two, shortage of solid int. However, Joint Operations Committee wants the Regiment to deploy. You will get as much int as we know now, and as it comes in during your flight and once on the ground.'

I thought, What the fuck are Euan and I doing here? Surely as Det operators it would be illegal for us to work outside Northern Ireland? I kept my mouth shut; if I started querying the decision, they might send me back and I'd miss out.

I looked around me and saw members of RHQ, the operations officer and the world's supply of Int Corps. The final member of the team was an ammunitions technical officer, a bomb-disposal expert on attachment to the CT team.

Someone I had never seen before moved towards the stage, a teacup in one hand, biscuits in the other. He stood to the right-hand side of the stage by the lectern. There was an overnight bag by his feet.

'My name is Simmonds and I run the Northern Ireland desk for the intelligence service from London. The people behind you are a mix of service and military intelligence officers. First, a very brief outline of the events that have brought us all here today.'

Judging by the bag, it looked as if he would be coming with us. The lights were dimmed and a slide projector lit the screen behind him.

'Last year,' he said, 'we learned that a PIRA team had based itself in southern Spain. We intercepted mail going to the homes of known players from Spain and found a postcard from Sean Savage in the Costa del Sol.'

A slide of the player came up on the screen. 'Our Sean', Simmonds said with a half-smile, 'told Mummy and Daddy he was working abroad. It rang a few alarm bells when we read it, because the work young Savage is best at is bomb-making.'

Was he making a funny? No, he didn't look the sort.

'Then, in November, two men went through Madrid airport on their way from Malaga to Dublin. They carried Irish passports, and in a routine check the Spanish sent the details to Madrid who, in turn, passed them with photographs to London. It turned out that both passports were false.'

I thought to myself, Stupid timing by them really. Terrorist incidents in Northern Ireland tended to decrease in the summer months, when PIRA took their wives and kids to Torremolinos for a fortnight of sun and sand. The funny thing was that the RUC also took their holidays in the same places, and they'd all bump into each other in the bars. By travelling to Spain out of the tourist season these two characters had drawn attention to themselves; if they'd passed through Malaga airport during the holiday season, they might have got away with it.

It turned out that one of the passport holders was Sean Savage, but it was the identity of the second man that had got everybody flapping.

Simmonds showed his next slide. 'Daniel Martin McCann. I'm sure you know more about him than I do.' He gave a no-fucking-way sort of smile.

'Mad Danny' had really earned his name. Linked to twenty-six killings, he had been lifted often, but had only been put away for two years.

To British intelligence, he said, the combination of McCann and Savage on the Costa del Sol could only mean one of two things: either PIRA was going to attack a British target on the Spanish mainland, or there was going to be an attack on Gibraltar. 'One thing was for sure,' Simmonds said, 'they weren't there to top up their tans.'

At last there was a round of laughter. I could see Simmonds liked that, as if he'd practised his one-liners so the timing was just right. Despite that, I was warming to the man. It wasn't often that you got people making jokes at a briefing as important as this one.

The slide changed again to a street map of Gibraltar. I was listening to him, but at the same time thinking of my infantry posting there in the 1970s. I'd had a whale of a time.

'Gibraltar is a soft target,' Simmonds said. 'There are several potential locations for a bomb, such as the Governor's residence or the law courts, but our threat assessment is that the most likely will be the garrison regiment, the Royal Anglians. Every Tuesday morning, the band of the 1st Battalion parade for the changing of the guard ceremony. We think the most likely site for a bomb is the square that the band march into after the parade. A bomb could easily be concealed in a car there.'

He might have added that, from a bomber's point of view, it would be a near-perfect location. Because of the confined area, the blast would be tamped and therefore more effective.

'Following this assessment we stopped the ceremony on 11 December. The local media reported that the Governor's guard-house needed urgent redecoration. In fact, we needed time while we gathered more intelligence to stop it needing rebuilding.'

Not as good as his last one, but there were still a few subdued laughs.

'The local police were then reinforced by plain-clothes officers from the UK, and their surveillance paid off. When the ceremony resumed on 23 February, a woman, ostensibly holidaying on the Costa del Sol, made a trip to the Rock and photographed the parade. She was covertly checked and was found to be travelling on a stolen Irish passport.

'The following week she was there again, only this time she tagged along behind the bandsmen as they marched to the square. Even one of the Rock apes could have worked out that she was recceing for the arrival of an active service unit.'

There was loud laughter. He'd done it again! I wasn't too sure if we were all laughing at his jokes or just at the fact that he kept on telling them. Who the fuck was this man? This should have been one of the most serious briefings ever. Either he just didn't give a fuck or he was so powerful no-one was going to say a word against him. Whatever, I could already tell his presence in Gibraltar would be a real bonus.

Simmonds stopped smiling. 'Our intelligence tells us that the bombing is to take place some time this week. However, there is no sign that either McCann or Savage is getting ready to leave Belfast.'

He wasn't wrong. I had seen both of them, pissed as farts, outside a bar in the Falls Road just the night before. They didn't look that ready to me. It should take them quite a while to prepare for this one – or maybe this was part of the preparation, having their last night out before work started.

'This is where we have a few problems,' he went on. He was working now without his notes. Did that mean no more one-liners? Certainly there was more of an edge to his voice.

'What are we to do with these people? If we try to move in on them too early that would only leave other PIRA teams free to go ahead with the bombing. In any case, if the ASU travel through Malaga airport and remain on Spanish territory until the last minute, there is no guarantee that the Spanish will hand them over, not only because of the dispute with the UK on the question of Gibraltar, but also because the case against them could only be based on conspiracy, which is pretty flimsy.

'So, gentlemen, we must arrest them in Gibraltar.' The screen went blank and there was only the light from the lectern shining up on his face. 'And this throws up three options. The first is to arrest them as they cross the border from Spain. Easier said than done; there's no guarantee we'll know what kind of vehicle they're in. There would be only about ten to fifteen seconds in which to make a positive identification and effect an arrest – not an easy thing to do, especially if they're sitting in a car and probably armed.

'The second option is to arrest the team once they're in the area of the square, but again this depends on advance warning and positive identification, and their all being together with the device. At the present time, therefore, we are going for the third option, and that's why we are all here.'

He took a sip of his tea and asked for the lights to come on.

'The Security Service will place surveillance teams to trigger the PIRA team into Gibraltar.' He looked around for each group as he talked. 'The two soldiers who have just arrived from the province must give positive IDs before the civil authorities will hand over the operation to the military. The four men from your counter-terrorist team will make a hard arrest, but only after they have planted the device.'

The two soldiers who have just arrived from the province. Now I understood. That was Euan and me.

'Once arrested,' Simmonds went on, 'they are to be handed over to the civil authorities. Of course the normal protection will be given to the team from any court appearance. The two operators from the province will not, repeat not, conduct any arrest or contact action. You understand the reasons why?'

He managed a smile. 'I think that's enough, gentlemen.' He looked at Frank, the CO. 'Francis, I understand we fly to RAF Lyneham in ten minutes to link up with the Hercules?'

Just over three hours later I was sitting in a C130 with Euan, who was busy worrying about a black mark on his new trainers. Kev was checking the weapon bundles and ammunition and, more importantly as far as I was concerned, the medical packs. If I got dropped I wanted fluid put into me as soon as possible.

We landed at about 11.30 p.m. on Thursday, 3 March. The whole Rock was still awake; lights were on everywhere. We moved off to the military area, where trucks were waiting with our advance party to get us away quickly and without fuss.

Our FOB was in HMS *Rooke*, the Royal Navy shore base. We had requisitioned half a dozen rooms in the accommodation block and turned them into living space, with our own cooking area and ops room. Wires trailed everywhere, telephones were ringing, scaleys ran around in tracksuits or jeans, testing radios and sat comm links.

Over the din Simmonds said, 'Int suggests there could be a third member of the team, and probably its commander. Her name is Mairead Farrell. Pictures will be here within the hour, but here's some background for you. She's a particularly nasty piece of work' – he paused to time his delivery to perfection – 'middle class, thirty-one, ex-convent schoolgirl.'

When the laughter died down he told us more about her. She'd served ten years in prison for planting a bomb in the Conway Hotel, Belfast, in 1976, but as soon as she was released she reported straight back to PIRA for duty. There was a slight smile on his face as he explained that her lover, unbelievably named Brendan Burns, had blown himself up recently.

The meeting broke and we mooched around looking for a brew. A scaley came over and handed out street maps. 'They've already been spotted up by the Firm,' he said.

As we started to look at their handiwork, he carried on. 'The main routes from the border to the square are spotted in detail, the rest of the town fairly well, and, of the outlying areas, just major points.'

I looked at it. Fucking hell! There were about 100 spots to learn before the ASU came over the border. I didn't know which was tougher, the PIRA team or the homework.

'Any questions, lads?'

Kev said, 'Yeah, three. Where do we sleep, where's the bog and is there a brew on?'

In the morning, we picked up our weapons and ammunition and went onto the range. The four on the CT team had their own pistols. The ones we had were borrowed – our own were still in Derry. Not that it mattered that much; people think that blokes in the Regiment are very particular about their weapons, but they aren't. So long as you know that, when you pull the trigger, it fires first time and the rounds will hit the target you're aiming at, you're happy.

Once at the range, people did their own thing. The other four just wanted to know that their mags were working OK and that the pistols had no defects after being bundled up. Euan and I wanted to do the same, but also to find out the behaviour of our new weapons at different ranges. After firing off all the mags in quick succession to make sure everything worked, we then fired at 5, 10, 15, 20 and 25 metres. Good, slow, aimed shots, always aiming at the same point and checking where the rounds fell at each range. That way we found out where to aim at 15 metres, for example, and that was at the top of the target's torso. Because of the distance, quite a lot for a pistol, the rounds would fall lower into the bottom of his chest and take him down. Every weapon is different, so it took an hour to be confident.

Once finished we didn't strip the weapons to clean them. Why do that when we knew they worked perfectly? We just got a brush into the area that feeds the round into the barrel and got the carbon off.

Next job was getting on the ground to learn the spots system, at the same time checking our radios and finding out if there were any dead areas. We were still running around doing that when, at 2 p.m., Alpha came up on the net. 'Hello, all stations, return to this location immediately.'

Simmonds was already in the briefing area, looking like a man under pressure. Like the rest of us he'd probably had very little sleep. There was two days' growth on his chin and he was having a bad hair day. Something was definitely on; there was a lot more noise and bustle from the machines and men in the background. He had about twenty bits of paper in his hands. The slime were giving him more as he talked, as well as distributing copies of the rules of engagement to us. The operation, I saw, was now called Flavius.

'Just about an hour and a half ago,' he said, 'Savage and McCann passed through Immigration at Malaga airport. They were on a flight from Paris. Farrell met them. We have no idea how she got there. The team is complete. There is just one little problem – the Spaniards lost them as they got into a taxi. Triggers are now being placed on the border crossing as a precaution. I have no reason to believe that the attack will not take place as planned.'

He paused and looked at each of us in turn. 'I've just become aware of two very critical pieces of information. First, the players will not be using a blocking car to reserve a parking space in the target area. A blocking car would mean making two trips across the border, and the int is that they're not prepared to take the risk. The PIRA vehicle, when it arrives, should therefore be perceived as the real thing.

'Second, the detonation of the bomb will be by a hand-held, remote-control initiation device: they want to be sure that the bomb goes off at exactly the right moment. Remember, gentlemen, any one of the team, or all of them, could be in possession of that device. That bomb must not detonate. There could be hundreds of lives at risk.'

I was woken by the noise of engines in reverse and wheels on tarmac. It was just after 6 a.m. I had been asleep for three hours. It was still dark and the rain had eased quite a bit. I leaned over to the back. 'Kelly, Kelly, time to wake up.' As I shook her there was a gentle moan. 'Oh, OK. I'm coming.' She sat up, rubbing her eyes.

With the cuff of my coat I started to tidy her up. I didn't want her walking into the airport looking wrecked. I wanted us looking as spruce and happy as Marie and Donny Osmond on Prozac.

We got out of the car with the bag, and I locked up, after checking inside to make sure there wasn't anything attractive on view.

The last thing I needed now was a car park attendant taking an interest in my lock-picking kit. We walked over to the stop and didn't have long to wait before the bus arrived to take us to departures.

The terminal looked just like any airport at that time of the morning. The check-in desks were already quite busy with business fliers. Some people, mostly student types, looked as though they were waiting for flights that they'd got there much too early for, and had got their heads down in sleeping bags spread across three or four seats, with a massive backpack alongside. Cleaners with polishing machines trudged across the tiled floors like zombies.

I picked up a free airport magazine from the rack at the top of the escalator. Looking at the flight guide at the back I saw that the first possible departure to the UK was at just after 5 p.m. that evening. It was going to be a long wait.

I looked at Kelly; we both could do with a decent wash. We went down the escalator to the international arrivals area on the lower level. I put some money in a machine and bought a couple of travel kits to supplement our washing gear, and went into one of the disabled toilets.

I shaved as Kelly washed her face. I scraped the dirt off her boots with toilet paper and generally cleaned her up, combed her hair and put it in an elastic band at the back so it didn't look so greasy. By the end of half an hour we were looking fairly respectable. The scabs on my face were healing. I tried to grin, but they hurt too much. No Prozac, but we'd pass muster.

I picked up the bag. 'You ready?'

'We're going to England now?'

'Just one thing left to do. Follow me.' I pulled at her stubby ponytail that made her look like a 4-foot-tall cheerleader. She pretended to be annoyed but I could tell she liked the attention.

We went back up the escalator and walked around the edge of the terminal, seemingly looking at the aircraft out on the tarmac. In fact, there were two quite different things I was looking for. 'I need to post something,' I said, spotting the FedEx box.

I used the credit card details on the hire car agreement to fill in the dispatch form. Fuck it, Big Al could pay for a few things now he was rich.

Kelly was watching my every movement. 'Who are you writing to?'

'I'm sending something to England in case we are stopped.' I showed her the floppy disk and back-up disk.

'Who are you sending it to?' She got more like her dad every day.

'Don't be so nosey.'

I put them in the envelope, sealed it and entered the delivery details. In the past we'd used the FedEx system to send the Firm photos that we'd taken of a target and developed in a hotel room, or other highly sensitive material. It saved getting caught in possession. Nowadays, however, the system was obsolete; with digital cameras you can take pictures, plug in your GSM mobile, dial up the UK and transmit.

We continued walking around the edge of the terminal. I found the power point I was looking for at the end of a row of black plastic seats, where two students were snoring. I pointed to the last two spaces. 'Let's sit down here. I want to look at the laptop.'

I got it plugged in and Kelly decided she wanted something to eat. 'Give me five minutes,' I said.

From what I'd seen already, I understood Gibraltar was a set-up, but it still didn't explain what Kev had to do with it. As I read on it became clear.

It seemed that in the late 1980s the Bush administration had been under pressure from Thatcher to do something about Noraid's fund-raising for PIRA. With so many millions of American-Irish votes on the line, however, it was a tricky call. A deal was struck: if the Brits could expose the fact that Noraid money was being used to buy drugs, it would help discredit PIRA in the USA and Bush could then take action. After all, who would complain about a US administration fighting the spread of dangerous drugs?

When the British intelligence service started to gather int about PIRA's drug connections with Gibraltar, it seemed to present a window of opportunity. After the events of 6 March, however, the window was slammed shut. Those votes were too important.

By the early 1990s the US had a new administration – and the UK a new prime minister. In Northern Ireland, the peace process began. The US were told – and the message was delivered at the highest level – that unless they put pressure on PIRA to come to the peace table the UK would expose what was happening to Noraid funds raised in America. It would look to the world like a failure by a power that preached so readily to others, to fight the drug war in its own backyard.

Another deal was struck. Clinton allowed Gerry Adams into the USA in 1995, a move that was not only good for the Irish-American vote but made Clinton look like the prince of peacemakers. He also appeared to be snubbing John Major's stand against PIRA, but the British didn't mind; they knew the agenda. Behind closed doors, Gerry Adams was told that, if PIRA didn't let the peace process happen, the US would come down on them like a ton of steaming shit.

A ceasefire was indeed declared. It seemed that it was now time to talk for real instead of the years of covert talks that had got nowhere. Clinton and the British government would be seen as peace brokers, and PIRA would have a say in the way the deal was shaped.

On 12 February 1996, however, a massive bomb exploded at Canary Wharf in London, killing two and causing hundreds of millions of pounds' worth of damage. The ceasefire was broken. It was back to business as usual.

But it didn't end there. Kev had also discovered that PIRA had been trying to blackmail certain Gibraltarian officials, with some success. It seemed Gibraltar was still the key to Europe. Spain was far too much of a risk. They had also targeted some important personalities in the US, so they could continue to operate their drugs business with impunity. One of the victims was high up in the DEA. Kev's problem was he didn't know who.

I did; I had the photograph of his boss.

And now I knew why McGear, Fernahan and Macauley had been in Gibraltar. Whoever the official was, they'd been there to give him a gypsy's warning, and to try to blackmail him with the shipment documents and photographs to get the route open again. Maybe ETA had wanted too big a cut of the profits in Spain.

I closed down the laptop. I had to get back to the UK. I had to see Simmonds.

Kelly had been watching me. 'Good,' she said. 'Can we have breakfast now?'

I walked with her to Dunkin' Donuts. She had a carton of milk, I had coffee and we both got stuck into some big stinking doughnuts. I had six.

At ten o'clock we went back down the escalator to international arrivals. I needed passports – British or American, I didn't care. I scanned the international flights on the monitor. Chances were we were going to end up with American documents as opposed to British, purely because of the number of families streaming back from the spring break.

Just like before, there were people both sides of the railings, waiting with their cameras and flowers. Kelly and I sat on the PVC seats near the domestic carousels on the other side of the international gates. I had my arm around her, as if I was cuddling her and chatting away. In fact I was talking her through some of the finer points of theft.

'Do you think you can do it?'

We sat and watched the first wave of domestic arrivals come and collect their luggage.

I pinged a potential family. 'That's the sort of thing we're looking for, but it's two boys,' I smiled. 'You want to be a boy for the day?'

'No way. Boys smell!'

I put my nose into my sweatshirt. I agreed. 'OK, we'll wait.'

A flight arrived from Frankfurt and this time we struck gold. The parents were late thirties, the kids were about ten or eleven, a girl and a boy; the mother was carrying a clear plastic handbag with white mesh, so you could check everything was where it should be. I couldn't believe our luck. 'See them? That's what we want. Let's go, shall we?'

There was a slightly hesitant 'Yeahhh.' She didn't sound too keen now. All mouth and trousers, my mother would have said. Should I let her do this? I could cut it right now. As they walked towards the toilets I had to make a decision. Fuck it, let's carry on and get this done.

'She's going in with her daughter,' I said. 'Make sure nobody's behind you. Remember, I'll be waiting.'

We followed on casually. The husband had left with the boy, perhaps to visit one of the vending machines, or to get a taxi or their car.

They both went into the toilets via the ladies' entrance, chatting and giggling. The woman had the bag over her shoulder. We entered via the men's on the right of the disabled toilets, and immediately went into one of the large cubicles.

'I'll be in this one here, OK, Kelly?'

'OK.'

'Remember what you have to do?'

I got a big, positive nod.

'Off you go, then.' I closed the door and held it in place. The toilets were large enough for a wheelchair to manoeuvre in. The slightest sound seemed to echo. The floors were wet and smelled of bleach. The timesheet on the back of the door showed that the place had been cleaned only fifteen minutes ago.

My heart was pumping so hard I could feel it underneath my shirt. My whole future pivoted on the actions of a seven-year-old girl. She had to slip her hand under the cubicle, grab the handbag, put it under her coat and walk away without looking back.

Not difficult, just majorly flawed. But without passports we couldn't get out of the country, it was as simple as that. There was no way I could go back to Big Al's. Besides the risk of the journey, I couldn't trust him, for the simple reason that I had no idea what he'd been doing since I left him. It was just too fucking complicated. We needed to get out of this country, and now.

I was shaken from my thoughts by a sudden *knock, knock, knock* and a nervous, 'Nickkk!'

I opened the door quickly, didn't even look, and in she ran. I closed and locked it, picked her up and carried her over to the toilet.

I put down the lid and we sat together. I smiled and whispered, 'Well done!' She looked both excited and scared. I was just scared, because I knew that, at any minute, all hell would break loose.

And then it came. The mother was running out of the toilet, shouting, 'I've had my bag stolen! Where's Louise? Louise!'

The girl came out and started to cry. 'Mommy! Mommy!'

I could hear them both run off screaming. Now was not the time to get out. People would be looking; attention would be focused. Let's just sit tight and look at the passports.

We'd just robbed Mrs Fiona Sandborn and family. Fine, except that Mr Sandborn didn't look at all like Mr Stone. Never mind, I could do something about that later on. But the names of both kids were entered on each of their parents' passports, and that was a problem.

I pulled out the cash and her reading glasses. The toilet cistern was a sealed unit behind the wall. There was nowhere to hide the bag. I got up, told Kelly to stand and listened at the door.

The woman had found a policeman. I imagined the scene outside. A little crowd would have gathered round. The cop would be making notes, radioing Control, maybe checking the other cubicles. I broke into a sweat.

I stood at the door and waited for what seemed like an hour. Kelly tiptoed exaggeratedly towards me; I bent down and she whispered in my ear, 'Is it all right yet?'

'Almost.'

Then I heard a banging noise and knocking. Somebody was pushing back the doors in the vacant cubicles and knocking on the doors of the others. They were looking for the thief or, more likely, to see if the bag had been dumped once the money had been taken. They'd be at our cubicle any second.

I didn't have time to think. 'Kelly, you must talk if they knock. I want you to—'

Knock knock knock.

In the echo chamber of the disabled toilet, it sounded like the slam of a cell door.

A male voice shouted, 'Hello. Police. Anyone there?' He tried to turn the handle.

I quickly moved Kelly back to the toilet and whispered in her ear, 'Say you will be out soon.'

She shouted, 'I'm coming out soon!'

There was no reply, just the same thing happening at the next cubicle. The danger had passed, or so I hoped.

All that was left to do was dump my pistol and mags. That was easy. I slipped them into Fiona's bag and crushed it into a package that would fit in a bin.

It was an hour before I decided it was safe to leave. I turned to Kelly. 'Your name is Louise now, OK? Louise Sandborn.'

'OK.'

She didn't seem fussed at all.

'Louise, when we leave here in a minute, I want you to be really happy and hold my hand.' With that I picked up the bag. 'OK, we're off!'

'To England?'

'Of course! But first of all we've got to get on the plane. By the way, you were great – well done!'

We got into the departures area at 11.30 a.m. Still several hours to go before the first possible flight, the BA216 to Heathrow at 17:10.

I went to a phone and, using the numbers in the airport

magazine, called each airline in turn to check seat availability. The British Airways flight was fully booked. So was United Airways' 918 at 18:10, the BA at 18:10 and the United at 18:40. I eventually managed to find two spare seats on a flight with Virgin at 18:45, and gave all the details of Mr Sandborn, who was on his way to the airport right now. Payment was courtesy of the details for Big Al's plastic on the car hire form.

I wandered past the Virgin desk for a check, and found it didn't open until 1.30 p.m. One and a half hours to sit and sweat.

Terry Sandborn was a little older than me and his shoulder-length hair was starting to go grey. My hair was just below the ear and brown. Thankfully, his passport was four years old.

To the delight of Kelly and the terminal's barber-shop owner I underwent a number one crew-cut, coming out looking like a US Marine.

We then went into the travel shop and I bought a pack of painkillers that claimed to be the answer to a woman's period pains. Judging from the list of ingredients, they were certainly the answer for me.

All the time, I kept hoping that the police had assumed the motive for the theft was money, and, rather than pursuing the matter further, had left it to the Sandborns to report the cards and passport missing. I didn't want to turn up at the ticket sales desk and be jumped on by several hundredweight of cop.

Still thirty minutes to go before we could check in. One more thing to do.

'Kelly, we have to go to the toilet up here for a while.'

'I don't need to go.'

'It's for me to get into my disguise. Come and see.'

We went to the disabled toilet in departures and closed the door. I took out Fiona's glasses. They were gold-framed and had lenses as thick as the bottom of Coke bottles. I tried them on. The frames weren't big enough but they looked OK. I turned to Kelly and crossed my eyes. Then I had to stop her laughing.

I got the painkillers out of the holdall. 'I'm going to take this stuff and it's going to make me ill. But it's for a reason, OK?'

She wasn't quite sure. 'Oh, OK, then.'

I took six capsules and waited. The hot flushes started, then the cold sweats. I put my hands up to show it was OK as six dough-nuts and a coffee flew out of my mouth into the toilet bowl.

Kelly watched in amazement as I had a rinse in the basin. I looked at myself in the mirror. Just as I'd hoped, I looked as pale and clammy as I felt. I took two more.

There were few customers at the long line of check-in desks and only one woman on duty at Virgin Atlantic sales. She was writing something and her head was down as we approached. She was in her mid-twenties, black and beautiful, with relaxed hair pulled back in a bun.

'Hello, the name's Sandborn.' Because of the codeine my voice was lower and coarse. 'There should be two tickets for me.' I tried to look disorganized and fucked off. 'Hopefully my brother-in-law has booked them?' My eyes looked to the sky in hope.

'Sure, do you have a reference number?'

'Sorry, he didn't give me one. Just Sandborn.'

She tapped that out and said, 'That's fine, Mr Sandborn, two tickets for you and Louise. How many bags are you checking in?'

I had the laptop on my shoulder and the holdall in my hand. I dithered, as if working out if I'd need the laptop. 'Just this one.' I put the holdall on the scale. It didn't weigh much, but it was bulked out respectably with the blanket.

'Could I see your passport, please?'

I looked in all my pockets without apparent success. I didn't want to produce Sandborn's documents straight away. 'Look, I know we were lucky to get seats at all, but is it possible to make sure we're sitting together?' I leaned a little closer and half whispered, 'Louise hates flying.'

Kelly and I exchanged glances. 'That's OK, baby, that's OK.' My voice dropped again. 'We're on a bit of a mercy mission.'

I looked down at Kelly and back at the woman, my face pained. 'Her grandmother's . . .' I let it hang, as if the rest of the sentence would be too terrible for a little girl's ears.

'I'll see what I can do, sir.'

She was hitting the keys of her PC at such a speed it looked as if she was bluffing. I put the passport on top of the counter. She looked up and smiled. 'No problem, Mr Sandborn.'

'That's marvellous.' But I still wanted to keep the conversation going. 'I wondered, would it be possible for us to use one of your lounges? It's just that, after my chemotherapy, I tire very easily. We've been rushing around today and I don't feel too well. I only have to knock myself and I cut.'

She looked at my scabs and pale complexion and understood. There was a pause, then she said, 'My mother went through chemo for cancer of the liver. The therapy worked, after all that pain she came through.'

I thanked her for her concern and message of support.

Now just get me into the lounge, out of the fucking way!

'Let me find out.' Smiling at Kelly, she picked up the phone and spoke. After several seconds of weird airline vocabulary she looked at me and nodded. 'That's fine, sir. We share facilities with United. I'll fill out an invitation.'

I thanked her and she reached for the passport. I hoped that, by now, she knew me so well it was just a formality. She flicked it open and I turned away and talked to Kelly, telling her how exciting it was going to be, flying to see Grandma.

I heard, 'You'll be boarding at about five thirty.' I looked up, all smiles.

'Go to Gate C. A shuttle will take you to the lounge. You both have a pleasant flight!'

'Thank you so much. Come on, then, Louise, we've got a plane to catch!' I let Kelly walk on a few steps, then turned back to the woman and said, 'I just hope Grandma can wait for us.' She nodded knowingly.

All I wanted to do now was get airside. First hurdle was

security. Kelly went through first and I followed. No alarms. I had to open up the laptop and switch it on to prove it worked, but I'd been expecting that. All the Flavius documents were now in a file entitled Games.

We went straight to Gate C, walked through and into the shuttle bus. There was a five-minute wait while the bus filled up, then the doors closed, the hydraulics lowered and we drove about half a mile across the tarmac to the departures lounge proper.

The area was plush and busy. I heard a lot of British accents, mixed in with snatches of German and French. Kelly and I headed for the United lounge, via a detour to the pick-and-mix stall.

We sat quietly with a large cappuccino and a Coke. Unfortunately the down time just gave me time to think about whether I'd made any mistakes.

A security man walked into the reception and talked to the people on the desk. My heart beat faster. We were so close to the aircraft on the other side of the glass that I felt I could reach out and touch them. I could almost smell the aviation fuel.

I told myself to calm down. If they'd wanted us, they would have found us by now. But, in truth, so many things could still go wrong that one of them almost certainly would. I was still sweating good-style. My head was glistening. And I didn't know if it was the capsules or my flapping, but I was starting to feel weak.

'Nick? Am I Louise all day today or just for now?'

I pretended to think about it. 'The whole day. You're Louise Sandborn all day.'

'Why?'

'Because they won't let us go to England unless we use another name.'

I got a smiling, thoughtful nod.

I said, 'Do you want to know something else?'

'What's that?'

'If I call you Louise, you have to call me Daddy. But just for today.'

I wasn't sure what kind of reaction to expect, but she just shrugged, 'Whatever.' Maybe that was what she wanted now.

The next three hours were grim, but at least we were out of the way. If I'd had any heart problems I would probably have died, the blood was coursing through me so fast and hard. I could hear it pumping in my ears.

I kept saying to myself, You're here now, there's nothing you can do about it; accept it. Just get on that fucking aircraft!

I looked at Kelly. 'You all right, Louise?'

'Yeah, I'm all right, Daddy.' She had a big smile now. I just hoped she kept it.

I watched the receptionist move to the microphone. She announced our flight and told us she had really enjoyed having us stay in the lounge.

There were about a dozen others who stood up and started to sort themselves out, folding papers and zipping up bags.

I got to my feet and stretched. 'Louise?'

'Yep?'

'Let's go to England!'

We walked towards the gate, father and daughter, hand in hand, talking garbage. My theory went: if I talked with her, they wouldn't talk to us.

Four or five people were ahead of us in the queue; like us, families with young children. Passports were being checked by a young Latino; he had an ID card on a chain around his neck, but we were too far away yet for me to make out what it said. Was he airline security or airport security?

Two uniformed security men came up and stood behind him, talking to each other. It was the kind of chat that looked so casual it probably wasn't. I used my sleeve to mop sweat from the side of my face.

Both the uniformed men were armed. The black guy cracked a joke as the white guy laughed and looked around. Kelly and I shuffled forward.

354

I held her beside me, the protective parent anxious in a crowd. The laptop was over my shoulder. Kelly held a teddy under each arm.

We moved three steps forward; another wait, then it was our turn with the Latino.

I wanted to make it all very easy for him. Smiling, I handed him the boarding pass and the passport. I was convinced the uniformed guys were looking at me. I went into boxer mode: everything was focused on the Latino; everything else was in the distance, muffled, distorted, peripheral. A bead of sweat fell down my cheek and I knew he'd noticed it. I knew he could see my chest heaving up and down.

Kelly was just behind and to the right of me. I looked at her and smiled.

'Sir?'

I silently exhaled in preparation and looked back at him.

'Just the passport, sir.' He handed me back the boarding pass. I grinned, the inexperienced dickhead traveller.

He flicked through the pages of the passport, stopping at Sandborn's photograph. He glanced at me, then back at the passport.

I'm in the shit.

I let him see I was reading his thoughts. 'Male menopause,' I grinned, rubbing my hand over what was left of my hair. My scalp was drenched. 'The Bruce Willis look!'

The fucker didn't laugh. He was making up his mind. Eventually he closed the passport and tapped it in his hand. 'Have a pleasant flight, sir.'

I went to give him a nod, but he was already paying attention to the people behind me.

We moved two paces towards the girls from Virgin and handed them our boarding passes. The two security men didn't budge.

We started to walk onto the airbridge and I felt as if I'd been trying to run through waist-high water and was suddenly on the shoreline.

The Latino still worried me. I thought about him all the way onto the aircraft. It was only when I'd found our seats, put the bag and laptop in the overhead locker, settled down and picked up the in-flight magazine, that I took a deep breath and let it out very very slowly; it wasn't a sigh of relief, I was boosting the oxygen levels in my blood. No, the fucker wasn't happy. His suspicions had been aroused, but he hadn't asked any questions, hadn't even asked my name. We might be on the shoreline, but it was far from being dry land.

The aircraft was still filling up. I kept taking deep breaths to try to control my pulse rate.

Officials were moving in and out of the aircraft with manifests. Every time it happened I was expecting to see the two security guys in tow. There was only one entrance, only one exit. There was nowhere to run. As I worked through the scenarios in my mind I just had to accept the fact that the die was cast. I was a passenger now and, for a fleeting second, I had the same feeling that I'd always had on any aircraft, military or civilian – I was in the hands of others and powerless to decide my own destiny, and I hated it.

Still people were filing on. I nearly burst out in nervous laughter as the speakers played Gloria Gaynor's 'I Will Survive'. I looked at Kelly and winked. She thought it was great, sitting there trying to strap in her teddies.

One of the male flight attendants came down our aisle, still wearing his Virgin suit, not yet in shirtsleeve order. He came down as far as our row of seats and stopped. Judging by his line of sight he seemed to be checking our seat belts. It was too early or that, surely? I nodded and smiled. He turned back and disappeared into the galley.

I watched the entrance, expecting the worst. One of the female flight attendants poked her head out and looked directly at me. Kelly's teddies were suddenly very interesting.

I could feel tingling in my feet. My stomach tightened. I looked up again. She'd gone.

The male attendant came out again, carrying a bin liner. He approached us, stopped and squatted down in the aisle next to Kelly. He said, 'Hiya!'

'Hello!'

He put his hand into the bin liner and I waited for him to bring out the .45. Good ploy, letting me think he's a member of the crew doing something for the kid.

He pulled out a little nylon daysack. Splattered all over the back was the Virgin logo and the words 'Kids With Altitude'. 'We forgot to give you one of these,' he said. I nearly hugged him.

'Thank you very much!' I grinned like an asylum inmate, my eyes 100 per cent larger through the lenses of Fiona's glasses. 'Thank you so much!'

He did his best not to look at me, as if I was indeed some sort of weirdo, then offered us a drink before take-off. I was gagging for a beer, but I might have to start performing the other side and, anyway, I just wanted to get my head down. We had an orange juice each instead.

Sharing the in-flight guide with her, I said, 'What film are you going to watch, Louise?'

'*Clueless,*' she grinned.

'Whatever,' I said.

Twenty minutes later, right on schedule, the aircraft finally lifted off from the runway. Suddenly I didn't mind being in a pilot's hands after all.

36

We went through all the nonsense of the introduction by the captain, how wonderful it was to have us on board and when we were going to be fed. My body heat was slowly starting to dry out my sweat-drenched shirt. Even my socks had been wet. I looked over at Kelly. She had a sad face on. I shoved her with my arm. 'You OK?'

'I suppose. It's just I'll miss Melissa and I didn't even tell her that I'm going to England.'

I knew how to get out of this type of thing now. 'Well, all you have to do is think of good things about Melissa and that will make you feel happy.' I was waiting for her reply. I knew the sort of thing it was going to be.

'What do you think about to make you happy, about your best friend David?'

Easy; I was prepared. 'Well, nearly twelve years ago, we were working together and he was rebuilding his house and needed a new wooden floor.'

She was enjoying this, stories at bedtime. She certainly looked as if she would go to sleep soon, cuddling up to me. I carried on telling her how we'd both nicked a squash-court floor from one of the HQ Security Forces bases while in Northern Ireland with the Det. We were there at three o'clock in the morning with spades, hammers and chisels. We put the boards in a van and brought them over to the mainland. After all, HM Government spent all that time and money training us to break in and steal things. Why not use it for ourselves? The next three days had been spent laying the hallway and kitchen of the house near Brecon with his nice new flooring.

I grinned down at her for a reaction, but she was already sound asleep.

I started to watch the video but knew I was going to fall asleep any minute – so long as the capsules wore off and I could stop my mind going back to the same question over and over again.

There was an unholy alliance between PIRA and corrupt elements of the DEA, of that there was no doubt – and it very much looked as though Kev's boss was at the centre of it. Kev had found out about the corruption, but not who was involved. He wanted to talk to somebody about it. So was it his boss that he'd unwittingly phoned for an opinion on the day I arrived in Washington? Very unlikely, because Kev would have included him on his list of suspects. Much more probable was that he'd spoken to someone unconnected with the DEA, someone who would have known what he was talking about and whose opinion he would have valued. Could it have been Luther? He knew Kev; would Kev have trusted him? Who knows? Whoever he called, he was dead within an hour of putting down the phone.

The cabin light came on a couple of hours before landing and we were served breakfast. I gave Kelly a nudge, but she groaned and buried herself under her blanket. I didn't bother with the food. From feeling almost elated at having got away with it, I awoke profoundly depressed. My mood was as black as the coffee in front of me. I'd been mad to let myself feel relieved. We weren't out of the woods by a long way; if they knew we were on the aircraft, of course they wouldn't do anything about it until we landed. It was at the point that I walked off the aircraft and stepped onto the ramp that they'd lift me. Even if that didn't happen, there was Immigration. The officials trying to keep out undesirables are much tougher and a lot more on the ball than those in charge of waving you off. They vet your documents that bit more closely, scrutinize your body language, read your eyes. Kelly and I were on a stolen passport. We'd got through at Dulles, but that didn't mean we could pull it off again.

I took four capsules and finished my coffee. I remembered that I was an American citizen now. When the attendant came past I asked her for an immigration card. Kelly still wouldn't wake up.

Filling in the card, I decided that the Sandborns had just moved and now lived only one door away from Mr and Mrs Brown. Hunting Bear Path was the only address I could talk about convincingly.

If I was lifted at Immigration, it wouldn't be the first time. I'd come into Gatwick airport once from a job. I gave my passport to the immigration officer, and while he was inspecting it a boy came up on either side, gripped my arms and took the passport from the official. 'Mr Stamford? Special Branch. Come with us.' I wasn't going to argue; my cover was good, I was in the UK now, everything was going to be fine.

They strip-searched me in an interview room, firing questions left, right and centre. I went through the whole routine of my cover story: where I'd been, what I'd been doing, why I'd been doing it. They telephoned my cover and James supported my story. Everything was going swimmingly.

Then I got put in the airport detention cells and three policemen came in. They wasted no time; they piled in like rugby forwards, two holding my arms, one throwing punches, then taking turns. They filled me in severely. No word of explanation.

Next I got taken for an interview and was accused of being a paedophile and procuring kids in Thailand – which was strange, considering I'd been on a deniable op in Russia. There was nothing I could say, it was just down to denying and waiting for the system to get me out.

After about four hours of interviews I was sitting in my cell. In came people from the intelligence service, to debrief me on my performance. It had been a fucking exercise. They'd been testing all the Ks as we came back into the UK; the only trouble was they'd picked the wrong charge to pull us in on. The police obviously didn't wait for niceties like court rooms when it came to dealing with child molesters, and everyone who was lifted got taken to one side and given the good news. One bloke, who'd flown into Jersey, got such a severe kicking he ended up in hospital.

Kelly was still half asleep and she looked as rough as I felt. She looked as if she'd been sleeping in a hedge. She yawned and made an attempt to stretch. As she opened her eyes and looked around, completely bewildered, I grinned and offered her the carton of orange juice. 'How are you today, Louise?'

She still looked lost for a second or two, then got back with the programme. 'I'm all right.' She paused, grinned and added, 'Daddy.' She closed her eyes and turned over, trying to sort herself out with the pillow and blanket. I didn't have the heart to tell her we were landing soon.

At least I got to drink her orange juice as a Welcome to London video came on the screens, loads of pomp, circumstance and pageantry, the Household Cavalry astride their horses, Guardsmen marching up and down, the Queen riding down the Mall in her carriage. To me, London had never looked so good.

Then the aircraft landed and we became actors again.

We taxied and stopped at our ramp. Everybody jumped out of their seat as if they were going to miss out on something. I leaned over to Kelly. 'Wait here, we're in no rush.' I wanted to get into the middle of the crowd.

Eventually we got all the bits and pieces back into Kelly's day-sack, organized the teddies and joined the line. I was trying to look ahead, but couldn't see much.

We got to the galley area, turned left and shuffled towards the door. On the ramp were three men – normal British Airports Authority reception staff in fluorescent jackets, who were manning the airbridge, helping a woman into a wheelchair. Things were looking good; freedom felt so close.

We walked up the ramp and joined the spur that led to the main terminal. Kelly didn't have a care in the world, which was good. I didn't want her to understand what was happening.

There was heavy foot traffic in both directions, people running with hand luggage, drifting in and out of shops, milling around at gates. I had the daysack and laptop over my shoulder and held Kelly's hand. She carried the teddies. We reached the walkway.

Heathrow is the most monitored, most camera'd, most visually and physically secure airport in the world. Untold pairs of eyes would already be on us; this was no time for looking furtive or guilty. The travelator stopped by gates 43–47, then a new one started about 10 metres later. As we trundled along, I waited until there was a gap each side of us and bent down to Kelly. 'You mustn't forget I am your daddy today – OK, Louise Sandborn?'

'As if!' she said with a huge smile.

I just hoped we were both smiling in thirty minutes' time.

We came to the end of the walkway and took a down escalator, following signs for passport control and baggage reclaim. From halfway down the escalator I could see the Immigration hall straight ahead. This was where we'd stand or fall.

There were about four or five people waiting to go through each of the desks. I started joking with Kelly, trying to give myself something to do instead of just looking nervous. I'd entered countries illegally hundreds of times, but never so unprepared or under such pressure.

'All set, Louise?'

'I'm ready, Daddy.'

I passed her the daysack so I could get the passport and visa card out of my pocket. We ambled up to passport control and joined the end of a queue. I kept reminding myself about an

American friend who'd travelled from Boston to Canada, and then from Canada back to the UK. He'd picked up his friend's passport by mistake while they were sharing a hotel room; he couldn't get back to exchange it, so he'd had to bluff it. No-one had even batted an eyelid.

We waited in line. Still with the laptop on my right shoulder, I was holding Kelly's hand with my left. I kept looking down at her and smiling, but not excessively so; that was suspicious behaviour and I knew that people would be watching on monitors and from behind two-way mirrors. The business type in front of us went through with a wave and a smile to the official. It was our turn. We approached the desk.

I handed my documents to the woman. She ran her eyes down the details on the card. She looked down at Kelly from her high desk. 'Hello, welcome to England.'

Kelly came back with a very American 'Hi!'

I guessed the woman was in her late thirties. Her hair was permed, but the perm had gone slightly wrong.

'Did you have a nice flight?' she asked.

Kelly had Jenny or Ricky in one hand, hanging by her ear, and the other one's head was sticking out from the top flap of her day-sack on her back. She said, 'Yes, it was fine, thank you.'

The woman kept the conversation going. 'And what's your name?' she asked, still checking the form.

Could I trust her to get it right, or should I butt in?

Kelly smiled and said, 'Kelly!'

What a farce. We'd come so far, we'd come through so much, only to be caught by a line straight from a B movie.

Straight away I smiled down at Kelly, 'No, it's not!' I didn't want to look at the woman. I could feel the smile drain from her face, could feel her eyes burning into the side of my head.

There was a pause that felt like an hour as I tried to think of what to do or say next. I pictured the woman's finger hovering over a concealed button.

Kelly got there before me. 'I know, I'm joking,' she giggled, holding out a teddy. 'This is Kelly! My name is Louise. What's yours?'

'My name's Margaret.' The smile was back. If only she'd known how close she'd been to a kill.

She opened the passport. Her eyes flicked up and down as she studied first the picture, then my face. She put the passport down below the level of the desk and I saw the tell-tale glow of ultra-violet light. Then she looked back into my eyes and said, 'When was this picture taken?'

'About four years ago, I guess.' I gave a weak smile, and said in a low voice that Kelly wasn't meant to overhear, 'I've been having chemotherapy. The hair's just starting to grow back.' I rubbed my head. My skin felt damp and cold. Hopefully I still looked shit. The capsules certainly made me feel it. 'I'm bringing Louise over to see my wife's parents because it's been quite a traumatic time. My wife's staying with our other child because he's ill at the moment. When it rains, it pours!'

'Oh,' she said, and it sounded genuinely sympathetic. But she didn't hand back the passport.

There was a big lull, as if she was waiting for me to fill the silence with a confession. Or maybe she was just trying to think of something helpful and human to say. Finally she said, 'Have a good stay,' and put the documents back on the desktop.

There was that urge just to grab them and run.

'Thank you very much,' I said, picking them up and putting them back into my pocket, then carefully doing up the button, because that was what a normal dad would do. Only then did I turn to Kelly. 'C'mon, baby, let's go!'

I started to walk, but Kelly stood her ground. Oh fuck, now what?

'Goodbye, Margaret,' she beamed, 'have a nice day!'

Then that was it. We were nearly there. I knew there wasn't going to be a problem with the luggage because I wasn't going to collect it.

I checked the carousels. There was a flight from Brussels that was also unloading, so I headed for the blue channel. Even if they were watching and stopped us because Kelly had a Virgin Airlines bag, I would play the stupid person routine.

But there weren't any Customs on duty in the blue channel. We were free.

37

The large sliding doors opened up into the arrivals hall. We walked through into a throng of people holding up cards for taxis, or waiting for their loved ones. Nobody gave us a second look.

I went straight to the *bureau de change*. I found I'd done well last night with Ron, Melvin and the Sandborns, ending up with over £300 in cash. Like a nugget, I forgot to ask for a small-denomination note for the machine and we had to queue for ages for tube tickets. It didn't seem to matter; even the hour-long ride to Bank station was enjoyable. I was a free man, I was amongst ordinary people. None of them knew who we were or was going to pull a gun on us.

The City is a strange mixture of architecture. As we left the station we passed grand buildings comprised of columns and puritanically straight lines – the old Establishment. Turn a corner and we were confronted by monstrosities that were built in the Sixties and early Seventies by architects who must have taken a 'Let's go fuck up the City' pill. One of these buildings was the one I was heading for, the NatWest bank in Lombard Street, a road so narrow that just one car could squeeze down it.

We went through the revolving steel and glass doors into the banking hall, where rows of cashiers sat behind protective screens. But I wasn't there for money.

The reception desk was manned by a man and a woman, both in their early twenties, both wearing NatWest suits; they even had little corporate motifs sewn into the material of the breast pocket, probably so the staff wouldn't wear them out of hours. As Kelly would have said, 'As if!'

I saw both of them give Kelly and me an instant appraisal and could feel them turning up their noses. I gave them a cheery, 'Hi, how are you?' and asked to speak with Guy Bexley.

The woman said, 'Can I have your name, please?' as she picked up the phone.

'Nick Stevenson.'

The girl called an extension. The man went back to being efficient on the other side of the reception desk.

I bent down and whispered to Kelly, 'I'll explain later.'

'He'll be along in a minute. Would you like to sit down?'

We waited on a settee that was very long, very deep and very plastic. I could sense Kelly's cogs turning.

Sure enough: 'Nick, am I Louise Stevenson now, or Louise Sandborn?'

I screwed up my face and scratched my head. 'Umm . . . Kelly!'

Guy Bexley came down. Guy was my 'Relationship Manager', whatever that was. All I knew was that he was the man I asked for when I wanted to get my security blanket out. He was late twenties, and you could see by his hairstyle and goatee beard that he felt uncomfortable in the issued suit and would be far happier wearing PVC trousers, holding a bottle of water and raving all night bare-chested.

We shook hands. 'Hello, Mr Stevenson, haven't seen you for a long time.'

I shrugged my shoulders. 'Work. This is Kelly.'

He bent down and said, 'Hello there, Kelly,' in his best 'I've been trained how to introduce myself to kids' manner.

'I just need my locked box for five minutes, mate.'

I followed him towards the row of partitioned offices on the other side of the hall. I'd been in them many times before. They were all identical; each contained just a round table, four chairs and a telephone. It was where people went to count money or beg for a loan. He started to leave.

'Could I also have a statement on my Diamond Reserve, please?'

Guy nodded and left. Kelly said, 'What are we doing here?'

I should have known by now that she hated to be left out of things. Just like her dad. 'Wait and see,' I winked.

A few minutes later Guy reappeared, put the box on the table and gave me a folded printout of my account. I felt nervous as I opened up the paper. My eyes went straight for the bottom right-hand corner.

Four hundred and twenty-six thousand, five hundred and seventy dollars, converted at a rate of 1.58 dollars to the pound.

Big Al had done it! I had to control myself as I remembered Bexley was still standing there. 'I'll just be about five minutes,' I said.

'Tell reception when you're ready; they'll put it back in the vault for you.' He left with a shake of my hand and a 'Bye, Kelly!' and closed the door behind him.

The box was 18 inches by 12 inches, a metal file-container I'd bought for a tenner in Woolworths, with a very cheap lock on the top that opened under pressure. I'd been planning to rent a proper safe deposit box, but then I'd remembered about the Knightsbridge raid years before. Also, it meant I'd have to turn up with a key, and I couldn't guarantee I was going to have that with me. This way was easier; the only problem was that, if I had to do a runner out of the country, it could only be during banking hours.

I flipped the lock and pulled out a couple of old *Private Eyes* I'd put on top in case it accidentally opened. I threw them over to Kelly. 'See if you can make any sense of those.' She picked one up and started to flick through the pages.

The first thing I took out was the mobile phone and recharger. I switched it on. The battery was still working, but I put it in the recharger anyway and plugged it into the wall.

Next I pulled out a clear plastic carrier bag which contained bundles of US dollar bills and pounds sterling, five South African krugerrands, and ten half-sovereigns that I'd stolen after the Gulf War. All troops who were behind enemy lines in Iraq were issued with twenty of the things as bribes for the locals in case we were in the shit. In my patrol we'd managed to keep ten of them each; we said we'd lost the rest in a contact. To begin with I'd only kept them as souvenirs, but they'd soon increased in value. I left them in the bag; I was only interested in the sterling.

I dug out a European leather *porte-monnaie* with a strap, in which I had a complete set of ID – passport, credit cards, driver's licence, all the stuff I needed to become Nicholas Duncan Stevenson. It had taken years to get cover in such depth, all originating from a social security number I'd bought in a pub in Brixton for fifty quid.

I then got out an electronic notebook. It was great; it meant that, anywhere in the world, I could fax, send memos, do word processing and maintain a database. The problem was I didn't have a clue how to use it. I just used the phone number and address facility because it could only be accessed with a password.

I had a quick look over at Kelly. She was thumbing through the *Eye*, not understanding a word. I pushed my hand to the bottom of the box and extracted the 9mm semi-automatic Browning that I'd liberated from Africa in the late Eighties. Loading the mags with rounds from a small Tupperware box, I made ready and checked chamber. Kelly looked up, but didn't give it a second glance.

I powered up the notebook, tapped in 2242, and found the number I wanted. I picked up the telephone on the table. Kelly looked up again. 'Who are you phoning?'

'Euan.'

'Who is he?'

I could see the confusion on her face.

'He's my best friend.' I carried on pressing the phone number.

'But . . .'

I put my finger to my lips. 'Shhh.'

He wasn't in. I left a message on the answering machine in veiled speech. Then I put the laptop into the box, together with everything that I wasn't taking with me – including the print-out.

Kelly was bored with the *Eyes* now, so I took them off her to put back in the box. I knew there was a question on its way.

'Nick?'

I just carried on packing. 'Yes?'

'You said David was your best friend.'

'Ah yes. Well, Euan is my best friend. It's just that sometimes I have to call him David because . . .' I started to think of a lie, but why? 'I told you because, if we got caught, then you wouldn't know his real name. That way you couldn't tell anyone. It's some-thing that is done all the time. It's called OPSEC – operational security.' I finished packing and closed the box. She had thought about it.

'Oh, OK. His name's Euan, then.'

'When you see him he might even show you the floor we talked about.'

I poked my head round the corner and waved at the reception-ist. She came in, picked up the box and left.

I turned to Kelly. 'Right, then, time for a shopping frenzy. Let me see, we'd better buy some nice new clothes for us both, and then we'll go and stay in a hotel and wait for Euan to ring. Sound good to you?'

Her face brightened. 'OK!'

Once this was all over I would have to set up a different named account and move the money, and I'd stop being Stevenson. A pain in the arse to organize, but I could live with that for $426,570.

The cab ride to Trafalgar Square became a tour given by me to Kelly. I was more into it than she was, and I could tell by the taxi driver's expression in his rear-view mirror that I was getting most of the details wrong.

We were going down the Strand when I spotted clothes shops on both sides of the road. We paid off the taxi and shopped for jeans, T-shirts and washing kit. Once done, we got another cab and I asked for Brown's Hotel.

I said to Kelly, 'You'll like this place. It's got two entrances, so you can enter from Dover Street and come out the other side, on Albermarle Street. Very important for spies like us.'

I switched on the phone, got hold of directory enquiries and called the hotel to make a reservation. Less than half an hour later we were in our room, but only after showing off to Kelly and discovering that the Dover Street exit was no longer open. Finger on the pulse.

The room was a world removed from the ones we had been used to. It was plush, comfortable and, best of all, it had a mini-bar with Toblerones. I could have killed a beer, but not yet; there was work to do.

Jet lag was starting to kick in. Kelly looked exhausted. She flopped onto the bed and I undressed her and threw her between the sheets. 'You can have a bath tomorrow,' I said. She was a starfish in about two minutes flat.

I checked that the phone had a good signal and that the charger was working. Euan knew my voice and my message – 'It's John the plumber. When do you want me to come and fix that tap? Give me a ring on . . .' would have done the trick.

I decided to have a quick nap for ten minutes, maybe shower, have something to eat, then go to bed. After all, it was only 5 p.m.

Ten minutes later, at a quarter to six in the morning, the phone rang. I pressed receive. I heard, 'Hello?' in that very low, very controlled voice I knew so well.

'I need a hand, mate,' I said. 'I need you to help me. Can you get to London?'

'When do you want me?'

'Now.'

'I'm in Wales. It'll take a bit of time.'

'I'll wait out on this number.'

'No problem. I'll get a train, it'll be quicker.'

'Thanks, mate. Give me a call about an hour before you get into Paddington.'

'Yep, OK.'

The phone went dead.

I had never felt so relieved. It was like putting down the phone after a doctor's just told you the cancer test was negative.

The train journey alone would take over three hours, so there wasn't much to do apart from enjoy the lull in the battle. Kelly woke up as I caught up with the election battle in the copy of *The Times* that had been slipped under the door – no walk to the street corner with some change at Brown's. I phoned room service and tried out the TV channels. No *Power Rangers*. Great.

In lazy time, we both eventually got up, showered, changed and were looking good. We took a leisurely stroll to the station through Piccadilly Circus, Leicester Square and Trafalgar Square. I delivered another tour lecture that Kelly didn't listen to. All she wanted to do was feed the pigeons. I kept on looking at my watch, waiting for Euan to call, and while Kelly was still being overrun by pigeons having a feeding frenzy in the square, the phone rang. It was 9.50 a.m. I put my finger in my other ear to block out the traffic and the screams of delight from Kelly and the other kids as birds tried to peck their eyes out.

'I'm an hour from Paddington.'

'That's great. I'll meet you at platform three, Charing Cross station, OK, mate?'

'See you there.'

The Charing Cross hotel was part of the station complex and just two minutes' walk from Trafalgar Square. I'd picked it because I knew that, from the foyer, you could see the taxis pull into the station and drop off their fares.

We waited and watched. The place was full of package-tour

Americans and Italians. The Americans were at the tour-guide desk, booking every show in town, and the Italians just moved from the lift to the exit door in one loud, arm-waving mob, shouting at each other and all trying to get through the glass doors at the same time.

It was about half an hour later that I saw a cab with a familiar figure in the back. I pointed him out to Kelly.

'Aren't we going to go and meet him?'

'No, we're going to stay here and look because we're going to surprise him. Just like we did in Daytona, remember?'

'Oh, yes. We have to stand off.'

I watched him get out. It was so wonderful to see him that I wanted to jump up and run outside. He was dressed in jeans and wearing the kind of shoes you see advertised in a Sunday supplement. Hush Puppies were positively cutting-edge fashion compared to these. He was also wearing a black nylon bomber jacket, so he'd be easy enough to pick out in the station. I said to Kelly, 'We'll give him a couple of minutes, then we'll go and surprise him, shall we?'

'Yeah!' She sounded quite excited. She had two lumps of bird shit on the back of her coat. I was waiting for them to dry before picking them off.

I stood off for five minutes, watching his arse for him. Then we walked towards the station and through a couple of arches to the ticket offices. The station was renovated Victorian, with W. H. Smith and all the other normal outlets. We looked for platform 3, and there he was, leaning against the wall, reading a paper. The same feeling: I wanted to run over there and hug him. We walked slowly.

He looked up and saw me. We both smiled and said, 'Hi. How's it going?' He looked at me, then at Kelly, but he didn't say anything; he knew that I'd tell him at some stage. We went off to the side of the station to steps that led us down towards the river. As we walked, he looked at my head and tried to hide a grin. 'Good haircut!'

Outside Embankment station we got into a taxi. Drills are drills, they're there for a reason and that is to protect you: the moment you start falling down on drills, you start fucking up. We took the driver a roundabout route, covering our arses, taking twenty minutes to Brown's instead of the straight-line ten.

As soon as we got back to the room I turned on the TV for Kelly and phoned room service. Everyone was hungry.

Euan was already chatting away with Kelly. She looked pleased to have somebody else to talk to, even if it was only another grown-up and a man. That was good, they were getting a relationship going, she was feeling comfortable with him.

The food came; there was a beefburger and chips for Kelly, and two club sandwiches for us. I said to Kelly, 'We'll let you eat in peace. We're going into the bathroom because you're watching TV and I want to talk to Euan about some stuff. Is that all right?'

She nodded, mouth already full.

Euan smiled, 'See you in a minute, Kelly. Save us a chip.'

We went into the bathroom with our coffees and sandwiches, the noise of the TV dying the moment I closed the door.

I started to tell him the story. Euan listened intently. He was visibly upset about Kev and Marsha. I'd got as far as the lift by Luther and co when he cut in. By now he was sitting on the edge of the bath.

'Bastards! Who were they? Do you think it was the same group that zapped Kev?'

'Must be.' I sat next to him. 'Kev knew the three who killed him. Kelly confirmed that Luther worked with Kev. Then there's the question of that phone call to "get the ball rolling".'

'You reckon it was Luther?'

I nodded. 'Fuck knows where he fits into the picture, but my guess is he's DEA, and also corrupt. It looks like some of the DEA are bent and working for drug money.' I told him about the

McGear killing and what I had found on the back-up disk once de Sabatino had opened the GIFs.

Euan understood so far. 'So it all has to do with PIRA running drugs into Europe? To keep the route open it needs backhanders, blackmail and threats. But what about McGear – did he say anything?'

'Not a word. He knew he was going to die anyway.'

'This guy de Sabatino? Does he have any copies of the int?'

I laughed. 'You know I'm not going to tell you that. OPSEC, mate, OPSEC!'

'Fair one,' he shrugged. 'Just being nosey.'

I carried on and explained what I had found in Kev's house. Euan didn't speak. He just sat there letting it all soak in. I felt suddenly exhausted, as if, by somehow passing on the baton to Euan, everything that had happened in the last ten days could at last catch up with me and take its toll.

I looked at him. He looked pretty drained himself.

'I can see only one thing wrong with what you're saying.'

'What's that, mate?'

'Wouldn't the Colombians have anticipated that a bomb would heighten security on the Rock, making it harder to get the drugs in?'

'It was a warning. They were sending out a gypsy's to anyone else who might not want to keep business going. I tell you, mate, this is far too big for me to be messing around with. I just want to get it to Simmonds and wash my hands of it.'

'I'll help any way I can.' He opened a packet of Benson & Hedges; he'd obviously taken up the weed again. I stood up, out of the way.

'I don't want to get you directly involved. Kev, Pat, me, we've all been fucked over – but I'm going to need you to back me if things go wrong.'

'You just have to name it.'

I could smell the sulphur from his match. He smiled as I started to wave the smoke from my face. He knew that I hated that. Even under extreme pressure some things never changed.

I said, 'Tomorrow afternoon, you should receive copies of the files by FedEx. If anything happens to me or Simmonds, it's basically down to you.' By now we were in a cloud of smoke. Any minute now the alarm was going to go off.

'No problems with that, mate,' he said in his very slow, very calm, very calculating way. If you told Euan he'd won the National Lottery he'd say, 'That's nice,' then go back to stacking his coins or folding his socks.

'How many copies of the disk are there besides the ones you're sending me?'

'I'm not going to tell you, mate. Need-to-know!'

He smiled. He knew I was protecting him.

'One more thing,' I said. 'I don't want to take Kelly with me to the Simmonds meet. He wasn't too pleased with me the last time we spoke. If this turns into a gang fuck I don't want her caught in the crossfire. You're the only person I can trust her with. It's only going to be for one night, maybe two. Can you do that for me?'

I expected an immediate answer and I got one. 'No problem.' A smile crossed his face. He knew I'd let him talk freely with Kelly so they'd get to know each other.

'Will you take her back to Brecon?'

'Yeah. Have you told her I live in Wales?'

'I've told her you live in a sheep pen.'

He threw the butt in the toilet because he knew I hated that smell, too.

I put both my hands on his shoulders. 'This has been a fucking shit week, mate.'

'Don't worry about it. Let's just go back in the room and finish off the brew. Then you just go and sort your shit out with Simmonds and get it over and done with.'

'How was the burger?'

'Fine. I saved Euan some fries.'

I sat on the bed next to her. 'Listen, Kelly, me and Euan have been talking, and because I've got to do some stuff in London we reckon it's a good idea if you go to the countryside with him and stay at his house. It's only for one night, I'll be back tomorrow. What do you think? Hey, you can even see the floor we laid. Remember I talked about it?'

She suspected she wasn't being offered any option and her face said so.

I said, 'I won't be long and Euan's house has sheep all around it.'

She looked down at her fingers and mumbled, 'I want to stay with you.'

I said with mock surprise, 'What, don't you want to go? You'll see all the sheep!'

She was embarrassed. She was too polite to say no in front of Euan.

I said, 'It won't be for long.' Then, like a bastard, I closed the trap. 'You like Euan, don't you?'

She nodded, never losing eye contact with me in case she made it with Euan.

'It's just going to be for one night. I'll be calling you anyway; I'll be able to talk to you.'

She looked very unhappy about it. After all, I'd promised not to leave her again. I caught sight of my mobile and had an idea. 'What if I give you my telephone; I'll show you how to use it.' I started playing with the buttons. 'Here you are, you have a go. If I show you how to use it, you can put that under your pillow tonight, all right?'

I looked up at Euan, trying to bring him into it. 'Because she'll have her own bedroom, won't she?'

'That's right, she'll have her own bedroom, the one that over-looks the sheep pen.'

I said, 'And I believe there's a TV in her bedroom, isn't there?'

'Yes, there's a TV in there,' he nodded and agreed, probably wondering where he was going to get one from.

There was an acceptance; she wasn't over the moon about it,

but that was good enough. I switched on the phone, tapped in my PIN number and handed it over. 'Just plug the charger into the wall when you get back and it'll keep working, OK?'

'OK.'

'Then put it underneath your pillow, so when it rings you'll be sure to hear it. All right?'

'Whatever.' By now she understood that she definitely had no choice.

Euan said, 'I'll tell you what, we'd better get your teddies organized if we're going to the country. What are their names? Have they ever been on a train before?'

She warmed to him. We went downstairs and got in a taxi to Paddington station.

38

We bought her ice creams, sweets, drinks, anything to keep her mind off what was happening. She was still deciding what comic to have as Euan looked at his watch and said, 'Wheels turning soon, mate.'

I went with them along the platform and gave her a big hug at the carriage door. 'I'll ring you tonight, Kelly. I promise.'

As she climbed up, Jenny and Ricky were looking at me from the Virgin daysack on her back. 'OK.'

The guard was walking the length of the train, closing the doors. Euan lowered the window so Kelly could wave.

'Nick?' She leaned towards me through the open window and beckoned as if she wanted to whisper something.

'What?' I put my face near hers.

'This.' She threw her arms around my neck, squeezed, and planted a big kiss on my cheek. I was so taken aback I just stood there.

The train started moving.

'I'll see you tomorrow,' Euan called. 'Don't worry about us. We'll be OK.'

As the train slowly disappeared from the platform I felt the same wrench as at the moment I'd seen Pat's body being loaded into the ambulance, but this time I couldn't work out why. After all, it was for the best and she was in safe hands. Forcing myself to see it as one more problem out of the way, I headed for the pay phones.

I got a very businesslike reply from Vauxhall: 'Extension, please?'

'2612.'

There was a pause, then a voice I recognized at once. 'Hello, 2612.'

'It's Stone. I've got what you needed.'

'Nick! Where are you?'

I put my finger in my ear as a departure was announced.

'I'm in England.' Not that he needed me to say that when he could hear that the Exeter train was leaving in five minutes.

'Excellent.'

'I'm pretty desperate to see you.'

'Likewise. But I'm tied up here until the early hours.' He paused to think. 'Perhaps we can go for a walk and a talk. Let's say four thirty tomorrow morning?'

'Where?'

'I'll walk towards the station. I presume you'll find me.'

'I'll do that.'

I put the phone down with a feeling that at long last the dice were rolling for me. Kelly was safe, Simmonds sounded amenable. With luck I was only hours from sorting out this mess.

Back at the hotel I ordered a hire car to go and pick up Kelly from Brecon after the meeting, and had something to eat. In my head I ran through exactly what I was going to say to Simmonds and the way I was going to say it. Without a doubt, I had in my possession precisely the sort of evidence Simmonds had asked for. It was a shame I didn't have the videotape to back some of it up but, even so, the stuff I had was probably more than he could have hoped for. The worst-case scenario now was that I'd get the slate wiped clean and be let loose. At least I had a few quid to start a new life with.

I thought about Kelly. What would become of her? Where

would she go? Would she have been affected by everything she'd seen and all that had happened to her and her family? I tried to cut away from that, telling myself that it would all get sorted out – somehow. Simmonds could help there. Perhaps he could orchestrate the reunion with her grandparents, or at least point me in the direction of the right kind of expert help.

I tried to get some sleep, but failed. At 3 a.m. I retrieved the hire car from an NCP car park and headed for Vauxhall Bridge.

I went a long way round, going all the way down the King's Road to World's End, then turning for the river and heading east again, mainly because I wanted to organize my thoughts one last time, but also because, to me, the drive along the deserted Embankment and past all the historic, floodlit bridges offered one of the most beautiful sights in the world. This particular night the lights seemed to shine a bit brighter and the bridges seemed more sharply in focus, and I found myself wishing Kelly was there to see it all with me.

I got to Vauxhall Bridge early. I drove east along the road that follows the river towards the next bridge, Lambeth. Nothing looked suspicious at the RV point on the drive-past. The petrol station on the opposite side of the road, about halfway towards Lambeth Bridge, had about four cars on the forecourt, groups of kids buying fuel and Mars bars and some early-morning office-cleaning vans filling up before their shift.

Further along the river, and on the other side, I could see the Palace of Westminster. I smiled to myself. If only the MPs really knew what the intelligence services got up to. According to the news on the radio, chances were that we'd have a new government soon. Not that I could vote for anyone. I hadn't existed in real time as Stone, Stamford, Stevenson or anyone else for years.

I did a full circle of a roundabout and headed back on the same road towards Vauxhall for one more drive-past. I still had time to kill, so I stopped in the garage and bought a drink and a sandwich.

The RV point still looked fine. My plan was to pick up Simmonds, make distance and angles as we walked to my car, and go for a drive. That way I controlled the environment. I could protect myself as well as him.

I parked up about 400 metres west of the RV. While eating my sandwich I checked out my route back to the car. I got out and walked down the road, arriving at five minutes to four. There was still nothing to do but wait, so I window-shopped at the bike shop, resolving that I really would buy one as a gift to myself. No, more than a gift – a reward.

At four twenty I moved into the shadows of the railway arches opposite the exit point that I knew Simmonds would use. There were one or two people wandering about, clubbers on their way home, or to another club. Their drunken laughs shattered the still morning air, then there was silence again.

I could tell it was him straight away, leaning slightly forward as he bounced along on the balls of his feet. I watched him branch right from the exit and stand at the pedestrian crossing, intending to head for the metal footbridge over the five-way road junction to the railway station. I waited. There was no rush; I would let him come to me.

As he crossed the road I came out of the shadows at the bottom of the footbridge steps.

He smiled. 'Nick, how are you?' He kept walking, nodding left towards Lambeth Bridge. 'Shall we walk?' It wasn't a question.

I nodded the opposite way, towards my car. 'I've arranged a pick-up.'

Simmonds stopped and looked at me with the expression of a disappointed schoolteacher. 'No, I think we'll walk.'

I was sponsoring the RV, he should have known that I'd organize for our safety. He stared at me for a few more moments and then, as if he knew I was going to follow, continued on walking. I fell into step beside him.

Ahead of us, on the other side of the Thames, the Houses of Parliament glowed in the dark like a picture postcard. We were on a wide pavement that abutted a grass section, and then there was another pavement that serviced the shop outlets that were part of the archways.

Simmonds looked the same as ever, his tie about half an inch loose, the shirt and suit looking as if his wardrobe was a carrier bag.

'So, Nick, what have you got?' He smiled but he didn't look at me. As I told him the story, he didn't interrupt, just kept his eyes on the ground, nodding. I felt like a son unloading his problems onto his dad, and it felt good.

We'd been walking for about a quarter of an hour and I'd come to the end of my presentation. It was his turn to talk. I somehow expected him to stop, or at least find a bench where we could sit, but he carried on walking.

He turned his head towards me and smiled again. 'Nick, I had no idea you'd be so thorough. Who else have you spoken to about this?'

'No-one else, only de Sabatino and Euan.'

'And has Euan or this de Sabatino also got a copy of the disks?'

I lied. 'No, no-one apart from me.' Even when you come to someone for help, you never play your full hand. You never know when you might need an edge.

He remained incredibly calm. 'What we have to ensure is that no-one else finds out – not for the moment anyway. This is more than low-level corruption. The links with PIRA, Gibraltar and, it seems, the DEA mean this is very grave indeed. You seem to have made a pretty good fist of this so far, so let me ask you something.' He paused as if he was a judge about to give his deliberation. 'Do you think it goes further?'

'Fuck knows,' I said. 'But you can't be too careful. It's why I wanted to talk to you on your own.'

'And where is the Brown child now?'

I lied again. 'In a hotel, fast asleep. I'll be needing some help to pass her on to her grandparents.'

'Of course, Nick. All in good time.'

We walked on a while in silence. We got to a bar on the corner of a car tunnel under the railway line. Simmonds turned to the right, taking us under the arches. Then he spoke again, and it was as if there was no question of me not complying with his demand. 'Before I can do anything to help you, what I need from you, of course, is the evidence.' He was still not looking at me, but making sure he avoided the puddles of water stained with engine oil.

'I haven't brought the disks with me, if that's what you mean.'

'Nick, I shall do my best to see that you both have protection. But I do need the proof – and all copies of it. Can you get them for me now?'

'Not possible. It won't be for a few hours.'

'Nick, I cannot do anything without them. I need all copies. Even ones you'd normally leave in that security blanket of yours.'

I shrugged. 'You must understand that it's for my own protection.'

We turned right again and were now heading back towards the station, paralleling the railway. For a couple of minutes we moved in silence along narrow, warehoused streets. Simmonds was deep in thought. A freight train rumbled above us on its way to waking up the residents of south-west London. Why the fuck was it so important for him to know how many copies there were and get his hands on all of them?

'Believe me,' I shouted above the noise, 'I've got that side all under control. I've been fucked over enough. You know as well as I do that I've got to protect everyone, including you.'

'Yes, of course, but I need to control all the information. Not even you should have it. There is too much risk involved.'

This was getting stupid. 'I understand that. But what if you get zapped? There would be nothing to back up what I'm saying. It's not only the Americans' corruption, don't you see? Gibraltar was a set-up. It includes us.'

Simmonds slowly nodded at a puddle in the gutter.

'A few things puzzle me,' I said. 'Why were we briefed that the bomb would be initiated by remote control? How come the int was so good about the ASU, but so wrong about there being no bomb?'

Still he gave no reply.

Things weren't adding up here.

Oh fuck.

I felt as if I'd been hit on the back of the head by a fire extinguisher again. Why hadn't I thought of it? The freight train's rumbling was now in the distance. The early-morning silence had returned. 'But you know all this, don't you?'

No reply. He didn't even break his stride.

Who had briefed us that the Gibraltar bomb was going to be initiated by remote control? Simmonds, who was there at Alpha to oversee it. Why the fuck hadn't I thought of it before?

I stopped in my tracks. Simmonds kept walking. 'This isn't just an American/PIRA thing, is it? It's much bigger. You are part of it, aren't you?'

The rear arches were more light industrial than retail – carrepair shops, sheet-metal works, and storage units, most with company vans that had been parked outside for the night. On our left, about 20 metres away, was a grassy area that belonged to a council estate, then flats beyond that. All around us were metal refuse containers and large red recovery vehicles, with yellow warning lights on their roofs.

He turned to face me and took the six steps back to where I stood. For the first time, we had eye-to-eye. 'Nick, I think you need to be aware of something. You will give me all the information – and I mean all of it. We cannot take the risk of other copies being in circulation.'

The look on his face was of a chess grand master about to make the decisive move. The shock and horror on mine must have been plain to see.

'We didn't necessarily go along with the Americans' determination to kill you, but you should be in no doubt that we will do so now if we have to.'

'We?'

'It's much bigger than you think, Nick. You're intelligent, you must realize the commercial and political implications of a cease-fire. Exposing what is on the disks would mess up much more than just what you know. It's very unfortunate about Kevin and his family, I grant you. When he told me what he'd discovered, I did try to talk my American colleagues into a subtler course of action.'

So that was why I'd been ordered back to the UK so apruptly. Once Simmonds had talked with Kev, he wanted me out of the US – and quick. He didn't want me speaking to Kev – or interrupting his murder.

I thought of Kelly. At least she was safe.

It was almost as if he was reading my mind. 'If your choice is not to give me all the information, we will kill the child. And then we will kill you – after extracting what we need. Don't be naïve, Nick. You and I, we're the same. This isn't about emotion, this is business, Nick, business.' He looked at me as a father would a wayward son. 'You really have no choice.'

I tried to fight it. He had to be bluffing.

'Euan sends his regards, by the way, and says that he managed to get a television set for her bedroom. Believe me, Nick, Euan will kill her. He rather likes the financial benefits.'

I shook my head slowly from side to side.

'Think back. Who initiated the contact?'

He was right, it was Euan. Simmonds was there to direct it, Euan was there to pull the trigger. But I still fought against the idea.

He opened his jacket and pulled a mobile phone from his inside pocket. 'Let Euan explain; he was expecting a call later anyway.'

He turned on the power and was waiting to put in his PIN number. He smiled as he looked down at the phone's display. 'This is how the Americans found you, you know. People think that detection can only take place when the phone is in use. Not so. As long as they're switched on, these things are miniature tracking devices, even if no calls are made or received. It's actually a form of electronic tagging. We find it terribly useful.'

He tapped in his PIN number, the tones blaring out of his hand. 'However, once you'd given them the slip at Lorton, our only option was to let you make entry back into the UK. I needed to know what you'd found out. I have to say, I'm so glad your cancer treatment was successful.'

Fuck! He hadn't even mentioned my lack of hair. That was because he already knew. But Euan. He'd been aware enough to mention it. I felt sick knowing he was using his skills against me.

Simmonds smiled. He knew he had me by the bollocks.

'Nick, I'll say this again. I really do need all the disks. You know the child would suffer greatly; it's not something that we would enjoy, but there are important matters at stake.'

I wanted so much for him to get through to Euan. I wanted to speak to him, wanted him to confirm that it was a bluff. But in my heart of hearts I knew that it wasn't.

Simmonds had nearly finished tapping in the number.

I had no choice. I couldn't risk Kelly. He wasn't going to make this call.

With my right arm in a hooked position, I swung round hard and connected with his nose. There was a dull crunch of fracturing bone and he went down with a muffled moan. While he writhed on the ground I kicked his case under one of the recovery trucks and, in the same motion, picked up the phone in my left hand, got behind him and positioned it at the front of his throat. Grabbing the other side with my right hand, I jammed it firmly under his Adam's apple.

I looked to the right and left. We were too exposed where we were, and what I had in mind would take several minutes to complete. I shuffled backwards, dragging him in between two of the trucks. I got down onto my knees, all the time pulling back on the phone. He was kicking out, his arms flailing, trying to rip my face apart.

His whimpers and chokes filled the air. I responded by leaning forward, using the weight of my upper body to bend his head down so that his chin was more or less on his chest. At the same time I pulled even harder. Just another two minutes and I'd be done.

After thirty seconds he started to struggle furiously, with all the frenzied strength that a man draws on when the knows he is dying. But no matter what he did now he wouldn't be getting up.

His hands still scrabbled at my face. I bobbed and weaved to avoid them, but maintained the pressure on his throat. Already the scabs from the fight with McGear had been pulled off, but I couldn't feel much blood. Then he managed to get his fingernails into the cut just below my eye. I stifled a scream as his three nails started to make entry into the already damaged soft skin. I made the injury worse by pulling my face away; as I did, Simmonds's nails took my skin with them.

I didn't bother now to see if anyone was watching. I was beyond caring. I was fighting for breath myself with the effort, and sweat stung the injuries on my face.

Gradually at first, his movements subsided to no more than a spasmodic twitching in his legs. His hands stopped grasping. Seconds later he was unconscious. It crossed my mind just to get up and walk away, to leave him to suffer the effects of hypoxia and be brain-damaged for life. I decided against. I wanted this fucker dead.

I gave it another thirty seconds. His chest stopped moving. I put my fingers on the carotid pulse and felt nothing.

I dragged him to the wall and sat him up against the doors of a unit. Then I got to my feet and started dusting myself down. Keeping to the shadows, I tucked my shirt in and wiped away the sweat and blood with my sleeve. I checked the phone. It had been turned off in the fight. I wiped my prints off it, then just left everything where it was and casually walked away. If anybody had seen me, so what? It didn't really matter. I had more important things to worry about.

I drove west, holding my coat cuff against my eye to stop the bleeding.

The whole situation was still spinning around inside my head, slowly beginning to make sense.

I now knew how Luther and co had found me – they must have beaten the number out of Pat and traced the signal while I had it switched on waiting for his call.

If I'd let on to Euan or Simmonds that there was only one more set of back-ups in my laptop and had handed it over, I'd have been dead. They were covering their arses but retrieving the information.

Had Simmonds arranged to phone Euan some time after our meet? Euan was over three hours away and Simmonds's body would be discovered soon. If Euan found out, he wouldn't take any chances. He would move location, maybe even kill her straight away. Either way, I'd have lost her. This time there was no question of just leaving her. I could call her on the mobile and tell her to run, but what would that achieve? She was in the middle of nowhere; even if she ran for half an hour it would make no difference. Euan's house was in the middle of acres of mountains, grass, rocks and sheep shit. He would find her.

I could call the police, but would they believe me? I could waste hours trying to convince them, by which time it would be too late. Or they might take it on themselves to raid Euan's house and the result would be the same.

For a fleeting second I thought about Big Al. I hoped he'd be well out of it by now. He didn't have getaway accounts for nothing. If he'd transferred 400 grand into mine, for sure he'd have taken 800 for himself. Old Melon Head would be OK. I cut him from my mind.

The motorway services just before Heathrow were being signposted. I had a thought.

I pulled off onto the slip road and drove into the car park. Now all I had to do was get to a phone and make a call.

39

The service station was busy. I'd had to park 100 yards from the main entrance. I got out of the car just as the heavens opened. By the time I reached the bank of four telephones outside the Burger King, I was soaked. The first two I tried only accepted cards. I had about £3 in change in my pocket – not enough. I ran into the shop, wiping my face to get some of the blood off. I bought a news-paper with a fiver and walked out, the woman looking worried at the state of my face. I then went back in and got a packet of Rolos with a £10 note. The woman looked even more scared. Maybe she thought I had seen her staring. She was just happy for me to take my change and see me leave.

As I dialled the number I felt a knot in my stomach, as if I was a teenager phoning to arrange his very first date. Would she have charged it and left it switched on? Why shouldn't she? She had never let me down before.

It started to ring.

For a moment I felt like a child in a sweet shop with his dad, hardly able to contain my excitement. Then I had new things to worry about. What if Euan had the phone now? Did I hang up or did I try to bluff it and maybe find out where she was?

It was too late to think. The ringing stopped; there was a pause, then I heard a quiet, hesitant, 'Hello, who is it?'

'Hi, Kelly, it's me, Nick,' I said, trying for all the world to sound Mr Casual. 'Are you on your own?'

'Yes, you woke me up. Are you coming back now?' She sounded tired and confused. I was trying hard to think of an answer; thankfully she carried on. 'Euan said that I may be staying with him for a while now because you have to go away. It isn't true, is it, Nick? You said you wouldn't leave me.'

It was a bad line. I had to put a finger in my other ear to hear her above the noise of the rain on the glass of the phone box. A lorry driver in the next box was shouting loudly and angrily, arguing with his boss that he couldn't go any further because of his tachograph, and he wasn't going to lose his licence just to get a few boxes of bloody anoraks up to Carlisle. On top of that was the steady boom of traffic on the motorway and the noises of people coming in and out of the services. I had to block all that out and concentrate on the phone call, because I couldn't ask Kelly to speak up.

I said, 'Yes, of course you're right, I will never leave you. Euan is lying to you. I have found out some bad things about him, Kelly. Are you still in the house?'

'Yes. I'm in bed.'

'Is Euan in his bed?'

'Yes. Do you want to speak to him?'

'No, no. Let me think for a minute.'

My mind was racing now, trying to think of the best way to say what I wanted.

'Of course I'm coming to get you. In fact, I'll be there very soon. Now, listen. I need you to do something very difficult and very dangerous. You only have to do this one thing for me and everything will be over.' The moment I said it I felt like a lowlife.

'I don't have to run away from the people again, do I?'

'No, no, no – it's not like that this time. But it's the most special job a spy ever does.' I didn't want to give her time to think, so I just carried on. 'But I want to check something first, OK? You're in bed, aren't you? Get under the covers and only talk to me in a whisper, OK?'

I could hear all the rustlings as she got underneath the covers. 'What are we going to do, Nick?'

'First, I want you to look at the front of the telephone and press a number. It will then light up. Tell me if you can see a picture of a battery. How many blocks are there where the battery sign is? Can you see it?'

I heard some scufflings.

'I can see that.'

'How many blocks are there in the picture?'

'Three. There's three blocks. One of them is flashing.'

'That's good.'

It wasn't really: two blocks meant she hadn't recharged it and the battery was down to less than half-power, but I was going to need a lot of air time to talk her through the whole process.

'What's that noise?' she said.

The truck driver was now really pissed off and was hollering down the phone, the roll-up in his hand making the phone box look like a steam room.

'Nothing to worry about. Kelly, I'm going to tell you what to do, but you need to keep listening to me on the telephone. Can you do that?'

'Why is Euan bad, Nick? What—'

'Listen, Kelly, Euan wants to hurt me. If he finds you doing this thing for me, he will hurt you too. Do you understand that?'

I could hear lots of rustlings; she was obviously still under the bedcovers. Then there was a very quiet 'Yes'.

She wasn't sounding a happy bunny. I was sure there was a better way I could be going about all this, I just didn't have time to think what it might be.

'If Euan wakes up,' I said, 'or if the telephone stops working, I want you to leave the house very, very quietly. I want you to go down the track to the road and hide behind the trees, just by the big gate that Euan drove through to get to his house. Know where I mean?'

'Yeah.'

'You must hide there until you hear a car come and stop, but don't get out from your hiding place unless it toots its horn two times. Then come out. Do you understand that? I'll be in the car. It's a blue Astra, OK?'

There was a pause. 'What's an As . . . Astra, Nick?'

Shit, she was seven years old and American. What was I expecting?

'OK. I'll stop in a blue car and come and get you.'

I got her to repeat it and, for good measure, I said, 'So if Euan wakes up and sees you, I want you to run to the trees as fast as you can and hide. Because if Euan catches you doing what I want you to do, we will never see each other again. Don't let me down, OK? And remember, don't you come out from behind those trees, even if Euan calls for you, OK?'

'OK. You will come and get me, won't you?'

There was a bit of doubt in her mind.

'Of course I will. Now, first of all, what I want you to do is get out of bed, then put the phone on the bed and get dressed, very slowly and quietly. Put on a nice thick coat. And you know those training shoes that you've got? Make sure you take those as well, but don't put them on yet.'

I heard her put the phone down and start rummaging around the room.

For fuck's sake, hurry up!

I forced myself to calm down.

It was almost two minutes before I heard 'I'm ready, Nick.'

'Now, listen to me very carefully. Euan is not a friend; he has tried to kill me. Do you understand, Kelly? He has tried to kill me.'

There was a pause.

'Why? I . . . I don't understand, Nick . . . you said he was your friend.'

393

'I know, I know, but things change. Do you want to help me?'

'Yes.'

'Good, then you must do exactly what I tell you.' I want you to put your trainers in your coat pockets. OK, now it's time to go downstairs. I want you to keep the telephone with you. All right?'

'Yeah.'

Time was running short and so was my money.

'Just remember, you must be very, very quiet, because otherwise you will wake Euan. If that happens, you run out of the house towards the hidey-hole – promise?'

'Cross my heart.'

'OK, I want you to creep very, very gently down the stairs. Don't talk to me again until you're in the kitchen; from now on what we must do is whisper all the time. OK?'

'OK.'

I heard the door open. As she came out of the room I imagined her passing the bathroom on her left. Ahead of her, up a half-landing and about 12 feet away, would be the door to Euan's room. Was it open or closed? Too late to ask her. A few steps now and she'd be at the top of the main stairs and next to the old grandfather clock. On cue, I heard its slow, ponderous tick-tock; it reminded me of something out of a Hitchcock movie.

The sound receded very slowly: good girl, she must be going down the stairs very carefully. Only once did I hear the creak of a board and I wondered again about Euan's door. Did he usually sleep with it open? I couldn't remember.

At the bottom of the stairs she'd be turning back on herself to the right, heading towards the kitchen.

I tried to imagine where she was, but lost her in the silence. At last I heard the barely perceptible sound of a protesting hinge; that was the kitchen door. I felt a stab of guilt for using the girl like this; but she knew the score – well, sort of. Fuck it, the decision was made; I just had to do it. If it worked, fine; if it didn't, she was dead. But if I didn't try it she was dead anyway, so let's get on with it.

She whispered, 'I'm in the kitchen, but I can't see very much. Am I allowed to turn the light on?'

It was the loudest whisper I'd ever heard.

'No, no, no, Kelly, you've got to speak very slowly and very quietly – like this.' I demonstrated. 'And don't put the light on, that would wake Euan up. Just go more slowly, and listen to me all the time. If you don't understand anything, just ask, and remember, if anything goes wrong or you hear a noise, stop and we will both listen. OK?'

'OK.'

The problem with her being quieter on the phone was that it was harder to hear her. The lorry driver had now finished, slamming the phone down and storming into the Burger King. A woman took his place and was gobbing off to a girlfriend.

The kitchen was two areas knocked into one: the old back room of the house and what had used to be an alleyway between the house and the old sheep-pen wall. The alleyway had been covered by a conservatory, with all the kitchen units arranged galley-style in one long range beneath it. There were plants on pedestals and a large circular wooden table in the middle of the area; I hoped she wouldn't knock anything over onto the squash-court floor. Thinking of the night we'd spent 'rescuing' the wood made me shudder at all those years of friendship, trust and even love. I felt let down, used, fucked over.

There couldn't be much battery time left.

'Everything OK?' I said. I tried hard not to convey any sense of panic, but I knew we would be in trouble soon. If the phone went dead, would she remember what I'd told her to do?

'I can't see anything, Nick.'

I thought for a few seconds, trying to remember more of the layout. 'OK, Kelly, go very slowly to where the sink is. Go and stand by the hob.'

'What's that?'

'It's the bit you cook on with saucepans. You see it?'

395

'Yeah.'

'OK, there's a switch on the right-hand side. Can you see that?'

'I'll look.'

A moment or two later she said, 'Nick, I can see now.'

She must have switched on the small fluorescent light that illuminated the worktop of the kitchen; she sounded relieved.

'Good girl. Now I want you to go back and very gently close the kitchen door. Will you do that for me?'

'OK. You are coming for me, Nick?'

I wasn't feeling confident about this at all. Should I stop it now and just get her to open the door for me and wait? No, fuck it. He might be getting a phone call any minute about Simmonds's death.

'Of course I am, but I can't come unless you do what I say, OK? Keep the telephone to your ear and, very gently, close that door.'

I heard the tell-tale creak.

'What I want you to do now is go and have a look under the sink, and put all the bottles and things on the table. Will you do that for me?'

'OK.'

There was silence, then a soft clatter as she moved bottles and cans around.

'That's everything out now.'

'Well done! Now, very quietly, read out the labels to me. Can you do that?'

'No, I can't.'

'Why not?'

'There's too many things and it's too dark, I can't do it.'

She was sounding under pressure now; there was that wobble in her voice.

Fuck, this is taking too long.

'It's OK, Kelly, just walk over to the light switch by the door and turn the light on. Don't rush. Will you do that?'

'OK.' It sounded as if her nose was blocking up. I knew the sound so well by now. The next stage, if I wasn't careful, would be tears – and failure.

I heard the shuffling towards the light switch.

'I can see now, Nick.'

'OK, now go back and read to me what the labels say, OK?'

'OK.' She moved back to the table and I could hear her pick up the cleaning products.

'Ajax.'

'OK, Kelly, what's the next one?'

Fucking hell, this was outrageous. I held the phone hard against my ear, almost holding my breath as I silently willed her to succeed. I was really pumped, I could feel my heart going. I was writhing like a madman in a straitjacket, twisting and turn-ing in the kiosk, miming Kelly's actions to myself. I looked across at the other box; the woman who was talking to her friend had wiped the condensation from the glass to get a better view of me and now seemed to be relaying a running commentary. I must have looked like a mass murderer, with cuts and scratches on my face and my hair and clothes soaking wet.

The loud noise of metal clattering onto wood made me jump.

'Kelly? Kelly?'

Silence, then the phone was picked up.

'Sorry, Nick. I knocked a spoon off. I didn't see it. I'm scared. I don't want to do this. Please come and get me.'

It wasn't long before the crying was going to start.

'Kelly, don't worry. It's OK, it's OK.'

I heard sniffing on the phone.

No, not now, for fuck's sake!

'It's OK, Kelly, it's OK. I can't get you unless you help me. You must be brave. Euan is trying to kill me. Only you can help me. Can you do that for me?'

'Please hurry, Nick. I want to be with you.'

'It's all right, it's all right.'

It wasn't all right, Nick, because Nick's fucking money was dis-appearing. I was down to my last few pound coins. They weren't going to last. I put another coin in and it rattled out into the coin return; I had to scrabble for another one.

397

She started to go through more of the labels. Most of the words she couldn't read. I asked her to spell them. As she got three letters out I worked out the rest. 'No, that one's no good. Read the next one.'

My mind was now racing, trying to remember ingredients and formulae. At last she read out something I could use.

'Kelly, you must listen very carefully. That's a green can, isn't it? Put it where you can find it again. Then I want you to creep out to the room next door, where the washing machine is. You know the one?'

'Yes.'

Euan had a place for everything, and everything in its place. I even knew that his forks would be lined up beside each other in the drawer.

'Just by the door is a cupboard and in it there's a blue bottle. The label says antifreeze.'

'What?'

'Antifreeze. A–N–T–I . . . I want you to bring it to the table, OK?'

The phone clunked onto the worktop. I started to flap even more.

After what seemed an eternity, she came back on. 'I've got it.'

'Put it on the table and then open it.'

I heard the phone go down again and lots of heavy breathing and sniffing as she struggled with the bottle top.

'I don't know how to do it.'

'Just twist it. You know how to open a bottle.'

'I can't. It won't go. I am trying, Nick, but my hands are shaking.'

I then heard a soft, long moan. I was sure it was going to turn into crying.

Shit, I don't need this. It isn't going to work.

'Kelly? Kelly? Are you OK? Talk to me, come on, talk to me.'

I was getting nothing.

Come on, Kelly, come on.

Nothing. All I could hear was her holding back tears and sniffing.

'Nick . . . I want you to get me. Please, Nick, please.' She was sobbing now.

'Just take your time, Kelly, just take your time. It's OK, everything's OK. I'm here, don't worry. OK, let's just stand and listen. If you can hear anything, you tell me on the phone, OK, and I'll try to listen at the same time.'

I listened. I wanted to make sure Euan wasn't awake. I also wanted a cut: there needs to be a cut in the action at a time like this, otherwise the errors snowball and people start tripping over themselves; so let's take our time, but at the same time be as fast as possible. I knew exactly what I needed to do, but the frustration lay in trying to interpret it to this child, under pressure, and to get her to work quietly – and all the time I was running out of money and the mobile was running out of battery life.

The woman left her booth and gave me a grin of appeasement, in case I was going to lunge at her with a meat cleaver.

'Are you OK now, Kelly?'

'Yes. Do you want me to unscrew the bottle still?'

I couldn't understand why she couldn't do it. I started giving her more instructions. Then I remembered – the bottle had a child-proof screw top. As I started to tell her how to undo it there was a soft bleep.

Battery. Shit!

'Yes, remember to push the top down before you turn. We just have to be a bit quicker, or the phone is going to stop before we finish.'

'Now what do I do, Nick?'

'Is that on the table with the top undone?'

Nothing.

'Kelly? Kelly? Are you there?'

Was the battery dead?

Then I heard 'What do I do now?'

'Thank goodness, I thought the battery had gone. Is there anything you can open that green can with? I know, use the spoon, Kelly. Very, very carefully now, pick it up, put the phone on the table and then open the can. OK?'

I listened, running through all the different options there were left if this scheme fucked up. I came to the conclusion there were none.

'Now, here comes the hard part. Do you think you are good enough for this? You've got to be pretty special to do this bit.'

'Yes, I'm OK now. I am sorry I cried, it's just that I'm . . .'

'I know, I know, Kelly. I am, too, but we will do this together. What I need you to do now is put the phone in your pocket with your trainers. Then take one of those big bottles from the table and walk to the front door of the house and open it just a little bit. Not wide open, just a little bit. Then put the bottle behind the door, to stop it swinging shut. Now, remember, it's a big heavy door so I want you to do it really slowly, really, really gently, so it doesn't make a noise. Can you do that for me?'

'Yeah, I can do that. What happens after that?'

'I'll tell you in a minute. Now, don't forget, if the phone stops working and you can't hear me any more, I want you to run to the trees and hide.'

Chances were, Euan would find her, but what else was there to do?

'OK.'

This was going to be the wriggly bit. Even if he was sound asleep Euan's subconscious was likely to detect the change in air pressure and ambient noise when the door was opened and make something of it in a dream, giving him a sort of sixth-sense feeling that something was wrong.

If so, at least she'd have a head start – so long as she remembered what I'd told her.

'I'm back in the kitchen – what do I do now?'

'Listen to me. This bit's very important. How much can you count up to?'

'I can count to ten thousand.'

She was sounding a little happier now, sensing the end was in sight.

'I only want you to count up to three hundred. Can you do that?'

'I can do that.'

'You've got to do it in your head.'

'OK.'

'First, I want you to go to the hob again. You know how to turn on the gas?'

'Of course! Sometimes I help my mommy with the cooking.'

I had never felt so sad.

I made myself concentrate again. There was no room for distractions. She might be dead soon anyway. I felt enough of a bastard for getting her to do my dirty work; while I was at it I might as well make sure she did the job properly.

'That's good. So you know how to turn on the gas in the oven and all the rings on the hob?'

'I told you, I know how to cook.'

A coachload of teenage kids returning from a school holiday trip was streaming into the burger bar. A gang of six or seven of them hung back and headed for the phones, laughing and shouting in newly broken voices, all trying to cram into the one vacant booth. The noise was horrendous; I couldn't hear what Kelly was saying. I had to do something. 'Kelly, just wait a minute.'

I put my hand over the mouthpiece, leaned out of the box and shouted, 'You – shut the fuck up! I've got my aunty here, her husband's just died and I'm trying to talk to her, OK? Give us some time!'

The kids went quiet, their cheeks red. They sloped off to join their friends, sniggering with mock bravado to disguise their embarrassment.

I got back on the phone.

'Kelly, this is very important. The phone might stop soon because the battery is running out. I want you to turn on all the gas on the cooker. Take the phone with you so I can hear the gas.

Go there now while I talk to you.'

I heard the hiss of the bottled propane that Euan used.

'It's very smelly, Nick.'

'That's good. Now, just walk out of the kitchen and close the door. But be very quiet outside the room. Remember, we don't want to wake Euan. Don't talk to me any more, just listen. Go outside the room and close the kitchen door, OK?'

'OK. I won't talk to you any more.'

'That's right.'

I heard the door close.

'Nick?'

I tried to keep calm. 'Yes, Kelly?'

'Can I get Jenny and Ricky to take with me, please?'

I tried harder to keep myself in check. 'No, Kelly, there is no time! Just listen to me. There isn't time for you to talk. I want you to count up to three hundred in your head, then I want you to take a really, really deep breath and walk back into the kitchen. Don't run. You must walk. Go into the kitchen and pour all the antifreeze into the green can. Then I want you to walk out of the kitchen – don't run! – I don't want you to wake Euan.'

If she tripped up and hurt herself, she could get engulfed by what was about to happen.

'Walk out very slowly, close the kitchen door behind you, then go out of the house and close the front door, really, really gently. Do not collect Jenny or Ricky.'

'But I want them – please, Nick?'

I ignored her. 'Then I want you to run as fast as you can up to the trees and hide. When you're running you will hear a big bang and there will be a fire. Don't stop and don't look back. And don't come out until I get there, no matter what happens. I promise I will be there soon.'

It was at times like this that I was pleased I'd done all the laborious, parrot-fashion learning of techniques for making incendiaries and improvised explosive devices. At the time, many years ago, it had been mind-bogglingly boring, but it had to be done because you can't take a notebook on the job with you. I learned, off by heart, how to make bombs from everyday ingredients and how to make improvised electrical devices. As clearly as even atheists remember the Lord's Prayer from the time it was drummed into them at school, I remembered the formulae and step-by-step mechanics for making everything from a simple incendiary like the one I was going to use to kill Euan – Mixture Number 5 – to a bomb that I could initiate by using a pager from the other side of the world.

The phone started bleeping urgently and then it just went dead. I visualized the glycerine in the antifreeze working on the mixture. In forty or fifty seconds it would ignite. If it was damp, maybe a little longer.

Kelly had less than a minute to get out of the house; the instant the gas was ignited there was going to be a massive explosion and then a fire. Hopefully it would take Euan down, but would it take her with it?

Please, please, please don't go after those fucking teddy bears!

I ran back to the car and started driving west. First light was just trying to fight its way through the clouds.

40

It was the worst journey of my life.

I saw a sign saying 'Newport, 70 miles'. I raced along at warp speed for what I guessed was 30 miles, then another sign told me, 'Newport, 60 miles.' I felt as if I was running on a treadmill to nowhere and the treadmill was waist-deep in water.

My body had calmed down from all the excitement and was telling me I was hurt. My neck was agony. The flow of blood had stopped, but the eye Simmonds had gouged was starting to swell up and affect my vision.

Euan, the fucker. The friend I had trusted for years. It was almost too painful to think about. I felt numb. I felt bereaved. In time, maybe, that numbness would turn to anger or grief or some other thing, but not yet. In my mind's eye, all I could see was the look on Kelly's face as the train left the station – and the smile on Euan's.

Where did I go from here? No fucker was going to move against me because they'd know that I still had the files. If the plan worked, Euan's package would sit in the sorting depot now there was no-one to deliver it to. The killing of Simmonds would be covered up, no matter what. If some zealous policeman started getting too close to the truth, he'd get stitched up. John Stalker wasn't the first it had happened to, and he wouldn't be the last.

It all made sense to me, now, that every time peace talks began PIRA, or someone claiming to be PIRA, had dropped a soldier or policeman or bombed the mainland UK. And why? Because it was good business to keep the Troubles alive.

There were plenty on our side who profited from conflicts like Northern Ireland and didn't want them to end. The RUC is probably the highest-paid police force in Europe, if not the world. If you're its chief constable, it's your duty to say that you want an end to the war, but the reality is that you've got a massive police force under your command and limitless amounts of resources and power. Within that force there are mini-empires that have evolved purely because of the Troubles, each of them getting whatever material and manpower they ask for to further their fight against terrorism.

Even if you're a twenty-four-year-old RUC constable, married with two kids, why would you want the Troubles to stop? You earn enough to enjoy a high standard of living, have a nice house, take foreign holidays. Why would you want to see peace and, in turn, redundancy?

The British army doesn't want it to stop, either. The province is a fantastic testing ground for equipment and training ground for troops – and, as with the RUC, it means the army gets a bigger slice of the cake. Every year the Army has to justify its budget, and it's up against the Navy, who are asking for more funds for Trident submarines, and the Air Force, who are banging on about needing to buy the Eurofighter 2000 or at least replace the flying coffin, the Tornado. With Northern Ireland on the agenda, the Army can talk about a 'now' commitment, an operational imperative – and nobody's going to argue against the need for funds to fight terrorism. As for the squaddies, they don't want to lose the chance of six months a year in Northern Ireland on extra money, with free food and accommodation. After all, they joined the Army to go on operations; that was what I had done and I thought it was great.

British industry stood to lose substantially from a ceasefire.

Major defence manufacturers designed equipment specifically for the internal security role and made fortunes out of the operational conditions. Equipment that was battle-proven in Northern Ireland was eagerly sought after by foreign buyers. No wonder the conflict had made Britain one of the top three arms exporters in the world, with beneficial effects on the UK balance of payments.

I knew now why McCann, Farrell and Savage had had to die. Enniskillen. The backlash against PIRA. People signing books of condolence. Irish-Americans stopping their donations. There must have been a real danger of a time of dialogue and reconciliation. Simmonds and his mates couldn't have that. They had to create martyrs to keep the pot boiling.

And me? I was probably just a very small glitch in a well-oiled machine. Come to that, Northern Ireland was probably only one item among many in their company accounts. For all I knew, these guys also provoked killings and riots in Hebron, stirred up Croats against Serbs, and even got Kennedy killed because he wanted to stop the Vietnam War. As Simmonds had said, it was business. There was nothing I could do to stop them. But I wasn't worried about that. What was the point? The only thing I had achieved was revenge for Kev's and Pat's deaths. That would have to be enough.

I got off the motorway and onto the dual carriageway to Abergavenny. The rain had stopped, but it was a stretch of road notorious for repair works. Euan's house was about 10 miles the other side of the town, on the road towards Brecon.

I weaved in and out of the traffic, other drivers hooting and waving their fists. Then, in the distance, I saw the red of brake lights. The morning rush hour had started. I slowed with the volume of traffic heading into the town and eventually came to a complete standstill. The jam was caused by resurfacing work and it looked as though there was a mile-long tailback.

I drove onto the hard shoulder. As I sped past them on the

inside, stationary motorists honked angrily. The noise alerted the workers laying the tarmac up ahead. They ran and shouted, trying to wave me down, gesticulating at the roadworks sign. I didn't even acknowledge them. I only hoped I didn't get caught by the police. I dropped a gear, made speed and changed back up.

I got to Abergavenny and stayed on the ring road. I got stopped at a long set of traffic lights and bumped up onto the kerb, edging my way to the front of the queue.

Once I was over the other side of the town I started to come into the cuds and the road narrowed to a single carriageway. I put my foot down and bombed along at 70 to 80, using the whole road as if it was my own. Seeing a left-hand bend, I moved over to the far right-hand side. I could hear the hedgerow screech against the side of the car. From this position I could see more of the dead ground round the bend. Not bothering with brakes, I banged down through the gears to second just before turning. Once on the bend, I put my foot down and made use of rubber on tarmac. Out of the bend, I block-changed to fourth and kept it there.

After a mile, a slow-moving truck was taking up most of the road. Its large container of sheep on two floors had a sticker on it asking me if I thought the driving was OK – if not, to ring head office. I had plenty of time to read it, labouring behind the fucker at 20 m.p.h.

The road twisted and turned; he could see me in his mirrors, but there was no way he was going to pull in for me to overtake. The speedo dropped to 15 m.p.h. and I looked at my watch. It was nine thirty-five and I'd been on the road for just under three hours.

I kept pulling out, looking and tucking back in again. Even the sheep were looking at me now. The truck driver was enjoying himself; we had eye-to-eye in his wing mirror and I could see he was laughing. I knew this road, and I knew that unless he let me overtake I was doomed to several miles of driving at his pace. By now the road had a 2-foot mud bank on each side, then trees and hedges. It was wet and slippery, with small streams running along each side. I'd have to take a chance and just hope that nothing was coming. On this road, all corners were blind.

Preparing for the next bend, the truck driver shifted slowly down through the gears and I accelerated past him on the wrong side of the road. If there was anything coming round the bend we'd both be killed. He flashed his lights and honked, probably doing his best to distract me and force me off the road. For the first time today I was in luck. The road was clear and I'd soon left the truck far behind.

A quarter of an hour later I was at the turn-off for Euan's valley. I threw a left and, within 100 metres, the road petered out into a single lane. If I came up behind a tractor or farm machinery there would be few passing places, but luck stayed with me and there was nothing ahead. Another twenty minutes and I got to the valley. And as I approached the brow of the hill I could already see the spiral of smoke.

41

The walls were still intact, but most of the roof had collapsed and there was smoke and scorch marks around the window frames. Two fire engines were in attendance and the firemen were still damping down. They looked wet, tired and stressed. On the other side of the house was an ambulance.

A handful of people had gathered, locals in their Barbours and wellies, who'd driven from the other side of the valley to rubberneck.

I drove on and stopped by the gate. A couple of firemen turned round, but they didn't say anything; they were too busy doing their work.

I got out of the car and ran across the road to the small copse about 50 metres away, hollering and shouting like a madman.

'Kelly! Kelly!'

Nothing.

'It's me, Nick! You can come out now!'

But she wasn't there. Deep down, I'd probably known all along that she wouldn't be. She'd been dead from the moment she'd picked up the phone.

I turned away and walked slowly up the track towards the throng of spectators. They gave me the once-over, obviously not liking the look of my damaged face, then turned back, more interested in the remains of the house.

'Was there anyone in there?' I asked nobody in particular.

A woman spoke. 'His lights were on last night and the ambulance crew have been inside. Oh, it's such a shame. He was such a nice young man.'

I walked beyond the group and a fireman came towards me, lifting a gloved hand. 'Excuse me, sir, if you could stay well back. We haven't made the area safe yet.'

'Radio Wales,' I said, trying to make myself sound official. 'Can you tell me what happened?'

I looked over his shoulder. Other firefighters were dragging out charred contents of Euan's house and placing them on a pile that was being damped down. I could now smell the burning.

I looked back at the fireman. He said, 'It looks as if there was a fire and then the gas bottles blew up. If you could move back, sir.'

'Was anyone killed or injured?'

As I asked, something one of them threw on the pile caught my eye. It was Jenny or Ricky, one or the other, I could never tell which was which. Not that it mattered now. Whichever one it was, it was burned black, with only half an arm left.

'It will take some time before we know for sure, but no-one could have survived that blast.'

He was right. In any other circumstances, it would have been an explosion to be proud of.

Kelly was dead. Maybe it wouldn't be too bad. It would be a fucker, but I'd get over it. What could I have offered her?

Kelly would have been in shit state when she realized what had happened to her and would have needed psychiatric treatment. Besides, she'd been starting to like the way we'd been living. Her death would tidy things up. I wouldn't have to protect or worry about her any more.

I turned and started back towards the car, deep in my thoughts. What was done was done; I couldn't change it, couldn't turn the clock back. I'd find out more from the news.

Behind me, in the distance, I heard the squawk of a bird, maybe a crow. It almost sounded like my name.

I stopped and turned.

And there she was, running towards me from beyond the trees.

I started to run towards her, but checked myself. I wanted to make it look casual, even if my insides were shaking off the Richter scale.

She flew into my arms and buried her face in my neck. I pulled her back and held her at arm's length. 'Why weren't you at the trees?' I was half angry, half relieved, like a parent who thinks he's lost a child in a crowd, and then finds her again and doesn't know whether to give her a good old bollocking or just a hug and a kiss. I didn't know what to do, but it felt good.

'Why weren't you by the trees where I said?'

She looked at me in disbelief. 'As if! Because you always make sure you stand off and watch. You told me that!'

I got hold of her hand, grinned and said, 'Yeah, fair one.'

Still smiling, we carried on along the track. She was soaked, her hair matted to her head.

We reached the car and got in without exchanging another word.

I looked at her in the rear-view mirror. We had eye-to-eye. She smiled and I snapped, 'Put your seat belt on!'

I turned the key in the ignition and we drove off.